# A Blend of Magic

## KATE KENZIE

# Dedication

For those who believed even when I didn't

# Contents

1.  Chapter One                                          1

2.  Chapter Two                                          8

3.  Chapter Three                                       19

4.  Chapter Four                                        32

5.  Chapter Five                                        38

6.  Chapter Six                                         44

7.  Chapter Seven                                       52

8.  Chapter Eight                                       60

9.  Chapter Nine                                        73

10.  Chapter Ten                                        81

11.  Chapter Eleven                                     93

12.  Chapter Twelve                                    100

13.  Chapter Thirteen                                  103

14.  Chapter Fourteen                                  105

| 15. | Chapter Fifteen | 109 |
| 16. | Chapter Sixteen | 112 |
| 17. | Chapter Seventeen | 121 |
| 18. | Chapter Eighteen | 128 |
| 19. | Chapter Nineteen | 133 |
| 20. | Chapter Twenty | 139 |
| 21. | Chapter Twenty-One | 150 |
| 22. | Chapter Twenty-Two | 156 |
| 23. | Chapter Twenty-Three | 169 |
| 24. | Chapter Twenty-Four | 176 |
| 25. | Chapter Twenty-Five | 188 |
| 26. | Chapter Twenty-Six | 194 |
| 27. | Chapter Twenty-Seven | 198 |
| 28. | Chapter Twenty-Eight | 203 |
| 29. | Chapter Twenty-Nine | 210 |
| 30. | Chapter Thirty | 215 |
| 31. | Chapter Thirty-One | 222 |
| 32. | Chapter Thirty-Two | 230 |
| 33. | Chapter Thirty-Three | 239 |
| 34. | Chapter Thirty-Four | 245 |
| 35. | Chapter Thirty-Five | 251 |
| 36. | Chapter Thirty-Six | 255 |
| 37. | Chapter Thirty-Seven | 259 |
| 38. | Chapter Thirty-Eight | 264 |

| 39. | Chapter Thirty-Nine | 268 |
| 40. | Chapter Forty | 271 |
| 41. | Chapter Forty-One | 276 |
| 42. | Chapter Forty-Two | 284 |
| 43. | Chapter Forty-Three | 287 |
| 44. | Chapter Forty-Four | 298 |
| 45. | Chapter Forty-Five | 310 |
| 46. | Chapter Forty-Six | 316 |
| 47. | Chapter Forty-Seven | 320 |
| 48. | Chapter Forty-Eight | 323 |
| 49. | Chapter Forty-Nine | 327 |
| 50. | Chapter Fifty | 333 |
| 51. | Chapter Fifty-One | 339 |
| 52. | Chapter Fifty-Two | 344 |
| 53. | Chapter Fifty-Three | 348 |
| 54. | Epilogue | 355 |
| About the Author | | 361 |
| Acknowledgements | | 363 |
| Mythic Alley | | 367 |
| Heart of Stone By Jessica Haines | | 369 |

# Chapter One

**Eight Years ago**

It was the black cat's fault Willow was there, but to her surprise, it was nowhere to be seen, not even lurking in the shadows with the estate agent, Clive. His reluctance to show her the property showed in his every step. There was no cheerful spiel telling her the highlights of the location or jovial banter as they walked through the labyrinth of cobbled streets in the coastal town. Only the call of the seagulls, waves crashing against the harbour wall, and the squeak of Willow's battered Converse boots filled the silence. The suave man she'd met moments earlier shrank further into his oversized coat the closer they got, like a turtle retreating into its shell. The swagger he had in the estate agency was reduced to a slow shuffle. His grey face matched the turbulent clouds rolling in, and his perfectly groomed hair drooped in the fine drizzle. In contrast, hers took advantage of the damp to ping into a mass of blonde, frizzy curls to match the increasing bounce of her pace. She checked the property details again.

*The Old Apothecary*
*Black Cat Alley*
*Fenwick's Yard*
*Whitby*
*North Yorkshire*

His colleagues had stood open-mouthed at her request to view it while his boss instructed Clive, the youngest employee, to take her. His face flashed with anger when he cast his judgemental eye over her appearance, taking in her ripped jeans and battered coat, convinced it would be a fruit-less viewing, a folly, and a waste of his time.

Once they entered the covered snicket, he thrust the bunch of rusty keys towards her and refused to go any further, citing a dust allergy.

'Not scared, are you?' she joked, only to receive a frosty glare. Willow could understand his trepidation; the enclosed courtyard lived up to the nickname one estate agent spluttered out: the Witch's Yard. Clive's dislike was clear, but to her, the unkempt and abandoned building emerging from the trapped swirling fog was a thing of beauty, even with its peeling paintwork and missing roof tiles. It bulged as if its red-bricked neighbours were trying to remove the blight of the town by force. Their overlooking windows were bricked up years ago to avoid seeing it, and the large old gas lamp above the alley entrance failed in its duty to light up the square. Two bay windows flanked the store's door, which, to her delight, had an intact stained-glass window above. With a clean, she could make the colours gleam.

She inserted the key into the lock. It stuck.

'Come on, please.'

She jostled it until it clicked, and the door creaked open.

Willow stooped to avoid a large cobweb hung low across the doorway. Darkness loomed in front of her and she floundered against the wall to locate the light switch. The empty property had lingered on the estate agents' books for decades; no one knew if the electricity was even still connected. The lights switched on, but it made no difference; the bulbs were hidden beneath a thick shade of webs and dust.

She stepped in. The floorboards sprang beneath her feet, causing her to proceed gingerly, and she sneezed as the dust motes danced. Maybe Clive had a point. Through stinging eyes, she saw a wall covered with shelves full of boxes and jars with yellow peeling labels, and opposite an old wooden counter ran the length of the long room. She couldn't resist trailing her hand along it, feeling the wood beneath and its potential. To her joy, the removal of a ghostly cloth revealed a traditional brass cashier's till. A satisfying ting rang out when she pressed a stiff button. Despite the display showing shillings and pence, it would have to stay.

She turned to face more shelves which rose to the ceiling, lined with jars full of things unknown and drawers of all sizes, many tiny. A large pair of scales stood on the counter, and a miniature brass version for precise measurement stood on the workspace behind. When Willow looked up, she saw the shadow of her smiling reflection in a mirror speckled with age declaring, 'Brightly Beans cures all'. The property details were right. It was an old apothecary, or a chemist at least.

At the back of the room, Willow noticed a door hidden in the gloom of the shadows. Locked. She juggled her phone to switch on the torch to hunt for a matching key as the dim overhead lights refused to reach this corner. The air grew cold; goosebumps formed on her arms while the hair on the back of her neck prickled.

On a nearby stool sat an old man hunched over the counter, sifting through paperwork. The distinctive outline of an overall coat covering a suit grew more distinct, and a dark tie came partially into view. She could see his furrowed brow as he peered in concentration over the metal-framed glasses perched on his crooked nose. His nimble but arthritic fingers flicked through the barely visible pages. He stopped, sensing her as she sensed him.

*Okay, not just a loop of time then*, Willow thought.

Was this the ghost that provoked Clive's allergies and the reason the property had remained empty for decades? They studied each other, his eyes scanning her up and down. Biting back her fear, she smiled, and to her relief, he returned the smile and nodded before continuing his eternal work.

Once through the labyrinth of shelves stashed full of dusty boxes, the next room opened up to be a deceptively large office. An old desk sat beneath a sash window while an aged coke burner for heat stood in the corner. She sat on a saggy, cracked-leather armchair and studied the room.

*Would that heat the water?* she thought, before acknowledging for the first time the spark of an idea she'd had on her midnight stroll had formed into a distinct possibility.

Willow made her way up the shop's creaking, gloomy staircase and explored the flat. *It's another time warp. Just a different decade.* Thick dust gathered on the kitchen cabinets, dulling the cheery yellow beneath. She screwed her nose up at the dark sticky residue on the faded, peeling wallpaper and ceiling near an aged cooker, revealing the last owner's love of a fry-up. She hid her displeasure when she saw two chairs sitting opposite each other over a chipped Formica table, as if the occupiers had hastily left. Maybe the gentleman downstairs wasn't the only resident in the building. The gaudy geometric carpet in the living room would have to go, she decided. Even in its muted state, it promised hallucinations or migraine if she looked at it too long. The windows overlooked the front of the shop, and Willow watched as Clive rubbed his hands and stamped his feet with cold. She would put him out of his misery soon, after she had explored the garden she'd spied from the bedroom window.

While secret yards like this were common in the town, hidden from tourists and treasured by locals, private gardens were not. Willow forced the back door open, and it hit the weeds and brambles threatening to climb the building like its own fairy-tale castle. The plot's size was manageable, though it would take grit and hard work to clear. It was perfect for her own witch's garden. Movement along the wall caught her eye. A dark shape emerged from the shadows; one she was expecting.

\*\*\*

Willow always struggled to sleep, or rather, stay asleep. When darkness fell, even with a burning night light, sleep would evade her, and when her eyes finally closed, lung-crushing panic would wake her. Often snatches of the dreams fled before she had a chance to catch and analyse them, leaving behind anxiety and unease. Other times, they were filled with memories she would rather forget. She'd tried herbal concoctions, spells, even hypnosis, before she succumbed to seeking help with conventional medication, but that led to her being trapped in her fear, unable to escape, paralysed until the drugs wore off. Never again, she had decided, so she ran. She sprinted through the night until exhaustion took hold and she collapsed into a dreamless sleep.

Last night was no exception, despite her hopes the sea air and cosy room in Mrs Ramsey's B&B would act as a sleeping draught and lull her to a deep sleep. Willow found herself on the clifftop bending over her burning thighs, fatigued from climbing the famous 199 stone stairs which wound up the hillside to St Mary's Church and Whitby Abbey. She forced herself to sync her breathing with the waves crashing on the rocks below. *Inhale.* The salty, fishy air shocked the anxieties silent, a numbing relief from the continual scream left over from her disturbing nightmares. *Exhale.* Her fears and crushing panic were released into the brisk North Sea air. Her heart rate slowed, and body calmed. She uncurled and stretched, allowing herself to look down at the slumbering town and harbour. Shrouded in the darkness, the rambling streets she had left were quiet, a contrast to the hustle and bustle she'd experienced earlier in the day. The occasional light shone from houses, and Willow wondered what the residents' stories were. Were they awake soothing a crying baby, burning the midnight oil for a deadline, or were they like her, haunted by dreams they couldn't escape from?

The cool breeze hit her face, urging her to unclasp the clip holding back her hair. With her face tilted to the heavy moon, she stretched and felt alive, revitalised after a long hibernation. If Louise could see her now, she would have burst out laughing, encouraging Willow to savour the moment and hold it tight, like she did the last time they were here. On this cliff.

A nudge and pressure against her legs forced her to look down. A black cat wound itself around her. Its intense amber eyes, glistening in the moonlight, stared at her. She bent to stroke the silky feline, but it disappeared, only to materialise metres away on a wall. As she approached, it darted away towards the steps, urging her to follow. It led her past the shops and cottages of Church Street, through lanes and short cuts she recognised and some she didn't. Disorientated, she saw the cat once more in the entrance of a shadowy ginnel. Instinct took over common sense, and she entered the dark, damp alley. Moonlight led the way as it shone on the courtyard ahead, revealing the derelict shop. The cat waited on the step before it faded away. Willow stood enchanted, not by the store with its twin bay windows, but by the tingle of excitement bubbling inside her and the potential she could see. For the first time, the wanderlust that had seen her travel and live from a backpack vanished and was replaced with the desire to stay and have a place to call home. The battered *For Sale* sign propped against the wall clinched the idea.

***

Now, with the sun straining to filter through the clouds, the witch and the cat met again. They acknowledged each other and Willow whispered her thanks before it melted away. Witch's Yard was where she belonged. It was the perfect place to put down roots. The perfect place to hide.

# Chapter Two

**Present day**

Willow fastened the trademark silver cat charm and blue ribbon around the package with a flourish and finished the sale. She forced another smile at the next customer while sneaking a look at the clock. Only half an hour to go until she could lock the door, but every minute dragged for a lifetime, as did the mellow song in the background. Next year, she'd play popular Christmas music with lyrics. Rosa, her assistant, might hate her for it, but at least she could sing along rather than strain to guess what the tune was supposed to be. As the door swung open, the bell jangled, bringing in a blast of icy air. The woman she'd just served stepped aside to allow another in. The shop floor had seen a steady flow of customers all day.

The golden glow from a traditional gaslight acted as a beacon to all who stumbled down Black Cat Alley. It guided them to their reward for walking off the beaten track and following their instinct rather than any advertisements. The cream-painted compact building stood proudly between its encroaching neighbours, and the worn flagstones in the small courtyard still glistened with frost and ice. *The Enchanted Emporium,* painted in silver followed by a sprinkling of stars, stood out against the midnight-blue shop frontage, and a sign with a silhouette of a large cat sitting on a crescent moon swung in the gentle breeze. Two small trees stood sentinel to the entrance, and their twinkling fairy lights bounced off the crystals hanging in the bay window as part of the winter display while the A-board declared the shop's wares: *Lotions, Potions, and Tea.*

Rosa approached the recent arrival, a young woman in an expensive red coat who scanned the store with her nose in the air. *Great, a snobby customer to end the day.* But the shop would work its magic. It always did. Especially this time of year when it was dressed to impress inside and out with glossy green foliage and red berries, which complemented the lady's shoes perfectly. A tiny fir tree sat on the counter decorated in natural cones, orange slices and cranberries adding to the festive aroma. Its fairy lights reflected in the surrounding glass jars, polished until they gleamed.

'Can I help you?' asked her assistant.

'No, thank you,' came a curt reply.

The American drawl Willow detected surprised her. Not by the accent, but why a sophisticated, high-heeled-Jimmy-Choo-shoe-wearing tourist would be in the small coastal town in the depths of winter so close to Christmas. Summer, yes, but in winter it was unheard of. Besides, those shoes were a health hazard on the cobbled streets in normal weather, never mind when it was icy. She must have a death wish. Willow realised she was the only one to think so as she saw Rosa's glazed expression when the woman barged past. Shoe envy. At five foot three, her assistant had an unhealthy obsession with any shoes that could make her taller. She would be adding those to the top of her virtual wish list.

The woman walked around the Emporium, and Willow wondered what would make her stop and widen her eyes with glee. There was always something, a moment when the store performed its magic and drew the person in: a candle, trinket, wand, or crystal ball, and it revealed more about the customer than talking ever could. This customer ignored most shelves but lingered at those devoted to a range of tea. She trailed her fingers across the rows of jars containing unique blends personally selected by Willow for their taste, herbal properties, and ethics.

'You can try some if you like.'

Rosa collected a glass pot full of amber liquid warming on a teapot holder and poured some into a small espresso cup with a saucer. No plastic cups for Willow's clients.

'How can a customer have the full tea experience from a plastic cup?' Willow explained when Rosa moaned at the washing-up. At their first meeting, Willow knew her employee considered tea as just tea. It was something you grabbed a box of at the supermarket, and when you fancied some, you threw a teabag into a mug of boiling water before adding milk minutes later. There was no finesse in her tea-making technique as evident when, as part of the job's interview process, Rosa made Willow a brew. Only politeness made her not splutter.

'You have a steep learning curve ahead of you when you work here,' she'd said. 'Your tea is atrocious.'

Rosa's hard work and determination paid off to become a valued employee and she now readily accepted the truth in Willow's favourite saying: 'Tea is a little bit of magic, available to everyone.' There was still much for her to learn. The intricacies of tea were an art form she'd yet to master. The Emporium's unique selling point was the complimentary sachet of tea given with every purchase and hand-picked from the small old drawers running behind the counter. The opportunity to discover what they needed in life via the tea chosen drew even the reluctant customers in. Some locals remained afraid of the Emporium's owner due to the folklore surrounding the once-abandoned shop. Both tingled with magic, and while the witchcraft products, proudly and elegantly displayed, encouraged some visitors, others told themselves it was a quirky gift shop while buying their herbal remedies and birthday cards.

For Rosa, the knack and ability to match tea with the customer remained elusive, so she stuck to the more generic messages. Everyone needed happiness, calm, and hope.

The aroma of cinnamon and cloves wafted up from the tea Rosa held—Christmas in a brew. It relaxed even the most stressed customer, and they'd had many over the last week. 'It's perfect on a day like today. It will help you warm up.'

'No. Thank you.'

The woman moved on to the collection of beauty products. It was there Willow saw it. The lady in red reached for a jar from the Wishing Spell range, her eyes wide and expectant.

The magic was complete.

\*\*\*

*Tap, tap, tap* on the parquet floor announced her arrival at the counter.

'Is this the 'original' Wishing Spell range?'

'Of course.'

'Only online it said it was out of stock.' The woman stared at her accusingly.

'Well, it was, but I prepared this batch earlier. And—'

'You're Willow Anderson.'

'I am.' Willow's stomach churned with trepidation. What now?

'Oh, my gawd! I need a photo. No one will believe it back home when I tell them, and Clara will be ecstatic that I've bought this direct from you.' The façade of superiority slipped to reveal the customer's childish excitement. She produced a mobile, and *click*, took a selfie holding the prized product. Willow's bemusement fell into shock when strange arms embraced her and another shot was taken with the glass jar held high.

'Thank you sooo much. My friends will be sooo jealous. We talk about your products all the time and Clara will wish she'd come for this herself rather than send me. Sabrina never got a photo.'

Everything slotted into place. Sabrina Williams, celebrity, model, and now successful actress was the reason the tiny shop had customers world-wide and why Willow couldn't keep up with demand for the bewitched beauty products and oils. After a chance visit, the American-based actress gave an interview declaring an enchanted moisturiser and tea from the Emporium's Wishing Spell range had rescued her scandalous career. Orders worldwide flooded in, rescuing Willow's own teetering business and the boutique shop flourished.

Willow deftly wrapped the small bottle in silver tissue paper dotted with blue stars before placing it in a now-famous box tied with a blue ribbon and silver cat charm. She slipped it into a bag with a complimentary sachet of tea for Clara. On impulse, Willow reached behind her for a second pre-wrapped package and selected another sachet from a drawer.

'This gift and the tea are for you. Only you. Drink it when you get back, boiling water—no milk,' she said, adding them into a separate bag.

'Really?' The woman couldn't hide her delight.

'Really. Now, have a happy Christmas.'

'So, what did you give her?' Rosa asked when the bell signified her departure, and both watched her treacherous walk across the courtyard, swinging her bags.

'Only a bath soak to remove the day's negativity.'

Rosa burst out laughing. 'You do know who that was. Or at least, who she works for, don't you?'

'Well, I assume for someone called Clara.' Willow shrugged while tidying the counter. The lull of customers Willow desired was here.

'For a supplier of the rich and famous, you really do need to read the papers, or at least follow Instagram.' Rosa loved the celebrity pages full of gossip, but her boss was nonplussed with it all.

'One celebrity, Rosa, just one.'

'Well, make that two now. She must work for Clara—the Clara! Rival of your best mate Sabrina. Whereas everyone loves Sabrina and wants to be her best friend, Clara is renowned to be as bitchy as she is beautiful. That girl you served will need bucket loads of that bath soak to survive working for her.'

'If this Clara is so attractive, why does she require a lotion created to attract the opposite sex?'

'Maybe the men around her aren't as shallow as they appear. But I wonder how she'll react with it being plastered on social media right—now.' Rosa dug her mobile out of her apron and showed it to Willow. The photo showing the beaming customer, @LibbyJ56, and Willow holding the love potion in all its glory was being reposted at an alarming rate.

'Can we take it down?' A nudge of anxiety grew as Willow read some comments. 'I don't need to be dragged into a celebrity feud or frenzy. I just want to be invisible with a few customers.'

'No, we can't and no, you don't. Anyway, it'll be fine. Clara'll love the attention and so will your bank balance before it all gets forgotten. It's a bit different to the last Christmas, isn't it? What was the tea?'

'Clara's was to aid gratitude.' Willow grimaced, hoping Rosa was correct and her fear of being seen was an overreaction. She sipped some leftover mulled wine brewed for the customers. 'But LibbyJ56—to give courage to follow the heart. Give her a few hours and she'll buy a plane ticket back home to America.'

'I don't know how you do it. You instinctively find the right tea for each person every time. It's like magic. Even Amber can do it.'

'It is magic, and I blended most of them. As for Amber, her mum was a witch. It runs strong in her blood. It's a whisper in the air, a longing. Anyway, you're learning.'

Rosa laughed. 'Customers who come to me get the generic confidence boost or a good day. Unless Old Percy gives me a nudge in the right direction.'

'See, you are learning. When you first came here, you couldn't feel Old Percy never mind recognise when he was offering help. Don't ever under-appreciate a good day or boost of confidence, it can change a life.'

Old Percy was the affectionate name given to the resident ghost, the elderly apothecary. He nodded, unseen by Rosa, in agreement. One day, she might see him.

'Is it okay to sneak off early? It seems she was the last customer. My mum has Alejo, and he'll be jumping off the walls with excitement and sugar. They're baking gingerbread men.'

'Of course. Thanks for your help. I wouldn't have survived today without you, but first ...'

Willow slipped into the back room and returned with a huge bag of gifts. 'For Alejo.' She lifted a smaller bag. 'For your mum for being a star at minding him, and this is for you.' A small exquisitely wrapped parcel sat among Alejo's gifts. 'But no peeking until Christmas Day. I will know.'

'I'm sure you will.' Willow froze when Rosa gave her a quick hug, but she knew not to expect one back. 'Now, are you sure you don't want to come to ours? Mum'll be cooking, and she always goes overboard for the three of us.'

'I'll be fine. Christmas dinner is just a fancy roast, isn't it? And I've made those.' A snapshot of gravy sliding down the kitchen walls and heavy fists slamming on the kitchen table sneaked into her mind, but she forced it away. Ghosts from the past didn't belong here. Not this year, not ever. For the first time in her forty-one years, she was in charge of Christmas, and she was determined to make it perfect. Her fridge and cupboards overflowed with food, and she'd already ticked several items on her detailed list of preparations off. She would embrace the experience rather than concentrate on the invasion of people to her home, where it was decorated to impress not just herself. Doubts crept in. Trading slouchy pjs and watching movies where others played happy families for being a hostess terrified her. Rosa's offer was tempting; she could cancel her friends and agree to be the visitor. There would be no culinary pressure, and her flat would remain her own. She scolded herself for considering it. It would break her god-daughter's heart and it wasn't as if Amber hadn't stayed over after long lunar study sessions before and Glenn had popped in a few times since their friendship grew. It would be fine. She could manage for a few hours and then her space would be hers again, with sanctuary restored.

'After all, my attempts will easily surpass Glenn and Amber's effort last year when the fire brigade arrived to douse out the flaming oven,' Willow added.

'Mmm, I wouldn't mind a sexy firefighter to brighten up my Christmas, but not sure Mum would babysit at such short notice. But if it happens again this year, I still expect to be on speed dial.' Rosa grinned with a faraway look Willow often saw when Rosa got lost in romantic thoughts.

'I can't believe you never contacted the one who gave you his number. Not even for one date.'

'One date can lead to more and then to complications. Vincent is the only man I need,' Willow said.

'Vincent's just a cat and—'

'Merry Christmas, Rosa.' Willow cut short the conversation they had repeated many times. Through the warped glass of the shop window, Willow watched her employee and friend cross the flagstones and disappear through the snicket.

With the door locked, Willow kicked off her shoes. All day she had longed for solitude, and now it was here. Loud songs quickly replaced the musical drone she had heard on a loop for hours and she sang along, swirling and dancing to the music while tidying for the last time that year.

The tempo of the music changed, allowing Willow time to pause. She nibbled a leftover mince pie that Rosa had put out for the customers and sipped some more mulled wine. The shop was everything she'd imagined it could be on the day she viewed it, from the colour scheme to the cat logo inspired by Vincent.

Where was that cat? It was unlike him to not be winding around her legs, catching stray crumbs. He had been with her from the beginning and had seen the store transform with her. The old dark interior was full of light despite keeping most of the original oak fixtures, and the old till gleamed. They only used it as storage, but during the night she could hear its distinctive ting as Old Percy continued his ghostly duties. She'd hidden her true witch self for many years, the shop gave her the opportunity to step away from the shadows and embrace the magic which ran through her being. Cauldrons, athames, crystal balls, and even broomsticks, made to order from a talented witch she had befriended, stood proudly among the rows of glass jars containing specialist herbs and tea. It still made her chuckle seeing the shock on non-magic customers' faces when they read the labels of *Eye of Newt* and *Bats' Wings* before they read the more recognisable and mundane names of wild mustard seed and holly underneath. Her idea of making magic acceptable to a wider audience worked by introducing specialist teas and, of course, the famed Wishing Spell range: handcrafted cosmetics and candles with added spells to be used daily, including the popular moisturiser, with a confidence spell woven into the mixture.

The Yule decorations and lights added an extra sparkle and fragrance she loved. A small Christmas tree stood on the counter decorated with cones, dried fruit, and berries. Willow favoured natural decorations except for a lone vintage bauble. She made it spin, remembering all the trees it adorned in her childhood. The one ghost she wished would visit never did, but she spoke to her, anyway.

'Merry Christmas, Mum. Next year will be a good one, don't you think? Things have come together.'

Would her mum be proud of the success? She hoped so, despite her mum's negative view of magic. She knew her mum would change one thing. 'I know you'd like to hear gossip about my love life and the patter of tiny feet, but I'm happy. You'll just have to accept the Emporium and Vincent are my babies.'

Arms stretched, Willow spun round on her stockinged feet and danced to the quickening beat of the music. Talking of Vincent, where was that he?

A loud knock on the door interrupted her thoughts. A dark shadow loomed behind the closed blind. Willow swallowed the rising apprehension, acutely aware of the Emporium's isolated spot, and whoever was behind the door emitted anger in waves. She edged towards the counter and retrieved a small vial she kept for emergencies and unlocked the door. The blast of cold air and the tall man standing there shocked her.

'I believe this—' he paused, grappling to find the words to describe the enormous ginger cat squirming in his arms, '—monster belongs to you.'

'To be fair, he believes I belong to him, but yes, he lives here. He doesn't need an escort. He knows the way home.' Fear dissipated; she slipped the vial in her pocket but her own anger rose. Vincent might be large, unruly at times, but he was no monster.

'He does when he appears in *my* house and refuses to leave. He's stalking me.' The man's rant continued, but her attention was on her cat and his was on the shadow moving at the edge of her vision. She recognised the glint in his eyes, a look she knew too well. Shit, Black Cat!

'No!' she yelled. The warning came too late. Vincent's hackles rose. He launched himself from the stranger's arms into the shop, hissing at the ghost cat that taunted him. The force propelled the man backwards. His windmilling arms failed to gain his balance.

*Crash*.

Willow's suppressed giggle escaped with a splutter when she visualised several cartoon birds flying around the prone man's head. He was as tall and broad as his shadow suggested, but he lost any sense of menace as he lay spreadeagled on the tree, previously standing guard near the door, tangled with fairy lights. She was amazed Vincent could floor this giant.

'Sorry, it's not funny.'

'No, it's not.' Any residual laughter disappeared with his icy glare and tone of voice.

Willow resisted the temptation to leave him there and offered her hand to help him up. As soon as he grabbed her hand, she felt it. The tingle. An electrical pulse ran up her arm. What the hell? Who let go first she couldn't recall, but if it was him, did he feel it too? What did it mean?

The flurry of questions stopped when Willow's body lurched forward. She screamed as the ground got closer in slow motion yet speeded up, making it impossible to break the fall. Pain exploded in her head as she hit the cold flagstone, then nothing. Everything went black.

# Chapter Three

**Days earlier**

The hum of the engine and monotonous vibration confused him as he struggled to open his eyes. His head thumped with every rotation of the car wheels, hitting the window he slumped against. All he could see was a vast amount of inky sky. Where was he? His neck muscles protested as he straightened, and the throbbing pain throughout his head intensified. The car dipped and lurched sharply to the left, his stomach following it. Nausea hit. The smell of the cream leather interior and air freshener swaying under the rear-view mirror, mingled with the stale alcohol emitting from his crumpled shirt, amplified the feeling.

'Stop!'

The car climbed another hill.

Come on, thought Nate, as another wave of sickness hit. The driver pulled into a passing place when it reached the snowy brow. Nate flung the door open, staggered out, and threw up. Freezing air hit his face, and he took some deep breaths, each one soothing his heaving stomach. Only when he knew he wouldn't be sick again did he look up. He stood in awe at the panoramic view of a vast, dark night littered with bright stars, the Milky Way running across the sky untouched by the artificial lights of a city.

'Here you go, Mr Reynolds.' The driver passed him a bottle of water, which he gratefully took.

'It's stunning, isn't it? You don't see that in the city.'

Nate nodded. 'Where are we?' he asked. The land dipped and peaked while the road, highlighted by the car's headlights, twisted and turned. No wonder he felt ill. A few silhouettes of trees dotted the landscape.

'The Yorkshire Moors, sir.' The driver studied his drunk passenger. 'Not far from Whitby. In fact, if you look over there, you'll see the Abbey.'

Nate looked and saw the ruins lit by multicoloured spotlights overlooking a black sea. He recognised the skyline from vague memories from childhood, or maybe a photo, but Nate was still none the wiser about why he was in North Yorkshire. What was he doing heading for Whitby? And why? He looked down to see himself dressed in a creased dinner jacket, a bow tie hung open round his neck, and a stain spread on his white shirt, the smell of whisky wafting up. Whisky. He could feel the burn in his throat and the warmth of his stomach as he recalled gulping down a shot before demanding another. He rubbed his brow as he caught snatches of the night before: Rebecca in her stunning red dress with a low-cut back which emphasised her curves, her pinned-up hair falling loose as she danced to the live music at the Hilton's Christmas Ball in London, the barman handing him another drink as he watched, and a concerned hand touching his shoulder. Nate patted down his pockets, pulled out his phone, and switched it on to a flurry of notifications of missed calls and text messages.

All variations of 'Where the hell are you?' With more expletives added with each new message.

\*\*\*

'This is as far as I can get, I'm afraid,' Rick, the driver, said, jolting Nate awake. The car drew up in a narrow, cobbled street, flanked either side by tiny traditional fishing cottages. Christmas trees sparkled in the windows and wreaths hung on the front doors. Shadows moved behind closed curtains as the morning inside began.  opened the car door and Nate climbed out to the sound of the hubbub of traders on a nearby street preparing for the day above the constant lapping of the sea against the harbour wall. The smoky aroma of kippers mingled with the saltiness and tang of the sea, making his stomach rumble despite the lingering nausea. He stood confused, clutching a bag gave him and willing his head to stop thumping. The church bells tolled seven, and his heart froze. He was supposed to be on a train to his office in London five hours away. There must be a mistake. He turned to get back in the car, but the rear lights disappeared around the corner, leaving him alone.

'There you are, love.' A lady with an oversized cardigan pulled tightly around herself appeared from a nearby cottage. 'You made good time. I'm Kelly. George called, so I was expecting you. I have the key, but maybe you'd like a cuppa or coffee? It's been a while since anyone stayed, so it'll be chilly in there. A cuppa will warm you up.'

Nate shook his head. George. He breathed a sigh of relief; if George was behind this, he would be okay. He hoped. He needed to remember, but the foggy patches of his memory refused to clear; a chill spread through him and a crushing knot in his stomach formed when he tried. Kelly handed him a key and directions, but he soon found himself alone when she was called back in by the children running through the house.

Sand Dale Cottage hid in a tiny yard of three sandstone-bricked houses squeezed into the small space. He unlocked the front door designed for people half his height and staggered straight into a small lounge with low ceilings, causing him to remain stooped. The air was stale, and the house was cold, as Kelly predicted.

Nate ignored the immaculate décor and furnishings but stumbled up the stairs to the first bedroom he could find. He flopped onto the bed and fell into a deep slumber, ignoring his vibrating phone as it rang again and again.

***

The incessant ring forced Nate awake and he wished it hadn't. The bright light intensified the pain in his head. *How much did I drink?* He sat on the edge of the bed, taking in the unfamiliar surroundings. *And where the hell am I?* Faint recollections of the car journey came back, but the rest remained lost in the thick drunken fog of his mind. The ringing continued. He stumbled down the stairs following the noise and answered the heavy corded telephone which predated the seventies. It felt alien in his hand, yet strangely comforting, reminiscent of his childhood.

''Llo,' he slurred.

'You got there in one piece, then. I thought I had better check since you haven't answered your mobile or emails.'

'George,' Nate said. 'What happened? Where am I? And why are you whispering?'

'You can't remember? I'm not surprised. The amount I saw you drink was enough to make your veins swim with alcohol, and I suspect you'd drunk more than that. You propping up the bar set a couple of tongues wagging, but most people were too drunk themselves to notice. Before you ask, I don't know why you were drowning your sorrows. But you said you wanted peace and quiet, and to escape. At such short notice and so close to Christmas, Sand Dale was the best I could do.'

'But why are you whispering?'

'You know what this place is like. Even your office has ears—before you know it, someone would overhear and realise you aren't dealing with an emergency in Strasburg. Your true whereabouts would be around the City in minutes. So, I'm in the gents where there is no one around.'

When Nate hired George over the string of young immaculate women waiting for an interview, it had raised a few eyebrows. He never thought the ability to have private conversations away from gossiping ears would be an extra advantage. When the battleaxe Mrs Ferguson, the PA he inherited from his predecessor, retired, it seemed the ideal solution. Despite her impeccable efficiency, he hated her; she looked down at him as if he was a scabby schoolkid dragged into being her boss. She resented any suggestion of change. Rebecca's endless comments and suspicions about the temps who filled in also wore him down. George might not be a qualified or experienced PA, but he was as efficient as Mrs Ferguson and came into work every day with a spring in his step, grateful Nate had given him a new career path rather than being forced to retire after being made redundant from a job he loved. His grandfatherly ability to get on with everyone while standing his ground made him the perfect candidate.

'Does Rebecca know?'

'No, but she is on the warpath demanding where you are. I expect a bonus for covering for you, and my missus expects an excellent review on Tripadvisor. Sand Dale is her baby.' Nate sighed with relief before tuning out as George gave him a lowdown on the house.

'Anything else I can help you with?' George said.

'Only one thing. Where can you get a proper coffee round here?'

The hot shower and paracetamol Nate found at the back of the bathroom cabinet eased his headache enough to walk into the town. The streets of Whitby heaved with last-minute Christmas shoppers searching for the ideal gift. Many were tired, stressed, and oblivious to the festive cheer the shops displayed, while others buzzed with excitement and caught up with friends over coffee and cake in the thriving cafés. The River Esk sliced the town in two. He joined a jostling crowd at the swing bridge, waiting for it to close so they could cross into the newer town. He heard the deep sighs and groans from partners of eager shoppers and child tantrums mingled with the intermittent hums of carols and gossip. A girl aged around five bounced up and down next to him, holding her father's hand.

'Can reindeer swim, Dad?' she asked, but he didn't reply, instead concentrated on the child on his shoulders who with every jiggle of excitement kicked Nate in the back. The boat they were waiting for sailed past and out to the sea below. They even decorated the boats with colourful lights wound around the mast and sides to join the festive cheer.

The warm fragrance of cinnamon and spice from the Scandinavian-style stalls in the Christmas market and the large tree decked with white shimmering lights tugged at his emotions, deepened his unhappiness. He was grateful to grab a takeaway coffee and bacon roll to eat on the beach, away from the crowds and festive atmosphere. The bitter north-east wind and salty air cleared the remaining hangover as Nate stood on the shore looking out to the horizon. *Maybe my drunken self was on the right track*, he thought. *I needed time away from everything, everyone.* His breathing matched the rhythm of the waves flowing in and out, and a sense of calm followed. He shivered. The coat he'd borrowed from the cupboard at the cottage offered no protection from the cold. If he was staying, he needed to get provisions, warm clean clothes of his own, and a charger for his phone, which lay dead in his pocket. Reluctantly, he headed back towards the crowds, unaware his every move was scrutinised.

***

Nate's icy hands struggled with the door key, but when it gave a satisfying click, he brought in the multitude of shopping bags, taking extra care not to hit his head on the door frame. Kelly, holding one small child and followed by two older ones, all bundled up in woolly hats and gloves, came around the corner.

'Hi.'

'Hello, love. You've a bit more colour in you now. Just checking you're all right and to give you this.' An older child offered him a small casserole dish. 'It's nothing fancy—just a bit of stew we're having, but I always make too much and I promised George I'd keep an eye on you, but it looks like you have stocked up. Are you staying for Christmas?'

*Am I?* he asked himself. It was only a few days away. *Am I really going to abandon Christmas at home to stay here alone?* His muscles clenched and his stomach churned at the idea of returning to London.

'Yes. I am.'

'Well, if you find yourself at a loose end, you know where we are. There's always room for one more at the table.'

He thanked her, eager to get into the warmth, but she continued to chat until the children squabbled. None of them noticed an uninvited guest silently slip into the cottage.

The blazing wood burner soon warmed the building. Nate slouched on the sofa, flicking through the TV channels; images of the ideal Christmas flashed by, giant trees, laughing children, and food galore. Even the grumpy characters he could relate to wore paper hats. He switched it off and flung the remote down. *This is a Christmas-free zone.* When George said his tiny seaside retreat was a doll's house, he wasn't joking. It could fit multiple times in the lounge of his flat, but George's wife had good taste and had achieved a modern look while keeping the original features and ambience. He had everything he needed: food, alcohol, Wi-Fi, and a TV.

'What the—? Where did you come from?'

A gigantic animal sat in the doorway. Its wide amber eyes intensely focused on him. Nate looked at his wine glass and the bottle on the coffee table, double-checking the amount he had drunk. He must be hallucinating—cats were never that big except in a zoo.

*Is there a Beast of Whitby, like the one on Bodmin Moor? But if so, it would be black, surely? Not ginger, nor so fluffy.* They studied each other. Its square head leant to one side inquisitively, long tufts of fur protruded from the top of his ears, and it even had a mane of longer fur around its neck. The tip of the long tail flicked. That wasn't a good sign, Nate thought vaguely, recalling all he knew about cats. Dogs he knew, liked, and could understand, but cats—they unnerved him with their look of superiority and claws. He hated them.

'I have nothing for you. Shoo.' Carefully, he rose from the sofa and edged to the front door and opened it to the blast of frosty air.

'Go. Get out of here.'

The cat ignored him, padded over to the log burner, and cleaned its enormous paws.

'Don't make yourself at home. You are at the wrong house.'

*Or are you?* George would have told him about another lodger, wouldn't he? Nate thought back to the earlier conversations with him, but the words were lost in the drunken haze. He was certain no cat was mentioned, but the seed of doubt nestled in. He grabbed his phone and switched it on.

A tirade of texts, missed calls, and message alerts flooded the screen. He switched it off.

'Fine. Stay!' Nate huffed and slammed the door. 'You've got until I talk to George. Just stay over there and leave me alone.'

Nate woke trapped against the back of the sofa by the cat sprawled next to him. He held the remote in one hand while the other subconsciously stroked the cat's long, dense fur, feeling the deep rumble of its appreciative purr. He snatched his hand away. *So much for leaving me alone?* A dull ache persisted in his bent neck.

'Get off me.' He shoved the cat, who sprang up in disgust, his long tail twitching. The scene unfolded second by second as the tail connected with a half-full glass of red wine. It wobbled, and Nate released his breath as it settled down. Another forceful swish of the tail tipped the glass over; claret drops sloshed onto the table and drip by drip fell onto the pale rug below.

'That's it. Out!' Nate raged. He stormed across the room and flung open the door. A wintry wind blew in stray snowflakes.

'I said out. I bet you don't even live here. Out.'

With a sigh and body as low as it could get, the cat slowly slunk out into the dark.

*What would George's wife say?* The stain refused to budge; instead it faded to pale pink and grew with every scrub of detergent. He hadn't even realised George was married, never mind her name. Nate had assumed George was a widower. After working together in close proximity, how did he not know that? Nate wondered whether the accusation of him not caring about anything but his work, spat out at him several times in the past few months, were true.

Twenty-four hours ago, his life was mapped out; he knew what he was doing and where.

Arriving home to his flat early, he'd looked forward to a long shower and swift drink before the Christmas Ball. They were not his thing, but as the boss he was expected to attend and Rebecca would have been devastated if he cancelled; it was circled in the diary and preparations had begun in earnest weeks ago—the dress, shoes, and bag. Who knows what else she had bought? As a social butterfly, she saw this as an opportunity to flutter and fly, soaking up any compliments, and an opportunity to network.

He kicked off his shoes before doing a double take as he saw another pair of shoes stranded in the hallway, followed by hearing a giggle from his room. He stealthily crossed the large open-plan living area, briefly noticing the stunning sunset across the silhouette of London from the ceiling-to-floor windows of his apartment. Through the opened door of his bedroom, he faced what he already knew: Rebecca straddling a vaguely familiar man in his bed, her long hair trailing down her naked back. He opened his mouth to speak and confront them, but he left in silence.

Hours later, Nate felt a sense of déjà vu when he flung his shoes off on his return.

'Darling, is that you? You're late. Please, can you zip up my dress?' Rebecca stood before him, stunning in a silk dress that hugged her body perfectly. She scooped her hair up before turning around. He zipped it up, and she purred her thanks.

He scanned the room for any signs of her lover's presence. There was nothing. Just the fragrance of her perfume, and he wondered if the excess was to cover up any lingering aftershave or smell of sex. He studied her as she finished getting ready. With her high cheekbones and a figure she worked hard for, she was as stunning as she thought she was. Maybe he had dreamt the last couple of hours driving round aimlessly, trying to make sense of it all. The evening passed in a blur, standing on the sidelines as he talked to colleagues and wished them merry Christmas. He watched Rebecca smile and laugh before talking to their wives. She fit into his world and looked the part more than he did. Everyone loved her, but as he waited for the anger to hit, he wondered if he did. Surely, he should feel angry and want to lash out after her betrayal, but he felt nothing. He ordered a drink and downed it in one gulp. The heat burned his throat.

He had another.

'All right?' George touched his shoulder.

Nate came out of his haze. 'Not really,' he slurred. 'Don't you just wish you could escape all this?' He gestured with his drink. 'Be by yourself, no cares and no bloody Christmas.'

Nate ignored George's scrutinising stare. After the day he'd had he deserved a drink or two and if he was getting drunk, it helped banish the images of Rebecca naked with someone else. 'Know anywhere?' Nate hiccupped and ordered another whisky.

'Strangely enough, I do.'

Within an hour and a flurry of phone calls from George, Nate fell asleep in the back of a car travelling north.

The wind whipped up outside, rattling the windows at Sand Dale. Swirls of white replaced the darkness of the night sky. The promised weather he'd heard murmurings about on the radio and news had arrived. *Glad I'm in here.* He poured himself another glass of wine. *I'd hate to be out in that.* Like the lumbering animal he'd thrown outside. Guilt kicked in, but it didn't live here. It was nothing more than a sponging and using creature taking its chance. Just like Rebecca. A newsreel showing her played in his mind. She was using his flat, his things, and his bank card. The rage kicked in and he stomped around the cottage. He opened a random cupboard in search of food. The images froze as he saw a box of cat kibble.

\*\*\*

The knock on the door vibrated through the small house. Nate staggered to the door and yawned. The low winter sun blinded him as he opened the door. He shivered, but at least the weather was calm. The storm had blown through, leaving behind a sludge of thawed snow.

'Mr Nathaniel Reynolds?'

'Yeah.' His heart raced. Had Rebecca tracked him down already?

'Packages for you to sign for.'

The man and his courier uniform came into focus. Nate grinned, allowing several boxes to be stacked inside.

'Great. Thanks,' Nate said. Unable to resist, he ripped open the largest box. Excitement bubbled up as he removed a top-of-the-range coffee machine. Now this was perfect.

'Wow! That is massive. Maine Coon, is it?' the courier said.

Confused, Nate shook his head. What was the delivery guy talking about? The machine wasn't that big. His hungover mind shrugged it off. He signed the electronic device, wished him a merry Christmas, and watched him leave. Along with a new laptop and other essentials, today would be an excellent day. The cheery over-enthusiastic radio DJ didn't grate so much now his mood lifted with the promise of caffeine. He sang and swayed to the music. The bitter aroma of fresh coffee filled the air with the comforting gurgle of the gleaming machine. Maybe it was too large for the petite cottage kitchen, but the taste was nectar, and the buzz running through his veins knocked the hangover away. Who needed the table to eat from, anyway? He wasn't planning on cooking anything beyond microwave food. A mournful cry came from the kitchen door. Nate flung it open and grinned. Today was getting better.

'You're back!'

The cat, looking no worse for his night outside, strolled in. Nate crossed over to the fridge and poured some cream, hoping it would help make amends. He regretted kicking the poor creature out into the storm and guilt had made sleep impossible. A cat like that was irreplaceable.

'You must be hungry too.' The cat finished lapping up its treat and licked his whiskers. 'You deserve to be spoiled.'

Over the next few days, they settled into a routine. During the day, the cat spent time with Nate before disappearing into the night for feline adventures. Nate discovered it enjoyed playing fetch like a dog, its fascination with water meant the bathroom door remained closed, and how much he enjoyed the animal's company.

Another movie watched, Nate stretched and took a call from George. After catching up with the news. Nate looked at the contented cat. He scratched behind its ear to be rewarded by a loud, rumbling purr.

'Oh, by the way, what's the cat's name?'

The purr stopped, and the cat edged itself off the sofa.

'What cat?' George chuckled. 'We don't have a cat.'

'You must do. It's been here since I got here. I found the cat food.'

'Cat food? That must have been left over from my sister-in-law's visit. Her cat always comes with her. Describe it to me.'

The flash of the phone's camera dazed the wide-eyed creature before he slunk towards the front door.

'Oh, that's Vincent. He's the witch's cat.'

# Chapter Four

**Present Day**

'I don't need to be here,' Willow said again. 'I'm fine.'

Nate ignored her protestations as he had done since he bundled her into the car and drove in excruciating silence across the Moors to the hospital. His eyes remained focused on the miserable Christmas tree in the corner of the A&E waiting room. It wasn't only real trees who drooped when unloved; old, dented baubles with chipped paint hung from balding plastic branches which the hastily thrown-on tinsel failed to disguise. The lopsided fairy looked like she needed counselling after all the trauma she had seen in this room. Fake festive wrapped gifts gathered below. Willow knew they were fake; several children and at least one adult had rushed over in delight but left disappointed once the packages were shaken. Her eyes burned under the bright strip lighting, and the incessant noise of the department, the clatter of trollies, clunk of wheelchairs, even the squeak of shoes, made her head throb more. They had been here for hours and she longed for the peace of her flat. Vincent would be sulking; not that he deserved sympathy, it was his fault she was here.

*What was he playing at?* In the eight years she had him, he had never been one to stray. He was a homebody apart from his daily jaunts around town. Yet he had forced himself into this man's life for days. *Why?* What made Vincent do it? It wasn't this man's personality; *Moody,* she decided. Anger and irritation radiated from the stranger, making her own temper bristle. He didn't have to stay with her. *Stubborn*. Despite telling him to go, he'd refused unless she contacted someone. With Rosa spending time with Alejo, and Glenn and Amber on their yearly trip to the panto, which she refused to ruin, she had no choice but to rely on him. *Sexy*. She shut the thought down. *No. I refuse to think about it.*

Willow concentrated on other people's dramas instead. An elderly couple argued about the husband's stupidity in climbing a rickety loft ladder, while he retorted it was her fault for demanding the special tablecloth they always used on Christmas day. He sat in a wheelchair with his swollen foot raised. A father cradled a young angel with her arm in a sling as she sobbed that her wings were crushed, while another child, dressed in a purple cloak bound with golden braid and crown, weaved himself through the chairs, an aeroplane held high in the air. His bruise forming on his head matched Willow's.

'If I stand up and play aeroplanes, can I go home?'

Willow hated hospitals. The oppressive atmosphere closed in as raw emotions of the patients' past and present bombarded her. More than one lone and disorientated spirit had walked by along the corridor. Nurses hurried by, harassed; she was wasting their time. It was just a fall. Willow stood up.

Her reluctant companion whipped round and glared. 'Sit down.'

Dizziness overwhelmed her, forcing her to comply. She found herself unable to stop staring at him. His eyes were brown and deep like the smoothest chocolate and it was difficult to tell where the pupils began. She wanted to take in every detail of his face and memorise it. The dark curls at the nape of his neck, the shadow of stubble forming. Her fingers twitched, longing to reach out to touch him. Her stomach somersaulted at the recollection of the electricity and warmth she felt when she grasped his hand moments before she fell.

He looked away and concentrated on his phone. Her gaze lowered towards his shoes. Willow cringed as she remembered.

\*\*\*

Nate's first thought when he saw the unconscious woman beside him was the song lyrics declaring the witch is dead. These were quickly replaced by *that will hurt*. Untangling himself from the foliage and lights, he cursed. After discerning she was alive, he carried her into the shop where music continued to bellow and the master of mischief who caused the accident was nowhere to be seen.

'Bloody cats,' he muttered. Once Vincent's identity was revealed, he'd felt betrayed and conned. First by Rebecca and now a cat. Anger had made him traipse around the town, hunting for the witch. Vincent refused to cooperate, forcing Nate to scoop him up and carry him; he was determined to return the cat. The longer it took, the more frustrated he became.

What had happened when he arrived at the store? The entire episode was a blur. One minute, the figure dancing in the shop mesmerised him, making him forget the squirming creature he battled to hold. The next he was falling thanks to that meddling cat, and something else. He lost some balance with Vincent's sudden leap through the doorway, but he was certain a force stronger than even an over-large Maine Coon was capable of had pushed him. Something from the shop. He shook his head, dismissing the idea except she was a witch. Had she cast a spell on him? And what had happened next? Her laughter aimed at him as if he was the clumsy one rang through the courtyard, flaring his irritation, but then she held out her hand. He grasped it only to see her recoil with horror and tumble to the ground. Why did she let go?

He looked down at the woman he cradled against his chest. When George told him about the witch of Whitby, he laughed. An absurd idea yet a clever business plan, a gimmick the tourists would love. She wasn't what he expected. No green skin, black hat, or matching black cat. A vague fragrance of apple shampoo drifted up. With high cheekbones and flawless skin, she was beautiful in ways different to Rebecca. She wore only a hint of make-up and the short-cropped hair gave her the appearance of an elegant elf. Her eyes fluttered, and she snuggled closer into his chest. He shivered, walking through a blast of cold air. The sudden drop in temperature brought her round. Her eyes opened wide.

'Put me down,' she screeched, kicking her legs.

Swearing, he strode into the back room and put her on the sofa harder than he should. She winced with pain, making him feel guilty, but he was only doing as she wanted. Rows of shelves, full of stock, filled most of the room except for the corner he stood. The small sofa and comfy chair, and a place to make drinks, made it into an improvised staffroom. An ancient coke burner added the much-needed heat. Herbs hung drying from a rack above her desk where melted candles stood in candlesticks, along with paperwork and a crystal ball. Crystals and pot plants lined the windowsill, and a broom stood near the door. There was no doubt he was in a witch's lair. Despite not believing in the supernatural, he felt disarmed and uncomfortable.

The sooner he could leave, the better.

'You need ice on that. Then I'll take you to the hospital.'

'No, I'm fine.'

Nate studied her closely. 'You've had a nasty bump on the head. It needs checking. I've had enough concussions from rugby to know. Either I take you or you phone someone else to.'

He passed her the phone. Standing up to her full height, she looked at him directly. 'I'll be fine. I've some salve to reduce swelling.' She continued to list other reasons she would be okay. His conviction wavered. She'd nearly convinced him to walk away, leaving her with her cat, when she paled further with a tinge of green. Before either could react, she vomited on his shoes.

***

'Willow Anderson?'

A nurse pulled the curtain open, walked in, and smiled at Nate scrunched up on a hard plastic chair. He smiled in return. His eyes sparkled as she reiterated what the doctor had previously told him, and he nodded. Willow longed to cough and declare she was the patient, but fatigue and apathy overwhelmed her. She wanted to go home and if it was quicker to let them believe they were together, it was a price worth paying.

'Okay, so we'll discharge you as long as you have someone with you for at least twenty-four hours, preferably forty-eight. I assume that is not a problem?'

Silence hung in the cubicle as both the nurse and the man waited for her response.

'No, that's fine.' She crossed her fingers behind her back. At this hour, Rosa would be asleep after an eventful evening with Alejo, and she refused to disturb Glenn and Amber on their traditional panto trip. Besides, she wouldn't be alone. Vincent would be there and the ghosts. No one was ever completely alone at the Enchanted Emporium.

'Great. I'm sure your man will spoil you, especially so close to Christmas. It's important to rest. So put your feet up and allow yourself to be pampered.' The nurse turned to him. 'With all head injuries, even slight concussion, it's important to keep an eye out for any new symptoms, including personality changes.'

'We've not known each other long, but I am assured she is always this grumpy,' he said. The nurse laughed, thinking he was joking. Willow's head throbbed when she scowled at him. *Who does he think he is?*

'Have a lovely Christmas, dears.' The nurse left with a cheery wave before going to her next patient.

'So then, Miss Willow Anderson.' His attention turned to her, and she hated the fact her heart fluttered despite her anger towards him. 'Your place or mine?'

'What?'

'You heard the nurse. You need to be with someone for twenty-four hours and unless you phone someone, I guess that person has to be me. Vincent doesn't count. And don't say you'll be fine. I have proof to say you lie where that is concerned.' He waggled his stained shoes. Mortified and reprimanded, all she could say was, 'I don't even know your name.'

'Nate, you can call me Nate.'

# Chapter Five

The bells chimed three over the sleeping town. Witching hour, thought Willow as she lay gazing at the moon high in the sky. All she wanted to do was sleep, but it remained elusive. This wasn't how she expected the early hours of Christmas Eve to be: a painful headache made worse by the tossing and turning she was doing to get comfy. Deep down, she knew her ability to sleep had little to do with comfort and more to do with Nate lying on her sofa a few feet below. No one stayed at her flat, yet there he was. Guilt added to her insomnia, guilt he had spent the evening at the hospital with a snappy ungrateful female followed by a night on a sofa not suited for anyone over five foot. She sighed. Would he be awake? She should apologise.

No matter how much she must have irked him, he remained a gentleman throughout. He barely flinched when he saw the mode of transport to get her to the hospital. Willow assumed they'd take his car, something posh and new, judging by his clothes. When he confessed to not having any, she hid a chuckle as he folded his large frame behind the wheel of the old, rusty Morris Minor van, complete with seventies-inspired painted flowers on the back. It was a leftover from her youth she was reluctant to leave behind. He took extra care tackling the winding roads across the Moors, and he started conversations only to be met with monotone, simple answers. On their return journey, when he tried to clear the air, she feigned sleep.

She cursed herself for not agreeing to go to his cottage; the lure of climbing under her own duvet had won her over. It wasn't his fault she was protective of her space, or that her cat had stalked him. It wasn't his fault she fell. The more she tried to recall the sequence of events, the less sense it made. Vincent was a large, powerful cat, especially if provoked by the ghostly black cat; he'd made her stumble more than once, but Nate was larger and strong. She would have expected him to step back at the most. There was no reason for him to slip. Her fear of being sued for negligence made her check for ice, but there was none nearby. He'd appeared to fly backwards. A piece of the story was missing.

It also wasn't Nate's fault that the fledgling bond Vincent had forged with him made her jealous. After years of being Vincent's only person, her cat, her familiar, was actively pursuing someone else. Her heart lifted when she saw Vincent standing guard in the shop window waiting for their return and forgiveness wasn't far away, yet when she unlocked the door, Vincent ignored her and rushed to Nate for attention. The snub's sting continued when he walked by Nate's side as she guided them through the staffroom and interconnecting door to the stairwell, the only place in the building that remained dark despite her efforts with the lighting and paint. A constant gloom and chill hung over it, which she could never decipher. Her head had throbbed too much to pelt up the stairs as usual to avoid it, and Nate didn't need any more reasons to think she was odd.

'Welcome to my home.'

Willow dropped the keys on the kitchen table. She knew he was tall, but it was only when he stooped under the door frame did she realise how much. If Rosa was there, she would pass comment on him being the perfect height to kiss with high heels on. Not that Willow wore heels, nor was she looking to be kissed. *Yeah, right.* A little voice reminded her of the flood of electricity when she held his hand. *Shut up*, she told it. She looked round and tried to see her flat through his eyes; chaos was the word that came into her mind. Her manic morning rush was evident with a used teacup on the side, unwashed pots in the sink, and a table full of paperwork. Vincent continued his adoration of Nate, mewing and chattering to him to demand food. The feelings were mutual as Nate bent down and scratched behind the cat's ear. Dejected, she sank onto the sofa when she was told to.

The unfamiliar clattering grated on her nerves. Her flat was her sacred space, her sanctuary; only Amber and Glenn came there regularly, and she saw them as family. She wanted to kill that cat until her ginger companion padded in and snuggled next to her, melting her mood slightly. 'You get away with murder,' she whispered, and he moved in closer.

'Here, have this.' Nate appeared, offering her a glass of water and painkillers. 'I'd make you a cup of tea, but couldn't find the teabags.'

'I don't drink tea using teabags.' She swallowed the medication.

'I noticed. You're a tea snob.'

'No, I'm not. The ritual of preparing tea is as important as drinking it. When done correctly the taste of loose leaf is far superior to teabags.'

He shook his head. 'I'm happy with the simple ritual of dropping a bag in the mug but you don't have those either. I bet given the choice, you'd rather teabag tea than none.'

Her temper prickled. 'You're wrong, not that it matters. It's late, I'm going to bed.' After dumping the spare duvet on the sofa, she flounced out of the room. In hindsight, it wasn't her finest moment. She had acted like a petulant child, and she needed to make amends. Hopefully, she could blame her mood on her head injury rather than his presence.

Willow flung back her duvet, exposing Vincent to the icy air. She grabbed her dressing gown and padded downstairs. All was quiet when she crept into the lounge. The tree's soft fairy lights illuminated Nate's sleeping form sprawled on the sofa, his long legs dangling over the edge. Who was he? Willow regretted spending the hours in his company in disgruntled silence. Maybe if she hadn't, she would know more than his name. Sleep had soothed the worry lines on his forehead and the angst she'd seen every time he looked at his phone. He treated it as if it were an undetonated bomb that he couldn't resist checking. The phone he still held in his hand. *What is your story?*

***

'What the hell do you think you are playing at?' Willow stood on the shop floor. Old Percy peered over the old brass till before dispersing. 'I know you're there. I can feel you.'

'You needed a little nudge to find a man.' A vague shape appeared, arms folded across her ample bosom and her nose in the air. The more righteous she became, the clearer Willow could see her.

*Mrs Marley.* Only the Enchanted Emporium could be haunted by its own Marleys.

'A nudge! You could have killed him. You could have killed *me*,' Willow continued, pointing to her swollen face. 'I'm happy on my own. I do not need interference from a stuck-up, hoity-toity gossip.'

A flash of hurt crossed the ghost's face. A lone wrinkled hand reached out to calm the atmosphere. Mr Marley rarely made a full appearance, usually a touch or a whispered, warning 'Moira' was enough to drag his wife back to the spirit world, but tonight she was on a roll.

'Happy? You are not happy. You need more than a successful business to be happy, you even keep your friends away. You need love, a husband. Children. You're not getting any younger, are you? What are you, forty? Forty-one? In my day you would be married by twenty.'

'Exactly.' Willow's voice rose. 'We're not living in the 1960s or whenever anymore.' The words enraged the ghost, who hated reminding time had moved on without her. 'Women don't need to marry.'

Mrs Marley shook her head. 'You'll end up on the shelf, a spinster if you're not quick. Even your cat knows it. Besides, have you seen his biceps? You must be blind if you haven't.'

They both heard the creak on the stairs and the apparitions faded.

'We are not finished yet, Mrs Marley. And don't you dare spy on him in the shower.'


'Everything okay?' Nate met her midway down the stairs. She nodded, not trusting herself to speak as she noted his shirt rode up, revealing a tanned stomach, when he ran his fingers through his hair, messy with sleep. Whatever he did for a living, he earned enough to go on holiday. She willed the butterflies waking in her stomach to calm down. Mrs Marley was wrong; she didn't need a man in her life, especially not this one.

'I just needed some salve. This calms inflammation better than any-thing.'

She showed him the small jar as they re-entered the kitchen.

'I thought I heard voices,' he said.

'Just me talking to Vincent,' she replied before registering Nate's look over his shoulder at the snoozing cat. *Blast.* 'Anyway, I'll go and put this on.'

'Here. Let me.' Nate unscrewed the jar's lid and dipped his finger into the cream. Gently, he applied it to her tender face. Closing her eyes, Willow couldn't help sighing under his touch and the aroma of comfrey and frankincense ointment mingled with his sandalwood aftershave. Her heart pounded. This wasn't a good sign. He stood close, dangerously close. She backed away and relaxed. Looking down, she saw what she was wearing. No one would look twice at her in her Christmas flannelette pyjamas.

As if he read her mind, he said, 'They suit you.'

'What? Childish and frosty?' She looked at the snowmen dotting the fabric. 'I need to apologise. For Vincent imposing on you for the last few days, I don't know what he was thinking. But mainly for my behaviour. I've been a lousy hostess and I do appreciate all you have done. Can we start again?'

'Apology accepted. It was one hell of a bump you had. It would put anyone in a bad mood. So yes, let's start again. Hi. I'm Nate.'

'Hi, I'm Willow. Welcome to my home.'

'I'd ask for a cup of tea, but I know you don't have teabags and I'm a teabag kind of guy.'

'No, I don't, but Rosa, my employee, does. She has a secret stash hidden under the sink in the back room. For when I'm not around.'

He laughed, and she noted how his eyes twinkled, threatening to make her swoon. 'What? Why didn't you say before?' Willow shrugged and he continued. 'Hang on, she thinks you're a tea snob too.'

'I prefer to call myself a tea connoisseur,' Willow conceded.

'That's just words. Are you up for an illicit cup of tea?'

'I could make one in the pot?'

'It's late. Live dangerously. I'll make you one. After all, I promised the nurse you'd rest.' He filled the kettle, and she headed to the door to retrieve Rosa's contraband. 'And if it makes you feel better, you can blame it and the rest of tonight on concussion.'

# Chapter Six

Willow woke. Her head pounded, but seeing the cup of tea and painkillers on her bedside table made her smile until she sipped the cold liquid. Still, it was a long time since someone had brought her a drink in bed. The memory of the early morning tea followed by melted cheese on toast when their stomachs growled was fresh in her mind. Despite the pain, maybe this Christmas Eve would not be as bad as she expected. The house was quiet. Silent except for Vincent's gentle snore. The folded duvet on her sofa confirmed what she suspected; Nate was gone.

'So much for following the nurse's orders. Not that I need mollycoddling. I've had worse hangovers.' Willow stomped across the kitchen and flicked the radio on, hoping the festive chatter would wash her disappointment away. It wasn't as if she needed him. She could continue her day as planned, but a nugget of loneliness settled in which she knew would be absent if yesterday hadn't happened. The boiling kettle released a satisfying whistle. Willow prepared her morning tea her way, vowing to return Rosa's teabags as soon as the tea revived her. The poky kitchen diner was a mishmash of retro fittings that came with the flat and from flea markets, but her favourite part was her wall of shelves displaying her collection of eclectic teapots and teacups. None matched, and they provided a splash of colour she loved. The chosen festive pot and cup refused to raise her spirits. As she looked outside, her garden, hidden beneath a white blanket, was untouched except for a lone trail of footsteps showing his departure.

'It's your fault I feel like this. You know the routine. Today is for relaxing, preparing for tomorrow and enjoying solitude after months of chaos, but your meddling has spoilt it. Bringing him here, making him stay. You're worse than Rosa with her matchmaking. What were you thinking?'

Vincent chirruped in response. His love for talking back was her favourite quality of the Maine Coon breed, but today she needed more.

'There's a reason I'm happy being the mad cat woman down Witch's Yard.' She slammed a bowl of food in front of him.

'Do you always talk to your cat like that?' Willow stood up too fast, causing her head to spin. Nate continued, 'Actually, don't answer that. I assume it is an occupational hazard for mad cat women.'

'You came back?' Willow blushed. Nate stood in the doorway, hair damp and his clothes sprinkled with snowflakes, holding a cardboard box.

'Of course. I promised the nurse I would and couldn't face being stalked another day by your cat, but if I am staying, I needed to change and bring provisions.' He gave her a paper bag; her stomach grumbled with the hit of cinnamon when she peered inside at the cinnamon rolls and Danish pastries.

Nate pushed a mound of paper and unopened mail to one side of the chipped Formica kitchen table to unpack his box. A coffee grinder, fresh beans, and a French press were revealed. 'You're a coffee snob!'

'No. I am, how did you put it? A connoisseur. Besides, have you seen your coffee? Not only is it instant, it requires a pickaxe to get it out of the jar.'

Willow reached inside the cupboard and grimaced at the thin layer of dust on the jar's lid. When she looked at the solidified mass, she was unable to defend herself.

'You're not the only one who likes a ritual. Now watch and learn.'

***

Willow sank into the steaming water, sending bubbles overflowing the bathtub, much to Vincent's delight. He batted the foam with his giant paws as it floated in the air.

'You never grow up, do you?'

Candles flickered in the draught from the windows, her eyes grateful for the subdued lighting. Her cheek smarted as she dunked, but the tension in her muscles eased in the heat. For the last few weeks, she had dreamt of this day: no boring music, orders to fulfil, or emotional customers to deal with. Despite the financial sense of opening on Christmas Eve to catch the last-minute shopper, it wasn't worth the mental exhaustion she'd experienced the first year she traded. Spellworking, even when performed subconsciously, required energy; once she'd locked the Emporium's door, she crawled up the stairs with exhaustion and she fell asleep on the sofa to wake on Christmas Day evening. She vowed never to do it again. Yule might have taken over as her mainstay celebration, but Christmas Eve retained the seed of magic planted by her mum, a complete Christmasphile even when times were hard. The belief that the impossible was possible lingered long after her belief in Father Christmas faded. It was her day to indulge in happier memories while watching her mum's favourite movies and eating freshly baked gingerbread. It was her time to relax, except today she couldn't. Not with alien sounds from downstairs, and not when the person making them made her want to seduce him.

At his insistence, for safety reasons alone, the bathroom door remained unlocked. She swirled her fingers in the water, a warning tingle gathered in her fingertips. Maybe if she wished hard enough, he would climb the stairs to check her well-being and come in.

*For God's sake, Willow, get over it.* The energy in her hands swiftly receded. Nate was only there because he had to be, not because he felt anything more than duty. Her emotions were at odds with her usual MO. Relationships longer than a night were rare and they were always on her terms; her home and talking about her past was strictly off limits, yet last night her guard had slipped, easing her into easy chat, laughing, and fuelling her desire for him.

When was the last time she felt like this? There was a crush she had at seventeen with the local bad boy she was convinced she'd marry and change his ways, then there was a guy at uni who was constantly drunk, but his handsome face and muscular arms made up for his beer breath and lack of intellectual conversation. More recently there was a man on his best friend's stag do whose Scottish burr made her swoon. That was one summer solstice night to remember; she smiled. One bonus of living in a tourist town was the potential for no-strings-attached summer flings, where they could both walk away after enjoying the chase, a lustful night, or days. A memory of the blazing sun warming her sun-kissed shoulders and dancing in the azure sea snuck in. Arms pulling her away from the gentle waves lapping over her bare feet, a shocked giggle—She slapped the image away. No, not even the ill-fated whirlwind summer she chose to scrub from her history was ever like this. Never did an inner voice unfurl from deep inside her and whisper it wanted more like it did last night when they shared food with Rosa's tea or now, as she imagined him stretched out on her sofa flicking through the TV channels. Her stomach flipped, urging her to listen, act, and ignore the alarm bells warning her not to get involved because if she did, she was playing with fire. The faint aroma of coffee drifted throughout the flat and Willow became grateful for its bitter aftertaste and the furry texture of her tongue. This sobering reality shook her from the thoughts of passionate embraces.

Thankfully, Vincent left her alone as she dressed, so he didn't witness the several outfits she tried before slipping on her battered leggings and faded, slouchy hoodie left over from her student days. If she couldn't rely on her own willpower to dampen her desire, this would prevent him from noticing her. Willow groaned when she realised the sweatshirt had been in her life for half of it. Time flew by at an increasing pace. *Forty years old*, she thought, looking in the mirror, *and I have a shiner only a clever use of make-up could disguise.* She dabbed her finger into the healing balm and massaged it into her swollen cheek, blocking the memories of Nate's fingers lingering on her face. They should change the head injury leaflet to warn patients about inappropriate attachments. She didn't fancy him, nor was there any other connection. Her feelings were just bruised neural connections and would subside with the headache, and life could continue as before.

***

The sound of the creaking and sloshing water while Willow bathed made Nate glance to the ceiling; he forced himself to focus on the figures acting out a dramatic scene until the actors drew each other into a passionate embrace. They didn't help dispel the image in his mind of her naked body immersed in water. He flicked through channels and increased the volume. Unlike his modern apartment, where noise was minimal, this building groaned; as the archaic heating heated the rooms, pipes clanged and clunked, giving it a rhythm of its own while enveloping the activity of its residents. Like the kitchen, the furniture in the lounge was a collection of mismatched, mainly pre-loved pieces. As far as he could see there was no theme or colour scheme, but together, they created a cosy, welcoming atmosphere helped by the glowing Christmas tree and blazing open fire beneath the mantelpiece decorated with evergreen foliage and berries. It was a contrast to his spacious open-plan apartment space overlooking the London skyline with its underfloor heating and mod cons. His Christmas decorations were coordinated in the current colour palette and kept to a minimum. Not that he had put them up himself. George hired a professional to tend to it while he was at work, yet he knew every pine cone and decoration on Willow's tree was hung with care and she probably dried and strung the berries and fruit herself. He imagined each bauble held tight to its own story. Had she sung carols while placing the fairy on the top of the tree and danced like she had in the shop when she thought she was alone? The ginger feline strolled in, leapt onto the sofa, and nudged Nate until he stroked him. Nate stretched out, relaxed and decided this room felt like a home.

'Feel better?' he asked when Willow came in, avoiding his eyes. The ice queen was back. He had hoped the tension between them had thawed after their shared tea and coffee, but the bath had rebuilt the wall. What was it with women? The monosyllabic reply and the following silence infuriated him. Her cat had been plaguing him for days and he was doing her a favour, but she refused to acknowledge him. She bore no resemblance to the woman he saw dancing through the cracks of the blind, being free and happy, nor the cautious but confident professional who'd opened the door of the store. Wearing an overgrown top that fell from the shoulder, emphasising her long neck, she looked vulnerable, especially curled up on the opposite chair, hugging a cushion as a barrier. She might be different to Rebecca in every way, but she was just as high maintenance.

Vincent abandoned him in favour of slinking onto his owner's lap.

'I can switch the TV off if the noise is too much?' he said.

'It's fine, carry on watching it.' She shrugged, making him sigh deeply. If the warmth he glimpsed last night and earlier over coffee didn't return, it would be a long few hours.

'Who's that?' The framed photo on a nearby shelf caught his eye. The candid shot was of a tanned man, a similar age to himself, he guessed. He had one arm draped around a laughing Willow and the other around a giggling teenager with tumbling red hair. Joy captured with a click of a button.

'Oh, that's Glenn, a friend, and Amber, his daughter. They are coming for Christmas dinner tomorrow.'

'A friend?' he said, still studying the photo.

'Yes, a friend. Hang on, you thought I was going to be eating a microwave dinner for one, while watching the Queen's Speech, didn't you?'

'It crossed my mind. You're rather prickly and you yourself said you were the mad cat lady. They are solitary by nature, aren't they?' he quipped, not mentioning the freezer drawer full of frozen meals for one he saw when searching for ice yesterday.

'I'm not that bad.'

'Your mood is just for my benefit then, or are you in caffeine deficit and in need of a cup of tea? I can put the kettle on.' He went into the kitchen after giving the picture a last glance. If she hadn't said differently, he would have sworn the photo showed a couple. A family.

After challenging Willow about her need for the extensive teapot collection, Nate sat on the floor beside the low table pulled into the centre of the room as she demanded. With Bing Crosby crooning in the background, he watched as a kneeling Willow arranged several bowls, teapots, and saucers on a deep bamboo tray. A cast-iron teapot sat on the hearth to keep warm.

'Every tea has its preferred temperature to stew, and method to make. Some of my collection is for aesthetic pleasure alone, others like these are used to make the perfect tea.' She poured warm water into a small clay pot and over the tiny delicate bowls. He dreaded picking them up, fearful his large hands would crush them. 'I first saw this in a tiny restaurant in Soho in London, and I realised how similar this ritual was to spellcasting, and how in the past tea made magic accessible, but now it gets lost in the desire for speed and convenience. The magic of tea isn't in the taste but in the preparation. It gives you space to take a deep breath and gather strength before helping a distraught friend. It is a momentary distraction from grief as the meditative ritual takes over or it creates bonds when people drink together. A cup of tea is more than a beverage but is used to show love, comfort, or it gives focus, energy. It's all about the intention.'

Nate's muscles relaxed while he watched Willow perform the mesmerising tea ceremony. Time slowed along with his breath and heartbeat as he focused on the clinking of the pots, the swirl of the water before it was poured down the slots of the tray into the well underneath, and her soft voice explaining the reason for each step. He closed his eyes when encouraged to smell the intoxicating fragrance before tasting. The delicate flavour preceded the fullness of the tea. When he opened them, he saw her watching him with a knowing smile.

'How do you feel?' she asked.

'Calm, relaxed but awake like I've had a good night's sleep,' He noted her transformation from a prickly guarded person to a serene, relaxed woman with a hint of fey—he was bewitched.

# Chapter Seven

The fridge door held a mosaic of photos and postcards precariously stuck in place by magnets. Sunsets, mountain ranges, and other landscapes were slotted alongside landmarks he recognised—Paris, the Pyramids, and the gothic streets of Prague. One fluttered to the floor when Nate opened the fridge for another beer. He bent down and studied it; a younger Willow stood in front of a steep mountain range that peeked through a thick mist. Unlike now, her hair was longer and dark, roughly scraped up into a bun, allowing stray ringlets to frame her face. It was a candid shot, catching her laughter as she shared a joke with the well-dressed Chinese man next to her.

'Where was this?' he asked.

Willow looked up from the gingerbread tree she was icing. She'd sat at the table after he ordered her to sit, despite her protestations and declarations that she was fine. He had the medical advice on his side, otherwise they knew she would have refused. The kitchen was a hive of activity as Nate took charge of all the food preparation for tomorrow's feast. It might only be the three of them, but Willow was determined it would be a celebration to remember with all the trimmings. 'Wuyi Mountains in Nanping, China. Mr Che taught me the tea ceremony I performed this morning. When I left uni, I was at a loose end. Not like the others, especially my best friend, Louise, who knew exactly where they were going with their lives. Rather than take the job I was offered, I was encouraged to take a gap year to travel and spread my wings.'

'Your parents actively encouraged you to travel? As soon as I graduated, I was expected to join the family firm in the City and start my career.'

'My parents are dead.' She paused, but not for long, eager to avoid sympathetic platitudes. 'It was Marian, my godmother, who told me to go. She also gave me Mavis, the Morris Minor you met last night. It belonged to her late husband. It was his pride and joy, but she decided it should be used. I doubt he'd have been impressed with the paint job Lou gave it, but the flowers made Marian laugh. She had the biggest belly laugh imaginable for such a small lady; it was infectious. She was one of the original flower power hippies.'

'I wondered how the psychedelic flowers came about. They aren't exactly you, are they?'

'Are you saying I'm boring?'

'No.' Nate held his hands up. 'Just you're not very hippy despite your alternative shop. Except in this photo. I can imagine you having flowers in your hair then.'

'Sometimes I did. Mavis's flowers grew on me and we shared many adventures as we drove across Northern Europe, so they were there to stay. My heart is in the East. I visited India, which led me to China, the home of tea, before a bush was smuggled into India so the British could get a cheaper brew. I worked on some plantations and the knowledge I gained complemented the lessons on herbal remedies my grandmother taught me. The seeds of the Enchanted Emporium were born there.'

'It must be nice to be passionate about something and make a career out of it,' Nate said, putting the photo back.

'You don't like work?'

'It's not my passion; I don't get up in the morning with a spring in my step to get there, which I imagine you do. It pays well. I'm successful, allowing me to live my life. Do I enjoy it? I haven't stopped to think about it.'

'Until now.'

'Until now. Do teenagers like homemade gingerbread cookies then?' he asked before taking one from the cooling rack.

'Amber eats them without complaining. Anyway, it's tradition. You can't have Yule celebrations without gingerbread. Don't you have something from childhood you do every Christmas?'

'I doubt fighting with your brothers counts. Christmas is overrated and always a let-down.'

'That's sad. I would never put you as a bah humbug type of guy.'

He shrugged, swigged some beer, and returned to peeling the spuds at the sink, lost in thought. What were his past Christmases like? Even in her darkest days, there was always something about this time of year which made it special.

They worked amicably next to each other talking about travel, university days, and childhood pets after Vincent caused an avalanche of vegetables with a misplaced jump onto the counter. Vincent was Willow's first pet of her own, while Nate still longed for the dog he was never allowed. He rolled the pastry while Willow filled the freshly cut circles with homemade mincemeat and covered them, ready to be baked before joining the warm batch cooling on a rack. Nate leant over and stole one, jumping out of her way to avoid the tea towel she swiped at him. He popped the whole pie in his mouth before she could retrieve it. 'Thief.'

'I'm checking they won't poison your guests. And it's a baker's prerogative to taste his wares.'

'Your wares? You didn't make them alone.'

'No, but you're only my apprentice today. I deserve the credit. Besides, I have never baked anything before.'

'What, never?'

'Never. There was never any need. Mum isn't the homemaker type and wouldn't dream of being in the kitchen with her sons doing something as frivolous as making mince pies when you can order them from Fortnum and Mason's. I must say there is something quite calming about doing it yourself. Maybe I should have pie making as my Christmas traditions.'

'Maybe you should. It's more grounding than opening a box of them.'

'But do they taste as good? I need another one to find out.'

Willow moved to guard them as he stepped closer. The air between them contracted and she could feel his warmth near her as she backed into the table. The electrical tingle she associated with his presence intensified.

'No, you don't.' She pushed him back. His firm chest against her hands didn't help her rising desire. It was clear his work schedule allowed him time in the gym. His pupils dilated, telling her she wasn't the only one aware of the change in tension. She broke eye contact and focused on the clock behind him. The countdown began as the second hand ticked forward.

Five, four, three, two, one.

'Well, that's it. Quarter past five. Your twenty-four hours of being my official supervisor and skivvy are over. Your caring duties are done. And I am still alive.' The sooner he left, the better. She stretched her arms wide to emphasise the fact, sending a shower of flour over the floor and herself.

'Technically, the nurse gave her instructions after ten o'clock, so you have a few more hours until freedom. Better to be safe than sorry.' Nate watched her carefully, hesitated before closing the gap between them again. He gently brushed some flour from her cheek. 'Unless you want me to go?'

Words failed her. Her mouth went dry and her heart thumped hard against her chest, so she was certain he could hear it. His lips were close, his aftershave mingled with spice, lingering on his breath from the stolen pie. *Would he taste of Christmas?* Her resolve to be alone faltered. She reached up, allowing herself to run her fingers through his hair, urging him closer.

A phone rang, slicing through the heat forming between them. He grabbed his phone from his pocket. The gap between them widened.

'Well, it's not mine,' he said.

Dazed, Willow listened. 'No, it's the shop's.' It stopped as abruptly as it started.

'Do you want me to stay?'

She nodded, wishing they could rewind time to recapture the last few moments.

'Good, because I've more pies to make.' He smiled and turned away, leaving Willow cursing whoever was on the phone as it rang again.

*** 

At Willow's insistence, they settled on the sofa to watch *A Christmas Carol*, the Muppet version, as her tradition dictated.

'I can't believe you've never watched it. Everyone needs to watch it, it makes you feel warm inside. What?'

'I'd never have associated the woman I met yesterday with someone gushing over a children's programme.'

'It's much more than a kids' movie. It's perfection.'

The opening song filled the room. Vincent draped himself over Willow's lap, forming a barrier between her and Nate, much to her surprise; after all he was the catalyst for the growing feelings she had for the man mesmerised by the singing puppets. Was her cat having doubts about sharing her time with someone else? She stroked him. Along with the bouts of incessant ringing from the store below, his position provided her space to think and distance herself from the idea of getting closer to Nate.

The film's credits rolled.

'Verdict?' Willow asked.

'I guess I've added another Christmas tradition to my meagre list,' Nate said while Willow replaced the film with another version of the Dickens tale. After their stomachs rumbled in unison, Willow attempted to order a Chinese takeaway. The restaurant owner took some convincing that the Enchanted Emporium wouldn't vanish when the delivery guy arrived.

Within weeks of moving in, Willow had discovered the problem of owning a store rumoured to have connections with the original Whitby witch. For decades, the building had hidden itself in the shadows of the alley, only revealing itself to a select few. It was a practice it was reluctant to give up. When she ordered products and booked builders for quotes, it took time to undo old protective spells, and she often resorted to begging the store to allow people to find it. All day she'd wait for the expected knock. Instead, she received frantic calls about being lost or, worse, accusations she was a time-waster because the address didn't exist. Some companies blackballed her for being a nuisance. The excuse of 'I own a spellbound building' failed to impress. The shop's reputation of being haunted preceded it. Several workmen refused to attend. It took many hours of research to find some who accepted its quirks, the cold patches and tools mysteriously moving on their own, and Vincent judging their every move. Double pay helped, but it crippled her budget.

To her relief, the food arrived on time, courtesy of a spotty teenager and his moped. He was eager to see the witch's house, but was only rewarded by a glimpse of a broom and a gracious tip. She also took the opportunity to tell Old Percy to 'sort out the bloody phone' to prevent it ringing again, which he did by pulling the landline from its socket. Some days, she loved sharing her space with ghosts.

The second version of Scrooge's story ended, and the takeaway packages were empty.

The twenty-four deadline was fast approaching. *Will he stay?*

'Let's go for a walk,' she said.

'What? Why?'

'Because it's Christmas Eve and Whitby is magical at night—come on, grab your coat.'


Willow led him through many alleys and yards to the streets of the old town, illuminated by the colourful lights strewn across the road from building to building. The sound of laughter and singing drifted from the pub. Nate wrapped his scarf around his neck tighter and they approached the steep, cobbled incline to the bottom of the famous steps. Vincent silently padded behind them. The area was busier than Nate expected. Snippets of conversation trickled down the hill as people of different ages climbed the winding stairs.

Some moaned about the weather, while others stopped to catch their breath on the benches.

Most were upbeat and excited.

'Where are they going?'

'To church.' Willow pointed towards a small church near the Abbey. 'For the midnight service. It is Christmas after all.'

'We're going to church?'

Laughing, Willow grabbed his hand, guiding him further upwards. He couldn't feel his fingers, nor her hand cradled in his, but he wished he could remove his gloves to feel her skin. His thoughts soon escalated to other things he would like to do. Who was this woman and what was he doing here?

She bounded up the steps and nodded to the parishioners she recognised, pulling him alongside her. The wind chill increased, biting their cheeks, but he embraced the feeling. It made him feel alive, happy and energised. Was this the Whitby magic she spoke of?

The squat church emitted a warm, welcoming glow and a general mumble of chatter as the vicar greeted his congregation at the door. Surprisingly, instead of following the stream of people, Willow turned left past the field of tombstones to the headland.

'No, we're not going to church. As lovely as the vicar is, our kind are not welcome by many. Besides, why cocoon yourself in a handmade structure when you have this.'

From their position, they could see the town below where Christmas lights shone, and their reflections danced on the sea, giving it an illusion of a beautiful fairy kingdom.

'Our kind?' Willow stared at him, and he wondered what he had been missing, feeling like a dunce. Then he saw her against the stars scattered in the black sky, forming constellations, and a faint glow flowed around her and he understood.

'The witch thing,' he said. Willow laughed again, but he detected something he hadn't noticed before—anxiety and concern.

'The witch thing,' she confirmed. 'But it isn't a thing. It's who I am.'

To the sound of 'Silent Night' playing in the church, Nate stepped closer, drew her into his arms, and kissed her.

# Chapter Eight

The alarm jolted Willow from her disturbed sleep and she fumbled to switch it off in the dark before falling back onto the bed with a groan, waking the snoring Vincent. 'Sorry, boy. You're not the man I wanted to wake up to this morning.'

The kiss was more than she imagined; it felt like coming home. When he wrapped his arms around her to shield her from the penetrating wind, his warmth heightened the anticipation of what would follow. Hand in hand, they returned through the labyrinth of alleys to the shop and Willow didn't doubt he would agree to a nightcap. Except he didn't. After a long smouldering kiss on her doorstep, he wished her a merry Christmas and turned away, leaving her shocked and frustrated. From her window, she saw his shoulders slump after checking his phone before he walked out of sight, adding confusion to the list of emotions that kept her awake.

If Louise was here, what would she say about him? First, she'd have gone through her mental list of requirements in a match. Job—tick. Job more than flipping burgers in a bar—big tick. Own place—tick. Handsome—tick. Hot—double tick. Able to hold an engaging conversation—tick, and make her body tingle with anticipation—tick. With everything answered, she'd turn to Willow and say with an enormous grin, 'Way to go, girl. You've turned a corner. Now get him back.'

It concerned Willow how the passing of time made it difficult to visualise her friend without the use of the photo sitting on her bedside table. Years might have passed since she received the phone call about the fatal fire, but her heart still ached every day. Louise's hair loosely tied back was easy to imagine; it was identical to Amber's before she dyed and straightened it. No one could forget her colourful bohemian style with the long skirts that swirled round her ankles and bare feet. She rarely wore shoes if she could enjoy the earth beneath her feet. Louise's desire to experience Whitby's energy had brought them to their special place. The place Willow took Nate. What was she thinking, taking him to the headland that was sacred to the two friends? And the place that made Willow fall in love with the coastal town. She knew Louise's smile would become fuller at the idea somebody had knocked down at least one brick in Willow's high defences around her heart. The smile might be harder to remember, but the memory of their first meeting was as vivid as the day they met.

\*\*\*

Willow had met Louise at York University on the night the freshers unpacked their belongings and said farewell to their families. All except Willow. Louise watched the tall, willowy girl make endless trips to an old, battered Morris Minor to retrieve boxes and return to the halls of residence.

Having already organised her room to her satisfaction, she went to offer help. Willow's instinct was to refuse and say she was fine, but she soon learnt nothing would stop Louise once she'd made a decision.

Willow's room was quickly sorted, and the two girls bonded over a cup of tea. They learnt they were studying different subjects: art predictably for Louise, with her flowing hippie-style fashion, and history for Willow; but the connection was forged when they discovered they were both witches. Louise was the first witch she'd met aside from her grandmother and the first who was proud of her identity instead of hiding it away like a shameful secret. It was Louise's idea to visit Whitby in the summer holidays to find the infamous Grandma Jax's house Willow had often spoken about, hidden low in the Yorkshire Moors. The place Willow felt most at home. So they booked a B&B in Whitby as a base for their search. In the evening, the girls climbed up the steps, past the Celtic cross to where Nate had kissed her. In the shadow of the Abbey, Louise stretched out her arms to soak up the moon's energy and called to the Goddess to ask for happiness. When she noticed Willow hadn't joined her, she urged her forward.

'Come on, Wills. Take them off,' she'd said, nodding at her big black boots.

'I'm fine—' not realising until then her friend was barefoot, '—thanks.'

'No, you're not. You're a pent-up ball of energy waiting to explode. You're a witch, it's in your blood and everything you do. You can't even make a cup of tea without turning it into a ritual. I've seen you. Watched you. Subconsciously, you murmur spells under your breath as you add the tea leaves. To calm people, give them luck for their exams, or get them out of your way. One slurp of your tea sent that creep with straying hands from room seventeen, scarpering quicker than any warning from admin could. Embrace it. Take off your boots and socks. Feel the earth beneath your feet, hear the waves crashing below, and the moon on your face. Join me and start being you. And be grateful, I'm not telling you to be sky-clad.' Louise's laugh rang out. 'That would get the locals talking, even in Whitby.'

So as the bells tolled midnight, they held hands, and their feet sank in the damp cold grass. Louise's skirt billowed in the breeze and her long hair flowed down her back, in contrast to Willow's, hidden under a hat, and her dark jeans.

'Can you feel it? The raw energy? Whitby may be famous for its Abbey, and the church has looked over the town for centuries, but the ancient energy the Vikings and those before them used still pulses under our feet. Can't you hear the wind whisper the town's past names—Sinus Fari, and Streanæshealh?'

And at that moment, Willow could, and every time she visited since.

*** 

Willow cursed the cold when she padded into the kitchen. She grabbed the jumper draped over a chair and slipped it on. One day, she would update the heating so there would be no more visible puffs of air first thing in the morning. Everything was as they'd left it last night before the walk. Pans of vegetables stood on the hobs, ready to boil, and a stack of tins containing the mince pies and gingerbread sat on the side. She opened one and inhaled the spice, remembering Nate's lips on hers. Sighing, she replaced the lid.

Vincent followed her down the stairs and she let him outside before unlocking the door to her workshop. The only place she deemed the turkey safe from the drooling cat. The single-storey building had once housed an outside loo and storage area but was now the creative hub for the Enchanted Emporium; it was where she processed herbs, bottled potions, and she experimented with herbal blends, remedies, and spells. Her cat sneaked in, and wound himself around her legs, making it difficult to carry the large bird back to the flat; the lure of food was more important than his early morning prowl around town.

With the turkey in the oven, Willow cradled her tea and planned the day. Amber and Glenn would be over mid-morning, giving her a few hours to fill with a relaxing shower and breakfast before curling up in front of the fire to read. She'd treated herself to a latest bestseller for this day, but her thoughts drifted to Nate. If she was Rosa, she would have googled his name and tracked down his social media accounts to discover all the tiny details he hadn't shared while peeling veg and watching old movies. The idea that her own life could be accessed by anyone sent shivers of terror down her spine, leading her to shun the invasive platforms, much to Amber's disgust. Willow regretted it now; as much as they talked, Nate revealed little of his life, making her curious. Who was he and was he thinking of the kiss as much as she was? If it wasn't for his text alerting her he had got back to his cottage safely and the organised kitchen, she would have assumed he had been a delusion caused by her aching head.

'Damn it,' she muttered. Her resolve broke with Bon Jovi pleading for his love to come home for Christmas from the radio.

*Fancy a Christmas cup of tea?* She typed a text and pressed send before she changed her mind.

Freshly showered, Willow dried her hair with a towel while checking her phone. *Message not sent* blinked on the screen and the signal bar failed to appear despite moving from room to room and standing on chairs. The more she thought about Nate, the more she needed to see him. A plan formed when she watched Vincent groom himself in front of the warm oven.

'Don't look at me like that. This works in the movies. Consider it your punishment for straying into someone else's home.' With a note attached to his collar, she turfed Vincent outside with instructions she hoped he would follow.

Willow stood in the lounge window, watching the courtyard for any activity. An emotional cocktail of doubt, fear, but predominantly excitement swirled in her stomach. The buzz of adrenaline needed a release. If her calculations were correct, Vincent, with or without Nate, should have returned. Unless he had become distracted, his deed undone, in the quest for a titbit at the harbour or a mouse. Different scenarios played in her head, including one where Nate scrunched up the note to throw in the bin, relieved he had had a lucky escape. *If he has*, she decided, *it didn't matter. This was just a fling.* A shadow emerged from the alley, Vincent followed by Nate. He looked up and as their eyes met, she knew inviting him in was a risk worth taking. He was a Christmas present for herself.

Willow opened the shop door, jangling its bell.

'I've never had post via a cat before. Is this a new witch craze because I thought it was owls these days?'

'You can't get hold of them easily any more. So, cats have to do.' Her cheeks ached from her constant wide grin. She couldn't believe he had come.

'Are you going to let me in or am I going to freeze to death or worse, get thrown into the bush again? Looking at it, I doubt it'll catch me this time.' The mangled plant bore scars of his fall and Willow made a note to herself to find a replacement, but first there were other things she must do.

Willow stood aside, allowing him in before locking the door. She felt his breath against her neck, and he slipped his arms around her waist. 'You do realise I only came back to reclaim my jumper,' he murmured.

'Jumper?' *What is he talking about?* She melted against his firm chest.

'This one.' He lifted the hem of her oversized sweater, grazing her bare stomach with his fingers, igniting a current of electricity through her. Looking down, she recognised the blue woollen top as his for the first time;

no wonder she couldn't forget his aftershave. Its continual presence teased her.

'Maybe I want to keep it.'

'It looks better on you, but maybe you don't need it on right now.' She turned to face him. Encouraged by the desire evident in his eyes, she silenced the conversation with a kiss.

The heat from the night before returned with more passion. He wouldn't leave her now. They stumbled backwards, and he lifted her onto the counter. She glimpsed an open-mouthed Old Percy before he vanished. The jumper discarded, his ice-cold hands made her shiver with delight as she hastily undid the buttons of his shirt, pulling him closer by his belt. The need for each other meant everything else slipped away.

\*\*\*

'Any chance of cancelling today?' asked Nate, kissing her neck.

'No,' she squealed in response, spraying him with bubbles from the sink. It was tempting to lead him to her bedroom and spend the morning together, but today was important for other reasons. 'In fact, they're here.'

Two figures appeared in the garden and followed the snowy path. A man strode behind a bounding teenager encased in a deep green Tolkienesque cloak; only her ripped black jeans and chunky biker boots revealed with every step showed she wasn't a movie extra. It took seconds from the downstairs door shutting for the shrouded figure to appear in the flat and embrace Willow.

'Merry Christmas,' the girl shrieked. Her hood fell back, revealing a shock of vibrant scarlet hair. 'Dad bought me this, with your help, I'm sure.' The velvet cloak opened wide, showing its black satin lining decorated with dragonflies. 'I love it—thank you. Who are you?'

'Ambs, this is Nate. Nate, this is Amber and her father Glenn.'

Amber scowled at the man drying the pots, taking in his socked feet and rolled-up sleeves. Her dad stood in the doorway. His surprise was also visible, but he smiled and held out his hand while balancing several immaculately wrapped presents. 'Hi. Sorry about my daughter. We weren't expecting anyone else to be here.'

'It was a last-minute decision.' Nate shook Glenn's hand.

Glenn gave the presents to Amber with instructions to put them under the tree before hugging Willow tight. 'Happy Christmas, Wills. Bloody hell. What happened to your face?'

Amber cast an accusing stare at Nate and Willow quickly intervened.

'Blame Vincent. He knocked me down the step at the front of the shop. Nate here rescued me.'

'He didn't catch you, though, did he?' said Amber, still suspicious that it wasn't an innocent injury.

'No, it happened too fast.' Willow omitted that Nate was in no position to help as he lay tangled in lights. The comical image made her smile again. 'But he picked me up and spent the evening in A&E with me. He was my knight in shining armour.'

'You should have called; I would've come over.'

'I know you would, Glenn, but it was panto night. I wasn't going to spoil your and Amber's evening away for this. How was it?' Willow deflected the topic to something more neutral.

'Oh, Willow, you must come next year. It was amazing. The set was wonderful.'

Amber gave a detailed description of the set and costumes.

'As you can tell, my daughter is into theatrical design. She hopes to work in the art department in the theatres once she has finished uni.'

'If I get to uni?'

Glenn rolled his eyes and gave his daughter a hug. 'Of course you will.'

\*\*\*

They retired into the sitting room. Amber knelt near the tree organising the presents into piles. Nate hovered in the doorway waiting to see where he could sit and noted it was a perfect Christmas scene; festive music played, candles flickered, and Vincent sprawled out in front of a blazing fire. The only difference was a Goth teenager replaced the usual overexcited child. The smell of turkey combined with the smell of the tree transported him back to his childhood, when Christmas was simple and exciting. When bulging stockings at the bottom of the bunk beds he shared with his younger brother made them jump up with glee and sit on the floor, ripping open gifts, eating the chocolate, and squabbling over who had the best presents. For the first time since he arrived, he thought of his family and what they were doing and whether they would miss him. He doubted it; he had missed many family Christmases through work responsibilities. His absence wouldn't be unusual. They would follow the same routine—church in the morning, followed by dinner and the grand opening of the main presents after the Queen's Speech. As a child, the delay drove him wild, especially when he discovered his friends opened their gifts before breakfast or even the night before.

His dad was strict; he had to wait as a child therefore so did Nate and his brothers. He wondered if his niece and nephew had to wait too. He hoped not, they deserved to have fun without the restrictions he had. Ten o'clock. His father would be bellowing out carols before listening to the sermon shivering on the family pew. Their church might have a new fancy heating system, but it did little to protect the parishioners against the bitterly cold draught that permeated the walls.

Glenn sat in the armchair chatting to Willow, and Nate couldn't help feeling he was the outsider until she reached for his hand, dragging him to sit next to her. 'Let the chaos begin.'

Before long, wrapping paper littered the carpet to the delight of Vincent, who practised his feline killing techniques on scrunched-up paper Amber threw for him. He caught them with his enormous paws before returning them to Amber for a repeat performance.

'Fetch is one of his many quirks. Who needs a dog if you have a Maine Coon?' said Willow.

'I'd still have a dog,' said Nate.

'So, you're a dog person? I doubt Vincent or BC would ever get on with a dog,' Amber told him. The air chilled between them until Willow nudged the teenager to dish out the presents. To Nate's surprise, she passed him some small parcels from Willow. He raised his eyebrows as he removed the layers of paper to see his favourite coffee beans and chocolate.

'How did you know?'

Willow shrugged but refused to elaborate. He held a pair of festive socks in the air.

'I think fate was being kind,' said Willow. In unison with Amber and Glenn, she ripped her present open. Looking at the goofy Rudolph jumper she received, and the equally garish jumpers Amber and Glenn were putting on, he had to agree.

'Time for a group photo,' Amber declared. Everyone clambered onto the sofa, posing for a series of selfies. Afterwards, Nate switched on his phone, swiped away the many notifications, and took some photos himself. He refused to think of anything but the family he had found himself in.

Amber stripped the paper from the last present, resulting in a delighted squeal at the large carved wooden box. The hinged front revealed shelves of aged glass bottles, small drawers, and compartments. Her fingers trailed over the objects, and her smile widened at the discovery of more vintage glass jars, a small set of brass scales, pestle and mortar, and stubby brass candlestick nestled in velvet padding.

'Oh my God I love it. Thank you.' Amber flung her arms around Willow.

'Every witch needs her own travel apothecary. You can take it to uni but no blowing anything up, brewing banned potions. or getting up to mischief.'

'Spoilsport. I bet you and Mum got up to mischief at uni.'

'Not as much as you think. The most I did was brew experimental teas. Your mum? Well, she was more explorative with her magic until she was nearly evicted for triggering fire alarms and many complaints about the obnoxious odours emanating from her room. Under there is a secret latch.' A hidden compartment pinged open. 'The perfect place for your Book of Shadows. Keep it safe and enjoy.'

They gathered around the table, their plates piled high with festive food.

'Can I get anyone a drink?' Nate produced two bottles of wine. Silence fell. Amber glared at him in disgust. Willow and Glenn exchanged a look before Willow said she would, but Glenn couldn't as he was driving. Glenn interrupted.

'Actually, I wouldn't anyway—I'm a recovering alcoholic.'

Nate cringed and wished he had been warned beforehand. 'Sorry, mate, I didn't realise.'

'It's fine. You weren't to know.' Glenn shrugged and turned to his daughter. 'Amber, it's fine. I don't need protecting or to keep it secret. It won't help. And I'm not about to fall off the wagon if I see someone else drink, including you.'

'Why would I want to? It tastes disgusting.' She crinkled her nose.

Nate poured him a Coke. 'How long has it been?'

'I've been dry for 785 days. Some of the hardest days, but well worth it.' The atmosphere relaxed as Nate and Glenn discussed his road to recovery and tales from his work. Laughter followed, allowing Nate to see Willow in her natural, relaxed environment.

She loved these people, but he wondered how they all fitted in.

'Time for the crackers,' said Amber. Willow offered one to Nate to pull. He noted the shop's logo and trademark colours of silver and blue. 'These are wonderful. I hoped we would have some this year. Willow makes them; each has a spell, gift, or potion to guide the recipient in the coming year. They sold out super quick. I made some this time—she didn't trust me last year.'

'I wonder why.' Willow chuckled. The satisfying snaps earned them all a disgruntled look from Vincent. A gold paper hat from Willow's cracker fell to the ground along with a small bottle of pale green liquid. Nate picked it up and gave it to her. The label read: *Protection*.

'Hey, I made that one. I hope it works, but why would you need it?' Amber said. Nate wondered the same thing.

'Probably against magical mishaps when you're in the workshop,' Willow deflected the conversation. She didn't seem concerned about the message so why did he feel uneasy? It wasn't as if he believed in this hocus-pocus. What would she need protecting from?

Amber received a bag of gems for confidence and reflection, and Glenn unwrapped a candle for romance.

'I don't think I'll need this, Wills.'

'Don't look at me. I've no control over what you're given. Take it up with the universe.' She put her paper hat on and nudged Nate to do the same.

'Let me take a photo, Dad. It might go viral like the one with Clara.' Amber snapped away.

'Please tell me that has settled down. If I'd realised the photo would be online, I would have stopped it being taken.'

'It'll calm down, and if she carries out the threat, I'll just hex her. Oh, don't look so worried. You know, I wouldn't really do that? What did you get, Nate?'

'What threat?' Willow's face paled, and Nate longed to reach out to her hand and soothe her anxious fingers stroking the bottle from the cracker.

'It was only said in jest, I'm sure, and it's trending on social media, which is a fantastic promotion for the Emporium. Everyone'll want to visit now. What did you get, Nate?'

He shook his cracker and a specialist sachet of tea fell into his palm with the simple message of *Clarity in the matters of the heart*.

'Do people really believe in these?'

Glenn laughed. 'If you asked me two years ago, I'd have said they were fools to, but if you hang around, you soon discover Hamlet was right when he said 'There are more things in heaven and earth, Horatio, than are dreamt of in your philosophy.'

# Chapter Nine

Willow snuggled against Nate as they lay in front of the fire and mulled over the day's events. Unable to resist, she helped herself to another segment of chocolate orange, relishing the smooth, silky texture followed by an explosion of citrus when it melted on her tongue. Another piece of heaven to add to a perfect day. The blazing flames warmed her skin while Nate traced a line from each flowering bruise on her hip to her arm and shoulder, as if connecting a surreal dot to dot. Considering how little she knew about him, it surprised her how easily he had dismantled the wall she had built around herself brick by brick over the years.

'How did you find your Christmas at the Enchanted Emporium?' she asked.

'It was different to any others I've had before and I never expected to be seduced by a witch in a Rudolph jumper.'

'It didn't stay on for very long once they left,' she replied, glancing at the discarded clothes scattered on the floor.

'Amber doesn't like me, trying to scare me off with that talk of ghosts which I know are not real. She's probably at home practising her voodoo on me.'

'She's not that bad. You were a surprise, that's all. She's used to it being just me.' Amber's reaction and reluctance to stop interrogating Nate surprised Willow as she was usually laid-back. After dinner, Willow had nearly throttled the teenager when she asked whether Nate knew about the ghosts. Like her home, Willow felt a powerful desire to keep them secret, to protect them and herself. The last thing she needed was for the building to be included on the list of Britain's most haunted properties. They were her secret to tell. She need not have worried; she discovered her apprentice had a natural flair for creepy storytelling worthy of Stephen King. Even the relatively docile Black Cat was embellished into a demonic creature, ready to attack strangers as they entered the store. She turned the truth into a fantastical tale no one would believe.

Nate poured out more wine, which Willow gulped down, reluctant to be drawn into a conversation about her spectral lodgers, especially as she was still reeling from the latest confrontation with Mrs Marley. Earlier, when Nate was in the shower, she'd turned on her phone, concerned with Amber's vague comments of the photograph being viral. The air grew cold behind her.

'Hussy,' Mrs Marley whispered into her ear. A tirade of disgust at witnessing such disgraceful behaviour in the shop followed. The rant would have continued if it wasn't for Mr Marley appearing. He coughed to attract his wife's attention before stating, 'July 1952.' It became clear by Mrs Marley's stuttering and the reddening of her near-translucent skin, Willow and Nate weren't the only ones to have cast away their inhibitions and given in to lust on the shop floor. In a blink, both ghosts disappeared, the temperature returned, and the phone was forgotten.

'Glenn's okay though. You must have known him a long time,' Nate said, interrupting her thoughts. She turned to face him.

'I had known of him but only met him a couple of years ago.'

'Only a couple of years? You seem closer than that.'

'We met during a traumatic time. That makes people bond quicker, I guess. He was Louise, my best friend's, husband. I was abroad when they met just after uni, but I received regular updates by post or, if I was in reach, by phone. While Lou was settling down, I packed up my rucksack to travel. It was only supposed to be for a year, but I caught the travelling bug so stayed on. I heard all about him, his quirks and loves, the house they had found. I didn't even get back for their wedding, despite her asking me to be her bridesmaid.

'Something I'll always regret. I let her down and should have come home even for a flying visit, but she understood. She always did. By the time I came back, she was a mum. Amber was about four when I finally met her while I was visiting Marian. I should have stayed. I knew Louise needed me, but she insisted I returned to India—I had a life out there, friends, a job. Weeks later, she died in a freak accident, but I never knew until I came back to England years later. I was Louise's witchy friend, hidden from view like a dirty secret.'

Willow paused and sipped her tea, remembering the shock and hurt of that day, thrust into grief but also a challenge that pushed her witchcraft ability to its limits. 'Not that I blame her. She loved Glenn, but he was sceptical about magic, so she repressed her witch side to keep him and didn't want me spilling any secrets. When he contacted me two years ago, Amber was critically ill. Louise's fears about Amber's strong magical powers consuming her when she became a teenager had come to fruition. They needed help, and I was determined not to let Louise down again.

As you know, Glenn was an alcoholic. His grief had destroyed him. His relationship with Amber was non-existent. We became close while she was getting better.'

'So Amber's one of you?' Nate stole the last segment of chocolate.

'If you mean, is she a witch? Yes, she is—see, you're learning how to spot us.'

'Mmm, it's hard not to recognise her as one since she is a Goth princess,' he added.

'Not all Goths are witches. Otherwise, Whitby would be awash with us at Goth weekend, and not all witches dress in black.'

'I figured that one out—you don't. So, it's not just a business gimmick to attract customers?'

'Is that what you thought? No, as I said before, this is who I am. I was born a witch, just as Louise and Amber were.' It had taken Willow time to accept her heritage and more than once it had crossed her mind that as she stepped away from the shadows of denial, Louise stepped into them.

'It's a hereditary thing, then?'

'Not always, but mainly,' replied Willow.

'And your mum was a witch,' said Nate.

'No,' she whispered. Her heart sped, and it tugged a memory she knew would trigger an avalanche of emotion. She tensed and felt Nate look down at her.

'You either take me as I am or leave,' she bristled. The bricks scattered around her heart were being rebuilt by unseen hands. The bubble of bliss she experienced wobbled and threatened to burst at his disbelief.

'Oh, I take it.' Her muscles relaxed with his kiss. 'You have bewitched me.'

Her body responded to his touch, and the taste of sweet smooth remnants of chocolate and wine. 'I hope so but not in the way you think.'

\*\*\*

Willow flung open the sash window, sending clumps of snow tumbling onto the shop's bay roof below, creating a powder puff explosion. A blanket of pristine snow covered the courtyard, and she fought the childish urge to run down and be the first one to make patterns with her footprints, or maybe a snow angel. Black Cat materialised and glanced up, challenging her to say something, forgetting the canvas would remain untouched with his prowling. She grinned. With Vincent still sleeping, the snow was all hers.

'Bloody hell! What are you doing?' yelled Nate from under the duvet, pulling her backwards onto the bed. Stray snowflakes stuck to her hair. 'It's freezing!'

'Well, it's even colder now you have dragged me down here. The window is still open.' She chuckled, thrusting her chilly hands onto his warm chest.

'You're evil.' He grabbed her hands. 'Or is this your way of saying you need warming up? Hang on—you're dressed.'

'Yes, I'm going out—are you coming?'

'It's Boxing Day, time to recover from yesterday's excesses and relax.' Nate snuggled back into the bed. As tempting as it was to undress and slip beside him, the lure of the outside won.

'Later. Come on.' She whipped off the duvet and appreciated his naked body before leaving him to swear.

\*\*\*

A deep row of people bundled up in their winter coats and hats gathered along the harbour wall, looking down at the beach below. The air buzzed with anticipation and chatter. Holding his hand, Willow weaved their way through the crowds until they reached the top of a slipway. She handed him her rucksack. His eyes widened as she shrugged off her coat and stripped to reveal a close-fitting black wetsuit. She rummaged in the bag to retrieve a bent and creased witch's hat.

'What the hell?' he muttered.

With a peck on his cheek, she placed it on her head and was gone.

Nate squeezed himself into a gap along the wall and shook his head at the surreal scene unfolding below. Despite the snow-laden clouds, people in various forms of fancy dress jogged up and down. With the loud klaxon and cheer rising around him, he caught sight of her pointed hat overtaking a large orange octopus as the medley of animals, book and movie characters, and more seasoned swimmers ran laughing across the beach into the incoming waves. Squeals rose above the roar of the sea when the first ones hit the water.

He watched the lone witch swerve past a lumbering T-Rex to run into the crashing waves with her arms stretched wide. His heart stopped when a pack of dinosaurs joined their friend, obscuring his view. Once they dispersed, she was nowhere to be seen. It jolted back to life when she materialised from the water clutching the drowned hat and it warmed at the sight of the pure delight on her face. Nate knew it was time to go home.

***

Fully dressed, Willow climbed down from the makeshift changing room in a coach to search for Nate in the crowd. Someone passed her a mug of soup. Grateful for the warmth, she thanked them and recognised him as a local trader. 'You're causing a bit of mayhem, aren't you?'

'Pardon?' Her teeth chattered together.

'I guess it's one way of getting customers. Send them over to us, will you, when you are done? Or I'll have to buy one of your wish candles the missus keeps harping about,' he joked before turning to talk to someone else. Confused, Willow continued her search.

A teenager ran up to her. 'Is it true? Does Clara really get love potions from you?'

She didn't reply. Every concern and question disappeared when she spied Nate in the distance, and he strolled towards her.

'That is the craziest thing I have seen. Why would you or any of them do it? It's freezing! There is snow on the ground, and more is about to fall.'

'It makes you feel alive and raises money for charity. I should have taken you with me.'

He shook his head. 'No way. Does this happen every year?'

She nodded. 'As far as I know. The first time I did it was for a dare with Louise. We both dressed up as witches. Later it became my tradition.'

'She made a big impact on you.' Nate draped his arm around her shoulder and pulled her close to stop her from shivering. They circumvented the bustling crowds and walked towards the swing bridge.

'She was the sister I never had. She made me believe in myself and brought me into the real world instead of hiding my magic. Magic always made my mum uncomfortable, and my stepfather hated it. It became a forbidden topic at home. She helped me see it was okay. It would have been her birthday today.'

'Amber never joins you?'

'No. She has her own way to connect and remember her mum.' They'd approached the entrance to Black Cat Alley when Willow heard a familiar rumble of wheels on a shopping trolley and shuffle of feet. Beaming, she waited for the elderly lady bundled up in a bobble hat and coat.

'Mrs Ramsey, what are you doing out in this weather?' Willow asked.

'I just needed to check whether that young journalist caught up with you?' she said.

'Journalist?' Willow paled. A chill gripped her heart, squeezing it tight.

'Yes, dear. Someone must have told him I knew you because he phoned trying to find out all about you and the store. Something about a love potion. Don't worry, I said he was mistaken, and I didn't know you, but thought you'd better know.' She patted Willow's hand and nodded at Nate before shuffling back down the street.

# Chapter Ten

Nate found Willow in a flurry of activity at the counter. She scrolled through the store's social media accounts on an open laptop while listening to many answerphone messages. He caught snatches of the conversations before they were deleted or frantic notes taken. Gone was the confident woman who made his heart jump when she emerged from the waves. Instead, she shrank and grew white as another request for an interview or comment was heard. He didn't know who Clara was, but he now understood why Amber had offered to hex her; she sounded like a bitch as the journalist explained the accusations against Willow. Nate was confident they were false, and Willow would never set out to destroy anyone's reputation as the sexiest woman in the industry to boost another actress's ratings. Amber might not like him, but he admired her protective nature. He'd do the same if it helped soothe Willow's anxiety. If he wasn't mistaken, she shimmered with adrenaline and her hand holding the phone trembled. Her wide eyes darting around reminded him of a feral cat he once saw cornered in a barn. It made no sense. After the dip, they were happy and joking about ways to keep warm after a hot shower when it changed in an instant. Once the old lady left, Willow fled down the alley and across the slushy snow in the courtyard, ignoring his calls.

'What's going on?' He approached her with care, noting Vincent standing nearby, and recalling the feral cat exploding from its spot with hisses and claws. Would the gentle giant do the same to protect his owner from a perceived threat? Her attention remained focused on the screen.

'Willow?' She looked up, tears welling in her eyes. 'What's up?'

'I should have checked when Amber mentioned it yesterday. I should have deleted it but I was distracted. I ...'

Nate looked at the screen to see a photo of a surprised Willow standing near a cheerful younger woman holding a jar. He squinted to read the label. A lotion to attract lovers, so what? The number of shares rose at an alarming rate. He registered the name Clara on the account and took a sharp intake of breath. How many followers? No wonder it was going viral.

'I don't understand why you're so upset. If you ignore the celebrity slanging match which has nothing to do with you, most want to buy your products. This is a good thing and will bring the business new customers from all over the world.'

'I don't want the Emporium to be famous nor be in the middle of two feuding celebrities and their fans. Some are accusing me of preying on the vulnerable but worse than that, my photo is out there, and journalists are snooping asking for my thoughts about the starlets' feud and explosion of interest in the store.'

'It's a nice photo. Hey, you aren't on the witness protection scheme, are you?' he joked.

'Of course not,' she snapped. Beneath the frenetic energy, the ice queen he met before was back. 'I just value my privacy.'

'I noticed Vincent is the star of your newsfeed. People love him and they'll soon forget about you and repost his photos again, but you will have new customers falling through your door with money to spend.' He studied her closely and watched her gain control of her emotions and shrug off the vulnerability to come back fighting.

'Fame and money are not what the Emporium is about. It's for those who need it, not for those who want to make a statement of their wealth or celebrity status or because it's the next new fad,' she said.

'Even celebrities and these unknown faces behind these endless notifications need help, Willow. The Enchanted Emporium is reaching out to them too. You can help more than those who stumble down Black Cat Alley. Most people never find it. I still get lost coming here and I know where it is. This place is excellent at hiding.'

Enveloping her into an embrace, he steered her away from the laptop. 'Come on, you're freezing. Time for that hot shower and this won't be so bad after a cup of tea.'

***

'Feeling better?'

A freshly showered Willow sank into the chair, cradling a mug of Yorkshire tea he offered her. She'd raised her eyebrows at his choice of vessel; mugs were on par with the teabags he'd used, but in this scenario, she welcomed the quantity and the thought. She nodded. The hot water washed away some initial fear and in her flat with flames roaring in the fireplace, Vincent draped on her knee and Nate watching her, she could believe her panic over the viral post was unfounded. Nearly. The truth still gnawed at the edges. How could she explain her anxieties were deeper than her hatred for social media without revealing her past? She couldn't. It was too much to dump on any relationship, never mind one hours old.

'This will help too. Thanks. I wasn't expecting you to make tea.'

'I needed the practice. I confess teabags were used but I did use the teapot and you're right, the process is relaxing.'

'Progress then. Next, you'll be hoarding a stash of different tea blends for different moods. Loose leaf, of course.' She grinned and sipped more tea for courage. 'I'm sorry for earlier, I overreacted. Social media scares me—I regret succumbing to Amber's pressure.'

'It can be a good marketing plan, but I understand your reluctance. I hate it and have accounts I don't use. Too much hassle and I'd rather talk in person, unlike my youngest brother, Jamie—he lives for it and turned his travel blog into a business. He'll do anything to boost his likes and followers. It's a fickle business and your post will soon be replaced by the next drama or big thing. It's just a slow news day,' he reassured her. Being with him, it was easy to believe his words and push her worries aside. The viral post would be good for business, like Sabrina's visit was. The added footfall might even pay for new heating in the flat.

'But if you don't want fame and fortune—what do you really want?'

Willow considered the question and felt the familiar tug of desire. Not for Nate this time, though she knew if he touched her all her current thoughts would disperse. She unfurled from the chair and walked to the fridge and the montage of photos to select one.

'I want this.' She thrust the photograph to him before she changed her mind. Nate took the battered picture, faded and discoloured with age. She sat next to him on the sofa, studying him closely while pulling a loose thread on her jumper. She couldn't confide in him about her fears, but she could tell him this. Something only Louise knew.

'That is what I want,' she whispered, pointing to the rambling, white-washed low cottage with the classic roses around the door. The hazy summer sun shone on the heather-strewn wilderness of the Yorkshire Moors in the background. Two figures stood in front of the open door. The stooped elderly woman leant heavily on a tall staff and her white hair was scraped tight into a bun. The lens captured her intense scowl at the photographer but the young girl next to her looked up at her with adoration.

'She looks terrifying,' he commented.

'She could be. She didn't suffer fools gladly. My stepfather hated her. She typified everything you read about witches in fairy tales, except she never wore a black hat. She even had a wart on her nose. That is my Grandma Jax.'

'And that's you?' Nate pointed to the child dressed in jeans and wellies with a mass of blonde ringlets. 'Your hair was wild.'

Willow touched her short hair and nodded. 'I think that pinprick of blue is the sea and that is the headland at Whitby. The house is the reason Lou and I visited Whitby in the first place. And then this shop became the reason I stayed, but the farm is where my heart is. It's home.'

*\*\*\**

'Again.' Young Willow watched the tea she'd painstakingly made pour into a bucket by the door. They'd use it to water the garden later. If her grandmother didn't appreciate her efforts, at least the flowers would.

'Remember the steps and concentrate,' the old woman said, giving her granddaughter the teapot back.

'I did,' Willow muttered under her breath, forgetting the sharp hearing Grandma Jax had.

'Obviously not. Otherwise, I would be over there with my feet up, drinking a much-needed cup of tea, rather than standing here with you. If you cannot perfect the art of tea making, how can you expect to make the potions you have your eye on? Now let's try again. From the beginning—warm this pot.'

Willow stood on a wooden handcrafted step, enabling her to reach the sink. From a young age, as soon as she was tall enough, it was her chore to wash up. Not that it was a chore; she enjoyed dipping her hands in the frothy water, sending bubbles in the air while cleaning the meagre amount of pots the pair created. She could watch the sheep grazing in the Moors through the window. At home, Willow wasn't allowed to touch anything in case it broke, and the only view from their windows were the grey drab council flats opposite. She always knew if she did the washing-up well, she could progress to tea making, and today was the day. Earlier, while Willow ate a thick slice of toast dripping with melted butter and homemade raspberry jam for breakfast, Grandma Jax declared since she was starting school next term, she was old enough to learn to make tea. Her excitement faded when she discovered it wasn't as easy as her grandmother made it look.

Tea was important at the cottage, and Grandma Jax took it seriously. She drank copious cups of all descriptions, many blended from the herbs she grew in the garden or foraged, and she never broke the ritual; she never poured boiling water over a teabag in a mug like Willow's mum did. If there wasn't time to brew the tea properly, there wasn't enough time to savour the end product. Even at five, Willow could see the truth in this. Her mum left endless mugs of half-drunk cold tea on the side, distracted by her chores, while Grandma Jax set the large farmhouse table with selected cups and saucers ready for the teapot to arrive under its cosy. Willow loved sitting at the table, swinging her legs without being told to be still, sipping the warm drink and listening to tales of the Moors and her grandmother's thoughts.

'Your mum would get more done if she took the time to sit for a while. The mind needs to gather its thoughts during the day, and teatime is the perfect time to do it.'

Every morning, Willow woke when the cockerel did and would sneak down the rickety stairs to discover her clothes warming near the range and a cup of tea on the table waiting. Grandma Jax was nowhere to be seen. At first, Willow believed fairies from the garden visited to do this while they were both sleeping like the shoemaker's elves in her favourite book, until one day she spied Grandma Jax's silhouette in the garden. Still as a statue, she stretched with her arms up to the sky. When Willow asked why she did this, her grandmother explained it was to welcome the day, be grateful for yesterday, and gain strength for the day ahead. From then on, two scarecrows overlooked the Moors at sunrise.

The holidays were over. Her mum would arrive shortly, but the excitement of showcasing her new skill overwhelmed the usual emotional tug of war of missing her mum and never wanting to leave Speedwell Cottage. The standing clock ticked loudly in the corner. Grandma Jax told her it was a grandmother clock rather than a grandfather one, which pleased Willow. She had never known her grandfather nor her dad, but when her mum had married Stuart, she'd met her stepfather's dad at the wedding and he wasn't how she imagined her new grandfather to be. He wasn't round and cuddly with a tickly moustache like in her stories, but tall and thin with cruel piercing eyes that watched her every move. She hid behind her mum's long ivory dress to avoid him, much to Stuart's annoyance, until her mum told her to be a good girl and go and play. Her mum resembled a queen that day, but she missed the mum from before, who always had time to play and laugh. Willow climbed onto a chair and traced the big hand and the little

one on the clock face to figure out how long it would be until her mum
arrived. She returned to her post at the window.

Willow had helped bake the chocolate cake and, to her delight, Grandma
Jax wasn't the perfectionist with baking that she was with tea. Weighing
was more fun using the old brass scales and how the mixture looked and
felt trumped accuracy. They murmured wishes and blessings with each stir
and Willow added extra ones for her mum's happiness. Did magic work in
cakes like it did with tea? She would have asked, but the sweet mixture she
licked from the spoon distracted her.

A tablecloth covered the small table near the fire and was set for afternoon tea, including a small jar of flowers they had picked from the garden.
Sweet peas. She hoped Mummy liked them. Willow hopped from one foot
to the other, watched by a black cat, Silas. He was Grandma Jax's shadow,
always close by, and even slept on her bed. He ignored Willow's attempts
to bribe him into her attic room. One day, she promised herself she'd have
a cat of her own. She loved her bedroom, with its sloping ceiling and views
across the Yorkshire Moors; the vibrant purple heather, trees, and glimpses
of the sea on the horizon made up for the lack of toys and possessions lining
the walls.

The crunch of the car tyres on the gravel alerted her to her mum's arrival.
She was alone, much to Willow's relief. Stuart had only been to Speedwell
Cottage once and Grandma Jax and he had not seen eye to eye. Willow felt
an undertone of unease between the two self-assured figures; the darkness
she always saw edging out of him was in full show under the old lady's
scrutiny. Willow was certain her grandmother could see it too, while her
mum remained oblivious to the angry colours swirling around him, unlike
the bright colours she saw around others. Her relief that someone else saw
it was short-lived as she squirmed at the questions Grandma Jax asked after
he had left. Willow knew what happened to telltales, so kept as quiet as

a mouse just as she did when whispered conversations and muffled sobs drifted through the thin walls at home.

Delighted to see her mum, she ran to the kitchen, reciting the steps her grandmother taught her. Fill the kettle, place carefully on the Aga's hot plate under the watchful gaze of Grandma Jax, then warm the teapot. Willow would make a perfect cup of tea.

It didn't go to plan. Willow enjoyed her mum's long, tight hug, soaking up her gentle smell she hadn't realised she had missed. Her mum ran her fingers through Willow's ringleted hair. 'This is as wild as ever and it's grown. And so have you. I've missed you sweetheart—so much.'

Willow sank further into the comfort of touch. Grandma Jax wasn't one for showing any signs of affection. The persistent kettle's whistle made her withdraw and guide her mum to the living room and prepared table.

'You need to sit, Mummy. And wait.'

Willow left her mum gazing out of the window, lost in her thoughts until she heard the gentle clattering of a tray. Willow returned carrying the cake; her tongue poked out in concentration while Grandma Jax followed with a tray holding a small teapot and milk jug. She nodded a greeting and sat down. From that moment, Willow was in charge.

'This cup's yours, Mummy. I chose it—yellow flowers are for happiness because you need some and I get to see you.' She noticed tears well up in her mum's eyes and was surprised when her grandmother reached over to squeeze her mum's hand, before she quickly withdrew.

'Carry on, Willow,' her grandmother urged her to continue and not get distracted. Willow whispered into the pot while stirring the seeping liquid, just like Grandma Jax taught her, before gingerly pouring some in each cup. She swirled milk in her mother's and handed it to her, beaming.

'I made it for you.'

'Thank you, sweetheart.' Tension eased from her mum's strained face with every sip of the drink. Pride bubbled in her chest. She had done it. She had proved she was a big girl. Maybe next holidays she would learn how to make potions. 'It's lovely. Just what I needed.'

'Now I know how I can make you tea at home. Grandma Jax taught me everything; I can make you tea every morning.' She gave herself an imaginary celebratory high five for that idea. It would be her mum's daily treat.

'What do you mean, everything?'

'Everything,' Willow squeaked, unsure what the change of tone in her mum's voice meant. She was supposed to be pleased, happy that Willow was being kind, but a thunderous look crossed her mum's face as she glared at Grandma Jax.

'Willow, why don't you go upstairs and check you have packed all your things?'

'I haven't served the cake.' The tension between the two women increased and Willow fled the table. Her mum didn't want cake. Raised voices and snatches of the conversation followed her to the stairs where she sat, hidden from view to listen, clutching her toy rabbit to her chest. Mummy was not happy.

'She is five! For God's sake. Too young to be making bloody tea on her own.'

'She is ready,' insisted Jax. 'She has proved herself more than once. You drank it. Tasted it. She makes a good cup of tea.'

'That is beside the point. You let her use the kettle. On the Aga. Anything could have happened.'

'Her father was the same age. It did him no harm.'

'It's dangerous. What else do you let her do while I'm not here?' The women moved towards the kitchen and Willow strained to hear their muffled voices until she heard her mum say louder, 'You can't be trusted.'

A door slammed, and Willow pelted up the stairs. Mummy ran into the bedroom and, in a frenzy, snatched up her daughter's belongings.

'Let's go.'

'But we haven't eaten the cake.'

'I said let's go,' her mum snapped.

The car reversed, sending a flurry of stones and dust in the air. Grandma Jax stood at the cottage door when they drove past at speed. She stooped lower than before but worse, her usual bright colours dancing around her body faded, replaced with a sludgy brown. Willow screamed and kicked her feet. She needed to say goodbye. The ferocity of her daughter's rage made her mum stop the car and allow her to run back.

Held in a rare hug, which Willow always remembered, she heard the rarer words, 'I love you,' before she was instructed to get back in the car. Her grandmother gave her a bundle and told her to remember the magic. When Willow unwrapped the patchwork quilt she usually had on her bed, she found her favourite cup and saucer. The first of her collection.

They sped down the motorway and the only reason Willow could think of to explain the event was Mummy preferred teabags.


Her mum's anger grew, and Willow watched it fizz around her in spikes of red. She banned any tea making as well as mentioning that 'bloody woman.' Her mother proceeded to say the words Willow dreaded—she was never going back. It wasn't safe. Her grandmother couldn't be trusted. Strangely, it was Stuart who fought her corner, and the following year, Willow returned. Years followed and every summer they packed her off to the Moors. She loved every moment: learning the names of flowers while tending the garden, making remedies for ailments and blending different teas for every occasion, and walking with Grandma Jax across the Moors to tend to her livestock. Her mum never stayed. The days of Grandma Jax and her mum sharing a gossip over a cup of tea were gone forever.

Willow's world shattered at eleven when they diagnosed her pale, gaunt mum with cancer. The visits to the Moors stopped; they needed Willow at home. Daily she made tea the way Grandma Jax taught her, stirring in words of healing; her mum was too ill to grumble about the appearance of teapots and for a while, Willow was convinced the magic was working where the traditional medicine was failing. Herbs grew in pots on every available window ledge, and the balcony became her apothecary. She only admitted defeat on the day her mother died four years later.

The call Willow never wanted rang through the flat in the winter she was fourteen. By a cruel twist of fate, Stuart answered, and he only revealed the significance of the call after her mum's death when Willow said she was moving to Yorkshire. Grandma Jax was no more. Too late to attend her funeral, Willow said goodbye the only way she knew. Slipping outside on the balcony at midnight, she looked up to the stars the city lights hid from view and toasted her grandmother's life with a cup of tea and vowed she would return to Speedwell Cottage and cherish it like the women of her bloodline had done before.

# Chapter Eleven

A wall of warm air and the aroma of hops greeted them when they pushed open the heavy door. The pub bustled with customers and she nodded to the few jovial locals she recognised, including the vicar. She unwound her scarf, grabbed Nate's hand, and snaked through the crowd to the bar.

'What do you fancy?' Nate caught the attention of the bartender and ordered a pint of beer.

'The same as you, please.' His choice pleased her. They might have different tastes in hot beverages, but they matched when it came to ale. She refused to analyse why this commonality was important. Her stomach rumbled. 'Grab a menu. We can eat here unless you want more turkey.'

She raised her voice over the cacophony of chatter, raucous laughter, and the eruption of the spontaneous sing-song in the corner. The upbeat atmosphere buoyed up her mood, battered by the day's events and recounting the past, an experience she'd found unexpectedly cathartic and hunger-inducing. Only Louise knew about Speedwell Cottage, but sharing its existence with Nate made it more real. When endless searches had come up empty, she doubted her memories and thought it was a figment of an elaborate dream. A weight had shifted from her shoulders, and it rekindled the spark to resume the hunt for the cottage. With help, maybe this time she could track it down. What was it about Nate that made her open up and talk, and when did she start thinking this relationship was beyond a few days nestled in a blissful bubble of fun and sex with no attachments or future? Ever since his first touch, a small voice replied, but she batted it away. Experience dictated happiness always burst with the slightest knock; it was just a matter of when.

They slipped into the empty chairs near the blazing fire. Nate caught sight of Vincent's lumbering ginger shape through the condensation-covered window. 'Does he follow you everywhere?'

'Only when I'm with a stranger.'

'Still a stranger, am I?' he teased. His fingers trailed up her arm, knowing the exact effect his touch had on her.

'In his eyes, anyone he hasn't known since he arrived on my doorstep is a stranger. Unless they bring him food, then he'll accept them for the time he takes to scoff the lot. He trusts no one.' Her cat's loyalty amazed her and she was grateful for his constant presence.

'Yet he was the one that came to me.'

'You must have had something he wants.' *Or he thinks I do.* 'Anyway, I think he is having second thoughts about having to share my bed with another man.'

Nate didn't have time to respond as Clive sauntered over. He had matured since their first meeting; his clothes grew more expensive as he progressed in his career and his sallow skin was now forever tanned from his many holidays in the sun. She suspected he topped it up with an occasional sunbed session so he would remain a hit with women. To her surprise, there were many. Fast cars, expensive holidays, and flashy dates were enough for some to make up for his snivelly character. Rosa assured her he could charm people with flattery in to using his agency and was tempted to date him herself before Willow warned her off. Her skin crawled the closer he came.

'Well, well, well, if it isn't the local crone and her familiar. Don't often see you in here.' The pint he held aloft sloshed onto the floor. His intense stare focused on Willow. 'The witch bottle must have smashed.'

'I think you'll find it is safely intact by the window,' Willow said. The attractive, vintage glass bottle stood among other olde-worlde paraphernalia designed to add ambience to the room. A throwback from the past when people believed its presence would deter witches from entering a building and trap evil spirits. Clive still gave credence to the old superstitions, unaware it was a modern fake with minimal power. She straightened her back and met his eyes. He took a step back, to her delight.

'You didn't take my advice then.' Clive turned his attention to Nate. 'It's your life, mate, but she'll entice you, capture you in her web of magic, and twist you until—'

'Clive! Just the man I need. My grandmother needs to sell her house.' A large rotund man approached, flung his arm around Clive, and escorted him away, interrupting his rant. He winked at Willow. She recognised him as a regular customer's husband who'd benefited from a tea created to perk up their relationship. Her invitation to their renewal of vows ceremony months later showed the tea's effectiveness.

'Well, he's a charmer and not your greatest fan. A distraught ex, by chance?' Nate asked.

'Not at all. Clive is the manager of—'

'Mercer's Estate Agents. I know. He was the one who told me where to find you. It amazed me how many locals recognise Vincent but know nothing about you. That wasn't the first warning he gave me. According to him, you're the devil incarnate bringing evil to the town, and my soul was in mortal danger.'

'Really? That's some reputation I have. He is Whitby's own Matthew Hopkins.' Nate's vacant expression confirmed he didn't know what she was talking about. 'He was the Witchfinder responsible for the death and persecution of witches in the 1640s. You need to scrub up on your history if you're involved with me. If I was around then, he would have taken great delight in dragging me to the ducking pond.'

'So, he hates you because he thinks you are a witch?'

'Mmm hmm.' Willow slurped her beer, watching Clive laughing across the room, buttering up a potential client. A swirl of hatred rose inside her, usually reserved for one other person. 'He had his reservations before he knew what I was. He was the original agent who showed me the derelict Enchanted Emporium. He hates this place so I bypassed him and completed the sale with his colleague, Michael. If you saw Clive's disdain for the property, you'd have done the same. Michael got the commission and promotion on the back of selling the unsaleable. But Clive seemed to forgive me for that. It was the witch thing that flipped his attitude. Some people are judgemental like that.'

Ultimately, would she discover Nate was one of those, too?

***

Involved. Nate mulled over her words. Was he involved? Despite the interruption from the creep of the estate agency, Willow continued to smile and chat, at ease in her environment. The traditional pub with its cask ale and original features celebrated its history rather than whitewash it in favour of the sleek futuristic bars favoured by Rebecca—for her, it was all about the possibility of networking and gleaning more business rather than relaxation. Willow's eyes sparkled as she regaled him with a tale about Vincent and the large fisherman standing at the bar. His heart plummeted and stomach clenched at the vibrating phone in his pocket. Another message. Yesterday he'd switched it off; he deserved one day free from his reality, but he needed to face it sometime. The arrival of food distracted Willow, allowing a sly check under the table. He breathed easy when he saw Jamie's name flash up; back from his latest jaunt in Australia, he was keen to catch up, but where the fuck was he? Unlike Henry, who was starchy, rigid, and boring, Nate enjoyed the company of his youngest brother. He was fun, spontaneous, and had retained the cheeky demeanour which kept him out of trouble throughout his childhood. It would be good to see him. Nate needed to go home, back to his life, but the pull to stay was like the tide ruled by the phases of the moon. Involved? He was getting too involved.

'So, did you ever go back to Grandma Jax's cottage?'

Willow nodded. 'After I met Louise, we were mainly inseparable. The first summer she insisted we had an adventure; Project Speedwell was born. With no Google Maps, sat nav, or clues except that photo, we drove Mavis into the Moors. Some witches are talented at search spells or have an uncanny knack of finding things, but not us. On the last day, we found it by chance. It appeared from nowhere. The building was tired but surprisingly okay, as if the fairies from my childhood had cared for it. The garden was a stunning display of colour. Much wilder than Jax would have liked, but it was under control. Unable to resist, we parked the car from view and explored. I showed her around the land and the orchard. I even found one of my old toys in the dilapidated chicken coop. A Wish Care Bear—you don't have a clue what one of those is, do you?'

Nate shook his head and pierced another chip with his fork. Cooked to perfection, they should have tasted delicious, but with his dry mouth and rising nausea they could have been cardboard. The thoughts of home refused to retreat. Focus, he told himself, on the here and now. His time with her was short.

'Then I saw Lou scraping around in the greenhouse. She'd remembered I'd mentioned Grandma Jax kept a spare key there for emergencies. We found it and went into the cottage. It felt so wrong, but oh so right. All her personal belongings were gone. The photos. Pictures from the wall. Her books. Some of the furniture was there, though. Her chair where Silas would sit, her cast-iron bed that creaked with every turn, and my room remained untouched. Forgotten. I wanted to stay. Climb under the eiderdown that was now damp and musty. Just stay.

'We heard a car approach, so we made a hasty retreat. We just got into Mavis when we heard the rumble of a removal van. We watched while a family bundled out of the car. I never came back. It hurt too much seeing strangers where she should be. I took my extended gap year, backpacking around tea plantations. Learning as much as I could. I only returned to England when Marian died and I needed to sort out her estate. On a whim I came to Whitby and Mrs Ramsey's B&B, hoping to find Speedwell Cottage again, buy it, but it remained elusive. Lost again, but one night I found the Emporium. The rest, as they say, is history.'

She paused and waited for Nate to respond but he remained silent gazing at his half full plate. Her hand squeezing his snapped him out of his own thoughts into the present.

'Look, Nate.' She stopped talking as Clive staggered back towards them with a full pint of beer in his hand. It sloshed over the rim with every swaying step. Willow's hand tensed and withdrew as she prepared herself for another outburst. Rage rose in Nate. What was it with this sleazeball?

'Bringing damnation to the town, you are. You're evil, spreading the disease of witchcraft with your tea.' Clive jabbed his finger close to Willow's face. 'Your large blue eyes don't fool me. She'll curse you. Give you nightmares you cannot escape from.'

Nate began to stand but the fierce look in Willow's eyes stopped him. Message received, he sat back down. It might be her battle, but he would fight if it escalated beyond her control. Her plan wasn't made clear to the landlord, who grabbed Clive and jerked him away, but not before he spat at Willow. A glob of spittle landed and swirled on the surface of her beer. Flushed with anger, she grabbed the glass and flung it towards him. And missed. A puddle of ale formed on the floor.

'I was always crap at throwing.'

With Clive ejected from the pub, Willow slunk into her chair and offered a weak smile to the landlord, who returned with a fresh drink and apologies. When he had gone, she turned to Nate.

'Look, Nate. I know.'

# Chapter Twelve

Willow snuggled against Nate. His chest rose and fell with each contented breath as he slept deeply. She relished being enveloped in his powerful arms, but sleep eluded her. The previous evening played on repeat. As much as she wanted to blame Clive for being the prick which burst the shimmering bubble protecting the couple from reality, she'd known before he appeared, the honeymoon period was ending. It was the way Nate's hands strayed to his phone in moments of silence and his faraway look when he thought she was distracted. It was over. He needed to go back to the life she knew nothing about. What did she know about him? From the snippets he revealed, she knew he was the eldest of three. One brother was serious, a stickler for the rules, while the youngest was a social media-loving free spirit. By the tone of Nate's voice when he spoke, he was Nate's favourite brother, who he missed greatly when he was travelling. His love of coffee rivalled her love of tea and he had a cinnamon rolls addiction, he loved dogs but tolerated Vincent, and he cried at the end of *It's a Wonderful Life*. Something he denied, but she refused to accept a sudden pine allergy. He had never struggled to pay his rent and never sofa surfed, unable to go home. Willow also knew how fiercely she wanted to keep hold of him when they'd made love for the last time and never let him go, but the weight of the unknown aspects of his life stopped her saying, 'Stay.'

It shocked them both when he asked if he could return for New Year. Her heart leapt with joy, but in the night's silence, she questioned how it would ever work. She would never fit in with his corporate life, and there was something else. A sense of unease, a niggle that hung in the corner of her mind. For once, she wished she could access the clarity of direction she experienced for others for herself. Instead, she faced a cloud of emotion and facts.

Swearing at the cold, she carefully untangled herself from Nate and grabbed his jumper to slip over her pjs. Vincent opened his eyes, stretched in preparation to follow her, but readily rolled closer to Nate when she said he could stay. The sight of both together was bittersweet and added to her melancholy. She needed tea to clear her mind.

Fronds of frost patterned the kitchen windows, obscuring the clear night sky. The town was quiet; too early for the seagulls to circle the harbour, and many locals would be dreaming like her men upstairs. The tea warmed Willow's hands and she debated going down to her workshop to catch up on some much-needed work. It was her favourite time of the day to blend remedies, make products for her Wishing Spell range, or brainstorm business ideas, but the lights from the tree and potential warming fire encouraged her to curl up on the sofa to rest. There was no rush to work. She kept the Enchanted Emporium closed until New Year to allow her to recover from the hectic month and restock the depleted shelves. It also gave Rosa much-needed time with Alejo and gave her mother a break.

With her in mind, Willow found her phone and switched it on for updates on their Christmas. Her inbox filled with photos showing the highlights of her friend's festivities. Alejo grinning with his stash from his stocking, his delight at opening his present from her, and a dinner table overflowing with food. Rosa hadn't joked when she said her mum went overboard. Willow replied to the texts but ignored the one about who the hunk was who made tongues wag in the pub.

She slurped her hot tea and fumbled her way onto Twitter as instructed by Rosa and Amber to read the updates from @LibbyJ56. Unlike her employees, social media wasn't her favoured place; she left it to them to promote and deal with the store's account but was obliged to be kept updated. She wished she hadn't.

In a series of posts, Libby recorded her review for the tea, her luck at getting a cancellation for a flight back to the States, surprise at her upgrade to first class and her parents' delight at her coming home for Christmas. Willow was glad she had made the journey, and it didn't surprise her to read her announce her resignation as Clara's PA. Willow received a personal thank you and mention of the shop. Willow had started a reply when she saw the comments.

The trending *#TheEnchantedEmporium* froze her blood. Clara and her legion of fans raged at Libby's departure and blamed Willow. They slagged Libby off and the photo of the love spell continued to cause uproar and memes. Her unease shifted to horror and disgust at the trolls' vile suggestions. Why did anyone think going viral was an excellent idea? She clicked on the direct messages. Icy fingers clenched her heart, forcing the blood to rush in her ears. She struggled to breathe; her lungs tightened as she gasped for air. Her vision went black, and the phone clunked to the floor.

# Chapter Thirteen

Willow rested her head against the cold tiles of the bathroom wall, catching her breath. Confident she would not retch or faint again, she gingerly stood up. It was a panic attack, that was all; thankfully no one had seen, not even Mrs Marley, who she expected would materialise once she registered the flat's spike in energy. Her panic receded as she forced herself to focus on her surroundings and the present, a technique taught her by Marian when panic attacks and nightmares were a daily occurrence. She was safe. The Enchanted Emporium would keep her safe. Splashing her face with icy water, she caught sight of her deathly pale reflection in the mirror: the dark purple bruise on her cheek and her short hair stuck up in spikes.

*I preferred your hair long, Goldilocks.* A simple generic comment in contrast to the vitriol of others, but that sent her hurtling to the past. He'd found her. After two decades and three continents, Rafe had found her.

Why hadn't she stopped the photograph being taken? Cocooned in her shop, she'd become complacent and expected time, a name change, and drastic hairstyle to be enough to remain hidden. It hadn't been enough.

Her mum always called Willow's hair her crowning glory, and she basked in her admiration. Inherited from her father, the blonde curls were the only connection she had with the unknown figure. She'd always assumed she'd always wear her hair long. Her most cherished memories of her childhood were her mum standing behind her, taming her ringlets into two plaits for primary school, or into a French braid as she got older. While her friends moaned about their mums babying them and independently experimented with their hairstyles, Willow loved those moments. It was time to catch up with news and discuss upcoming events or woes. Even when roles reversed after her mum's diagnosis and Willow washed and combed her mum's dark hair when her body was too weak, they enjoyed the time. Neither mentioned its thinness or the increasing number of strands the teenager fished out from the plughole that no spells could reverse. Her mum cried the day Willow shaved her hair in solidarity with her mum's chemo journey and made her vow to never do it again. A promise she didn't keep until she met Louise and the tight-wound anger and grief hidden behind dyed cropped hair uncoiled notch by notch. By the time she'd headed into her globetrotting adventure, her freshly reclaimed blonde locks curled past her shoulders. Glancing in the mirror again, Willow touched her short hair. Her mum would hate her current hairstyle.

Willow had cried the night when blunt scissors hacked off her ringlets, sending them tumbling to the floor with her identity and her past. She sat numb when gentle foreign hands slathered dark dye into her scalp. A sacrifice needed in exchange for freedom. No one would ever call her Goldilocks again.

Except now on her phone, in black and white, they had.

# Chapter Fourteen

The lamp's orange glow replaced the darkness with a click. Clutching her pendant for reassurance, Amber strained to hear the whisper which woke her, but the house remained silent. Just a dream. She snuggled down under her duvet, but her body refused to relax. It remained alert, aware of a shift and change in the air. She sighed and flung back her bedding. If sleep evaded her, she might as well make use of the extra time; besides, her creativity was stronger at night and, with deadlines for her art coursework looming, she needed it.

Beetle chuntered with joy at her impromptu art session. Released from his cage, he scampered across the paper-strewn desk and up her arm to drape his long, slender body over her shoulders like a scarf. While Vincent adopted Willow as his witch, a large polecat ferret with a distinctive black mask found Amber. Though Glenn didn't appreciate the slight musky odour or the mischief which followed the creature like a shadow, it had burrowed a place in his heart making it easy for her to convince him her pet should stay. What surprised her was his immediate acceptance of Beetle sharing her room. Maybe he knew Beetle would use his Houdini-like skills to sneak in to her anyway. He had proved his determination to be close to her several times. The bond between a witch and her familiar was too strong to resist.

There it was again. The whisper. A murmur. If she was stacking shelves at the Enchanted Emporium, she would have said it was one of the ghosts, demanding attention. Maybe even the elusive one on the stairs, but this house was phantom free despite Amber thinking it would be rather cool to live with ghosts. When they were house-hunting, Willow was adamant even the most benevolent ghost gets wearing. The father and daughter needed to use their energy to build their relationship and home, not feed any spectral visitations. This meant they reluctantly retracted the offer on the fisherman's cottage Amber loved when an old lady knitting appeared near a phantom range. Their current house was perfect and ghost free.

Through the open curtains, Amber watched the full moon illuminate the white-dusted extensive garden. It might be sleeping, ready to bloom in the spring, but Amber and Glenn's shared love of gardening was clear in the well-kept garden. Unlike the one in their previous home, which remained a blank canvas after a decade of living there, this one had evolved within two years. Together, they had worked to create an oasis throughout the seasons for themselves and nature. They researched and plotted before putting the plan into action. They dug borders, planted flowers, and weeded side by side, getting to know each other and heal the rift between them. A winding path led to the shed and greenhouse, past the recently created pond and the gnarly trees she loved. The vegetable patch allowed them to be self-suffi-cient as possible. Amber shuddered as she remembered life before Beetle and Willow, when she was drowning under the responsibility of running a home, schoolwork, and caring for Glenn because alcohol chipped away his ability to function. She recalled his apathy and his unbridled rage that focused on her because she'd survived the freak accident in the family home and Louise hadn't. She was the consolation prize he didn't want. The love for his wife was so powerful and all-consuming that in grief, it transformed into anger. Fire and magic destroyed his perfect family in an instant. Amber's magic.

Beetle's appearance was the catalyst that changed everything. He brought Willow into their lives and she formed a bridge between them, supporting Glenn while he went through the hell of detox, AA meetings, and counselling, and she helped Amber control her magic and learn to trust her dad again. Moving to Whitby, closer to Willow, had been a fresh start, and with New Year days away Amber was conscious another was on its way. If she remained motivated to study, she could claim her reward in the upcoming months. Studying art at university was within reach. It was all she had dreamt about for years and it kept her going through the terrible times. It was her opportunity to spread her wings, but doubts crept in every night. With her new independence, her dad would be alone. Would loneliness trigger him to take a sip of his favourite drink, then a bottle? If he slipped backwards, would it be her fault?

Amber forced herself to focus on the empty canvas. The world around her retreated until it only comprised her, the paints, and the image forming in her mind, conjured by the project's brief and her own interpretation. Her breathing slowed, and she instinctively swept and jabbed colours across the canvas, recreating the scene only she could see. She slipped into the creative zone. The brush dipped into the fresh water; black swirls rotated as she stirred it clean. The whisper became louder, urging her to look into the water, and the bowl appeared deeper than possible. A jolt of electricity shot through her as an image shimmered at the bottom. Ripples dispersed when she took the brush away, revealing Willow huddled on the shop's doorstep, staring into the night. She clutched Vincent tight as her body shook, and tears dripped onto his fur. Dark shadows under her red-rimmed eyes joined the purple bruise on her cheek. Willow's sense of loss overwhelmed Amber, shrinking the distance between apprentice and mentor. She tried to reach out to comfort her friend, but she remained a bystander. Frustrated by the limitations of magic, Amber groaned. The bond snapped, and Amber recoiled to reality with a jolt. She hated seeing Willow upset, but she felt relieved. It was over. Despite assurances from Glenn, and her boyfriend, Jack, when he saw the Christmas photographs of Willow and Nate laughing, she didn't trust him. It was the reluctance to talk about his life, the way his hands reached for his phone when no one was looking, and his mysterious arrival at Whitby that fuelled her suspicions. Everyone dismissed her worries and accused her of being jealous. They didn't understand.

'It's over, Beetle,' Amber whispered. Willow's heartache was painful to watch, but the relationship was young, just a brief Christmas affair. Willow would get over it and things would soon return to normal.

# Chapter Fifteen

In the dark, Willow stood alone on the shop floor, wringing her hands. Once her legs stopped trembling, she'd fled to the Emporium to check the locks and bolts. The aroma of the festive tea blends mocked her; only two days ago, she'd welcomed Nate into her life to celebrate Christmas, but now she had to let him go. They weren't meant to be together. For the wrong reasons, she'd suspected it yesterday. She knew it now. Fate cast the die on their relationship before it began the moment Libby entered the shop.

Willow refused to expose Nate to any incoming threat and her past. Panic returned. Was Rafe outside, waiting in the shadows? Had he typed the message from a local B&B and was now breathing the same sea air? Familiar shadows and shapes became malevolent. Her imagination ran riot, fuelled by her rising fear. Her heart raced and another wave of nausea threatened. The walls loomed above her and began to close in, consuming her. She gulped for air.

'There you are. It was getting lonely upstairs. I didn't hear you get up. That's one thing I'll miss when I get home. The sea air and its ability to give you a good night's sleep, though snuggling a beautiful witch helps too.' Nate padded into the shop with Vincent trailing behind. His voice snapped her back to the room, and the walls receded. Seeing him dressed in only his jeans, and his hair tousled from sleep. Willow fought the urge to step forward, to be enveloped in the security of his arms and feel his naked chest against her. She turned and looked into the courtyard. The full moon reflected on the frost forming on the paving slabs. There was no one there. 'I'll get my fix when I come back for Glenn's New Year's Eve party and—' He registered her reluctance to engage. 'What's wrong? Willow, you're shaking and freezing.' She flinched at his touch and backed away.

'Willow, talk to me. You're scaring me. Is it your head? Do I need to contact the hospital? They said—' Panic rose in his voice and he patted his jeans for his phone.

'My head is fine. I—' She faced him and faltered. The speech she'd planned vanished in his presence, hijacked by the part of her urging her to confide in him. Tell him about Rafe, the past she ran from, and make him stay. 'It's us. This thing we have … You need to go home.'

'I know, I'm going after lunch and then—'

'No, you don't understand. You need to go now. We won't work, we're too different. There's no use delaying it. Please, Nate, just go.' He stood in silence studying her and she mentally implored him to do as she asked. The longer he was there, the harder it was to fight her resolve.

'Please, I've made up my mind. You don't belong here. Just go.'

'Fine. If that's what you want.'

She bit her lip and nodded. Nate stepped back and walked out. The sound of his ascent on the stairs twisted her heart, and she struggled to hold back the tears. The temperature behind her dropped. A faint Mrs Marley appeared, followed by a concerned Old Percy. *Great. Now I have witnesses to my heartache*.

Nate returned, fully dressed, carrying a box of his belongings he'd accumulated in a short space of time. Vincent leant into Nate when he bent down to ruffle his mane. Vincent's intense stare willed her to stop this charade and tell him to stay. She shook her head, despite knowing she was breaking her cat's heart and hers.

'Bye, boy. Bye, Willow.' She made eye contact with him and wished he saw her pain, the unsaid words and fear. It was a battle of emotions as her head confirmed what her heart had been telling her since they first met, she loved him. Three days in his company and she had fallen hard.

She slid back the bolts and unlocked the door, and pulled it open. He strode past her, in silence, and with Vincent by her side, they watched him disappear out of sight through Black Cat Alley, but not out of their hearts.

# Chapter Sixteen

Huddled over the workbench, Willow blew into her blue hands. Hot air billowed from the fan heater but lost the battle against the icy draught seeping through the outside door. Originally an outhouse full of junk and old boxes of bygone products, a coal bunker and outside loo, the workshop never lost its chill. While she appreciated the coolness on blistering summer days, temperatures struggled to rise in the depths of winter. Shivering, she sipped her tea to halt her chattering teeth. The long hot soak in the bath had failed to ease the deep ache in her freezing bones, so had curling up under the duvet, breathing in Nate's aftershave on the pillow. *Well, no one forced you to sit outside in your pjs on one of the coldest nights,* she scolded herself. True, but as she watched Nate leave, she sank onto the doorstep where they'd met and her body refused to move, paralysed in shock that when she needed him most, she'd pushed him away. Vincent's constant nudging and mewing finally broke the spell, forcing her into the building. Her heart ached when she discovered the cup of tepid tea, with its matching saucer, on the kitchen table, and it shattered into shards when she lifted the tea cosy to reveal a warm pot. With no teabags in sight, he had performed the ritual of tea making for her.

*Don't think, just work.* This mantra had got her through bleak times before so it could again. Was it always this hard? Emotions swirled, consuming every part of her mind. Visions of him versus snapshots of the degrading online messages she was compelled to look at until she locked her phone away. Crushing grief versus gripping fear, and the desire to hide against the surge of adrenaline urging her to flee. All emotions fought for supremacy. Vincent had no conflict about the situation. He stood on guard outside. No matter how much she tried to entice him inside with treats, his need to protect took precedence over cuddles and comfort.

She lit more candles and a vintage paraffin lantern. If nothing else, they would add much-needed heat and light. The bright overhead light remained switched off. Its brightness dazzled and aggravated her brewing headache. She fumbled with a stopper of the bottle, sniffed it before adding two drops into the cauldron. Once the bubbling liquid released a satisfying fizz, she turned over the hourglass. The trickle of sand fell, and she took a deep breath, inhaling the floral aroma; her racing pulse calmed beat by beat. She was in her workshop. She was safe.

Of all the places in the Emporium, this was her favourite. It was truly her space, her haven. Created to her specifications, it was a blend of old and new. A collection of plants growing in the window's light and herbs drying above her bench were reminiscent of Grandma Jax's kitchen. Shelves and cupboards she rescued from flea markets and skips lined the walls and were full of meticulously organised ingredients and books. Handmade tiles decorated with alchemical symbols and sigils lined the wall behind the workbench. An extravagance she couldn't resist when she saw them online. She balanced her guilt of reckless spending with the cleanliness and hygiene requirement of the area. They were easy to wipe any creative or spell disasters away and they added to the ambience of the room. Despite the traditional tools of a witch, such as the cauldron, crystal ball, mortar and pestle, and wands standing next to modern appliances, it resembled a mad chemist's laboratory. A radio played softly when she wanted company, but most of the time, she was happy to work in silence, except today. She notched up the volume higher in desperation to drown out the incessant ringing of the shop's phone drifting through the walls. It was driving her insane.

Thank goodness the shop was closed until New Year's Eve; she wasn't ready to face people. Or ghosts. Another benefit of this room, it was ghost free. No pitying looks or opinions about her love life, much to Mrs Marley's frustration. Earlier, in the office, Willow saw her roll back her shoulders, ready to launch into an attack on Willow's actions, so she took delight in slamming the interconnecting door shut, leaving the ghosts behind.

The beat of the music drowned out the tentative knock. Willow jumped when the door flew open and a running child slammed into her.

'Thank you,' he squealed.

'Alejo.' Willow ruffled his hair. Looking over at him, she saw Rosa standing in the doorway. 'You're not supposed to be here.'

'Alejo wanted to say thank you for his Christmas presents and so did I. You spoil him.'

'The thanks could have waited.'

'I know but ... Okay. I needed a break from my mother.' Rosa rolled her eyes and sighed. 'And we were strolling along the beach when I bumped into John who said he saw you with a shiner at the pub with a man. And you were laughing!'

'So, you came here for the gossip?'

Rosa grinned and nodded. 'Of course. He wasn't lying about your bruises. They look nasty. I'll put the kettle on, but first, what is that stench?'

They both looked at the old, rickety door in the shadows at the back of the room. A green glow shone through the cracks and wisps of an emerald mist escaped. While the workshop was hers, the room beyond was not. Willow stroked the jar she'd received in the cracker.

Protection.

More ingredients were added into the cauldron and the resulting fragrance overpowered the sulphurous odour from the back room. Unsure what to say, Willow was relieved when Alejo interrupted.

'Frog legs. Are you cooking frog legs?'

'Frog legs. No. Slippery, slimy slugs maybe, but I can tell you there were no frogs involved in that brew,' she replied, looking at Rosa.

'Promise?'

'I promise. Why don't you see if there are any lollies left over in the jar?' He ran across the room, dragged a short stool to a table to reach for the treats. He mouthed a song to help him decide the flavour before choosing the red one, as he always did. Ever since she made the first batch of lollies using Grandma Jax's recipe to soothe a nasty sore throat, Alejo expected them to be available for every visit. From the original honey and lemon, she experimented with calming lavender, refreshing raspberry, and numerous combinations. Red, whatever the flavour, always won.

Rosa placed a fresh drink next to Willow but cradled hers for warmth. 'Mum got a French cookery book as a present, much to her disgust. She muttered about frog legs and snails all Christmas Day, much to Alejo's fascination. Personally, I fancy trying them, but in Paris after I have shopped in all the boutiques. She loved your present and so did I. Are you sure about it? It is very extravagant even before the offer of babysitting that little rascal.'

'Of course, I'm sure. You deserve a day being pampered and Alejo and I'll have a splendid time. It's a win-win situation. You can go there guilt free.' A new spa had opened in a local hotel earlier in the year and Willow knew Rosa had drooled over the idea of jacuzzis, massages, and pampering until she registered the prices. *She works hard*, thought Willow, *it would do her the world of good to have a treat.*

'Thank you, but don't dodge the subject. Who is he? Where is he? And what did you do to your face?'

'He was Nate and I imagine he is, if the traffic is clear on the M25, heading home.'

Willow returned to her work, hoping that was enough information.

'Not a local then. Come on, Willow, I've been cooped up with Mum for days. I need more. Where did you find him then? When are you seeing him again?'

Willow sighed and briefly recounted their meeting and Christmas, glazing over the last evening and a few hours. 'I'm not seeing him again. He is gone. It was just a fling.'

'You don't do flings.' Rosa checked Alejo was out of earshot. But bored with being in a room where touching anything was forbidden, he'd slipped into the garden under the watchful eye of Vincent. Arms wide, he spun in circles, making engine noises, reminding Willow of her emergency room visit and Nate. A hard lump formed in her throat; she would not cry. Not now. Not in front of Rosa.

'Pardon,' she said, aware Rosa was waiting for a reply.

'I said you don't do flings. One-night stands occasionally but never more than a few hours. It must have been some shag.'

Willow blushed and ground the herbs in the pestle harder. 'He knew what he was doing.'

'Damn. Vincent brought you a hot hero. Was he wealthy?'

'Strangely, I didn't ask for payslips, but he seemed to do okay.'

'Does he have any brothers?'

'Two actually. One married with two kids and the other is married to his phone and work as a globetrotting influencer.' Willow might have been unsure about what the role entailed, but, judging by the look of glee and excitement on her friend's face, Rosa was not. 'Enough please, Rosa. It was a Christmas affair. It's over.'

'It's a shame, that's all. John said you looked happy despite being bashed up. Are you sure you're okay? You look knackered and your eyes red. Has he broken your heart and you're plotting to poison him with a spiced green tea?'

'Of course not. I ended it with him, and the eyes are from burning frog leg stew in there, which has nothing to do with him.' They both studied the continual swirl of mist seeping from the far door. 'Tell me more about your Christmas?'

Willow allowed the chatter to wash over her and nodded hopefully in the right places.

The slap of a tabloid newspaper on the bench regained her focus on her visitors. Her face and Sabrina's shared the front page with a headshot of Clara. The feud between the two actors had intensified. A twisted plot they had dragged the store into.

'That's all we need. No wonder the phone has not stopped ringing. Even Old Percy has got fed up and pulled the phone from its socket for some peace.'

'It will calm down when Clara drinks your tea. Did you see Libby has made her way home for Christmas?—you have another loyal fan, though Clara is blaming you for her need to search for new staff. It'll be good though. Free publicity.'

Willow snorted. 'I don't want publicity. Have you seen the comments on Twitter? Some are lewd and ...' Willow wanted to tell her about her gripping fear when she read the words on the screen, but it would open up part of her history she couldn't share with her friend, or anyone.

'They are just trolls. Don't let them get under your skin, otherwise they'll do it more. Ignore them and they will disappear under the bridge where they belong. Trust me, this will put the Enchanted Emporium on the map, and it will go from strength to strength.'

*Not if I have anything to do with it*, thought Willow, decanting the current brew into a jar.


Willow stayed in the workshop as long as she could. Darkness fell, and Vincent groaned with hunger.

'Sorry, boy, I got distracted. Things to catch up on, you know.' Lies. More lies, but unlike Rosa, Vincent didn't believe her. For the first time since she moved into the flat, she didn't want to go home. The rooms were too empty and too large without Nate's presence. How could someone who flitted into your life for less than seventy-two hours leave a gaping hole so wide in her heart she doubted it would heal? The cheer on the TV amplified her distress, music reminded her of his foolish dancing, but the silence fuelled her fear. The fear ignited the paranoia of being watched and found. She flinched at every sound, convinced it was Rafe. Every room was checked for monsters and internet trolls in case they'd invaded her physical space and her mind. Satisfied she was safe, she curled up on the sofa exhausted, watching the flames dance in the hearth. Vincent draped himself over her until she gave him more space and she succumbed to heart-wrenching sobs until her throat hurt and eyes burned. She used the cuff of the jumper he had left behind to wipe away her tears and switched on her phone, hoping among the endless notifications there would be a text or a missed call from him. Nothing. There were messages from Amber and a missed call from Glenn. A return call would wait; she couldn't face talking to him. Hope rose with the receipt of an incoming text message and was dashed when it was just Glenn. Opening it, she sobbed at the influx of Christmas Day photos, the party hats, the sharing gifts, and the indulgent meal. Joviality filled each image. She studied the selfie capturing everyone, including Vincent squeezed on the sofa. They looked happy. Nate fitted into her life and she had pushed him away. At that moment, she'd had it all, but she had thrown it away.

'I had to,' she told Mrs Marley, flickering in her peripheral vision. 'It wouldn't be right to land him in the shit that is coming.' Ever since she decided to put down roots in Whitby, she'd feared discovery, knowing one mistake could bring Rafe back into her life. Time and distance had made her complacent, but the message was a warning. The bruises he'd inflicted might have faded, but his final threat remained real. As much as it hurt breaking up with Nate, it was better this way. Being single was her destiny.

An alarm shrilled. It was time. Vincent stayed close as she opened the aged door. With a scarf wrapped over her mouth, she went in. Rosa and Alejo were right, this potion stank and made her eyes sting. While the Emporium welcomed her presence, and the workroom was hers, this room never would be. It belonged to the original owner and hummed with a deafening energy that often overwhelmed her. She rarely entered. Builders had discovered the tiny room hidden behind a brick wall during the renovation. Their initial excitement dissolved the moment a witch's lair was revealed under a century's worth of cobwebs. Cupboards full of bottles and shelves of aged, handwritten grimoires lined the walls, leaving a space for the workbench already prepared for the witch's return. The intense atmosphere made the builders pale and tremble. Willow made strong tea to calm them, but one refused to return to work. Willow knew this was the hub of the store's power and the origin of the courtyard's name, the Witch's Yard. The walls resonated with the residues from the previous witch's magic, light and dark, and her emotions, love and hate. It was this extreme energy Willow needed to tap into. She had every faith in Amber's protection spell, but she required it to do more. She added a few drops of Amber's potion to the potent liquid brewing in the ancient cauldron and recited the words she had found in the dusty grimoire. The now-sludgy-green vapour retreated into the pot and the air cleared. The spell was complete. Willow ladled the potion into a bowl and locked the room.

Outside, she walked the perimeter of the garden, painting sigils on each wall, gate, and door with the viscous liquid. She repeated the actions at the front of the Emporium, drawing the final pattern at the snicket entrance. Satisfied she'd warded every potential entrance, Willow retreated to her flat.

The night deepened. A mist formed from the ground, swirling upwards. It thickened. A black brume bellowed into the street from Black Cat Alley until it shrouded the town. With the help of a sleeping draught, Willow slept.

# Chapter Seventeen

T he door opened and Willow found herself wrapped in Glenn's muscular arms before she could speak.

'Happy New Year. You made it!' he said, releasing her. 'No Nate?'

She shook her head, shrugging off her coat to add to the pile gathered on the newel post.

'Amber said he'd gone, but I still hoped the reason you weren't answering your phone was you were busy with him.'

'I was busy ignoring everything. Have you seen the papers? I've been lying low.'

'Easily done in this weather. Thank God that fog has lifted. Never seen it so thick or consistent. Not even in the cities. The older locals were calling it a pea-souper. Amber was convinced they would cancel the fireworks and beach party.'

Willow kept quiet. The intensity of the obscurity spell and its effectiveness impressed her. Only the most intrepid shopper battled down Black
Cat Alley. New Year's Eve was the first day opening after Christmas and
usually busy with customers wanting a spell or a candle to enhance their
willpower for their resolutions or tea to bring positive change. Today it
dwindled to a handful. While she welcomed the low footfall for her own
sanity, guilt about her neighbouring traders made her counteract the en-
chantment. Thank the Goddess she had; she'd forgotten about the beach
party, a highlight for Amber and friends. By the time she left the Emporium, the mist had receded and only remained over her building and the
entrance to the yard. It knew how to protect itself.

Mellow music from the lounge, where people of all ages mingled,
clashed with the deep bass vibrating upstairs. Furniture was pushed back
against the wall to give room for dancing, but many huddled in groups
chatting. The house absorbed the joyous atmosphere and memories to help
make it a home. She faked a smile, longing to be curled up in Nate's jumper
watching movies hidden from any threat, but she'd promised Glenn she
would come. She refused to let him down. This party signalled an important milestone for Glenn. He wanted to step away from the grief which
held him back for so long and celebrate with his friends new and old.
He was unrecognisable from the heartbroken, alcoholic man she first met
when he was spiralling into despair. Now his relationship with Amber was
strong, his new gardening business was thriving, and he was no longer a
loner. Louise would have been proud.

Two teenagers nodded at Glenn as they slid past, taking cans of beer
upstairs. Giggles drifted down, followed by a rush of clomping footsteps as
Amber descended.

'Hi Wills. You okay?' Amber asked as she gave her a brief hug. 'It's good
to see you—alone.'

Glenn flinched at her rudeness, but his rebuke remained unsaid with the arrival of a squabble of teenagers. 'I'll see you later, Dad.'

Before his lecture on safety and rules began, Amber reached up to put a finger to his lips.

'I know, Dad. I'll stay safe. Jack will bring me home, won't you?' A tall teenager nodded. Amber looked up and grinned. 'Mistletoe. Time to kiss Willow, Dad.'

To the sound of catcalling, Willow leant up and kissed a stunned Glenn on the cheek, satisfying the mob. With a quick hug, Amber and her friends waved goodbye and jostled each other down the path.

Willow sidestepped more sprigs of mistletoe hanging in the lounge's threshold to avoid any more unwanted encounters, particularly from Glenn's lecherous neighbour. Amber had gone overboard. She nodded greetings to people she recognised as she scanned the room, clasping the silver perfume bottle she wore round her neck. Containing a couple of drops of Amber's potion, it was enough to ground her and keep the panic at bay. She was safe. Rafe was not there. Not that she expected him to be. Always a keen student, Amber, with her own demons to hide from, protected the house with charms and magic. Willow hoped she was right to have faith in her apprentice's abilities, and they were powerful enough to keep him away.

'I guess Amber wasn't a fan of Nate's then. I thought she liked him.' Willow accepted the beer Glenn offered and welcomed the bitter taste despite the unease of drinking alcohol while Glenn sipped his Coke. The guilt was her problem; he was determined to show he could be around alcohol without succumbing to its power.

'It was a shock seeing him there. No warning. Just bam! We arrive at your doorstep and there's a man draped round you whispering sweet nothings in your ear. I don't think she ever thought about you and other people before, so the green-eyed monster showed up. She'll get over it—I liked him. It was good to see you happy and relaxed.'

'She won't have to get over anything. He's gone home. It was nothing. A fling,' she said.

'It didn't look like a fling. Anyway, from what he was saying, he travels up the country often, so it doesn't have to be just anything. I think— Oh!' It took a while for him to acknowledge her body language and reluctance to expand on her feelings.

'Yes, oh. I don't want to talk about it. There is only an hour left of this year and I intend to leave this year behind and start afresh with no regrets.'

'No regrets? Is that because you regret sleeping with him or dumping him?'

'Glenn, you're my friend and I love you dearly, but leave it. I don't wish to talk about my love life with you.'

'That's a shame, because I was hoping to discuss mine. Get a female perspective kind of thing, but if it's a no-go topic, I'll shut up.'

'You will not.' She dragged him outside into the garden strewn with fairy lights. The house was too noisy for a conversation like this. 'Tell me more.'

'I was thinking of going on a date.'

'That's great. Unexpected but great. Who with?'

'No one in particular, but I was thinking one of those dating apps. Know anything about them? I need tips.'

'No!' Willow spluttered, choking on her beer. 'But Rosa's the queen of them. She'll be happy to teach you all you need to know.'

'And maybe teach you? If Nate is out of the picture,' Glenn responded. 'It was seeing you happy that gave me the idea. Maybe it's time.'

'Maybe it is.' Knowing Louise and reading her diaries, she knew her friend never wanted him to be alone if something had happened to her. Their love was unique, and no one could replace her, but Glenn deserved another chance at love.

'What do you think Amber will think? We've only just built a relationship. I don't want to rock the boat.'

'You saw how she was with Nate and are worried she'd react the same? It might take her a while to get used to the idea, but she knows you love Louise. She won't be here forever. She goes to uni next year. I think it's a wonderful idea. You need a life too. It's time to make new choices, have new adventures.'

A hush descended in the house. The countdown to the end of the year began.

Five. Four. Three. Two. One.

Cheers erupted inside and fireworks exploded in the distance, brightening up the sky with green and red sparkles of light. They clunked drinks together.

'Happy New Year,' Willow said in unison with Glenn. Their eyes connected and time paused. The close space between them filled with tension. Was he going to kiss her? Her mind contemplated what it would feel like if he did. How would it compare with Nate? Much to her relief, Glenn stepped back, and she didn't have to know.

\*\*\*

Amber ran across the beach, her boots thumping on the compacted sand, dragging Jack with her. She laughed as he stumbled over a rock. She swooped it up and held it up in the light of the blazing bonfire, revealing a fossilised sea creature. 'A St Hilda's snake stone,' she murmured.

'Do you really need another one?' Jack asked.

'Nope.' But she slid it into her pocket, anyway, smiling as she felt its reassuring weight. No one was ever too old for fossils. They reminded her of her mum and their shared excitement as they went fossil hunting.

The original collection they once gathered had disappeared years ago, but Amber's one grew with every beach walk.

The pair joined the throng of people keeping warm by the fire. Jack slid his arms round her, and she leant back on his chest, watching the flames dance before her. Laughter and cheer seemed to fill the beach as someone switched on some music, causing some to break away to dance. A girl bundled up in a hat and scarf gave Amber a drink—'Mulled cider'—before the crowd swallowed her.

'You don't have to drink it,' murmured Jack against her hair.

'It's fine,' she replied, welcoming the cup's heat in her hands. She took a sip. Despite it being two years since her dad's last drink, the association between alcohol and loss of control was strong. She feared she'd slip into an addiction like him, but as she saw the crowd's joviality, she wanted to be like them. Just for once, it was New Year after all. The warmth tingled her mouth, the taste and intoxicating smell of apple and cinnamon hit the spot. She continued to drink.

'I think Dad wants to date.'

'What makes you think that?' Jack pulled her closer.

'I caught him looking at dating sites on his laptop. He hastily closed it when he saw me, looking sheepish. I stopped myself saying something.'

'So, how do you feel?'

'I don't know. When I first saw it, I was relieved it wasn't porn like Angie found on her dad's laptop but then I could feel myself getting angry. I hated it. Like he was replacing Mum. Me and him work now. I want nothing to change but ...' She gazed at the sea, watching the tide flow in and out. 'Things are changing. We're off to uni next year. Dad will be on his own. I don't want him to be lonely, be sad, or think too much. If he met someone like Willow, it could work.'

'Well, that explains all the mistletoe dripping from every doorway at yours. I thought it was for my benefit. Not that I need an excuse to kiss you.'

Amber turned to kiss him. 'But it worked, didn't it? They're perfect together; they both enjoy the garden, they're best friends and they know each other's pasts. And all about me.'

'It was a peck on the cheek. Not even a tentative kiss on the lips, Ambs.'

'Okay, it wasn't a sizzling passion-filled snog, but it's a start. It'll plant a seed. I just need to make sure it has the chance to grow.'

'What about Nate? Willow seemed pretty happy with him in the photos you showed me.'

'No. He's hiding something, I know it. Anyway, he is out of the picture. Crawled back under his rock in London. Willow needs someone like my dad.' The party mood intensified around them and the countdown began.

Five. Four. Three. Two. One.

A chorus of happy New Year rippled through the crowd along with hugs, slaps on the back and passionate embraces as fireworks exploded above. Colourful stars lit up the sky overlooked by the illuminated Abbey. A tingle of anticipation formed in Amber's belly. With the promise of uni, Jack, and her dad and Willow getting together, this would be the best year ever.

# Chapter Eighteen

Nate watched the sunrise over the city skyline from his balcony. The blaze of orange and pink glistened on the Thames below. The first day of a new year. At home, where he was expected to be. His eyes ached as a hangover threatened to hit. He longed for the crash of waves on the harbour wall to replace the drone of traffic and distant emergency sirens, and to smell the aroma of kippers and saltiness of the sea rather than insulting fumes from the streets below, and to hear the screech of the gull tapping on the roof rather than the cooing from the lone pigeon pattering on his neighbour's balcony. Since his return to London, he felt out of touch, out of place, like Alice returning from Wonderland. Before, he'd been content and proud of his plush apartment with its sleek and modern furniture and fittings, but now it felt cold, impersonal, and soulless. Even the large Christmas tree dressed in the best, most expensive designer decorations added no festive cheer. Not that he or Rebecca had decorated it. George had arranged for a professional to swoop in while he was at work. A ready-made Christmas scene. Nate shook his head. No wonder the Christmas spirit failed to arrive; it required active involvement, attention, and care.

He sipped his tea in his favourite mug and opened his phone again. Fresh disappointment hit when no new notifications showed. His fingers hovered over the keypad, tempted to wish her a happy New Year, check she was okay, or share the photo he had spontaneously taken of his new gleaming red teapot sitting in his monochrome kitchen. Sighing, he put the phone away. Willow had made it clear she didn't want contact. If only he knew why or what he had done wrong.

One minute he was happy, content, and full of anticipation of enjoying Willow's company before he left in the afternoon, and the next, he received an emotional punch in the stomach with no warning. It had started off a good day; Willow leaving the bed woke him, and he admired her shape as she gingerly walked across the room. He contemplated calling her name and enticing her back to bed into the warmth, but she whispered to Vincent to stay so he assumed she would be back shortly. Hopefully, with a coffee. Or tea—a drink he had become accustomed to despite his continual protestations. The rhythmic feline snore lulled him back to sleep. He woke to Vincent scratching incessantly at the closed bedroom door. Despite the space on the bed next to him being cold, he remained upbeat. When she'd said she knew the night before, a rush of guilt had frozen his heart. What did she know? He breathed out when she revealed she knew he had to go home, back to his life. He did but, in that moment, he knew; he didn't need the brew from the cracker to give him clarity of his feelings. He was deluding himself to think he could return to his normal life without her. She was a drug he had to have more of. He would go home, finish it officially with Rebecca, and return. Today wasn't the end. He whistled while he made tea, enjoying the relaxing steps, and pondered which cup suited the day ahead. His tune continued as he descended the stairs, expecting to find her in the workshop catching up with work. He shivered as if someone walked over his grave and was about to joke whether it was one of her ghosts when he saw her, standing in the dark shop. On hearing his approach, she straightened up, ready to fight. Her sorrow couldn't be disguised when with steely determination she declared it was over.

Nate grabbed his phone again and scrolled through the photos. Glenn and Amber beaming into the camera. The four of them crowded on the sofa. It captured her in mid-laugh as Vincent rushed by in a blur. Proof that it wasn't his imagination. Whitby wasn't a dream, despite the dreamlike quality to it. They were happy. He wanted to hear her voice and feel her. He wanted the woman currently sleeping in his bed, to be her.

***

Nate's first task when he arrived at his office was to strip it of the offending Christmas decorations the department's self-appointed elf, Linda, had insisted on strewing across his bookshelves and computer. Every workplace had one, someone who from the middle of November brimmed with excitement, whipped open a spreadsheet for Secret Santa and parties. Nowhere escaped tinsel and festive trinkets once December arrived. The last offending bauble failed to hit its intended target of the cardboard box on a chair but ricocheted off the wall and narrowly missed George as he entered, proffering Nate's morning coffee.

'One double espresso with a little cream and sugar on the side,' said George, scanning the now-bare room, his eyes lingering on the box brimming with the decorations. 'Would you like me to take them with me when I go?'

'Please, and tell the others I want all the decoration removed from their desks by lunchtime. It's a new year, we don't need any distractions.'

'Oh,' said George and Nate knew what was coming. 'They prefer to wait until the sixth as tradition dictates.'

'It won't hurt them this year.' Nate dug his heels in. He'd rather hear the discontented mutterings from his staff than be mocked by the festive season any longer, reminding him of what he had, however briefly, and what he lost. There was still no contact. The small spark of hope she'd send some New Year wishes snuffed out as the days passed.

'I'll tell them. My wife is over the moon with your glowing review of Sand Dale on Tripadvisor. She's a new booking already.' George grinned over his tablet, ready to tell Nate of the day's schedule.

'About that. I've a confession to make.'

'If it's about the rug, Kelly's sent a photo of the replacement and she'd be thrilled with it. And the coffee machine. Some visitors do like their coffee.'

'It's rather big for the space, so I can replace it with a smaller version. No, it's not the rug.' Nate shifted his pens around his desk. 'I borrowed a book.'

George chuckled and shrugged his shoulders. 'That's what the bookshelves are for, Nate. Books get borrowed, books get left. I assure you it won't be missed.'

'It wasn't from the bookshelf in the lounge. It was from the kitchen. A recipe book on baking.' Nate wasn't sure why he reached for it while making a hot milk on Christmas Eve. Sleep had proved impossible with the fresh memories of Willow's lips against his and his regret of leaving her on the doorstep of the Emporium instead of accepting her invitation of a nightcap. The battered cloth cover, yellowed, torn pages with smatterings of stains, and handwritten annotations beside the recipes soothed him. The calm he felt while weighing out the ingredients for the mince pies and gingerbread and the satisfaction of seeing the end product earlier replicated as he read. He itched to try some of the simpler recipes. He couldn't leave it behind.

'Again, I'm sure it won't be missed. All Josie's favourite recipes are in her head. Never saw you as a cook but maybe give bread making a go, she swears by its mood-modifying properties.'

# Chapter Nineteen

Rosa chatted while Amber perched on the stepladder, rotating the stock. Now the fog had lifted, a steady stream of customers eager to start the new year with a magical boost visited the shop. Amber suspected Willow had something to do with the unusual weather. Slight wisps lingered between the cracks of the courtyard's paving slabs and the store brimmed with protective energy. She shook her head; she loved Willow but the number of spells she'd conjured to keep journalists away was overkill. It kept potential customers away. Anyone susceptible to the charged energy would have second thoughts about walking down Black Cat Alley. When her dad had mentioned Willow's reluctance to engage in the hive of excitement around the store and determination to lie low, Amber disagreed with the logic. It made no business sense not to tap into the social media storm. The rivalry between the two stars threw the shop into the spotlight but thanks to @LibbyJ56's tea review, her thread documenting her journey home, and her resignation as Clara's PA, *#TheEnchantedEmporium* and *#TheWishingSpell* range were trending. Amber conceded some weirdos existed, making their warped opinions known, and Clara's fans were raging, but it was doing wonders for the shop's visibility. There was nothing like drama to attract new followers.

The pressure of looming exams forcing itself down on her didn't prevent Amber's mood rising with each like or share. She loved working in the Emporium, and serving customers, but her favourite time was learning the trade and magic in the workshop. Since returning to work, she was eager to show Willow her recent ideas, make products, and learn, but Willow remained elusive. Apart from the brief encounter on New Year's Eve, Amber hadn't seen her properly since Christmas and she missed her. She was even avoiding her dad thanks to Nate breaking her heart. The sooner Willow and Glenn got together, the better. Amber needed to activate her plan. The first on the list was to invite her over for Sunday lunch. It had been ages since they had done something together and if it became a regular thing, the pair would see how well suited they were.

Glenn's enthusiasm for his dating plan made him grateful when she helped set him up on the dating sites. He needed it. If he'd published his own bio, he would have no hope of success. Potential partners would have laughed at him. Acting the supportive daughter might be difficult, but this way, with the passwords safely tucked away, she could monitor his matches. Meddle if necessary. Not that she'd confided that part to Jack. He might be her best friend and boyfriend, but with his traditional family, he'd never understand, and he'd judge her. It was a perfect plan.

'What are you looking so smug about?' Rosa passed her another box and dismantled the empty ones.

'Just stuff.' Amber shrugged and considered whether Rosa was a potential ally with her romantic outlook and the endless consumption of romantic novels. There was no time to talk when Willow came through from the back room.

Immaculate as always, Willow's make-up couldn't hide the dull exhaustion in her eyes and her weight loss. Amber cursed Nate. How dare he hurt her friend like this, but Willow's distress could benefit her plan. Her dad could make it better. Willow was always the strong one and pulled them out of their terrible times. Now it was their turn.

'I've deleted the Enchanted Emporium's Twitter account,' said Willow.

'What!' Amber spun round, wobbling the ladder precariously. 'You've what?'

Willow repeated herself.

'But that's madness. Social media's the way to go, it's how successful businesses succeed. We're trending. You're overreacting, Willow. Everyone gets trolled. Just block them. Not—'

'Enough!' Willow raged. 'It is my business. The Emporium is no longer on social media.'

'You've deleted all of it? Even Instagram—it has the largest following. Vincent is the star of the show, please, not that.' Willow's anger shocked her into a quiet plea. She never got angry, not even when Vincent smashed a display of spell bottles when pursuing an imaginary mouse.

'I couldn't. You hold the password, but I want it gone. Now!' Willow retreated to the workshop with a slam of the door.

'Willow!' Amber shouted, jumping from the ladder. She wouldn't lose her Instagram followers. Rosa blocked Amber's path.

'Leave it, Amber. She's the boss and you have to respect her wishes.'

'You don't understand. You oldies are all the same. I worked hours on that account. Hours.' Any sympathy Amber felt for the situation drowned in her anger.

'Give her time. It's obvious this Clara business has affected her more than you think on top of her breakup with Nate.'

'She was with him for less than a week. Not exactly the romance of the century, was it?' Amber fled into the courtyard with another slam of the door, leaving Rosa and a perplexed Old Percy alone.

***

Amber stood on the beach alone. After an uneasy shift at the store, she couldn't face going home. Glenn would take Willow's side, just as Rosa had. The moon reflected on the water as she attempted to match her breathing with the ebb and flow of the incoming tide. Inhale as the crescent waves flowed towards her, exhale as they receded. She urged her anger to retreat, but it continued to brew. It was unfair. All her hard work over the last few months to attract and interact with followers, gone with a click of a button. Or not. Amber smiled, knowing removing yourself from social media wasn't as easy as Willow assumed. With another click, she could reactivate the accounts once she convinced Willow to agree, but the longer they were offline, the more followers they would lose. Whatever happened, she wouldn't delete Instagram. She'd invested too much time in taking the perfect shots of their stock, promoting their story, and making Vincent a star. Everyone loved him; they followed his latest antics and then bought the products. It was her baby. She wouldn't waste her hard work. Not for some callous remarks made by trolls and the twisted opinions of Clara's fans. Okay, she admitted some comments were worse, especially the weirdo who explained in significant detail what he would like to do to a witch, but they were on the other side of the screen. They meant nothing. Just scum.

Anger flared again, aimed at Willow, the trolls, and herself for not paying close attention to Twitter, allowing college work to distract her. A tingle gathered in her fingers, an electrical pulse with nowhere to go. She raised her hands and wondered, not for the first time, how it would feel to be powerful enough to stand on the headland and manipulate the tide, to raise the waves high before releasing them, sending them crashing down on the rocks below. A ripple of old energy ran beneath her feet. Forget the potions, teas, remedies, and divination Willow taught; she wanted to tap into it to see how far she could go. The release of energy would be immense and surely relieve the pressure she felt, but with every action, there was a consequence. She knew it. She glanced at the colourful beach huts behind her, quiet and locked up while the season was over. If the old magic was as potent as she suspected, they wouldn't stand a chance.

Amber bent down, selected a pebble, and threw it into the water with a plop. She repeated the process again and again. Each time, allowing her pent-up angst out. Lost in her thoughts, she didn't notice the man approach until he was near. He bent down to pick up a stone. He studied it, weighing it up in his hand, and launched it at the sea. It bounced on the water not once but four times before it skimmed the surface and disappeared.

Amber looked at him and the stone she held. In silence, he selected another pebble and repeated the process. Amber attempted to copy his throw, but her stone flopped lazily in the water. Failure wasn't helping her mood.

'It's in the pebble you choose. That's too round.' His voice was deeper than she expected, and she strained to recognise the slight accent. She wanted him to speak again. He strolled away, focused on the ground. He returned; his black, long coat flapped open with each stride to reveal dark jeans and boots. Thin leather straps held his long black hair into a low ponytail. Tendrils of a tattoo rose from his collar, making Amber wonder where the origin was and if it was the only one. Her heart flipped.

'Try these.' He handed her three flat stones.

He stood close, adjusted her arm, allowing her to see more tattoos under the cuff of his coat, and under his instruction, Amber threw again. It bounced three times. She grinned. She did it.

'See, it's easy when you know how.'

They continued to skim stones in silence despite curiosity welling up inside her. Who was he? The bag slung over her shoulder moved and inwardly she groaned. With a writhing bag, the moment she longed to last forever would surely end.

'Thanks, Beetle,' she murmured as his small face peeked out from the bag. He scrunched his eyes shut, yawned, and stretched out his small furry paw.

'Is that a ...?' said the stranger.

'Yes, this is Beetle. Beetle, meet ...' The ferret clambered up her arm to perch on her shoulder. Amber waited for him to fill in the blank, but a ping of a phone notification cut the air.

The man reached inside his coat and studied it. After typing a response, he said, 'I need to go. Keep practising,' and walked away.

Amber placed Beetle on the sand. He chuntered, sprang in the air in delight, and ran round in figures of eight before digging a hole. With an empty beach, she allowed him the freedom to play. Her anger slipped away. Willow's threats were forgotten. All Amber could think of was the mysterious stranger and how to meet him again.

# Chapter Twenty

W illow heard the door open behind her, and the clink of china and clomping footsteps gave the identity of the visitor away, but she kept focused on the task at hand. She was tired, and didn't want another argument. She couldn't face the fury of a teenager, especially not one who could cause havoc in a blink if she put her mind to it. Yesterday's run-in with Amber had added to her sleepless night along with the snarling face of Rafe competing with a hurt Nate.

'Tea.' Amber slid a cup on a matching saucer next to her. Willow took a sip. Calming chamomile, and a twist of passion flower for peace of mind. The perfectly balanced flavours swirled with the magic. Amber knew her stuff, and a tug of pride for her apprentice pulled at her bruised heart.

'Amber, I'm sorry. I sprang the deletion of the accounts on you. The Clara situation has spiralled out of control. It scared me,' Willow confessed.

'Mmm hmm. I get that. Some comments are horrid, but bullies feed off your fear. You taught me that. Trolls sit behind keyboards spewing out hate, hoping to hit a raw spot to make themselves feel better. They don't care beyond that. Their power lies in being anonymous. You may think they know you, but they don't. It's like those sham psychics you told me about who give cold readings. It only takes one thing that touches a nerve for you to believe them. They're clever, but they're not authentic.'

Was she right? Willow ran her fingers through her hair. Blonde, and since she had not had time to cut it for weeks, her natural curl showed. Goldilocks as a name wasn't much of a leap. A cheap shot thrown to cause a reaction. Those who believed they were cursed could have the same experiences as one who was hexed. *Come on, Willow*, she berated herself, *what are the odds of him stumbling over a photo online?* Had she mistaken paranoia for intuition and allowed the monster to rise from under the bed to haunt her night and day? There had been no more contact. Journalists had faded away. If it was him, maybe he had crawled back under his rock. And if that was the case, where did that leave Nate? She shook her head—one revelation was enough for now.

'When did you get so wise?'

'I learnt from the best,' shrugged Amber. 'Does that mean I can keep the social media?'

'Twitter goes. Instagram can stay. But if there is any bother ...'

'Thanks, Willow.' Amber gave Willow a distracted hug. Her attention was drawn to the door in the shadow. 'Now, will you tell me how you created the tremendous fog?'

Willow shook her head. 'I think that spell can remain where I found it. But your protection potion is potent and definitely gave it a boost I wasn't expecting.'

Glowing with praise, Amber opened the Enchanted Emporium grimoire and helped Willow create stock for the Wishing Spell range, the next best-selling products after the specialised tea blends. Magic electrified the room as they worked as a team.

Willow passed Amber a jar of dove's foot and watched as her mentee checked the label, opened it, and took a moment to smell the wild geraniums before scooping up the required amount. Once inspected, she added it to the cauldron. She was learning well. Like brewing tea, the quality of ingredients mattered; mouldy or contaminated herbs potentially caused havoc with unexpected results for customers. Willow recalled an irate customer complaining when her night of planned passion with her husband descended into a farce with the unintentional addition of a rare fungus. Who knew an organism so small held such power? She now cultivated it in a jar, just in case she ever required it. The night wasn't a complete failure; Willow still saw the middle-aged couple holding hands, strolling through the streets like love-struck teenagers. Maybe they needed the evening of the unexpected to force conversation, laughter, and reveal the true person to each other again.

Spellcasting used all the senses to detect any subtle changes in the plant's composition. It took practice and concentration. To see Amber instinctively use her teachings made Willow hope Louise would be proud. She also hoped Louise wouldn't be too disgruntled by Willow's teaching methods. Their different approaches to witchcraft had caused teasing and arguments. Louise could never understand Willow's desire for perfection, rarely deviating from tried and tested spells she'd learnt from books or Grandma Jax. Tea blending was the only time she experimented, but even then ritual mattered. Consistency was key. She never rushed, allowing herself time to channel the relevant emotions and intentions into the concoction, a tiny part of her in every spell. Willow often described Louise's magic as slapdash. *Instinctive* was Louise's retort. Her technique was more random and fluid, with a pinch of this here and maybe add a drop of that, depending on what was close to hand. She followed no rules but accepted her many successes and shrugged off the failures.

Willow often feared the traditional teaching was letting her best friend down, especially when Amber fought against it. Only the promise she'd made the last time she saw Louise and love for her mentee made her muddle through. 'You'll help, won't you if I can't? Don't let her struggle to be a witch on her own or be forced to hide her true self like you did. Her powers are too strong to be contained, they'll lead her into trouble.' The prophecy proved correct two years ago when they nearly lost Amber because her magic remained unchecked.

At least Amber agreed ingredient preparation was essential. A flower picked under the watchful full moon was more potent and had slightly different qualities to one picked in the blazing sun. Willow tried to harvest her own, using the Enchanted Emporium's small garden to its full capacity, always envious of Grandma Jax's extensive herb garden or walks on the Moors providing a wealth of ingredients. Precise records on the plants' harvest were kept on the bottle and in the thick ledger. Willow believed this attention to detail was key to the shop's success. And as Willow drummed into Amber, belief was the secret for successful spells. It was the magic element.

'How's college?' she asked.

'Okay, I guess.' Amber wiped a loose strand of vibrant hair away from her face. 'They're putting the pressure on about our mock exams and applying for uni. Mrs Riozzli wants me to apply to the Royal College of Art in London.'

'Do you want to?'

'I do, but there's Dad. It's so far and I don't want him to be lonely.'

Willow grinned. 'He'll be fine. It's your life and you need to follow your dreams. Anyway, what's he up to tonight?'

Amber creased her nose in disgust. 'A date.'

'See, he won't be lonely. He has a life too.'

'But not with her! I saw the texts; she is not suitable at all.'

'Texts? Were you snooping? Amber! You can't moan about your privacy if you are invading his,' Willow said, staring at her charge.

Rebuked, Amber's shoulders slumped and she concentrated in silence on the potion. After a while, she reached for the bottle of dragon's blood.

'These spells aren't as exotic as I thought they were. When you realise dragon's blood is ...'

'I know. I remember berating Grandma Jax for cruelty to animals until she informed me of their true origins. I imagined her trudging over the Moors searching for dragons and trespassing the church belfries to capture the bats. She did have a pond on her property for the newts.'

'You miss her?' Amber said.

'Of course, but she's part of me. That'll never change.'

'I miss Mum. What do you think she'd say about college and Dad?'

'She would want you to embrace the opportunities that will arrive and let your dad move on to be happy. That's all she ever wanted,' Willow replied, knowing it would be true. She gave Amber a tight hug. 'It'll be fine. It will all be fine.'

***

Whitby was awash with romance and pink. Despite cutting through the town's many ginnels and yards, Willow couldn't avoid the paper hearts and red roses decorating shop windows urging customers to shower their loved ones with gifts of art, confectionery, and flowers. With her head down, she pulled her hood forward to avoid being tempted by the bookshop with its white-and-black chequered tiled entrance or seeing the many jewellers taking advantage of the romantic day. An ecstatic couple coming out of one forced her off the kerb into a deep puddle. They were too busy gazing into each other's eyes and admiring a ring to notice. She cursed and a tug of jealousy added to her foul mood. Usually, Willow would have preferred to stay in rather than dodge umbrellas and tourists not fazed by the rain, but she needed to escape the Emporium. If she tied another ribbon around a gift while listening about someone else's love life, made another love potion, or smelt more roses, she would scream.

Willow used Amber's artistic skill for the tasteful window display drawing customers in; love potions and Wishing Spell candles promoting romantic nights were flying off the shelves, as were lotions to enhance confidence and harmony. Willow swallowed a chuckle, recalling Amber's furious blush at Mrs Cooper's request for a blend of tea known to act as an aphrodisiac. While Amber was horrified at the idea of someone over seventy having sex, Willow thought it was nice that after fifty years together, the passion was still there.

The abundance of rose quartz and creating love potions was an occupational hazard. It was impossible not to think of Nate. More than once, she forced herself not to text or stare at the Christmas photo of him like a love-struck teenager. She repeated the reasons the relationship wouldn't work over and over. Amber doodled hearts while speaking to the customers, giddy about her upcoming date with Jack, and Rosa repeatedly sneaked into the back to reply to messages on her dating apps. When the call came, she took the opportunity to slip out, leaving the overwhelming loved-up atmosphere behind.

The furore over Clara had quietened with no further threats. The trolls retreated or found a new victim to attack with the stroke of the keyboard, proving her wise apprentice was correct. There was no Rafe, but she still checked over her shoulder at regular intervals. She caught a man's stare through a window, also decorated with care, promising the house of your dreams. Mercer's Estate Agents. A witch ball hung in the window near the manager's desk and she could see a tiger's eye paperweight near his nameplate to keep witches away. Clive. Unable to resist, she flung back her hood and smiled a greeting. Watching him squirm made walking in the rain worth it. Cupping her hand over her phone, she checked the address she'd been given.

Vincent's daily strolls had increased, and he often disappeared for long periods of time. Where he went had remained a mystery until a phone call fifteen minutes ago from a woman called Kelly. The excess love potions in the shop must also be playing on Vincent's mind. Willow turned down a cobbled yard to see a soggy, bedraggled cat sitting on Sand Dale's doorstep.

'Oh, Vince.' Her heart broke at his solemn expression. 'He's not there. He isn't coming back. Someone else is staying here now. Nate wasn't meant to be ours, but I miss him too.'

***

The Emporium's bell jangled as the postman stomped in, shoved a parcel labelled fragile and letters towards Rosa before slamming the door behind him.

'Well, he was in a cheery mood,' she said. 'I guess he didn't get any cards this morning. Neither did I, but I'm not taking it out on the world.'

'That's only because the post doesn't arrive until now. You're still hoping there'll be one waiting at home,' joked Willow.

'Actually, I know there will be,' said Rosa, sorting out the post. 'Alejo will have made one without fail, and he's the only male I need. Not that it will stop my mum from going on about the lack of men in my life. She'll nag and then gloat. She had two cards delivered this morning—by hand.'

'It's the cooking, you know. Don't look at me like that. It is true what they say about a way to a man's heart,' said Willow as Rosa passed over the parcel and bills.

Absentmindedly, she unwrapped the brown-paper parcel and the bubble wrap. She gasped. Under the tissue paper was a teapot exquisitely hand painted with witches' hats, frogs, and ginger cats. It was unique and beautiful.

'Hey, it's Vincent! Where did you find that?' asked Rosa.

'I didn't,' Willow said. She searched for a note, but instead found several bags of Twinings tea and another parcel wrapped in orange tissue paper.

'See. Even you have a Valentine's gift and you have sworn to leave men alone.'

'It's not a Valentine's Day gift. It will be a promotion or ...' Ripping open the package, she pulled out a scrap of multicoloured material.

'What is that?' Rosa screwed up her nose at the intense colours.

Willow shook it out, chuckled when she slid it over her new teapot. The tea cosy fit perfectly—a small fabric gingerbread house with a pair of striped legs and enormous black boots poking out of the bottom. Her heart skipped a beat. She knew exactly who had sent it.

'It's the Wicked Witch from Oz.'

Once Willow had passed the potion a browsing customer would need to Rosa, she retreated into the back and popped the kettle on. A new teapot always needed testing. A quick photo on her phone documented its safe arrival, and she typed a thanks to Nate. And stopped. She wanted to press send, to open a conversation, but the same arguments against the relationship from December remained. Sod it. It was only polite to respond to a gift, and they could always be just friends. Couldn't they?

A loud squeal of, 'No!' preceded a loud crash. Phone forgotten, Willow ran into the shop.

Glass jars previously on the counter lay smashed on the floor, glittering crystals sparkled among the tea leaves, and the delicate aroma of Earl Grey permeated the room, while Rosa comforted a shocked customer. Old Percy stood over the mess, shaking his head in disgust, his smoky eyes firmly fixed on a forlorn ginger cat who attempted to shrink his sizeable frame and slink past Willow. He failed.

'What happened?' Willow asked.

'That bloody cat happened!' Rosa remarked as the lady left, leaving the basket of items she'd chosen on the counter. Willow watched as she shuddered when she walked through Old Percy's barely there form; he materialised stronger with indignation. Most of the time, the apothecary was happy for Willow to be in charge, but mess and Vincent made him angry. It would not have happened under his watch. 'I saw the crazed look he has when something catches his eye, but before I could tell him no, not that he listens, Vincent shot through the shop, over the counter, bowled straight into the customer and chased it. By the time he got there, it had vanished as it always does. He's a liability.'

'Vincent can't help it.' Willow instinctively defended her cat, despite agreeing with Rosa. Vincent was trouble, especially when the spirit of the Black Cat hung around. The bell jangled and Vincent escaped.

'He's in a hurry.'

'He's in disgrace,' replied Willow, brushing the evidence into a dustpan. 'Hi, Glenn. What brings you into town?'

Glenn looked sheepish and lifted the bags he was holding. 'Shopping. I have a date tonight.'

'So Amber said, but she was scant on the details.'

'I don't think she likes the idea of her old dad dating, despite helping me with the websites. I need your advice on what to wear. Amber laughs at everything I try,' he moaned, but not too much. He was grateful their relationship had improved enough for the moans and jest.

'I guess I had better put the kettle on again.' Willow guided him up to the flat.

Willow tucked her feet under herself, sipping her tea while Glenn, one by one, tried on different shirt combinations. Endless open bags hid the sofa.

'How much did you buy?' she said.

'I didn't know what to get, and the assistant wasn't much help. He wasn't interested, kept looking at his phone mumbling it's all right. He did say I could bring things back if I changed my mind.'

'I would have come with you. If you'd asked. It's ages since I've been on a shopping spree.'

'It would have been easier.' He slouched onto the chair. 'Christ, Wills, what am I doing? This entire thing is a stupid idea. Maybe I should cancel.'

'No! You are going on this date. Unlike the last one, she won't stand you up, and from what you have said about your online chats, you've plenty to talk about. Relax and enjoy her company. Do you want me to be your emergency caller if things go awry?'

'My what?'

'I text you at a set time. If it's going well, you ignore it, but if not, I'm your ready-made excuse to leave. Surely you know that?'

'No. It must be a girl thing. How to make me even more paranoid. Every time a date makes an excuse to leave now, I'll think it's because of me.'

'That one,' Willow decided as he modelled a blue shirt that matched his eyes.

'Are you sure? But what about the jacket?'

'It's a date. A dinner. After the first twenty seconds, she won't care if you're wearing a jacket or not. And if she does, she isn't worth it. It looks good. Chill out, otherwise you will hyperventilate and that isn't a pleasant look for anyone.'

'Shit, this is different to how it used to be.' Glenn sighed.

'If in doubt, show her your biceps and she'll melt in your arms. If you weren't my best friend, I would date you myself.' She cringed and wanted to retract the vocalised stray thought like a misjudged tweet. Would she really? If her heart didn't long for Nate, maybe, she decided. She assessed Glenn; he had changed from their first meeting. Gone was the belly, his drawn yellowing face and bloodshot eyes from the excess beer. Instead, he had a healthy glow, eyes that sparkled when he laughed, and defined muscles from his rekindled passion for gardening. Swopping office work for the outdoors suited him. She blushed, imagining falling into his arms and his lips close to hers. Remnants of the love potions must have drifted through the floorboards.

'Were you this nervous for your first date with Lou?' Mentioning her friend's name flushed away her inappropriate thoughts.

'Lou! God no. By the time we went on our first date, she'd seen me at my worst. Hungover in my boxers in the student digs kitchen that hadn't been cleaned since we moved in months before. It was vile. Not sure what she saw in me, really.'

'Maybe it was your six-pack.'

'I didn't have any then. I was as lanky as you could get. When we got together, I felt I was the luckiest man on Earth. I'll never find someone like her. Should I be doing this?'

'It's only dinner. You're not looking to replace her, but you want company. She'd want you to live your life. You won't stop loving her when you find someone new, it'll just be different. Hearts expand, they don't replace the love that is already there. It isn't overwritten like files on a PC.'

Glenn scoffed at the good luck crystal she slipped him as he left, but he clutched it as he trudged down the stairs. Did she really think they could be together? Out of the corner of her eye, she saw her new teapot, and she knew her heart belonged to someone else.

# Chapter Twenty-One

In London, Nate's senses were also experiencing the excess use of red roses, hearts and pink; all stores used them to display their wares, including one trying to convince the shopper the way to the affections of a loved one was a new household appliance. *More likely cause an argument. Who'd be conned by it?* Enough fools, he guessed, otherwise they would not do it. A lady selling overpriced roses on the street corner accosted him. Another thing that would cause a row, why buy a singular rose when they expected a dozen? His mood plummeted as the day progressed, and he registered George's relief when he said he was nipping out between appointments. Like a loyal dog, his foul mood followed him, making his responses to questions terse enough for one of his employees to leave his office on the verge of tears.

He rang the bell of the exclusive jewellers, and they ushered him in. Diamonds sparkled, and the gold gleamed under the bright lights. The compulsory red roses set the scene for romance. A couple gushed over the wedding ring collection and recounted their wedding plans to the smiling advisor. It sounded like Nate's worst nightmare. Why did everything have to be so excessive? If it were up to him, he would elope.

'Ah, Mr Reynolds. Here it is. Such a beautiful cut. It will impress the lucky lady, I am sure.' The jewellery advisor showed him the open box.

Nate mumbled under his breath and forced a smile. The ring was stunning. Rebecca would be suitably impressed—by the expense. As soon as it was on her finger and she was alone, she would research the design and cost. Unless she already knew; they'd visited many jewellers to browse rings—before Christmas and her affair. And Willow.

*What would she choose? Do witches even get married?* His thoughts of her were never far away. *Enough. It was over.* There had been no contact since he walked through Black Cat Alley, but he missed her. There were reminders of her everywhere. The Vincent photobombed photos showed when his finger slipped on his phone, the cracker gift lay in his sock drawer, and the gossip. Earlier that week, he was walking by one of his employees' empty desks when he spied a fashion magazine peeking from under some files. He didn't recognise the celebrity on the cover with her dark glossy hair, airbrushed skin, and catty eyes, but he knew the name. Clara. Unable to resist, he flicked through until he found the article. It documented her rise to fame, her steamy on and off affair with a famous musician, and her ongoing and long-standing feud with her rival, Sabrina. The words *the Enchanted Emporium* jumped out further down the page. Before he finished, he noticed a presence next to him. Alice, the owner of the magazine and office gossip, had returned. Despite reprimanding her for reading on work's time, he heard her chuckle when he strode away.

Willow might be miles away, but fate kept nudging her into his life, forcing him to question things over and over. What was he doing? Jamie, his youngest brother, had it sorted. He knew what he wanted and went for it, even if it was different from his family's wishes. With his cheeky grin, he always wrangled their support. Rebecca fought for what she believed in with stubborn determination, as the ring in his pocket confirmed. Nate? While his career was strong, he suspected he drifted into other people's plans, never acknowledging his own desires. Why else had he agreed to his brother's ludicrous plan? Most people would have refused to become involved, especially after his Christmas confession on top of Rebecca's betrayal. Everything was out of kilter: relationships, his flat, and his work. The rush of adrenaline from sealing a new deal remained elusive and only symbolised more money in his bank account. What he needed was to breathe in the refreshing coastal air to clear his mind, but instead the hectic streets of London called.

Distracted, Nate dodged the tourists blocking his path as they gaped and clicked their cameras at the arches and windows of the gothic church-like architecture of the Royal Courts of Justice. Under the watchful eye of Samuel Johnson's statue, he impatiently joined those waiting to cross the road. His heavy trench coat over his designer suit offered him some protection from the bitter icy wind but not as much as the coat he bought in Whitby with its arctic lining and hood. Why did everything remind him of that time? His phone vibrated in his pocket.

'Yes! I'm on my way. Give me five minutes,' he snapped, winding his way through the crowd. 'Actually, make it fifteen. I've got to go.'

He disconnected the call. Above the heads of the crowd, he spotted the golden sign of a famous tea company, Twinings, under the iconic golden lion and royal crest guarded by two seated men. How often had he crossed this road and never seen it before? It was easy to miss, he consoled himself, when he had had little interest in the beverage. Unlike now. He edged closer, drawn to it like a pesky moth to his bedside table lamp.

Similar to the Enchanted Emporium, it was squeezed between the two imposing grand buildings, making the pillared door to the single-storey property resemble a gateway to a magical land more than a business. Swinging open the heavy doors, he stepped over the mosaic tiled threshold into the narrow store and welcomed the warm escape from the wintry day. The aroma of different tea blends released the tension in his shoulders he never realised was there until they sagged. Shelves brimming with boxes and jars of tea and accessories lined the walls, under the watchful eye of the oil-painted figures. Did they haunt the place like Old Percy, offering advice or causing havoc? Willow would know. He threw open the Pandora's box of memories he struggled to contain daily, accepting the pain he would feel when he'd scramble to close the lid again. While he was here, he would allow himself to remember. To feel. Feel what? He wasn't sure, but he knew despite the brevity of their relationship, he missed her. He missed her flat, and he missed chatting over tea and coffee. Nate held a teapot, tipped it to imagine the tea flowing into a cup, judging whether it would pour well. It's all about the spout, he remembered Willow saying but the why was lost when he'd become mesmerised by the ritual she performed. His heart flipped at the memory and he swiftly returned the pot to its shelf.

A murmur of voices drew him further into the store, leading him to the museum with its potted history of tea hanging on the walls and objects in cabinets. *Willow would love it. Has she ever been here to the smallest oldest tea shop?* Her face would light up with her glee before she'd still to study the information. She'd grab his hand and pull him to the nearby testing booth where a blend of different languages, clink of teapots, and murmurs of appreciation of the tea they tried filled the room.

'Would you like to try some, sir?' a retail assistant said, holding a glass teapot of amber brew. His fingers skimmed the small box inside his pocket, reminding him of a promise made. He should be at work, but he nodded. Five more minutes, as he gazed at Willow's photo on his phone. Just five more minutes with his memories.

***

George brought in a tray of a cup and small teapot under a tea cosy. What he thought of the new routine of tea in the morning rather than strong coffee, Nate hadn't asked, but like most things he took it in his stride.

'You've a meeting at ten about the Blanchard account. Henry has slotted in another meeting with you at one, so I've changed your conference call to three. That'll provide a good excuse if Henry is giving you a headache.'

'Thanks, George.' Nate lifted his head up from the document he was reading. Thank goodness George knew Henry's ability to induce a migraine in everybody, but particularly Nate, with his overbearing, monotonous personality which would only get worse once Nate's plan came into fruition. He rubbed the frown lines that were becoming more prominent on his forehead. Doubts crept in. What had seemed the ideal solution to his apathy at work while at Whitby with Willow lying next to him, didn't with the passing miles and time. Too late now, he'd set the train of change on the track when he told his plans to his family: now only time would tell whether it would result in a painful crash or trip to paradise.

'My wife also sent this.' George handed over a folded piece of paper from his pocket. Nate opened it to read the petite refined handwriting. 'As another thank you. More reservations for Sand Dale have been made.' Bauernbrot. Nate had never heard of it before. 'She inherited it from her mother who was given it by her German penfriend. Has a nice taste and she thought you'd like it. She also sent this, a sourdough starter.' George passed him a small jar of frothy beige substance. Ever since his confession, George's wife had snuck him recipes and samples to try, quietly encouraging him on a journey he never thought he'd take, and as she expected feedback, he couldn't discard them into his drawer of to do later.

When Nate attempted bread making, he understood why George suggested it. The kneading and thumping of the dough released some of his brewing frustration. It made him easier to work for. 'Tell her thank you. I'll give it a go.'

'And Parson's Investigations phoned with an update. Told them you'd call them.'

'Thanks George. Hopefully it'll be good news.' George left with a small salute as if Nate was his superior in the forces. Stupid fool. Nate shook his head, he was under no illusion that he was in charge. George's organisational and personal skills kept the business running more than him. He picked up his phone and dialled.

'Parson's Investigation Agency, how can we help?'

This was another idea that was planted in Whitby which he hoped was a good one. Willow and magic might not have had luck finding her grandmother's cottage, but professionals might. He'd used them before when he needed background checks on dubious business connections or employees. They were discreet and good. Within minutes, he'd have an answer and a legitimate reason to phone her. The bewitchment she cast still held. His mood plummeted as he listened to the investigator; the update was, there wasn't one. With little to go on, an old photo with little landmarks and unreliable memories from a child, the task was proving difficult. Made harder by their only revelation. Beyond buying the Enchanted Emporium, they'd found no records of a Willow Anderson. Who was the witch who had captured his heart?

# Chapter Twenty-Two

An ear-piercing shriek and crash sent Willow running into the shop in time to see a flash of orange fly through the open door and across the courtyard.

'Not again,' Willow said. Boxes of tea lay scattered on the floor and *A Spell for Calm* candle rolled towards her. She scooped it up and mumbled, 'I wish,' under her breath. At least there were no customers this time to appease with apologies and complimentary tea. It was becoming difficult to explain the random behaviour of the usually genteel cat without mentioning the ghostly feline. They either didn't believe, became scared, or embroiled Willow into a discussion on hauntings which lasted forever.

'Yes, again,' said Amber as she retrieved the packages and continued to replenish the depleted shelves. 'I think Vincent and Black Cat have unfinished business.'

'Vincent and I have unfinished business. It's getting beyond a joke. I'll have no stock by the time they sort it out between themselves.'

'It isn't his fault. BC keeps appearing, provoking a reaction. Vincent has a reputation to keep up. He'll have gone to strut around town where he is king to feel better. Honestly, though, Black Cat is never normally so active. Can't you do something? Talk to him maybe,' said Amber.

'To Black Cat? The fact he's still here centuries after his first sighting is a testament to his perseverance of staying. I doubt I can do anything. He'll have retreated to wherever ghost cats go by now.' When she first moved into the crumbling shop, curiosity led her to dig into its history hoping to find more on Old Percy, his real name at least, but while the apothecary remained elusive, she was surprised to find records about a ghostly black cat wandering around the street in the 1850s. As with real black cats, some believed he was a warning of trouble ahead, others believed he brought luck. Since he showed Willow the store and her next chapter of her life began, she'd always believed in the latter, but the recent chaos he was creating didn't feel lucky at all.

'Well, he's hanging around for a reason. There is a change in the air, I can feel it,' Amber said, dismantling the boxes.

This echoed Willow's view, but to hear it out loud made her uneasy. What was coming?

'So, was love in the air at yours yesterday?'

'For me, at least. Look at what Jack got me.' Amber waved her arm making a silver bracelet with a dragonfly charm gleam in the light, 'He also made me dinner, candles, the works—the vegetarian lasagne was burnt but it didn't matter. It's the thought that counts, isn't it?'

Willow listened to her apprentice gush over her romantic evening. How simple youthful love seemed. Willow hoped it stayed that way for the pair. She'd witnessed Jack and Amber's friendship blossom into first love with the exponential rise of heart doodles and portraits of him on the Emporium's notepads and receipts. Every scrap of paper succumbed to graffiti when creativity hit if Amber's sketchbook was not in reach, reminiscent of living with Louise in their uni days. Willow would miss them when she went to university. Maybe BC's increased sightings were nothing to do with Willow, Nate, and a teapot with its zany tea cosy, but her junior apprentice. A warning of the challenges ahead for the young pair as they headed into a year of fresh adventures. It made sense, Willow decided, Amber was as integral to the Emporium as she was.

'What about your dad? He's not replied to any messages. He went, didn't he?'

It was a shame if his nerves stopped him going. The pair had been talking online for weeks after forming a connection over a shared love of gardening. Willow saw the potential chemistry flowing in the real world.

'He went, but I don't think it will be an everlasting love affair. But he is seeing her again at the weekend.' Amber shook with laughter, but she refused to elaborate under Willow's interrogation. It was his story to tell.

***

'Let's just say, Wills, it wouldn't have mattered what I wore, especially the finer details like the shirt buttons I was worried about. Her eyesight was dire, and she refused to wear glasses because they make her look old. Old. She was old enough to be my grandmother. Don't laugh. It was excruciating.'

Vincent opened a lazy eye as Glenn's voice echoed around the back room from the speakerphone and resumed his snoring curled up beside her feet while she caught up with paperwork at her desk. He had long been forgiven his antics. Rosa's voice serving customers drifted in from the shop floor. Willow visualised Glenn dressed up, expecting the beautiful slender woman he had seen on her profile, only to be confronted by the aged version, and felt his pain.

'She wanted a toy boy?'

'I don't think she did, not really. She's nice and liked the flirting but then we got on well. She wanted to come clean. Face to face. She was very apologetic for duping me.'

'But Amber said you were seeing her again at the weekend?'

'I am. We spoke about gardening and her late husband's roses. I'm going to hers in a professional capacity to see her garden. If the dating side of things isn't working, at least I'm getting new customers. What about you? Were you surprised by a dozen red roses on your doorstep?'

'No roses. No card. But I got a teapot and tea cosy.'

'Well, that's one way to get to your heart. From whom?'

Willow remained silent but doodled a series of interlocking hearts on a scrap of paper. *Bloody hell, I'm turning into a teenager.* She dropped the pen to the floor. Vincent pounced, ready for a fresh game.

'Ah, Nate. Have you spoken to him?'

'No. There was no name, it might not have been him.' She ripped off the offending page of drawings letting her know exactly what her heart thought.

'But you suspect it was? Just do it.'

'I don't want a relationship, Glenn.'

'It isn't a relationship; it is polite to say thanks. The gift was thoughtful. Go on. Just do it. Now.'

\*\*\*

'Every night, it's the same. As soon as I switch the fan on, he moans. I open the window and he moans about the seagulls. Seagulls, I ask you. He should experience the hot flushes I do, and he wouldn't moan about the bloody seagulls. This is the man who slept through our Susan screaming as a baby.' Willow forced herself to focus on Mrs Pugh but failed. She had heard it all before, and once Mrs Pugh started talking, she rarely paused for breath. Her mind drifted to the conversation with Glenn and cursed him; responding to the gift wasn't that easy. When she opened her phone, Nate's face filled the screen, sending her heart racing. His voice would draw her in, making it impossible to walk away again. From the corner of her eye, a gaggle of teenage girls hovered around the Wishing Spell range, all with their mobiles out taking selfies and texting. Probably to each other. Maybe that was the way to do it. A text, a brief message that was simple, impersonal, but polite.

'Don't you agree?' said Mrs Pugh. Willow hoped she nodded in the correct place and urged time to hurry so she could close the shop and be alone. Away from Rosa and the ghosts.

*** 

With tea brewing in the pot, Willow sat at the kitchen table with Vincent sprawled on it.

'Okay, let's do this.' Inspired by the teenagers, she snapped a photo of the teapot and its tea cosy followed by a short thanks, ignoring the last message he'd sent asking *Why?* She pressed send before she could delete.

Her phone pinged with an incoming message while she took her first sip of tea. She gingerly opened it.

'Glad you like it. How's the tea? That place lures you in like the Emporium.'

'What do I do now?' Willow asked Vincent who didn't respond, 'He'll expect an answer.' Torn, it was tempting to switch off her phone and ignore him. *It's a text, it means nothing.* Her phone pinged again. An image of a red teapot for one sat on an immaculate kitchen surface, unlike hers. It was easy to visualise the surrounding monochrome sterile kitchen with all the mod cons. What must he have thought of her mismatch of styles and old furniture?

'I even drink tea at work. You have converted me to at least one a day.'

'You make tea in a pot at work?' she replied. Willow wasn't sure exactly what he did except it was his PA's wife who let out Sand Dale cottage. There were so many things she didn't know.

'Of course, I have it on authority, teabags are for heathens. Well, George makes it. He finds the process quite relaxing.'

'Unbelievable. You make your PA make your tea–that doesn't count.'

The conversation pinged back and forth, making it easy to fall into the banter until her tea was cold. She spluttered out the icy tea. What was she doing? Her heart leapt with joy and a smile formed while the alarm bells rang louder, but she continued to type a reply.


Insomnia made her slip into the workroom to blend the tea for Mrs Pugh. A sleepless night was manageable if it proved to be productive. Her phone lit up, notifying her of another message. A photo of his kitchen appeared on her screen. Flour covered the once-clean surfaces. 'I can't sleep.'

'Me neither.' She answered with a photo of the workbench covered with spell-making tools. Her cauldron sending wisps of rose-tinted smoke into the atmosphere.

'What are you doing?' she typed.

'Bread. Tea isn't the only ritual I discovered is relaxing.' He drew her in again, she wanted to know more. Why was he baking bread in the middle of the night?

'You should try it. The smell when you wake up to fresh bread, the taste as you bite into it, is perfection.' She didn't want the bread, she wanted him, to taste him, feel him and inhale the familiar sandalwood of his aftershave. These desires were not part of the plan.

'Come on, Vincent. I need to clear my head.' *I need to stop this now.* She switched her volume off, slipped her phone into her pocket, and headed into the night. The street lights reflected on the cobbles and her footsteps echoed along the empty streets. It was just her and her cat. Up on the headland, the town below slept. It was her home, and the spot she stood belonged to her and Louise, but now it was also his. Forget the nights with Louise; all she could recall was him, his touch and the first kiss. The full moon hung low in the sky, blinding the neighbouring constellations. She retrieved her phone, snapped a photo, and shared to Nate. It failed to do the landscape justice; the captured impressive moon reduced to a pinprick of light. As she expected, it pinged.

'I miss it. I miss you.'

***

Willow scooped up the mail from the doormat and flicked the door sign over to *open* when Rosa sprinted across the courtyard, late as usual.

'Sorry I'm late. Alejo's teacher wanted to see me about … God, you look knackered. I thought I had a rough night with Alejo having nightmares and my mother giving her usual non-helpful advice.' Rosa shrugged off her coat and tied her Enchanted Emporium apron round her waist.

'The sleep spell's not working then.' Willow had created the spell for Alejo herself. Full of calming herbs and gems, the small pouch promoted relaxation and pleasant dreams.

'It didn't get the chance. Mum found it under his pillow and threw it out, declaring she didn't want that mumbo jumbo in the house. The sooner I find somewhere else to live, the better. I don't understand it. She's happy enough to drink her revitalising tea and use that herbal rub for her arthritis. But a simple pouch of—'

'I'll make another. Maybe put it somewhere more discreet.' Mrs Smith's reaction didn't surprise her. Many locals were happy to accept the benefits of the tea, but even after trading for several years, anything else still carried the age-old stigma against witchcraft.

'Why are you so tired? A spell gone wrong or is it something to do with that silly tea cosy and the inane grin on your face every time the mobile in your pocket vibrates. It's against the business ethic, you know.'

Heat rose to Willow's cheeks. It was one of the strict rules she often berated Amber for—no mobiles on the shop floor. It was bad enough the customers had an over-reliance on them, like the women browsing the jars for spell ingredients while consulting their Pinterest feeds. Only one bore the glimmer of a hereditary witch, but the others might learn. If they concentrated and relied less on their phones and more on intuition.

'I'll make tea.' Willow left Rosa's laughter behind her, carrying the mail. Secluded in the back room, she opened the new message. The first after his declaration, neither brave enough to expand their feelings more. An image appeared showing thick toast dripping with melted butter and a mug of tea with the caption:

'Wish you were here.'

*So do I but it is not an option.* 'It would be better with cheese,' she typed her safe reply.

The kettle on, she sifted through the post—bill, bill, junk mail—and raised her eyebrow at a cream envelope addressed to her but posted by hand.

An icy breeze swept by and a faint Mrs Marley craned her neck to see who the sender could be, her excitement strengthening her. Willow shook her head and shielded it from view.

'You're so nosy. It will only be a thank-you card.'

Rosa handed over the change to a contented customer clutching their package with the swinging cat charm when Willow came through to the shop and passed her the tea.

'That took forever to make. I guess you got sidetracked by your phone. Any gossip? Has he—? Is everything okay?'

Willow forced a smile and willed her hand to stop shaking. 'Yes. It's all good. Everything is fine.'

***

Everything was not fine. A trio of ghosts stalked Willow all afternoon, chilling the shop to teeth-chattering temperatures without her rebuking them. When she waved Rosa goodbye and spun the shop sign to *closed*, her shoulders sagged, and despair replaced the fixed smile. Mrs Marley violently shuddered when Willow walked through her to the workshop. Only Mr Marley's hushes stopped his wife vocalising her disgust at the violation. Vincent remained at his witch's side as she locked the door behind her, leaving the spooks to gossip.

Willow wasn't sure how she'd got through the day with no further interrogation from Rosa, who readily accepted her boss's pale face and vagueness as symptoms of a brewing headache. The constant stream of difficult customers helped cover the lie as Willow worked on automatic, refusing to let her concentration slide to the cream envelope in her desk drawer until now. With trembling hands, she re-examined the envelope and, with a deep breath, slid the card out. Large blooms of lilies filled the card. Her mum's favourite flower. A glimpse of the exotic, she would say, especially when she was undergoing treatment, a reminder of all the places she wanted to see when she was better. Their floral meaning ranged from virtue through friendship to devotion, but to Willow, it always meant betrayal and hurt. Death. Before they married, Stuart would arrive with a bunch of lilies declaring his love. Later, they arrived after Willow woke to her mum crying or wearing a fresh bruise around her wrist or eye. After the funeral, the house brimmed with them; their cloying fragrance filled the air until she stamped on every bouquet before discarding the crushed, mangled blooms in the bin. No, she would not pin this card on the staff noticeboard with others.

Her lacklustre attempt at convincing herself it was cruel coincidence, a mistake by an unwitting customer wanting to express their gratitude, was crushed when she opened it to the wave of hatred the writer left with his capitalised penmanship. With no signature, the words themselves confirmed her fears.

*You should have been mine, my Goldilocks.*

The words were nothing; they were everything. This wasn't a troll reaching from the other side of a screen. It was him. He had found her. It was white lilies that brought him into her life and for a brief time she'd reduced her abhorrence to them to a simmering dislike, believing the twist of fate had turned in her favour.

He'd been waiting at the counter, ready to check into the hotel, when she began her shift. A posh Greek resort, it made a pleasant change from the bar work she often took to pay for her travels. She'd held her hand up instructing him to wait. Bemused, he watched her scoop up the flower display of the offending white lilies in front of him and throw them in the bin.

'What did they do to you? Not perfect enough for you, Goldilocks.' He chuckled at his own joke, flashing his perfect white teeth. The lilies weren't welcome but five minutes in the presence of this smooth-talking Spanish Adonis was. She wasn't interested in a relationship, but she found herself looking forward to his visits to the reception desk where he lingered longer than the enquiry needed. And then the bouquets arrived with no lily in sight. During his two-week stay that became four, his mission became to make her life perfect. Eventually, with the urging of the rest of the hotel's staff who were drunk on the possibility of romance, she agreed to a date. He always asked for her opinion, giving her three options like the fairy-tale protagonist he anointed her as. His charm, certainty, and his more affluent lifestyle swept her away. He made the impossible destinations true. Her plans for solo backpacking became a pair. Not satisfied with youth hostels and camping, he dined and slept in high-end hotels and destinations. She was living a dream, not knowing the nightmare to come.

Willow checked the envelope again. With no stamp, it was hand-delivered and that meant only one thing; he was in the locality. He could be anywhere, watching and waiting. He had invaded her space. The card fell as she sank to the floor. A chill crept through her veins; an icy fist clenched her heart as she tried to comprehend what it meant. Alone, she succumbed to the panic attack. Her vision blurred. Vincent nudged her, chattered, and forced his lumbering body onto her trembling knees. Her tingling fingers found his fur and his warmth gradually grounded her until the gasps for air developed into sobs.

***

Through the gap in the curtains, the moonlight illuminated the patchwork squares on her quilt. Vincent purred and his tail twitched as he dreamt. *At least one of us is getting some sleep.* Rafe knew where she lived. Willow couldn't escape the shredded card's toxicity that crept through her home. Its tendrils of hate squeezed her heart, forcing the long-sealed box of memories to fling open to the last day that began with, *'Goldilocks, my little Goldilocks.'* The innocent pet name her mum had called her soon twisted into something to hate. Except she wasn't his. She wasn't anyone's. He didn't belong in her current life, yet his resurgent power bombarded and crushed down on her, forcing her to gasp for air and forget how far she'd come. It took all her willpower to remember it. The angry witch inside her screamed for her to destroy the card, banish him, and cast his evil out of her life. Again.

With the flourish of a magician's assistant, she whipped the bedspread away and wrapped it around her shoulders against the chilly February air that seeped through the aged window frames. Vincent glared while she groped for her slippers and reluctantly rose from the bed to follow his witch down the stairs.

Willow retrieved the torn pieces of card from the workshop's bin and threw them in her cauldron. The flame of a black candle danced while she selected the required ingredients from the rows of bottles above the workbench. The old witch's room called, and Willow battled the temptation to find a more powerful spell in the old dusty books, one created by a witch who had no qualms about stepping into darker magic. No, the unknown consequences of using someone else's magic were too great. The New Year fog had protected her, but other businesses paid a heavy price in their profits. She had to do it her way. Herbs groaned and crunched under the pestle as she ground them against the stone mortar. She sprinkled them into the cauldron with a dash of black salt and a couple of drops of Amber's protective oil. It was too late to regret using it for conjuring the fog, but she was reluctant to use all the remainder now. What if things escalated? Using a blazing taper, she ignited the card. Wisps of smoke curled upwards, and she breathed in the herbal aroma, focused on Rafe's image, and chanted the banishing spell. Blue flames consumed the card's broken image until charred ash remained. His face wavered as the words pushed him away from her thoughts, the Emporium, and her life.

She unlatched the workshop door, pulling the quilt tighter around her. Hard frost clung to the leaves on the evergreen bushes in the Emporium's garden and white crystals on the path sparkled under the gaze of the moon. The cold nipped at her ankles and through her thin pyjama bottoms as Willow walked to the mosaic circle she had painstakingly created with pebbles, polished glass, and shells. Four lanterns hung on posts, one for each compass point. She cast her circle, lighting the candle for north, east, south and finally west. Standing in the centre, with Vincent by her side, she placed the cauldron on a dedicated, flat stone altar. The quilt fell when she extended her arms upwards, calling for the Goddess's help. An increasing breeze caught the ash; it rose spiralling towards the stars. Rafe's face, his arrogant smirk, faded into the shadows. Standing still, Willow waited for the surge of power flowing through her body to complete the spell and to feel the expected overwhelming calm, but nothing came. The sense of foreboding and panic remained. A black cat watched from the garden wall as the witch withdrew into the building in defeat.

# Chapter Twenty-Three

'You're not still interfering, are you?'

Behind Amber, the bed shifted and creaked and a folder jabbed her in the back as Jack edged closer to her. His open textbooks were strewn across the duvet while she'd stacked hers neatly beside her on the floor. Beetle snoozed, curled tight on her lap. Amber flipped the laptop lid down too late. He had already seen the open web page.

'I'm not interfering.' She paused, fumbled for the right words. 'I'm just tweaking things in favour of the preferred outcome.'

'You're cancelling your dad's date. What's wrong with her?'

'I don't want a stepmother only seven years older than me.'

'What? You can't expect everyone he dates to be in it for the long term. It's not all about fairy tales and weddings. He deserves fun, spontaneity, a laugh. And she has some interesting attributes.'

'So, you're saying he's looking for one-night stands—that's gross.' Amber cringed, thinking about her dad and what was her name being together. Emily-May. Her interesting attributes were obvious in her low-cut top. Were they even real? Her dad and her would not get together if she could help it.

'Willow will be much better ...'

'Stop it. Just stop it now.' Jack's voice rose with an unusual flare of temper. 'You'll be making love potions next. Christ, you have, haven't you?'

'No, of course not!' she said, relieved the tab showing the browser's results for love potions had closed earlier. She wasn't lying. She had done nothing, but not because of morality; she lacked the ingredients and was convinced the perfect spell lay out of reach, locked behind the old door in Willow's workroom. If fate didn't make Willow and Glenn see their potential, she was prepared to give more than a little nudge.

A textbook behind her banged shut, waking Beetle. Jack stood, sending a sprig of rosemary floating to the floor. She offered it back to him as he threw his belongings in his rucksack.

'I don't want it. It stinks.'

'It helps you concentrate and remember things.'

'Headache-inducing more like. A few leaves won't make me pass these exams. It needs a miracle.'

'Well, I can blend some ...'

'I said no. I don't want your potions or candles to light. I just want ...' He stared at her for a moment. The air tensed and time paused as she waited for him to continue. What did he want? He sighed, hoisted up his bag on his shoulder, and left without saying goodbye. She swiped away a tear as his footsteps thudded down the stairs and the front door slammed. It was all right for him with his perfect family. His happy secure parents and two younger brothers. And his warm and loving house which always felt like a refuge when she visited, especially in the early days of their relationship, when Glenn's alcoholism was at its worst. The constant hubbub of chaos underpinned by unconditional love fascinated her. She relished the noise his brothers made chasing round the kitchen table while his mum cooked homemade meals, and even when the baby screamed, it felt like paradise. Jack had no worries. Unlike her newly stitched-together family, whose strength had yet to be tested. She couldn't take the risk. Glenn needed someone like Willow, not some blonde-haired Clara wannabe with sly feline eyes. A few dates with her would lead to heartache for her dad and his wallet, Amber decided. She finished cancelling the arranged date and blocked her. It was better this way.

She was doing her dad a favour. A huge favour.

The silence in the house was unnerving. Beetle's attempt to lighten her mood by scurrying up her arm to nudge her face, failed. She never rowed with Jack. Jingling her bracelet, she couldn't believe it was only two weeks since their Valentine's Day celebrations. How had things spiralled out of control? Not just their relationship, but Willow, too. Jack had always been her dependable rock but recently they clashed over everything from the amount of study to do, date nights, her matchmaking scheme, and now even her use of magic. If only she could put her finger on why. She twirled the rosemary between her fingers before picking off the leaves one by one.

He loves me, he loves me not. He loves me. He loves me not. Confetti of green leaves surrounded her. He loves me.

*Well, he has a funny way of showing it.* One reason she loved him was his acceptance of who she was. He'd always believed in her magic and encouraged her when fear made her retreat from her emerging power, but his rejection exposed another crack between them. The other was Willow. When she tried to explain her concerns about her mentor, he accused her of relying too much on her perceived intuition and not on the facts. Glenn hadn't helped, either.

Distracted, he readily believed the lies Willow told, but Amber knew something was wrong.

Very wrong.

*** 

Two weeks before, Amber's first clue something was amiss was seeing the ghostly black cat sitting in the Emporium window among the display of candles and tea. Mr Marley in Willow's lounge window, watching her cross the courtyard, confirmed her unease. He tipped his head to greet her. Of all the ghosts, Mr Marley was the most aloof and ethereal. Yet she could see his solid form as clearly as the customers walking by. In the past, his faint outline only appeared when he dragged his wife away if her opinionated and busybody tendencies threatened to hurt someone, except the time she saw the couple embrace under the mistletoe. A scene she found sweet, an example of genuine love lasting across time and space. To her surprise, when she considered finding true love, the dark-haired stranger on the beach appeared instead of Jack. Was he the one? Her guilty heart leapt at the idea, but no matter how hard she tried, he remained impossible to find. Maybe he was a tourist visiting for the day. Whoever he was, she knew she had to see him again.

A wave of tension hit Amber when she entered the store. It overwhelmed the benefits of the calming music and fragrance of teas and herbs. Amber noted Rosa's strained smile and flushed face as she served a regular. Mrs Hartley-Booth. Tall and slender, with a harsh face, she was a customer Rosa and Amber both tried to avoid, and often bartered jobs so they weren't the one faced with her moans and quibbles. She required perfection only Willow had a chance of achieving. It was sod's law; she was here on a busy day, but it explained the number of people waiting.

Amber rushed into the back to retrieve the midnight-blue apron emblazoned with a Vincent's silver silhouette Willow insisted all staff wear. Compared to the spring day outside, the room's arctic temperature made her gasp. Shivering, her frozen hands struggled to tie the apron around her waist. Old Percy stood guard at the window, ignoring her in favour of watching over the small garden. What was the matter with them? She hadn't seen Mrs Marley, but she suspected, like the other ghosts, she would be more visible than usual.

She slipped beside Rosa and beamed at the next customer; relieved Mrs Hartley-Booth was striding across the courtyard, looking triumphant. Together they served the customers with a flurry of fingers, tying bows and adding charms to the trademark boxes until the crowd dwindled to a lone woman browsing. Not for the first time when there was a rush, Amber cursed Willow's demand for high standards and attention to detail. It would be easier if the products were placed in a bag and be done with.

'You gave Hartley-Booth a discount, didn't you?'

'Ten percent off for loyalty. Wish she'd find somewhere else to go. She takes the biscuit with her demands,' confirmed Rosa.

'That's why she comes. Shops in York wouldn't stand for her nonsense, but for some reason, Willow tolerates it. She is too nice for her own good. Where is she?'

'Flu. Got a text from her this morning to open up.'

'Flu? She looked fine yesterday.' Amber stared at her colleague. Willow was never ill.

'She looked peaky when I left. As pale as I imagine the ghosts are.'

'Maybe not. They're different today.' The Emporium was different and not just the temperatures in the rooms.

'Well, she chose a good time to be ill. It's been madness all day. Even Percy has abandoned me today. No nudges or drawers creeping open to show me the right blend to give people. Nothing. I'm so glad you're here. I can finally go for a wee.'

Amber sent her off for a break and mulled things over. Flu? Maybe, but her intuition screamed not. Rosa rushed into the store, giddy with excitement reminiscent of Alejo's excessive buoyant energy.

'I saw him. I saw Old Percy. Fancy, today of all days, I get to see my very first ghost. Is it always that cold when he's around? Does that mean I'm becoming more like you? A sensitive? A witch?'

*No, it confirms Willow doesn't have flu and the ghosts are absorbing energy so they can manifest and keep guard.* The only thing Amber couldn't understand was why.

Over the next few days, Willow ignored texts and refused to answer the flat door, pleading the contagious nature of her illness. Rosa left soup or an aromatic dish outside the flat's door daily, and Amber blended several healing remedies. She became increasingly frustrated that any magical attempts to connect with Willow were met with a dense, foggy barrier. No one would listen to her concerns. Both Glenn and Rosa believed everything Willow said in her vague texts. Besides the rare mumbles through the door, the only evidence Willow was alive was the creaks from the flat's floorboards. Despite accusations she was overreacting Amber knew something had to be done. Willow wasn't fooling her, and since it coincided with Valentine's Day, Amber bet it had something to do with Nate. She wished Willow had never met him.

***

Glenn knocked on the flat's door. With no response, he turned to leave, but Amber emerged from the shadows on the stairs.

'You promised, Dad.' Whether it was her incessant pleas or her promise to help him with a tricky customer's garden design, Glenn had finally promised he would check Willow in person.

'And you are supposed to be at work downstairs.'

'Please, Dad. I need to see she is okay.'

He knocked again.

'Come on, Willow. I need to see your face and make sure you haven't joined the other spooks of this place. I'm not leaving until I do, and I have enough provisions to keep me happy on the stairs for ...'

The door creaked open. Amber crept forward. Willow's pale, gaunt face with dark shadows under her eyes made her doubt her intuition and concede the mundane rational explanation of the flu was correct after all. Glimpses of the usual clean but homely flat showed disarray and the stench of old bins drifted down the stairwell.

'Go to work, Amber,' Glenn said. 'I've got this.' She protested; she could make a healing brew, she could— It was then she saw it. Without a word and with tears blurring the steps in front of her, Amber fled down the stairs, slamming the connecting door to the shop behind her.

# Chapter Twenty-Four

A dull grey light shone through the window. From the sofa, Willow could see the faint glimmer of the Marleys standing there, looking out over the courtyard. His arm wrapped round his wife in a tender embrace. *True love lasting through time.* Willow swallowed to dislodge the aching lump in her throat and bit her lip, but tears continued to fall onto Vincent lying beside her. Was it only yesterday the exchange of messages between her and Nate dismantled her resolve to keep him away and made her hope a relationship with him was possible? It seemed longer, hazy and fading like a dream as you woke. The spell had failed.

Rafe's hatred pushed against the protective barriers placed along the property boundary: how long they would hold? She wasn't sure. *If one spell failed, why not all?* Anger blended with her escalating fear. She couldn't even go to the police; the evidence was burned to ash. *Like the rest of my life.* Willow sank further into the cushions, deflated and tired.

Nate's name flashed on her vibrating phone. Her finger hovered over the *accept call* until it rang off. Throughout the night she had typed variations of *I need you* before deleting them. Would he come over the Moors in a Land Rover rather than a stallion to fight her demons and hold her like the Marleys? Willow never saw herself as a damsel in distress, she was always ready to fight her own battles, but now? She would welcome the help, but ask someone for it? Never.

Her phone pinged again. A photograph of two doorstop slices of toast oozing with cheese appeared. Her stomach turned and her heart splintered more than she thought possible. Only a few hours before, she was happy. The laughter of children and hubbub of locals getting on with their daily routine drifted through the cracks in the old windows. *I'm late. I need to go to work.* Her leaden legs refused to cooperate, and her racing heart warned of another imminent panic attack. It would only take a glimpse of his poison, an angry customer, or Rosa's friendly chat to strip away the remaining protective layers Willow had built around herself to reveal the beaten, vulnerable child beneath. Exhaustion overwhelmed her.

After a quick phone call, Willow curled on the sofa wrapped in the quilt, where she stayed.

The fall into depression surprised her. It grasped and dragged her down before she knew what was happening. Lost in the dark, she found herself alone in an uncharted alien world of sludge and grey. Adrenaline-fuelled anxiety had always kept it at bay, forcing her to take midnight walks, work harder, or flee when threatened. There was always someone to turn to and help keep the dark away. Marian, her mum's best friend, opened up her home when at sixteen she arrived on her doorstep with her rucksack and sleeping bag, unable to live with Stuart, her stepfather, any longer. Louise, the sister she never had, always had her back when Willow confided in her. Grief and their absence compounded her distress.

Doubts of her magical ability confounded her state of mind. Every word, taunt, and accusation people had said ricocheted around her head as she tried to focus on protection and calming spells. The loudest voice was Clive, just as it was when she first opened the Emporium and he encouraged petitions and active campaigns to close the store.

As days progressed, the flat chilled and the Marleys' presence grew stronger. Willow saw every wrinkle beneath Mrs Marley's meticulous make-up when they stood over her and the multiple snags in Mr Marley's jumper told her a dog once lived in the flat. Luckily, it had not joined its spectral owners; Vincent's relationship with one ghost animal was enough to contend with. Had Black Cat retreated into the shadows, she wondered, or was he ruling the roost downstairs while his nemesis was protecting his witch? The archaic heating system struggled to warm the building, so Willow dragged her duvet onto the sofa, watching endless movies. They refused to soothe her mood, but they distracted her from any noise her anxiety could grab and twist into something to fear. When the fire died down, Willow wished her uncurled hand would release a ball of energy to produce witch fire, a talent she lacked despite the many lessons Louise gave her. 'Maybe it's not in your genes,' her friend exclaimed, but Willow knew Grandma Jax could do it and her father. *One more failure to add to the list.* Willow's talents with herbs, tea and, insight into people's needs paled against Louise's ability to manipulate the elements and courage to experiment with all magic despite disastrous results.

'How am I expected to teach your daughter, Lou? I'm failing her like everything else.' There was no reply. Amber was one of a kind. It was obvious when Willow met her for the first time. Her scrying and spell making ability were exceptional without instruction, but there was an undercurrent waiting to be unleashed. The escapade with soul walking a couple of years ago confirmed it. Only time would reveal if Louise's prophecy about her daughter's powers were true, but she needed more guidance than Willow could give. *Another failure and a broken promise.*

Her only escape was sleep. While nightmares plagued her at night, triggered by the clunks of the pipes, creaks of the beams, and clawing of birds on the roof, the soothing sounds drifting from the shop in the day lulled her to sleep, taking her to the place she wanted to be.

Speedwell Cottage.

\*\*\*

*Bang. Bang. Bang.*

Willow hid under the duvet. Another repetition began. Firmer and more determined than before. She preferred Rosa's tentative knocks and Amber's muffled cursing to these. They were easier to ignore and the reward of hot food on the doorstep was always welcome, even if her appetite fled when she brought a spoonful to her mouth. She turned up the volume on the romcom playing on repeat. Mrs Marley shook her head before becoming engrossed in the goings-on of Colin Firth and the housekeeper on the TV screen. If Willow had known her penchant for movies, she would have left them playing while at work.

*Bang. Bang. Bang.*

'Come on, Willow. I need to see your face and make sure you haven't joined the other spooks of this place.' Glenn's continued speech convinced her he meant business. He would not leave until he saw her.

Sighing, she dragged her duvet around her and padded to the front door, where Vincent was already waiting. He reached up towards the handle, letting his view be known. Her company bored him. Willow fiddled with the chain and deadlock, opened it a crack, to see Glenn and Amber in the shadows. Vincent barged past her, opening it further. He sped down the stairs, eager for escape and to stretch his legs, knowing his witch had company.

'Jesus! You look like hell, no wonder you're not downstairs. You'd scare your customers away. And your kitchen—it resembles my student days,' Glenn remarked, but Willow didn't hear; she saw Amber's face transform from relief to betrayal as she looked over Willow's shoulder. Willow's sludge-filled mind delayed her ability to call out and explain before the sound of stomping boots descending the stairs echoed in the stairwell. The bottom door slammed shut. Glenn didn't flinch at his daughter's departure, but continued to study his friend.

'Flu has a habit of flooring you.' Willow longed to rush after her apprentice, but what could she say to make it better? Explanations wouldn't ease the tension; the truth would cut deeper.

'Flu? Are you sure? Amber said—'

'Flu! Snot, cough, fever, the works.' Her fingers instinctively crossed behind her back.

'You should have called.'

'I texted.'

'In a house full of spooks who near enough serve customers and answer phones that is not reassuring.'

'Only Old Percy does that, and he pulls the phone out of the wall not ...' Willow registered the concern in his face and guilt sneaked in. First Amber and now him, pulling her emotions in ways she couldn't deal with. 'Look. I'm okay. Alive, so you can go now. I'd hate to spread my germs.'

His foot prevented her from closing the door. 'Actually, I fancy a cuppa and you look like you could do with one. By my reckoning, you won't be contagious now. So, no excuses, I'll make it. Teabags?'

Giving up, she allowed him in and followed his gaze to Rosa's box of Yorkshire tea near the kettle. He'd discovered her guilty secret.

'Are these teabags? You never use teabags. They are environmentally unfriendly, and they take the magic away from the process—'

She swiped them from his hand and hugged them protectively. Now was not the time to explain that they reminded her of Nate and their first night together. Bittersweet memories in a sea of horror.

'I don't need a lecture.' Willow placed them in the cupboard along with the mug she'd raided from the Emporium's stock advertising the store. Another notch in her rigid tea beliefs. She conceded Nate was correct. Builder's tea did taste better in a mug in times of crisis.

'No—' he nodded, taking a step back and an exaggerated sniff, '—but you do need a shower or, even better, a soak. Wash your hair. Get changed. You stink.'

Running her fingers through her hair, she cringed at the greasy texture, allowing it to stick up in tufts. She screwed up her nose, aware of the stale odour wafting up from her days-old pyjamas stained with the wine she'd spilt while crying. Alarmed, words failed her.

'Just go. I'll put the kettle on.'

\*\*\*

'Feel better?' Glenn asked when she returned, wearing fresh leggings and a clean, sloppy jumper. One chosen in haste, so she didn't slip on the jumper Nate left, despite his lingering scent being overwhelmed by the staleness of the last few weeks. If Glenn wasn't there, she doubted her resolve.

'I do. Thanks.' Acknowledging the pleasure she felt taking a hot bubble bath. The relaxing bath oil from the Wishing Spell range didn't proclaim miracles, but her knotted muscles loosened and the tension in her shoulders eased. The floral scent encouraged her to submerge deeper into the water, removing grime and a layer of fear. She had tried before to shower but, naked and vulnerable, every noise or creak escalated her anxiety. It could have been Rafe invading her home, as he had her mind. The Marleys' attempts to reassure her with Mr Marley guarding the door outside and his wife soothing her with her words failed. It was easier to avoid bathing altogether. With Glenn in the flat, she could relax.

'You didn't need to have tidied up. I would have done it—eventually.'

Glenn shrugged and leant back on the kitchen chair at the table that was now clear bar the makings of tea. 'Consider it paying a debt. You did it for me many times, as I recall. Besides, days-old lasagne is no diet for a handsome Maine Coon. The red paw prints made the kitchen look like a crime scene.'

The kitchen was transformed. Gone were the collection of the drabbest cups she had used; the mouldy casserole dishes and bowls of uneaten soup which joined the colony of fungi were washed, and the bins taken out. The room sparkled. An open window circulated the air, dispersing the heavy cloud of depression. The saltiness of the sea and the call of the seagulls flying outside woke her senses, and the atmosphere shifted upwards.

'Thank you.'

'Flu takes it out of you. The flat would still be a hovel next week otherwise. If it was flu.' Glenn poured dark amber liquid from a teapot into a brightly coloured cup and pushed it towards her, urging her to sit.

'I don't know what you mean.' She sank into the chair opposite, focusing on the rising steam from her cup and the aroma of the well-chosen blend instead of the look of concern in his eyes.

'Amber wasn't convinced it was illness that's locked you away and don't tell her this, but she's rarely wrong. Not about emotions and stuff. But there is also that ...' He pointed over her shoulder at the mirror. The same mirror covered by a scarf that had caused Amber's storming down the stairs. Like his daughter, he knew what it meant. He had seen it all before.

'Worried Amber would spy on you, were you?' he pried directly.

'More concerned she'd be worried if she saw the flat in a state,' explained Willow. *And ask questions I'm not prepared to answer.* When witches entered the shop, a gentle hum vibrated in the air. The frequency differed depending on the witch's power and experience. It was how she recognised hereditary witches from novice ones discovering their skills, and differentiated those unaware of their latent nature and customers intoxicated by the town's gothic atmosphere but whose purchases would remain in cupboards gathering dust. The connection allowed her to customise her service to fit with their needs. It was different with Amber. Amber was different. She didn't only feel the electrical pull to interpret and unpick, she could amplify it, to delve deeper into that person. With Amber's ability to scry and tap into people's lives using reflective surfaces, Willow had no choice but to cover them and block her. She couldn't risk her having access to her fears and memories. Maintaining the mental barrier was exhausting, but if Willow's suspicions were correct, Amber didn't need mirrors for the connection. If she tried, kinship and focus would be enough.

Glenn placed his hand over hers. 'I know I'm not Louise or even female, but I consider you my friend. My only friend. If something's going on, I'm here. To listen, to fight if needed, or even just wash up.'

The words Willow longed to speak stuck in her throat, as she knew they would. As much as she wished she could tell him the truth, the years of keeping secrets, shame, and fear forbade her. Instead, she sipped her tea. She focused on every detail—the aroma, the swirl of the liquid, and the drop dribbling down the side to the saucer—when her hand shook. Placing the cup on its saucer, she studied the man in front of her. Her friend whose frown lines were deeper than she remembered and circles under his eyes reflected his worry about her. The Marleys, clutching each other, hovered in the doorway, waited for her reaction.

Taking a deep breath, she pushed her chair back and strode to the mirror and whipped the scarf away. The ghosts nodded and their solid forms faded. Whatever danger remained, Willow knew one thing: even with her secrets, she was not alone.

Glenn's visit gave Willow the impetus she needed. She uncovered every mirror, revealing the physical toll the last few weeks had on her complexion and weight. Her grown hair curled over her ears, revealing the blonde roots she wanted to hide. Only those closest to her would not believe she was recovering from illness. Natural light flooded the flat when she drew back all the curtains, and her mood lifted. A chink of light had broken through the gloom. She dragged her fusty bedding upstairs to the laundry basket, and layers of dust covering all surfaces were wiped clear. The sharp fresh sea breeze, gulls calling, and the general murmur from the town drifted through the open windows, making her feel alive. Exhausted, she sat on the edge of the bed. It wasn't perfect, but it was a start.

Once she heard the shop's lock click closed and Rosa tottered down Black Cat Alley, Willow forced herself down the stairwell. *He is not here*, became her mantra. The icy patch on the ceiling was no longer contained in a small area, but crept down the walls. Shivering, she walked past; it was a problem to be considered another day. With regret, she returned the teabags to Rosa's hiding spot along with a note of apology, but she wasn't surprised to see a fresh box. *While the cat was away, the mouse will play and all that*. She smiled. There would be a backlash from her staff after they heard of Willow's hypocrisy. Old Percy scrutinised her every move and lingered in the workroom's doorway when she opened it for the first time since the card's arrival. She stood speechless. *Was this how the shoemaker felt when the elves finished the exquisite shoes for the king?*

Amber had cleared away the evidence of her last spell; the room was spotless. Freshly made potions lined the correct shelves, the aroma of fresh tea blends filled the air, and new Wishing Spell candles hung in their racks. A list of stock they needed to order lay on the bench alongside several packages ready to post. Her young apprentice had picked up the reins of the business and carried on. A rush of pride and love for her warmed Willow and made her smile. Despite the hurt she'd inflicted on Amber, she still devoted her time to the Emporium for her. Thanks to her efforts, Willow had a business to return to. *I hope it didn't interfere with your revision.* Willow glanced at the calendar and calculated how many days, weeks, she had lost in the void. *Shit! Her exams.* Had she missed that? Drowning in her own sorrow, she hadn't been there for an important time for Amber. Her mocks could impact the university she chose. Who else had she let down?

*** 

Willow checked her phone while the tea brewed in the pot. A bright yellow teacup promised her hope she didn't feel. There were no new messages or calls from Nate. He had given up, and knowing it was for the best didn't stop the pain. Another person she had hurt, except, unlike Amber, she couldn't apologise to him.

Someone rapped on the door, and Vincent became animated as the aroma of fish and chips wafted into the room. Willow opened it and Rosa, with an excitable Alejo, bustled in with warm paper-wrapped packages and a bunch of flowers.

'Sorry to drop in unannounced and uninvited, but Glenn said you needed feeding up. Thought you'd want a change from Mum's Spanish fayre, and no one can resist chips.'

And she couldn't. The salty taste and dripping vinegar sent her taste buds into a frenzy. Her appetite came back in an instant. The vibrant daffodils placed in a jug on the table added brightness to the kitchen, as did Alejo's endless chatter and wonder at being in a witch's home. Having the duo in her personal space differed from being in the shop, but Willow found she didn't mind. She welcomed the company. Rosa gave the love sent from well-wishers, the gossip including her sighting of Old Percy and how people stopped her in the street asking about Vincent, concerned they hadn't seen him on his daily walks or visits to their homes for titbits.

'You would never guess he'd do that, would you?' Willow said as Vincent vocally demanded Alejo share his fish. Giggling, Alejo obliged.

'He's been missed and so have you. I've missed you.'

'And Amber?'

'She's worried about you, obviously, and is quite a bossy madam when you're not around, but she worked hard.'

'I saw. You both have. I don't know how to repay you.'

'You haven't seen the overtime sheet yet. It will make your eyes water. We're just glad you're getting better.'

Once dinner was eaten, they shared a tub of ice cream after Alejo insisted everyone needed pudding. Conversation continued until Alejo yawned. It was past his bedtime.

Rosa rummaged in her bag and pushed a box of Yorkshire tea across the table. 'For emergencies. And don't apologise—it's nice to know behind all the witchiness and perfection you're human after all.'


Every day Willow got up, applied make-up to disguise the sleepless nights and forced herself to trudge down the stairs to the shop floor and face the customers. Amber boosted Willow's protection spells around the building with her own enchantments, easing some anxiety. Cocooned in the Enchanted Emporium, there was no more contact. Maybe the banishing spell had worked after all.

Day by day, the darkness retreated with the help from her friends. Every evening either Glenn or Rosa and Alejo arrived to share dinner, ensuring she ate. The ghosts faded as the company of the living replaced the dead. Old Percy resumed his supervisory role of Rosa and ghostly stocktaking, while Mr Marley vanished with a roll of his eyes when his wife insisted on watching a repeat of *Pride and Prejudice* with Colin Firth. Willow knew things were more acceptable when she came home to a warm, empty lounge.

To her relief, Black Cat was nowhere to be seen, but apart from her scheduled shifts in the Emporium, neither was Amber. She continued to work hard and was pleasant to Willow, but avoided spending time alone with her. She'd even declined extra spell lessons, citing revision and seeing Jack. The rift forming between them needed healing. Willow had let her down once; she wouldn't fail her again.

# Chapter Twenty-Five

The scrunched-up paper ricocheted off the rim of the bin, much to Beetle's delight. He pounced on it several times before stashing it away from prying eyes. Amber ripped out another sheet of notes and tried again. It missed. She pushed her textbook away. It was no use. The longer she studied, the more the words swam on the page, making her head ache. Books piled high on the desk were a constant reminder she had to do this. She couldn't slack. Her mock results were a disappointment and without Jack to discuss the lessons and theories, her motivation waned. He was right about one thing. No amount of rosemary would get her a good grade. She missed him. If he was there, he would hug her, encourage her to carry on, and remind her of the fun they planned for this summer. But he wasn't there. She was on her own. Ever since he'd stormed out, there was an undercurrent she didn't understand. He turned away to answer texts, cancelled more than one date, saying he had to look after his brothers, and avoided her after lessons. Something was going on.

The house was too quiet, and she regretted declining her dad's invitation to go to Willow's for tea, citing her revision as an excuse. The warmth of the Emporium's flat and company would be welcome, but it was better this way. No matter how much she missed time with her dad and longed to discuss her worries. Willow and Glenn needed time alone for their relationship to bloom. Now more than ever.

It wasn't the sense of betrayal when she saw the extent Willow went to to shield her life from Amber that sent her fleeing down the stairs and biting back tears while serving customers that day; it was the shock of Willow's appearance. Her vulnerability. The figure huddled beneath the duvet was an unkempt, shrunken version of the strong person she knew. Her weight loss emphasised her high cheekbones, and against her pallor, her eyes were larger and dull. If the elegant, confident mentor Amber aspired to be crumbled under pressure, what chance did she have? The force of emotion scared her, followed later by the guilt. Willow had shown unwavering support for her when she needed it, yet instead of stepping forward to give her a hug and help, she fled. Maybe if she stayed, Willow would have confided in her and explained why she'd discovered remnants of a banishing spell in the workroom and why, when the flat door opened, a fleeting look of terror crossed Willow's face. It was too late now. The best thing to do was to maintain the protection spells around the Emporium, keep a low profile, and trust her dad to fall in love. He would protect her from the danger Amber detected lurking in the shadows.

The sketch emerged on the page, making Amber's heart flutter as the man from the beach's face took shape with each pencil stroke. At least something was looking up. After weeks of searching, she had seen him again.

\*\*\*

It was a chance sighting. Fate, she decided afterwards, a sign their meeting was meant to be. Jack had not only stood her up for the study session at the library, but snapped at her when she phoned him to see where he was. The desire to revise vanished as she fumed; with Willow still absent from work, she had begged an overworked Rosa to cover her shift so she could catch up with him and resolve their differences. Her plan—to study, make up, and return to hers for movies and pizza—was destroyed. Checking the time, it was early. If she went to the shop, Rosa could leave to collect Alejo from school, but it would entail the third degree. Rosa was like a terrier hunting prey when it came to gossip, and a premature appearance would make her zoom in.

Avoiding the swing bridge in case the pull of the store's magic proved too much to resist, Amber explored Whitby's new town. With more modern shops, and flashing lights and music playing from the arcades ready for the new holiday season, the atmosphere was different. Tourists encouraged by the spring sun blocked the paths, adding to her foul mood. She climbed up the steep slope until many of the shops and the crowds fell away. Bending down to tie her boot's shoelace that had come undone, Amber saw a familiar coat on the opposite pavement. A car honked as she ran across the road. If she hurried, she could catch up with him.

'Amber,' a male voice called behind her. She ignored it and continued up the road.

'Amber.'

Groaning, she spun round to greet the local postman jogging towards her. A jovial man suited to the job, any other day she'd be happy to see him, but if there was a competition between Rosa and him for time gossiping, he would win.

'You still work at the Emporium, don't you? I missed a letter out. Found it just a minute ago. You wouldn't be a love, would you, and take it with you? It would save these aching knees. They are playing up something chronic. Maybe Willow could give me something to help. The balm I used—'

'Yes, maybe. Fine. Got to go.' Amber snatched the cream letter from his hand and shoved it in her bag. Her prey was still in view higher up the hill, looking at a shop window. He went in. By the time she reached the building, her breath was ragged, beads of sweat gathered on her brow, and she knew, if she saw her reflection her face would be as red as her hair. She didn't care. She needed to see him and couldn't lose him now. The door squeaked as she entered.

It took a while for her eyes to adjust to the gloomy light in the empty room. Someone had squeezed two overstuffed sofas into the compact space and several magazines cluttered the table in front. Framed prints filled every space of the walls; she stepped closer and monochrome tattoo designs of varying detail drew her in. Her fingers itched to wipe the glass of dust to see the contour of the dragons, creatures of the deep, and cartoons more clearly. *Was he getting a new tattoo?*

'Can I help you?' A gruff voice snapped her out of her thoughts. A gargantuan man approached her, crunching his podgy knuckles before stroking his short, unruly beard. His greying hair pulled back into a pony-tail emphasised his receding hairline and his heavy-metal T-shirt strained over his stomach and chest. She cringed under his stare until she became mesmerised by the intricate dragon descending his arm. It gave her courage.

'I want a tattoo.'

'You want a tattoo? You need to be eighteen.' He retreated behind a reception desk and flicked open a magazine, dismissing her.

'I am eighteen. I have ID.' She slammed her rucksack on the counter and rummaged through her college books and sketch pads. She swore under her breath. It was there somewhere. If only she were organised, her ID card would be in her hand, ready to wave it under his condescending, bulbous nose. She unloaded her bag, finding it sandwiched between the pages of her English textbook. Amber thrust the provisional driving licence to him. He pushed it away without looking and continued to read his graphic novel. Unsure what to do, she reloaded her bag and hovered nearby. The clock on the wall ticked louder and the rustle of paper with every page turn added to her anxiety. What was she doing? The shop door invited her to leave, walk across the beach until she came to her senses.

'For fuck's sake. Just sit down over there,' the man snapped. 'Artie will be with you in a minute.'

With a brief nod, and cheeks burning, she perched on one of the sofas clutching her bag. A door opened in the distance. Heavy footsteps approached, and he strode out from an archway in the corner of the room.

'Thanks, Uncle Garth.' The voice was smooth like the sweetest chocolate, and, like their first meeting, Amber drowned in his deep brown eyes. Without his coat, the intricate designs covering both his muscular arms were visible; a fire-breathing dragon wrapped around his forearm. She longed to study it and know its meaning. This was Artie.

'Hey! It's the ferret girl. Tell me you haven't got him hiding in there?' He flashed a smile, pointing at her bag.

Her dry mouth and tongue refused to cooperate with a spoken response. It really was him. After dreaming and searching, she had found him.

'Come on. I've a free slot; we can discuss what you are looking for?' *You*, she thought. *I've been looking for you.*

The room she followed him to was bright and clinical, a contrast to the gloom they had left behind. The photographs displayed on the wall were stylish, modern, and showcased the best of tattoo designs. Amber settled into a reclining leather chair, watching Artie prepare his workstation.

'So, did you manage to bounce it?'

The low music in the background calmed her, allowing her to gather her composure. 'Several times.'

He rewarded her response with a warm smile and rolled the stool he sat on backwards so he could study her. 'Let me guess, you're after a tattoo of your furry friend. He was a surprise. I've never seen a ferret before, never mind on the beach.'

'No. I don't want him. I want a dragonfly—here,' she said, pointing to her inner forearm. Despite her impulsive visit, her decision to have a tattoo wasn't a whim; for two years she had mulled over the idea, born from a comment made in class as she doodled endless dragonflies darting across the page of history notes. 'That would look great as a tattoo,' made her consider it, research artists, establishments, and count down the days to her eighteenth birthday. Jack's discouragement and reluctance to see the attraction didn't faze her. He warned her it was a lifetime commitment, but that was the point. It would be with her always, a reminder of her past, and keep her grounded in the future. A sign of who she was. Stumbling across Artie and this place was meant to be.

Scanning the last page of the portfolio Artie had given her, she shook her head, None of the designs were right.

'Why don't you explain what you want again?' Artie took out his sketchbook, opened it to a fresh page, and hovered a pencil over it. 'Maybe I can do a custom design.'

Amber pulled out her own sketch pad from her bag, bulging with extra scraps of paper. Shrugging off her shyness of showing her work, she flicked through the pages until she found the right one.

'I want something like this.'

# Chapter Twenty-Six

The call of the sea was strong, urging her to visit the headland over-looking the town. To feel the wind kiss her face while soaking up the full moon's energy, inhale the cleansing salty air, and hear the crashing waves below. She assumed once she returned to work, exhaustion and the inability to have a nap during the day would force her body to rest and sleep soundly, but to no avail. The nights trapped her in a cycle of nightmares and insomnia, reliving the past and fretting about the future. Maybe connecting with nature would do the trick?

Vincent chattered and wound himself round her legs, as much as a lumbering ginger feline could, once he realised her intention. 'We can't go unless we find my trainers and you're not helping,' she said to him when he nearly tripped her up. She tracked her shoes abandoned under the sofa from the last jaunt to the Abbey, the night she sent Nate the photo of the night sky. Two whole moon cycles ago. No wonder she was out of sorts and the fingers of depression still caressed her, waiting for her to slip so it could tighten its grip.

Her hand trembled as she unlocked the exterior door into her garden. Vincent shot out down the path onto the garden wall. A ginger beacon to follow, but she couldn't. Her feet froze to the ground. Shadows grew where the moonlight didn't shine, reminding her he was still out there. It had been quiet with no contact as before, but he could be watching. Waiting outside the shop's perimeter for her guard to fall. Vincent detected her panic and returned with an impatient flick of his tail. Fear won. Together, they retreated to the safety of the flat.

'I'm sorry, boy,' she said, sipping the hot chamomile tea, allowing it to calm her racing heart. 'It was a bit too ambitious, wasn't it?'

He didn't respond. Once her panic attack subsided, he turned his back, ignoring her. She had let him down. 'You're not being fair, Vince. He could be out there waiting. I'm being cautious.'

She had not left the boundary of the Emporium since the card's arrival. In the day, she sent Amber or Rosa on errands and relied on online deliveries for the rest. There was no need to leave. She was safe, but she missed seeing the seasons change, soaking up the town's atmosphere, and living. Vincent missed it too.

The nightmare consumed her the moment she fell asleep. A childhood dream resurfacing to plague her nights. It was always the same. Speedwell Cottage looked as she remembered. The blazing fire in the hearth warmed Silas, the threadbare cat curled up on the mat. Grandma Jax's chair stood empty, with her cardigan hanging over the back where she always left it when it wasn't draped over her shoulders. Willow couldn't see her grandmother, yet the house was calm, waiting for her return. She wandered through to the kitchen area to discover the hot teapot ready to pour into the two teacups nearby. A sudden howl of wind whipped round the building, rattling the windows. The air chilled with a loud thump, bashing the old front door.

*Bang bang bang.*

Barefoot, Willow stepped forward, unable to resist the compulsion to open it. Silas woke. Alert, he blocked her path, hissing as she approached. Another bang and the door flung open. Her scream woke her, but she never could shake off the sight of the monster standing in the entrance. The gytrash with his drooling mouth, gnashing teeth, and fiery eyes.

Willow resigned herself to counting the hours until dawn broke. The dream must mean something. If only Grandma Jax was there to soothe her fears like she did when Willow's scream brought her into the attic bedroom. In rare moments of affection, her grandmother would cradle her and tell her stories until her eyes grew heavy and she slept. Her grandmother. Speedwell Cottage. Willow smiled as a plan formed in her mind.

She retrieved a battered suitcase from under the bed, blowing the dust bunnies away, and placed it on the lounge floor. She needed space. Inside was a bundle of letters from Louise, journals documenting her travels, old photos, and what she was looking for—the folded maps and scrapbook. Over the years, she'd hunted for Speedwell Cottage with no luck. Disheartened, she'd packaged everything away. It was time to try again. If it worked for the boy in the film *Lion* tracking down his family in India, it would work for her in the Yorkshire Moors.

Faded fluorescent orange marks highlighted the discounted areas on the map spread out on the floor. She read the extensive notes written from the memories she recalled from her childhood and added extra clues from her dreams. She sketched the cottage and drew a floor plan. Anything that could be a clue to unlock the location of Speedwell Cottage was recorded. Estate agents' sites were browsed in case a miracle happened and it was on the market. Google Maps became her favourite place as she travelled across the Moors in the given radius, based on the time it took Louise and her to get there from Whitby. Memories of their adventures comforted her, and she remembered her friend's dogged determination to find it. Willow resolved to do the same.

# Chapter Twenty-Seven

M ay's glorious sunny weather brought tourists to Whitby, with many finding their way down Black Cat Alley to the Emporium, forcing Willow out of the workroom onto the shop floor. The endless stream of questions and serving kept her busy and, to Amber's relief, she seemed happy. More like the Willow she used to know. In the jovial atmosphere, Amber enjoyed working side by side with a fellow witch. She loved Rosa, and they shared a laugh, but the pressure of being the one who could answer any questions beyond the available tea blends lay heavy on her shoulders. Amber finished serving her last customer and mopped her brow with her cardigan sleeve. Witch's Yard was a sun trap and even with the fans on, the temperature was baking in the shop.

With the shop empty, both witches became aware they were alone for the first time in months. The silence grew, and Old Percy paused, waiting to see who would speak first.

'How's college?' Willow asked.

'It's fine.' The more detailed responses Amber longed to say stuck in her throat. Where could she start? Her worry about her upcoming exams, Jack and Artie? Recent events and worries had tangled in a tight ball and were difficult to unpick.

'So, everything is okay? Your dad said he has hardly seen you since half term.'

'I've been busy revising. You know, at Jack's.'

As soon as she said it, she mentally kicked herself. Willow would detect the lie. No one could study in a house full of activity, with the loud TV blaring, arguments raging between his brothers, his mum's singing, and the tantrums of the toddler. Jack always studied at hers. Nothing happened. Willow didn't react.

'Ah, Jack. How is he doing? You both must be looking forward to the summer of freedom. No study, just fun until uni. Maybe when your exams are over and you have time, we could get back to our lessons.'

'That'd be good.' Amber nodded. It would. She missed the hands-on magic, creating and blending the store's lotions, potions, and tea. The workroom allowed her witch side to be free without interruption and being seen as odd or as something to fear. She loved it. Until now. Tempting as it was, working alone with Willow and needing to relax for the magic to happen was too risky. Amber couldn't let her guard down. Willow wasn't the only one keeping secrets.

'You could tell me what your secret ingredient for the last batch of Wishing Spell sleeping lotion you made was. It has had rave reviews.'

*There is no special ingredient*, thought Amber, surprised Willow didn't know.

The only difference between the spells Amber created was the proximity to the old witch's room; the closer you were when casting the spell, the more potent the effect. She privately named the room The Cobble, an abbreviation of her mum's favourite word and one which made her giggle as a toddler—collywobbles. The nervous sensation that produced the telltale roll of the stomach and queasiness. It was obvious whenever Willow approached the rickety door; she had an attack of them. If she could, Amber was sure she would brick the relic room up again. In contrast, Amber loved the room. She itched to enter and explore. If being close to it conjured up powerful magic, what could it contain? The rare times Willow opened it in her presence, she saw the poky space was a time capsule from centuries before when they feared and forbade witchcraft. Its heavy protection spell held its power despite the degradation in time. Driftwood-made shelves filled the space above the cluttered workbench and were full of old leather books and warped glass bottles hidden beneath the cobwebs. One book, with yellowing parchment and faded ink, lay open on a stand. The answers to her problems would be hidden in there. If only she had access to it.

'Aren't you hot in that?' Willow pointed at Amber's cardigan.

'No.' She shook her head and pulled the sleeves down further. For the last few weeks, she had avoided any confrontation about her tattoo by covering her arms. The cooler weather helped until this week's mini heatwave. Time was running out and everyone would know. She stretched towards the top shelf, returning the recently used jars and humming a song she had heard on the radio.

'Amber, tell me you didn't?'

'What?' She followed Willow's gaze to her arm, where her sleeve had crept up to reveal the bottom of her tattoo. She snatched it down. 'Okay. I didn't.'

'No, don't. Show me before the shop fills again.' Willow sidled up to her, giving her no choice but to peel off her cardigan, and she held her arm up for Willow to have a closer look.

'What do you think?' Still red at the edges, a delicate dragonfly was inked in flight on her pale skin. The green haze shimmering around it added to the magical effect.

'It is beautiful. One of your designs?'

Amber nodded. 'It felt right. A dragonfly to remind me Mum is always around and how far Dad and I have come.'

'The presence of spirit and transformation. It's perfect. I just hope you were careful and went somewhere reputable.'

'Of course, I did. I'm not stupid.' She snatched her hand away and regretted her reaction when she saw sadness flash across her mentor's face. 'I researched places and their hygiene ratings. It was fine.' It wasn't another lie. She had spent hours looking at places and written a list of her top places to go, but Bones Ink didn't come up in the search. If it had, she would have rejected it for its run-down façade and dusty reception, but once she saw Artie in an immaculate clean room, she knew she was making the right decision. She trusted him.

'Please don't tell Dad. He'll kill me.'

'You know he won't do that.'

'Please, Willow. He won't understand.'

'Okay, I won't, but he'll be fine.'

'Maybe.' She struggled to define her feelings. Tattoos never came up for discussion at home, so she didn't know if he liked them or not, but she couldn't stop thinking she had pushed an invisible boundary and was unsure of the fallout. What if he hated them? It was fine, Willow telling her Glenn would be okay. She knew the new Dad. The happy, confident, and sober version, but memories of when he raged over simple things sneaked in at times; she couldn't stop them. The fear remained that the old Dad would reappear, and she would discover their close relationship was an illusion. *No one understands*, she thought. *That's not true, Artie understood*. To her relief, when she showed him her art, he didn't laugh, but nodded while flicking through the rest of her work. After discussion, they decided on one of her prolific drawings of the favoured insect. He was easy to talk to and listened as a modified version of her childhood came out and she spoke of her reluctance to leave home. He confided in his complicated relationship with his mother, also a reformed alcoholic. Learning to trust was the key to move forward, he explained, as was talking. It made sense, but if she spoke to Glenn, everything could be revealed. There was too much at stake. For Willow. For her.

# Chapter Twenty-Eight

W illow released a sigh when Rosa disappeared through the ginnel, late as usual to pick up Alejo from school. Alone, the forced smile and mask of joviality slipped; hiding her persistent anxiety was harder than she imagined. Her reprieve was short-lived. The shop bell jingled with the arrival of her next customer. A flood of warmth filled Willow and a genuine smile formed as a short lady bundled up in a winter coat and hat shuffled in.

'Mrs Ramsey. It's been a long time since I've seen you. It's lovely to see the sun has brought you out.'

'Yes lass, it's been a long winter, but the lure of your special brew has brought me out of hibernation. And the sunshine, too.'

'Well, it's good to see you.' Willow weighed out her loyal customer's usual before pouring it into an Enchanted Emporium tea caddy Mrs Ramsey whipped out of her wheeled shopping trolley. *Why waste packaging, dear*, was always her motto. A woman after Willow's own heart.

'Now I just need to pick up some kippers for my guests and I can head home for this. It'll add a much-needed spring in my step, it will. If you don't mind me saying, you could use some too. Everything all right, dear?'

The immaculate make-up didn't disguise the haunted look and extreme fatigue from beady, observant eyes and Mrs Ramsey always noticed details others missed. During Willow's B&B stays, they'd often spoken over cocoa well into the nights when neither could sleep. The topics ranged from her plans for the Old Apothecary to the more personal memories of Louise and Mrs Ramsey's grief for her beloved husband. Her warmth and lack of judgement made her an easy confidante.

'Everything is fine,' she said. *Fine*, the small word that holds a multitude of lies. The old lady held on to the counter and rubbed her lower back.

'Those cobbles play havoc with my sciatica. Getting older is harder and more painful than you ever think possible.'

'I may have a balm for that. I made a fresh batch this morning. I'll grab you one from the back.' Willow slipped into the stockroom, passing Vincent, who never missed a fuss from Mrs Ramsey. It would not surprise her if he visited the B&B as he had Nate. On her return, she saw the cat purr as Mrs Ramsey bent down, whispering into his ear. Straightening up with ease, she looked sheepish.

'Do you fancy a rest and a cuppa while you're here? It may help your sciatica.'

'That would have been lovely, dear, but I'd better get back. I'm expecting a call from my son. Gone all hi-tech I have, one of those silver surfers, you know. It's wonderful. I can talk to him from the other side of the world. I'll see you later, dear boy.' Mrs Ramsey paid for the balm with a note she clutched in her wrinkled hand, and gave Vincent a last farewell pat.

As Willow watched her follow Rosa's footsteps across Witch's Yard, she couldn't help noticing a spring in her step that defied a bad back.

The next day, suspicions mounted when Rosa located the landlady's purse behind the counter display of candles. Unless Old Percy had developed a pickpocketing habit, it couldn't have got there by accident. A quick phone call confirmed them as Mrs Ramsey declared she couldn't possibly leave the house to collect it, but Willow was welcome for tea.

***

Willow stood at the entrance of Black Cat Alley. Vincent swept past her with his tail high in the air, down the tunnel to the busy street beyond. *At least one of us is eager.* Her heart thumped hard against her chest. Faster and faster. A loud whooshing pulsed in her ears, accompanying the dizziness, which threatened to overwhelm her. Touching the cold, damp wall shocked her into taking a deep breath. A murmur of voices and Rosa's laughter drifted from the busy shop across the courtyard. A few steps back and she would be safe. Mrs Ramsey would understand if she explained there was a rush of customers. Amber could drop the purse off after college. Vincent reappeared and scowled. His eyes boring into hers.

'Don't look at me like that. I know,' she said. 'I know. I have to do this.'

*Just one step. And another.* She focused on her cat at the end of the tunnel. People strolled by without a care, laughing and talking into their mobiles. They were living their lives. As she hit the high street, she realised the length of time she had remained in her sanctuary. Winter had long gone; shop displays celebrated spring and the promise of summer. The buzz of tourists already filled the air. Whitby had shrugged off its winter hibernation and come alive. *So many people for him to hide amongst.* Sensing her panic, Vincent fell in line with her steps and stood close as she waited to cross the swing bridge. The fresh sea air and saltiness kept her grounded, and as she came out of the town to the row of B&B's her fear receded. There were no footsteps behind her and no sense of being watched. She was still safe.

'Sit. Sit, dear.'

The sitting room hadn't altered since Willow's last visit years before, including the sofa, which now sagged further with age. A basket of wool and Mrs Ramsey's knitting sat near the cold, empty hearth. A thin layer of dust gathered on the once-immaculate surfaces and crumbs lay on the floor, missed by failing eyesight. The same, but different, just like her hostess. In her own environment and layers of clothing removed, she was thinner, more petite and fragile than Willow recalled. A sign of the passing years during which she had failed to visit.

'Where's that cat of yours?' Vincent replied with a mew and frantic scratching in the kitchen. Mrs Ramsey blushed and tottered out. The sound of a cupboard door opening and biscuits falling into a bowl and contented munching made Willow grin. *At least one of us has been checking on her.* On the table nearby, the collection of framed photographs had expanded since her last visit. Some she recognised from before, including the large sepia photo of Mr and Mrs Ramsey on their wedding day, and close family. Others she didn't. There were several photographs of Louise, Louise and Glenn on their wedding day and one with her holding a newborn. Amber. Another was taken the summer before Willow went travelling, the last one when she'd stayed here in the B & B with Louise. She picked it up. Between the two laughing witches stood a younger Mrs Ramsey, flustered at being included in the photo. It had been a wonderful holiday when both had high hopes for their futures.

'I remember the first summer you came. Bohemian Lou in her vibrant colours with a daisy in her hair, I believe, and you dressed in black looking haunted as if you were here for our Goth weekends. So different, but the bond between you was immeasurable.' Mrs Ramsey returned with Vincent trailing behind. She settled into her chair before passing Willow a scrapbook. On opening, Willow hid her surprise at seeing further photographs of Louise and her daughter, postcards Willow had sent from her travels and a few infant drawings from Amber. She never knew Louise had stayed connected with the beloved landlady, as she did. It would be something to tell Amber next time she saw her. She flicked over the page to see several newspaper cuttings about the Enchanted Emporium. Moments in time even she had forgotten about. She swallowed hard. Mrs Ramsey had spent time and effort collecting memories to create a book of love Willow never expected.

'Did you know I called you my girls? Every summer I'd tell everyone I saw my girls are coming. This house was always lighter and brighter when you were here. Full of laughter and gossip. Each year, I saw how you bloomed under Louise's care and how you grounded her. When you came back from your travels, all tanned and confident, I thought to myself, she has done it. She's come out of the shadows and living. I was so proud of you. Every time I see you and that monstrous cat of yours walking along the beach or see someone carrying a bag with your logo, I still think that's my girl.'

The threatening tears spilt over and trickled down Willow's cheeks. Mrs Ramsey rummaged in her cardigan pocket to produce a clean handkerchief and pressed it into her hands. 'Now that haunted look is back. As is that gytrash nightmare of yours.'

Sharing a house in the earlier days made it impossible to hide Willow's nightmares, often waking her with a jolt or a scream. Mrs Ramsey was the only person bar Louise she'd ever described them to. She'd remembered.

'Yet I don't see your silhouette up on the headland. Walked them away, you always did, and it worked. Now your fears are keeping you locked indoors. It never takes long before a sanctuary becomes a prison, especially when you apply the shackles yourself. Don't look so surprised, dear. I may not be a witch, but I have picked up a few bits of knowledge over my years.' Mrs Ramsey reached over and held both of Willow's hands. 'Don't let him destroy you, the dreams you have achieved, or the witch you have become. You're not the meek child you were when I first saw you. You don't need to retreat into the shadows. Remember the story of the gytrash. Now I've said my piece. It's time for that cup of tea.'

She settled back in her chair and sighed. 'Be a love and pour. My knotted hands are not to be trusted with my best china anymore.'

Blindsided, Willow did as she was told, and filled each china cup with tea mashed to perfection. She topped them up with a splash of milk and passed one over to Mrs Ramsey's waiting arthritic hands. She must drop off some soothing hand cream for them and vowed to herself to visit more.

'Thank you,' Willow murmured.

'What for? The ramblings of an old woman? It's nowt. Now help yourself to biscuits. Not homemade, but delicious all the same. Let me tell you all about my news. Our Joel is coming to visit from Australia next year. Can you imagine that young whippet of a grandson is old enough to travel across the world alone?'

Willow sank into her chair with Vincent by her side and listened to Mrs Ramsey's enthusiastic chat about her family and plans for the future.

Much to Vincent's delight, Willow made a detour from Mrs Ramsey's to the beach, past the bright beach huts. She nodded to people she recognised and smiled at the nudges tourists gave each other at the sight of a large cat strolling on the beach. At the shoreline, she watched the shallow foamed water flow over the sand and shells towards her before drawing backwards. The endless cycle of growth and retreat. With the help of her friend's words, the gentle breeze and warm sun on her face, the last grey clouds of depression departed. Willow had fought for survival before, succeeded, and she could do it again. It was time to take control, starting with a new blend of tea she could taste on her tongue. Maybe she should allow Amber to restart the social media accounts. If Rafe contacted her again, she would not shy away from facing him, not again. It was time to fight for herself, her business and magic.

# Chapter Twenty-Nine

From her bedroom window, Amber watched Glenn dig over the border, getting ready to plant the tray of bright primroses and seedlings they had nurtured since spring. They always did it together. A shared love of gardening bonded them while they healed their relationship, and the garden flourished under their care. Her favourite time of the year was passing while she was cooped up studying. She longed to close her laptop, pull on some tatty clothes, and join him. They rarely spent time alone recently. His visits to Willow, long hours at work, and her study always got in the way. And secrets. Despite Willow's assurances, she still had not told him about her tattoo. She had to soon. She couldn't expect Willow to keep quiet and he was asking questions about why she insisted on wearing long sleeves in the blistering heat. The newly healed dragonfly looked better than she expected. There were no regrets. Every time she trailed her finger over the delicate lines, she remembered Artie's touch and smile.

To Garth's disapproval, she had returned to Bones Ink several times; Artie's smooth voice and ability to soothe her fears drew her there. He understood her and her art. With his encouragement, she produced a portfolio of work, and a couple of his clients had commissioned a bespoke design. The buzz she had from seeing her art on someone's skin was addictive. As with tea blending, it was instinctive to add an intention, a spell, for that person alone to give them what they needed. A sigil for protection hidden in the leaves of a flower, or healing drawn in the scales of the mermaid's tail. If she could ink the person herself, the options to help were endless. Better, though, she didn't need a degree to learn. With her ability to study waning at least there was a backup plan when results day would confirm her fears. She doubted she would pass her exams. Until then, Bones Ink was another secret to keep.

She pulled out a cream envelope from her sketchbook addressed to Willow Anderson.

All day she carried it with her, waiting for the opportunity to pass it on, but when the time came, she couldn't do it. The Willow she knew and admired was back, chatting with customers and even walking up onto the headland. What right did she have to pull the rug under her again? It didn't take a crystal ball to see her friend's face crumble or hurtle back into depression once she read the letter.

Amber unlocked the concealed drawer in her apothecary's box and retrieved the bundle wrapped in silk and herbs. Once a quick fresh protection spell was cast, she unwound the fabric. Hatred and anger spewed into the room despite her attempts to neutralise its source, several envelopes matching the one in her hand. Every one identical. The same brand of envelopes, font, and no clues to the sender.

The first one had arrived while Willow was sick. On her way to the Emporium, she discovered the new postman leaning against the alley wall clutching several letters to his chest. Beads of sweat beaded on his grey skin while he struggled to breathe. Amber pulled her phone out to call emergency services, shocked someone not much older than herself was having a heart attack, but as she approached him, she felt it. The pulse of an activated protection spell pressing against him, barring entry. As she guided him to sit on the edge of the kerb away from the ginnel, she scooped up the letters he dropped. All were addressed to Willow. He quickly recovered. Confused and embarrassed, he refused help beyond a drink of water from a nearby shopkeeper. Dehydration could do strange things, he insisted, but he never did the round again nor ignored the rumours of spooky goings-on in Fenwick's Yard. The Enchanted Emporium protested when she took the mail in, and she cautiously sorted them. Bills, invoices, and junk mail. There was nothing to provoke a reaction until she saw it. It wasn't magical, but the negative energy was palpable, and the hatred it emanated made the back of her neck tingle. She ripped it open. The words made her sick. Everyone knew about internet trolls but to hold a penned letter spewing vile rants about the evil of witches and her mentor felt more personal, more threatening. Unsure what to do, she shoved it back into the envelope and her bag. It was a one-off, something she didn't need to worry about or concern Willow with, she decided, but they kept coming. Most days, the regular postman whistled as he walked through the ginnel and across the courtyard. If it was quiet, he chatted to Rosa over a cup of tea. This day, he came in silently. While Rosa served a customer, he approached Amber, asking for Willow. When she explained her illness, he looked sheepish. A few moments passed before he said there was a letter he couldn't deliver. He'd left it in the prearranged place for Willow to collect, like the old days. Her puzzlement showed. After checking the conversation would not be overheard, he explained further. When the shop refused mail by magical means, he would leave them with a neighbouring shop who were happy to act as a go-between. When Amber collected the now-familiar letter, everything slotted into place. The discovery of the remnants of a failed banishment spell in the workroom, Willow's absence, and the ghosts being on guard duty. The more her concerns for Willow's welfare were dismissed, the harder it was to confide in someone, and she didn't want to betray her friend's trust. It had snowballed out of control. Her only solution was to track down the perpetrator and make them stop. If only she knew how.

More conventional means of ticking off suspects revealed no answers. As much as she distrusted Nate and blamed him for being the catalyst for the year's downfall, this wasn't his style. With no further evidence, she had reached a dead end. Scrying gave nothing away, nor did her mum's Book of Shadows and journals she had inherited. Like love spells, finding the origins of letters was not on her mum's agenda. The Cobble's grimoires might have a spell she could adapt, but without the key, it was impossible. Beetle might be the ultimate thief with his ability to sneak into the smallest space, but it would be a recipe for disaster, adding him to the vicinity of Vincent and Black Cat. The sooner Willow and Glenn realised they were made for each other, the better. Her dad would protect her.

***

Amber jolted awake with a gasp. She sipped some water, hoping it would ease the rolling wave of nausea. Jack had ignored her. He saw Amber standing in the shop doorway and turned away, continuing his walk down the street, pushing Joe in his stroller and attempting to control the squabbling twins. She wanted to run over and wrap the boys into an enormous hug as she always did and be part of the group, but she couldn't. It was just a dream. But as much as she told herself and repeated the phrase over and over, she knew it was a lie. It was more than a dream. It was his dream.

They'd discovered her ability to dream walk into his dreams by accident. All couples dream about each other. This particular day Jack had recalled his latest dream, and she finished it, describing every minute detail from the colour of the buildings to the coin he discovered on the dusty road. Amber witnessed it all from a window and he'd seen her. The following night, he dreamt the same landscape and when he acknowledged her standing in a doorway, they discovered they could consciously interact and mould the dreams to their wishes. Who needed to worry about curfews and rules when anything was possible as they slept?

His refusal to interact hurt more than his distancing in actual life. She could rationalise that with exam pressure and family commitments, but this was different. Meeting in his dreamscape was their time to relax and have fun. Whatever was going on with his life, as far as she was concerned, with this snub, their relationship was over.

# Chapter Thirty

'Thanks for that. Tea?' Willow served Glenn a glass of iced tea from the jug she'd placed on the small patio table moments before he phoned, declaring he was on his way with two bags of compost he had over-ordered for a job. She didn't believe for one minute his reason for visiting. If anything, he could have used them for his garden but now her friends deemed her recovered enough to remember to eat, the routine of nightly visits had slipped by. Surprisingly, she missed it.

'No worries. It's better you use them than the faff of returning them to the supplier.' Glenn sank onto the wobbly garden chair. Straight from work, he looked exhausted and the usual exhilaration of doing a day's work in a job he loved was tainted with concern. She waited for him to speak, knowing silence would encourage him to offload more than questions. Like father, like daughter.

She sipped her drink, welcoming the refreshing coolness. Summer had arrived early, with blazing temperatures. How Glenn worked in it, she didn't know. The flowering wisteria offered them much-needed shade in the small kitchen garden. She used every available space for plants she could harvest for the Enchanted Emporium's remedies and spells. Under her care, it flourished, providing her with a feast of colour and scent while wildlife buzzed with activity. An abundance of butterflies covered the buddleia and bees enjoyed the lavender and a brave bird hopped close to the slumbering Vincent sprawled on the patch of catnip she'd grown for his benefit. It was her oasis after long hours at work.

'I'm giving up dating,' declared Glenn.

Willow whipped round to look at him. This was the last thing she was expecting.

'Can I ask why? I thought things were going well. I mean, you haven't met the woman of your dreams, but it sounded as if you were having fun.'

'I was, but it doesn't matter. It'll wait. I'm worried about Amber. I need to focus on her right now.'

'Now she has her exams and reduced her hours, I've hardly seen her. It's revision or Jack. During her last shift, she was panicking about this week's exams, but she's worked hard. She knows that deep down, so she'll be fine. More to the point, what are you concerned about?'

'Jack? Well, this week, that's up in the air. She has ignored any message and calls from him and when he couldn't get through, he phoned the landline. I had strict instructions to say she was out.'

'It'll be a tiff and blow over, judging by the heart doodles I found on the invoice forms. They are teenagers, it happens.'

'I know, but there is something more. I think she's self-harming or has lost weight and has an eating disorder.'

'We are talking about Amber. The girl who has been known to eat tea round yours and then go to Jack's for more. What made you come to that conclusion?'

'She's evasive, avoiding me and always wearing long sleeves. It happens. I've read up on it and with the childhood she has had, dealing with me, maybe—'

'Stop! Right now. I can safely say she doesn't have an eating disorder nor is she self-harming.'

'But it's summer. She should be wearing short sleeves like normal. You know what it is, don't you?'

Willow nodded and squeezed his arm. 'I do. I wish I could tell you, but you know I can't break my confidence. Our relationship took a battering with my depression but talk to her. She wants to tell you but doesn't know how and, for goodness' sake, when she does, remember your fears and give her a big hug.'

Her heart tugged at the relief showing on his face. 'You're a good dad and you will deal with this teenage stance of independence, like Louise would have done.'

'Thank you, I think. I just worry there will be a repeat performance of two years ago.'

'She has grown to be a confident young witch with an excellent head on her shoulders. She may have her teenage trials, but she wouldn't put herself in danger. Not again.'

***

'Beetle! Where is it?'

Amber's dragonfly bracelet was missing. The last time she had it was a week ago when she threw it across her desk in disgust after Jack's betrayal.

She needed it. Her exam was hours away and whatever she thought of Jack it would bring her luck. A heap of discarded books, paper, and clothes piled into a higher mountain as she checked everything on the desk and floor. Beetle appeared from her college backpack carrying her house keys.

'Oh, no you don't.'

Her attempt to grab him failed as he darted across the room, dragging her keys in his mouth. He squirmed away to slip into his den under the bookcase.

'Beetle, bring them back.' Despite Amber lying on the floor chirping to lure him out, it was no use. Once he ferreted his treasure away, he would not voluntarily give it up.

'Okay. Have it your way.'

There was one thing he loved more than his hoard: fresh egg yolk. With him distracted by the treat and safe in his cage, Amber pulled out his stash. Odd socks, lipstick, pens, scrunched-up paper, her keys, and the missing dragonfly bracelet. She released the breath she didn't know she was holding. A wave of regret washed over her as she slid it on her wrist. It was only months since Jack and she were happily planning the summer. How could it have fallen apart so quick? *Enough, you don't need him.*

Artie listened to her and understood her far more than he did. Any spare time she had, she gravitated to Bones Ink. The creative atmosphere ignited ideas for her own work and when Artie set her challenges to push her designs out of her comfort zone, she was in her element. A brief description given, her hands itched to draw her interpretation. If she could prove she was skilled and determined enough, maybe he would consider taking her on as his apprentice.

She rummaged in Beetle's nest some more; make-up sponges, hair bobbles, and a leather strap. She recognised it instantly, and Jack was forgotten. It must have slipped from Artie's hair when Amber made an impulse visit to the parlour with Beetle hidden in her bag. Once he took a shine to an object, he was determined to nab it by whatever means. People didn't call ferrets little thieves for no reason. Holding it in her fingers, she could see Artie deep in concentration while he tattooed a client's arm. Would he ignore her in his dreams like Jack did? Did he even think of her beyond an interested artist? He was only nine years older. Age meant nothing, did it? There was a spark between them. She felt it as they spoke, and he would not spend time with her if he didn't think there was something. Maybe he dreamt of her like she did him; the thong could provide a connection she needed to walk into his dreams. It was tempting to try, but despite what Jack thought, she had red lines she refused to cross. Family and friends were off limits. At times, when the emotional connection lured her in without her trying, she walked away.

'I wouldn't be able to do it, anyway. I don't know him well enough.' But what if she could? What if psychometry worked alongside dream walking?

The idea formed. Scrying had failed to find the person writing the letters. A thick fog blocked her view. The person knew how to push a witch away, but people's defences came down in sleep, they might let her in. A tweak of doubt urged her to reconsider. Two years ago, she'd nearly died after inexperience with magic and astral projection led her to danger. For weeks she ended up in intensive care, hovering between life and death, unable to return to her body. She'd promised she wouldn't do it again, but dream walking was different. The risks would be less, surely. She didn't need to interact with the dreamer; watching from afar would be enough to see who it was. It would be minutes. Seconds. Any dangers were minimal, and she wouldn't be breaking any promises. The result would be worth it. Excitement grew; she needed to gather objects to practise with but first she needed to do her exam.

\*\*\*

Amber could walk into Jack's dreams with ease. His consent and the bond they shared meant it took seconds to see him waiting. All she needed to engage and manipulate a dream was for the dreamer to bring her into their mind's narrative by acknowledging her. A nod, facial expression, or a word in her direction was enough. Otherwise, she remained a bystander watching the scenes unfold behind a looking glass. Connecting to a stranger's dream proved more taxing. A collection of random objects she picked up around town lay on her desk. A bookmark from the library, coffee cup from the beach, receipt, and a baby's sock.

The baby was the easiest and most fun to use and she didn't have to wait until night-time to try it out. Locking her bedroom door, she held the sock in her hand while allowing herself to drift off. The toddler sat in the crib watching the mobile and smiled as soon as she saw Amber in the corner. With a flick of her hand, Amber made the toys jiggle and dance to a soothing melody of 'Clair de Lune'. Giggles encouraged her to conjure more magic until she heard a woman's voice, and the child woke, thrusting Amber back to her reality in an instant.

Adults were harder, requiring her to push through a dense barrier. The effort showed with the dark shadows forming beneath her eyes and constant yawning during the day. As she browsed the different dream-worlds, she concluded people were either stranger than their daily façade or more mundane. From elaborate tales of espionage and deceit to witnessing the methodical making of a coffee, the human mind conjured up it all. Labyrinths of corridors were a popular dream leading to endless rooms of different sizes, but nightmares were the worst. When they belonged to children, their readiness to see her allowed her to lead them to safety. Adults were different; she stood helpless to change the horrific scenarios, and she never wanted to think about the images a teenage boy conjured after she used his dropped Coke bottle. Ew!

The time came to use the letters. With additional protection spells, Amber slept. There was nothing. Did this person ever dream? It seemed not.

# Chapter Thirty-One

With her hands on her hips, Rosa looked sternly at Willow, her Mediterranean temper simmering beneath her usual calm, bubbly exterior.

'Just go! Stop making excuses.'

Willow's desire to go to York for the day faded as the time to leave crept close and she regretted texting Rosa with her plans when the impulse grabbed her in the night. If anyone could hold Willow accountable, it was her employee and friend. Poor Alejo had no chance of getting away with chores. One glance made you comply with her wishes.

'You haven't been out of this town since last year. It'll do you good. I'll keep an eye on Vince, and Amber will be in later. And you can pick up some of those delicious brownies from the market.'

It was true, her ability to leave the Emporium was back, but she needed to push her boundaries of security. Now was the perfect time to go to the city, and it was only for a few hours. Mrs Marley fussed as Willow dressed, insisting she wore a summer dress instead of jeans, and urged her to be more daring with her make-up. Neither woman would let her back out of this trip.

A while later, Willow conceded both Mrs Marley and Rosa were right. The journey through the dramatic Moors relaxed her even when Mavis groaned at the steep inclines and twisty roads, and despite the struggle to find a parking space, being out was just what she needed. York's unique energy lifted her mood, as did window shopping. The products the shops sold changed over time, but the history of those who went before lingered, no more evident than in the cobbled narrow street of the Shambles. It was a step back in time with ghosts mingling in with the crowds, ignored by many, but their presence accepted as part of the fabric of the ancient city.

The bells rang from the Minster as she wandered to one of her favourite places, the unique Tudor-built Mulberry Hall that housed her favourite store, Käthe Wohlfahrt. She lost herself in the dazzling intricate Christmas display behind their warped-glass window. Forever Christmas, the shop was a deep contrast to the blistering sun heating her bare shoulders. Her mum would have loved it. Like the Enchanted Emporium, this building oozed its own special magic, luring customers in, and she wasn't immune. Before she crossed over the threshold, an icy patch crept down her back. Shuddering, she backtracked. Someone was watching. She weaved through the crowd gathered round to gaze at the decorations.

'You're not thinking of going in, are you? It's only June.'

'Nate?' Her heart skipped a beat. It couldn't be. Dressed in a suit that accentuated his broad shoulders and frame was the man she desired. He nodded and stepped across the narrow road in a couple of strides; the sea of tourists divided without hesitation to let him pass. Standing next to him, she resisted the temptation to reach out to touch him, to make sure he was real.

'Willow.' He gave a nervous smile that revitalised the dormant butterflies in her stomach. 'I never expected to see you here, never mind drooling over Christmas baubles in the summer heat.'

'I wasn't drooling.' At least not then. She broke his gaze. His eyes were drawing her in. Six months since she saw him, but her body remembered every caress and wanted more. Time hadn't dampened her feelings for him. She needed to walk away. 'I wasn't expecting to see you here, either.'

'Business trip, but the meeting finished early. Do you have time for a tea?'

'I don't think it's a good idea.' Alarm bells rang. She needed to walk away now.

'Come on, Wills. Tea. York. How can you resist? Didn't you say at Christmas I needed to try a Fat Rascal at Bettys? Now is a perfect time to do it and I'd prefer to go with company.' His hand grazed her arm, sending a familiar flood of electricity through her.

'I've got to go.'

Nate stepped back but strode beside her as she walked towards the Minster.

'Come on, live dangerously. Who's at the shop?'

It was the living dangerously she was worried about. When apart, it was easy to ignore her feelings, her wants, but being close to him made it impossible. All she wanted to do was wrap her arms round him, draw him close, and never let him go. Being in touching distance from him, catching the faint scent of his aftershave, and being able to look into his deep chocolate eyes, her resistance crumbled; the cracks in her self-built protective wall spread until she couldn't refuse. *It is just tea. I'm allowed a cup of tea*, she decided as she murmured, 'Rosa and Amber.'

'They'll be fine. Their boss sings their praises often enough and I'm sure they would agree you deserve a cup of tea. You could take them back some goodies.'

***

Light streamed through the long windows in the art deco room and, with the grand piano playing in the background, Willow easily imagined slipping back in time. The walnut-panelled walls and intricate marquetry oozed an opulence she was unaccustomed to. A waiter in his white shirt, black waistcoat, and white apron covering his black trousers served their order.

A mobile phone vibrated on the table beside the teacups and saucers.

Nate caught her critical gaze and swooped it up to place in his pocket. 'Sorry. That ruined the illusion, didn't it? I keep expecting to see men in suits and ties and women in 1940s dress walking by down below, but it's all jeans and shorts.'

Willow knew what he meant. They sat overlooking the hustle and bustle of a modern York street, including the snaking queue to get into Bettys itself. The queue she usually joined to get cakes to go. Sitting in was beyond her expectation. How much money and influence did Nate have to gain a table in the Belmont Room on a whim without booking in advance? There were so many things they had not discussed. He remained a stranger despite the closeness she felt.

'You look different in a summer dress. It suits you.'

Willow blushed and the heat radiating up her body intensified when he placed his hand on hers. Reluctantly, she pulled her hand away to pour the tea.

'What, more than my pjs or your shirt?' It was his turn to be at unease.

'Well, this is very civilised and not how I expected my afternoon to be. How are you going to eat all that?' Nate pointed at the three-tiered cake stand full of confectionery delights, cakes, sandwiches, and scones. A feast designed for one.

'I'll manage, I'm sure,' she said, selecting a tiny chequered Battenburg cake. 'Besides, that's what doggy bags are for. As you say, Rosa and Amber will be happy.'

Silence grew between them and she was relieved the ritual of tea making distracted her from the fear he would mention her lack of response to his text. To be on the safe side, she whispered a calming spell while she stirred the pot. They would have tea, enjoy each other's company, then leave for their separate lives.

'How are Amber and Glenn? She hasn't discovered black magic and is planning to destroy the universe with that ferret of hers?' Nate asked, taking a sip of his drink. His large hands emphasised the delicate china cup he held.

Willow shook her head. 'Not that I am aware of. Though I've seen little of her recently. First revision took priority, and now it seems enjoying the freedom from study is more important than learning magic. Tourist season is always manic in the Emporium, so her shifts are mainly on the shop floor.'

'You miss her.'

His statement hit home. She missed the teaching and companionship of the young witch more than she'd expected. Her love for her was as it was for Louise. She was family. If only they could rewind time, she'd make sure this year would be different.

'I do.'

'It surprises me. I thought the Emporium was her second home and magic was her true love and nothing, not even exams, would interfere with that.'

'No, her first love is art. It always has been.'

'No way. I disagree. I may not know her like you do, but on Christmas morning when she opened that box you gave her—her eyes sparkled much more than with any of the art materials she received. Even those she claimed she had always wanted. Given the choice between art and magic, it'd be magic every time.'

'You're forgetting the raging teenage hormones and sense of adventure. It changes everything. So, how about you? Still forcing your employees to make cups of tea for you?'

'I've learnt my lesson. I'm pleased to report I make them myself. Have you been to Twinings in the Strand? It is an amazing place.'

'I have years ago, but should visit again.'

'You should. We could explore together. There are many places I could show you, including a tea emporium you would love. Different to yours in many ways, but it's always good to look at the competition.' She listened to him ramble, entangled in his vision of an itinerary of places he'd love to show her. His hand grasped hers.

'A tea emporium? What happened to the man who would only drink coffee?'

She was determined not to be sucked into his fantasies, but it was hard as his touch sent tingles of desire up her arm.

'I'm a changed man—in many respects. You'll see my collection of teas when you come down.'

'Or you could send me a photo.' Willow needed to pull her hand away. They were treading in dangerous waters, but her body refused to move. Resigned, she allowed herself the contact she craved. 'How else have you changed?'

'I've stepped back from the business. One reason I'm here is to tie up loose ends before my brother takes over.'

'Your globetrotting influencer brother is coming into the family business?' A quick internet search had produced many hits on the Jamie's

Travel blog. The carefree tanned version of Nate didn't look like a person to thrive on making deals wearing a suit.

'No way. Jamie has just signed up with a new sponsor and—' Nate paused, a deep frown formed on his brow, and he restirred his tea lost in thought before he continued. 'He is very much doing his own thing. It's the middle one, Henry.'

'So, what are you going to do? Apart from bake bread and drink tea.'

'I don't know. Travel, I guess, that's what you do at a crossroads, isn't it? Since I've got into this baking lark, I'd like to visit different places, the Mediterranean obviously but also further afield. When I've travelled for work, there's been little time to explore outside hotels and the boardroom. Never mind try authentic recipes and experience the surrounding culture rather than those in generic cookbooks, but beyond that.' He shrugged. 'Who knows?'

'You'll be joining Jamie with a baking travel vlog next. I can see you now chatting about food in the Andes while he does skydiving in the background,' Willow joked. She'd missed this easy chat and listening to his future plans, even if they were without her.

'Don't you start. Jamie has already floated the idea, talking about sponsors he could get and collaborations.'

'Are you tempted? The two Reynolds brothers taking over social media.'

'No. I don't want my face out there for everyone to see. I've seen the reaction he gets out and about. I'd rather do it just for me, though as insane as it sounds for a novice, I'd love to own a bakery.'

Listening to his enthusiasm for his newfound passion lulled Willow into relaxing and enjoying his company and his idle touch of her hand. Their conversation progressed to Glenn's disastrous dates, George's shocked face with the teapot's arrival at the office, and Vincent's antics. The world and time slipped away as they laughed until they heard the returning waiter's cough. They had overstayed their welcome and, looking at the time on her phone, so had she. By the time she got home, Rosa would have locked up.

'Please, Willow. Don't go.'

# Chapter Thirty-Two

Amber and Rosa served the steady stream of customers. To Amber's relief, many were regulars who knew what they wanted, or tourists interested in grabbing a famous Wishing Spell candle or tea rather than requiring in-depth knowledge and time. Fatigue wore her down, and she doubted she could hide her impatience for dithering customers much longer.

'So, does he know yet?' Rosa asked, looking at the dragonfly prominent on Amber's bare arm. It was proving a talking point for many.

'Who? My dad? Yeah, it all came out, so no more jumpers in June,' Amber replied, keeping a close eye on two girls she recognised from college browsing the shelves.

'That's a relief. It must have been a worry. Keeping secrets always is. I remember having to tell Mum I was pregnant with Alejo. Every time I tried, I visualised her anger, her disappointment, and backed out. It took me six months and by that point she had noticed, anyway. That was my only teenage rebellion.'

Amber always struggled to remember Rosa was only in her early twenties and as close to Willow's age as she appeared. Their lives were a mile apart.

'I think I'd rather confess to having a tattoo than pregnancy,' Amber conceded.

'I bet your dad preferred it too.'

'Yeah. He thought I was self-harming and ready to demand I go back to counselling. Only showing him the tattoo convinced him otherwise.'

Glenn's reactions had surprised her. One evening, he insisted she help in the garden and show her arms. His relief was clear as she rolled her sleeve to reveal the dragonfly, and the rage never came. He adored the design. With warmth he said words Amber treasured. 'You are so like your mum. She would be proud of you.' They worked side by side in the garden, and he shared memories of Louise's plan of having a tattoo. One she had also designed herself only to bottle out as she sat in the chair. Later that evening, he found her mum's sketchbook so she could see the design herself. With a tweak here and there, Amber could see how to develop it and vowed to herself to have it inked onto her ankle as her mum had planned. The gap between father and daughter narrowed.

As Rosa said, she felt lighter, but a heaviness surrounding her relationship with Willow remained. She missed their chats, her lessons, and hearing stories of Louise. When her dad spoke of her, a raw pain reflected in his eyes, but Willow chatted as if Louise had just popped into the next room. *Soon*. She'd be able to have that back soon. Her hopes of discovering the person behind the letters were fading. The dream walking had so far come to nothing. It was as if he didn't exist, or was a witch performing magic to block invasion. Plan A of matchmaking took priority and today, Willow's spontaneous retail therapy provided the helping hand she needed. It was fate. Once she knew Willow was safe and Glenn happy, things could return to normal. No more avoidance of lessons or sneaking to Bones Ink. No more secrets.

Under the pretence of harvesting some herbs for Mrs Pugh's tonic, Amber slipped into the Emporium's garden. It wasn't a colossal lie. She was gathering herbs but for her own devices. Vincent wound his large, lumbering body around her legs, hindering the progress through the abundance of plants vying for space in the small garden. It was a witch's oasis and contained all she needed for the love spell she'd discovered online. Her mum's notebooks and grimoire failed to provide her with any clue on matters of the heart; Louise's priority was nature, raising the elements, and latterly teething and childhood nightmares. *Not much use, Mum.*

A flash of movement in the upstairs window caught her eye. Mrs Marley looked down. That was all she needed, a snooping ghost spying on her. Forcing a smile, she waved, and the figure melted away. *Phew.* She was safe, but for how long, who knew? Ever since Willow took her under her wing, there was an agreement Amber could help herself to what she needed, but if she knew which herbs were being taken, she would put two and two together, thwarting Amber's plan. The cat continued to nudge her.

'Vincent! Enough. I haven't got time.'

He flopped down on a patch of flattened herbs before rolling on his back and purring, intoxicated by their aroma and the heat of the sunrays catching his orange fur.

'Yes. Catnip is needed. If it works on you, I guess it works on humans too.'

Amber shrieked as Vincent swiped his clawed paw at her hand. Droplets of blood rose to the surface of the scratch; she hastily sucked it. Had he figured it out? She shook her head.

'You're just an oaf of a cat protective of his precious catnip.' She pushed him out of the way to snip off the leaves, surprised as always at his weight.

'Don't look at me like that. This is no worse than your meddling at Christmas.'

Her conscience niggled when he strutted away with his tail high in the air. Thank heavens he couldn't talk. Besides, she had to do it. This was for her dad and for Willow.

Amber returned to find Rosa on the phone.

'No. That's fine. Amber's here and she's nodding. She agrees.'

She raised her eyebrows, mouthing, *'What?'* as Rosa continued to speak.

'Will do. Have fun.'

Rosa hung up. Amber strode across the shop floor with a sense of trepidation as she glimpsed Black Cat strolling across the courtyard. 'What've you agreed to on my behalf?'

'Only to feed Vincent. I'm locking up as Willow's bumped into an old friend, so will be late home.' Rosa buzzed with excitement at the potential for gossip tomorrow. 'I wonder who it is? Does she know anyone in York?'

Amber shrugged. 'Probably someone from her uni days. She studied there.'

'Really? I didn't know that.' Forget tomorrow, Rosa latched on to the possibility of gossip today. 'What did …?' Amber heard her frustrated sigh when a customer arrived. *Saved by the bell.* Talking about Willow's life, knowing how little she shared, felt a betrayal of trust, and she didn't want more guilt. Black Cat slipped in before the shop door closed. *He's a sign. Today things will change*, and with the final ingredients securely in her rucksack, Amber was certain her potion would set the course.

\*\*\*

'Hi Vince. Your owner's abandoned you for a night out on the town. But here's your dinner.' He appeared when Amber shook the cat biscuits but kept his distance. 'Still angry at me? Well, the feeling's mutual. I'm doing what's right for both of them. You had your turn with Nate and now it's Dad's time.'

It felt odd being in the flat alone, the atmosphere stilted; even the Marleys were absent. Yet there was a sense of being watched, of something holding its breath to see what she would do next. *Nothing. I'm doing nothing. Not yet anyway.* The essence of Willow was everywhere, from the extensive collection of teacups to the mementos from her travels, including the blanket she brought back from Peru draped over a kitchen chair. Maybe when she got together with her dad, they would travel to far-out places. *Na, they're both too much of homebodies now.* Amber knocked the table as she walked by, sending a magazine to the floor. As she placed it back, she saw it. A large ornate key. This had to be to do with the change in fate Black Cat had hinted at earlier. A large grin formed on her face. With Vincent happily munching the food in his bowl, Amber slipped it into her pocket. Forget Pinterest and other online searches. If she wanted a spell guaranteed to work, the answer lay in the Cobble.

The key lay heavy in her hand. A faint tingle of magic forced her to question her actions. She looked over her shoulder and listened for any sign she shouldn't proceed. There was nothing. No creaking floorboards, slamming of doors, or ghostly interruptions. The scratch smarted as she placed the key in the lock. *Am I really doing this? Hell yes!* An image of her dad sitting alone flashed into her mind. Despite Jack's disapproval and the dire warnings drummed into her at her first magical lesson, that love spells were the most dangerous to perform, this was the only way her dad and Willow would see each other the way Amber knew they should. Her attempts at more traditional meddling had failed, but she knew there was a chemistry between them. Okay, she admitted there was no explosion of passion when they looked at each other, and not even a fizz when they sat nearby, but all that would change with a forceful push. She would have a stepmum of her choosing by the end of the year, one who fit into the family dynamics and wouldn't push her out, one who would care for her dad and bring security, not upheaval, and definitely not a bimbo extraordinaire with pumped-up breasts and mouth like Emily-May. Glenn would, in turn, support and protect Willow from mortal dangers. The house would be full of love and laughter.

The lock clicked, and she heaved the creaky door open. Her nose tickled, a sneeze threatened, and her eyes stung as dust motes danced in the air, disturbed after years of settling on the surfaces. She located a lantern on a hook by the door, and with a roll and flick of her hand, a blue ball of energy bounced from her fingertips to the wick. The resulting golden flame illuminated the tiny room.

'Wow.'

Amber wished she could think of a more appropriate word, a clever word fitting her amazement at the sight before her. *How could Willow not use this room?* This was a witch's paradise. A low hum of residual magic radiated from the walls. Whatever potion she created using a spell here was bound to have the potency required. All doubts faded as her excitement grew. She was in the Cobble.

A mishmash of ancient shelves lined the room above a stained workbench. Some were driftwood and hastily put up, but someone had clearly handcrafted others with care and love. She ran her fingers over the intricate runes and symbols carved into them. Rows of medicinal bottles and jars filled many of the shelves, their yellowing and peeling labels hidden under layers of dust and grime. The small window gave little light despite the blazing summer sun outside, thanks to the maze of cobwebs created by several spiders, and the creeping ivy outside concealing the room from the garden.

An iron cauldron stood empty on the workbench, along with candlesticks smothered with melted wax, and a pestle and mortar. Abandoned poison bottles, parchment and quill gave the impression the first witch long ago was disturbed mid-spell. Amber spied the book she had glimpsed previously and bent forward to read the spell on its open page. *Fog of discretion.* She knew it. Willow had used old magic to cast the mysterious fog. The room wasn't as disused as she'd thought, but Amber still couldn't understand why Willow hadn't used old magic to banish the person behind the letters. Behind the threats. The rule of three? The same reason she had not attempted it herself. Would she pay a price for her planned love potion? If she suffered heartbreak to get Willow and her dad together, it was a price worth paying.

She set aside the book, her attention drawn to others, crammed onto a shelf in the darkest corner of the room. Light from the lantern failed to banish the shadows there, heavy with an oppressive magic. Whoever this space belonged to, they hadn't shied away from using dark energy. A tremor ran down her back as she trailed her hand over a cracked leather spine. This was the one. She eased it out. The air shifted, magic crackled, and a sudden sense of being watched made her turn. No one was there. Logic told her to be fearful, but curiosity took its place. The old witch still remained. She felt her presence, her impotent resentment.

'I'm just borrowing it. I'll return it shortly. I promise.'

Amber needed better light to see. 'I'll sit just outside this door so you can see me. I'm only looking.' She took the lack of response as a grudging agreement and backed out of the room. Cross-legged, she sat on the workshop's floor, and gingerly placed the ancient tome near her in full view of the Cobble. Time stood still while she studied the yellowed pages and faded ink. Handwriting styles had changed over time as different witches had added their own sketches and notes. Symbols and formulas she didn't understand littered the parchments, but there were place names she recognised: Streonshalh, Eoforwic, and Elfaen. She murmured the words.

'Can I just ask you a question?' she asked the void of the Cobble. The door slammed shut. 'I guess the answer is no, then.'

Amber returned to her quest. At times, images manifested before her, snatches in time showing different hands flowing across the page—wrinkled hands with swollen joints, slender smooth ones, and the most recent wore an impressive engagement ring. All were left-handed. She scrolled through the abundance of love-related potions, lotions, and amulets. Ways to attract a lover, binding one to you, or how to lure someone away. They were all there. She discounted those which were too complicated, impractical, or disgusting. Who would ever believe giving their potential lover menstrual blood in coffee was the way to passion? She needed a vegetarian option.

She continued. They already sold Aphrodite's tea in the shop, but getting her unadventurous dad to drink apple tea would require another spell. It was either Yorkshire tea or nothing in his eyes. 'Love. I need a spell to amplify love.'

A slip of paper peeked from the bottom. She flicked to the marked page and grinned.

'Perfect.' It was subtle, flavourless, and the ingredients were readily available in the garden and hedgerows. Notes in a fresher ink filled the margin with slight adjustments and tips, and Amber jotted these down in her notebook along with the spell. She closed the book, dislodging a letter. Dated 1921 in faded ink, it pleaded Vi not to use magic but to leave matters of the heart to fate alone. It was signed *your loving sister, Kate.*

Amber wondered whether Vi had followed the advice. A postscript gave the answer written in the same handwriting as the matchmaking and heart-breaking witch.

*My dearest sister,*
*I'm sorry your warning has come too late.*
*A girl needs to have some fun. Be nice. You may be my bridesmaid.*
*Your loving sister, Vi.*

Amber traced the loops and swirls of the words, allowing an image to emerge. The music of the Charleston filled the room with a joyous laugh. It was the owner of the engagement ring. With an endorsement like that, Amber had to try it.

Thanking the guardian of the Cobble, she reluctantly returned the book. If her calculations were correct, this month's new moon was on Friday only days away, making it the ideal time to brew this spell. Black Cat was right, things were changing. Everything would be okay.

# Chapter Thirty-Three

The hot water from the monsoon shower pelted her skin, washing away the indulgent but complimentary shower gel. *This is heaven.* It was a far cry from the lacklustre, often cold, shower at home. Once snuggled in the soft luxurious white dressing gown, Willow padded into the bedroom, her bare feet sinking into the thick pile of the carpet. Nate snored gently, star-shaped on the king-size bed, naked apart from the sheet draped over him. She considered waking him, but a cup of tea called.

She perused the collection of teabags on offer while the kettle boiled. If Nate woke, he would insist on room service for tea in the pot despite the late hour. Her confession about her use of teabags had yet to be made. Pulling back the curtains, she sank into a chair. If she were at home, the sliver of the waning moon and sprinkling of stars would ground her heightened emotions, but here the lamps illuminating the historic city walls hid the night sky. The suite, larger than the footprint of her flat, oozed class, opulence, and money. How had she ended up in one of the poshest hotels in York? When he asked her not to go, she'd asked him why. His reply made her freeze as they echoed the words she wanted to say.

'Because I miss you, and every time I think you are part of my life, you disappear. Stay.'

He stepped forward and kissed her. As their lips met, she knew she was in trouble. Her head caught up with her heart and accepted she was in love and couldn't let him go. Her fate was sealed when he dragged her to the Christmas shop. His eyes sparkled as the shop's magic took hold, revealing his childlike self when they held hands and browsed the decorations. His bewilderment at the traditional glass gherkin for a tree made her laugh until tears ran down her face until she explained the story behind it. He teased her when she confessed she didn't own this essential decoration. Together, they studied the cuckoo clocks with awe and actively planned their ideal tree. Willow could visualise it standing in the flat's corner while they celebrated Christmas again. From the shop, it was only a short distance to his hotel, and neither could turn away.

She watched his chest rise and fall with each breath. She loved him, but if they were to move on together, he needed the truth about her past and present. He had to decide if he wanted to stay.

Willow shrugged off the dressing gown and slid into the bed, snuggling close to him. He wrapped his arm around her, drawing her closer to the warmth of his body, and she rested her head against his chest, comforted by his sandalwood aftershave and hearing the pace of his heart in sync with hers.

'Morning,' he said, his breath kissing her hair. 'Is it morning?'

'It's turned midnight, so technically it is.' His hand trailed across her hip, and dipped to her lower back where his fingers lingered on her silver scar on her left side. Each circular movement cemented her resolve, he needed the truth.

'You've lost weight.'

'Hmm hmm. It's been a difficult few months.' Once they'd stumbled into his hotel room, there was no time to talk, no time for anything except to strip off their clothes and feel each other again.

'The Clara and Sabrina feud?'

'And some.'

'Want to tell me about it?'

Cocooned in the safety of his embrace, she nodded and gripped his hand tight in hers, using his strength to bolster the courage needed to throw open the locked box of her past and reveal herself to someone else. For him to understand the present, he needed to understand what came first. Where to begin? The day she rolled up at Marian's house with her rucksack and sleeping bag after her mum died, unable to live with her stepfather anymore, and how with her blessing and care she encouraged her to travel, setting everything in motion? Just the fateful day itself? Nate needed to know about him. Concentrating on an inky smudge on the hotel wall, the only blemish she could see in the perfection the room portrayed, she took a deep breath.

'At Bettys, you said you fancied exploring the Mediterranean for your baking. Europe was my first stop for my globetrotting adventure. Prague, Paris for a weekend on my own but I promised to return when I was in love, then the Greek islands to catch some sun with plans to explore the rest of the Med: Italy, Spain, Malta and then over to Egypt, you get the picture. It didn't happen.'

'Why not?'

'I got engaged. His name was Rafe. Raphael Amenábar. It wasn't love at first, not for me anyway. He always told people differently. My first impression of him was he was a drunk, posh git with an inflated ego and I wanted nothing to do with him and told him so.'

***

The bar buzzed with the holiday excitement emanating from the tourists and the excessive consumption of ouzo and cocktails. Edging through the crowd, she hadn't expected to gain the attention of a suave chino-wearing Adonis with breath smelling like a brewery. He hadn't accepted her rejection following a corny chat-up line that made her eyes roll but instead a tray of complimentary drinks arrived for her and the backpackers she'd befriended earlier. Rather than act on her first instinct, she accepted the red wine while refusing to acknowledge him. Who was she to turn down a free night out when funds were low, and she needed to save for the next leg of her trip? While the bar wasn't her preferred venue, unlike the small quiet taverna some locals introduced her to, she appreciated the hustle and bustle of people that allowed her to slip out unnoticed back to her room. Willow never expected to see him again.

Greek life suited her, and she'd just sent Marian and Louise another postcard explaining her intention of spending more time there. The job she'd found at a hotel offered her the security of cheap accommodation, the pay wasn't bad and she liked the staff she was working with. The azure sea and white sand were her constant companions. Her heart lifted with the sound of the cicadas serenading from the olive trees lining dusty roads. With no responsibility apart from herself, and connecting with the sea, earth, and nature, she walked taller, slept easier, and was eager to start the day. 'You're healing,' Marian declared when they last spoke, and she had to agree. The pain of the last few years, looking after her mum after her leukaemia diagnosis with little help from Stuart, had taken its toll. His preferred help focused on how much he could drink and womanising. Never mind his anger. Marian had done her best to soothe her, but travel was what she needed. It was a good life.

The second time she saw him, he wasn't drunk but standing at the hotel reception desk. Holding her hand up, she forced him to wait while she snatched up the display of white lilies someone had placed on the desk.

'What have they done to you to deserve that?' he said as she pounded them into a nearby bin. 'Don't you like flowers, or are they just not perfect enough for you, Ricitos de Oro?' He laughed at his own joke. Her beginner Spanish lessons had paid off when she recognised a name she hadn't heard for years: Goldilocks.

'I like flowers, just not lilies.' She refused to say why, but the next day she came in for her shift and a fresh bouquet arrived with no lily in sight. More followed every day. Daily he greeted her with her Spanish nickname that sounded wildly inappropriate in his silky voice followed by a new proposal for a drink or meal. He wore her down to agree to one date. She was flattered by his determination and her inability to move in her room for floral displays. There were only so many she could tolerate before they felt claustrophobic.

The evening wasn't as bad as she imagined. She agreed to another and then another, swept up by his certainty, endless charm, and his lifestyle. It seemed nothing was out of reach, or impossible in his quest to make her life, his Goldilocks, perfect. He always offered her three options in line with the fairy-tale persona he'd appointed her. She felt special, like the queen of the story, not realising until later she'd learnt to recognise the subtle inflection of voice, the shift in his stance urging her to the correct decision. Why go camping, which she loved, when he could afford a posh suite in a five-star hotel? Forget trekking across dusty roads, with a rucksack on your back loaded with water and cheap sandwiches, and relying on vintage buses. He had a car ready to use. His rational arguments were impossible to defy until all her own plans paused, and then were forgotten, but she was adored, happy, and believed this was the devotion Louise felt.

\*\*\*

'Those around me thought his actions were romantic. It was close to mass hysteria when I came into work, and they unpicked my dates or when he spontaneously delivered a gift. This frenzy escalated when he proposed in a private cove with only the seagulls to witness it. If I'd told Louise and if Grandma Jax were there, they'd have told me to run a mile. To take heed of the alarm bells I'd tried to silence but still clanged in my head every time he took control of my life, rearranging my shifts so I could spend time with him and commandeer my time. They'd have recognised his family name and warned me what the inevitable outcome would be.'

'You didn't tell Louise?'

'Not Marian either. Not until after the event. I wanted to keep him secret until I could show him off when I came home. Show how far I'd come from the angry teenager who relied on nobody on the top of Whitby's headland. Stupid, really. Paid for it tenfold.'

Nate tensed behind her, and his arms circling her drew her closer to him in anticipation of the next instalment of her story. It was tempting to stop, roll over to kiss him, and push the past away—

'What happened next?' He refused to let her backtrack. She'd come this far.

'We went to visit his family to share the news of their engagement. In his native Spain.'

# Chapter Thirty-Four

**Then**

Straddled behind him with her arms wrapped around his waist, Willow took in the lush green landscape of peaks and falls. The ragged Pyrenees looming in the distance were awe-inspiring without the additional thrill of the twists and turns of the motorbike. Dubious at first, she protested at his idea of travelling to his parents' on a bike once they arrived in Spain, but now she could understand the appeal. Travelling at speed, her connection to the environment was one she'd never experienced before. It distracted her from the tumult of nerves plaguing her since he'd slipped the exquisite diamond ring on her finger, much fancier than she ever imagined her ring would be, if she'd ever considered tying herself to another person.

But her colleagues' enthusiasm reassured her she would get used to it. She was just being picky.

Once she'd met the Amenábar clan, they planned to go home to Marian and Louise to share the good news. She couldn't wait to see their surprise when he stood next to her when she knocked on their door. Only her anxiety clouded the scenario. What would he think of her home? The grey council estate bordering suburbia was a far cry from the region of La Rioja, full of vineyards and dramatic atmosphere. Fancy her falling in love with the heir of a vineyard estate selling wine globally? She was entering another world.

Maybe if she'd had more knowledge of Spanish history or her mum encouraged her to embrace her witch heritage, rather than demonise the magic running through her blood, the mention of his birthplace would have flagged up as a cause of concern. Instead, she rested her head against him as they sped towards his family's vineyard and home.


Surrounded by lush green fields of vines, the villa was as immaculate and polished as Rafe, but Willow's fears of fitting in were unfounded when his family rushed to embrace her once she crossed the threshold. His younger sister, Anna, grabbed her hand to inspect the ring along with his mother, while his father and brother patted him on the back with a flurry of excited congratulations. Only the aged, shrunken lady dressed in formidable black hung back from the welcome, scrutinising her every move. Francesca Amenábar, his matriarchal grandmother. Rafe noticed, and squeezed her hand, assuring her his lone grandparent was only protective of the family and she'd come to love her as much as he did by the time the week was out. Willow doubts trebled when Francesca turned and walked away.

Willow fell in love with the area, for its contrast from the dusty, often stark landscape of the Greek island with its ever-changing seascape. Surrounded by birdsong and immense swathes of patchwork fields, it reminded her of the holidays with Grandma Jax. The place she called home. Maybe this would be an excellent alternative? Rafe took her on the bike to explore the area, gave her a guided tour of the distillery, giving her a deeper appreciation of the wine they drank with their meals, and showered her with attention. During the evening meals, Anna introduced her to the intense red Patxaran, and she discovered more about the family she was about to join. With each nugget of information, the more she respected Francesca, whose business acumen had made the vineyard flourish and the Amenábar brand expand. Willow's only hope was that behind the steely stare Francesca still cast her way there was a seed of warmth and acceptance to ease Willow's transition to becoming an Amenábar after the wedding.

That morning, before breakfast, Willow plunged into the swimming pool for a refreshing swim, a habit she'd formed over the last few days. The warm water washed over her as she did repeated lengths, cleansing any worries conjured in the night. A chill ran up Willow's spine with the distinct feeling of being watched. Francesca stood on the side, her arms folded. Willow gave a cheery wave and swam to the steps. While no one was around, maybe this was the ideal opportunity to talk to her and pave the way to a better relationship.

She strode to one of the sunloungers to grab her towel to dry off and cover herself up with the sarong. Some conversations weren't to be had wearing only a bikini. She bent down, and *Ow*. Arthritic fingers grabbed her arm, digging deep into her flesh. The sarong slipped from her hand and the red material floated on the pool water.

'Bruja! Bruja!' The old lady spat the words out, followed by a stream of Spanish Willow struggled to understand. She tried to straighten, but Francesca pushed down. Her wet feet slid on the damp tiles, sending her skidding into the chair and landing hard on her knee. She winced, but the pain was overtaken by the yank and firm hold of her hair. Panic gripped her. Taking advantage of Willow on the ground, Francesca loomed over her, holding her in place by a fistful of hair. She couldn't escape the continuing onslaught of words peppered with *bruja* raining down on her. Flecks of spittle hit her cheek. She wanted to fight back, to escape and push her away, but this was Rafe's grandmother. Was she suffering from dementia? The disturbance drew the family out of the house. Rafe froze on the poolside with his mouth gaped open. Why wasn't he helping?

Finally, Anna and her mother stepped forward, cajoling her grandmother in a flurry of rolling Spanish. Hands released Willow, allowing her to stand. Rafe rushed over, but instead of wrapping her in his arms to comfort her and explain what was going on, he spun her round and Francesca jabbed her lower back. Her tattoo. All this because of a tattoo she'd drunkenly got on a night out with Louise. An opposing pair—a moon for her to represent her desire to move in the shadows and a sun for Lou, who shone bright. This was ludicrous. She tried to explain but Rafe's icy scowl, reflecting his grandmother's hatred, silenced her.

Twisting her arm behind her, he frogmarched her into the house, ignoring her tears and sharp intakes of breath as her knee protested with her weight. Household staff usually hidden in the shadows gawped, witnessing her downfall.

'Tita says you are a witch. Is it true?' he said as soon as the patio door slid shut, forming a transparent barrier between the ongoing commotion across the pool with much heated gesturing and glances towards the house. Only Anna stood away from the others, fear reflected in her face. Willow wished she could console her, but she had her own fear to contend with that refused to abate with tense Rafe still clutching her.

'Well, yes. I'm a witch.' She shrugged him off, rubbing the pained skin.

'So, you admit it?' His anger rose, and the air between them brimmed with a red-tinged atmosphere beyond that she'd experienced with Stuart at home. 'Saves dunking you, I suppose.' His words made no sense. She'd swum in the pool for days debunking the myth about witches sinking or floating.

'You knew,' she muttered, assessing where the exits were in the room. The French doors weren't an option, but the one in the far corner led to the lounge then the main hall away from him.

'No, I did not. You think I'd have dated you, lavished you with gifts, proposed to you if I knew?'

She hadn't hidden it from him. She might not explicitly have declared it in words but the signs were there. The permanent altar set up in her room, crystals in her pockets and night-time promenades on the beach to celebrate the phases of the moon. Others around her figured it out, and often asked for unsolicited herbal advice or spells, why not him? *Because you stepped into his life*, a small voice piped up. He'd only visited her cramped room once and his attention was more on drunken fumbling in the dark than assessing her decor. Rituals had fallen to the wayside with spending time with him becoming an increasing importance. Panicked, she had no defence.

'You must have bewitched me,' he ranted. A pulse throbbing in his temple and his gesturing mirrored his grandmother's. Her toxic contagion taking hold. Willow backed away, but he blocked her path to the connecting door to the rest of the house. To freedom. 'You've infiltrated my family, made them love you. I showed you the inside workings of the business. Was that the plan? Marry me and destroy everything we've built up from within?'

Willow shook her head. Now would be a good time to be a witch like Louise, who'd conjure a fireball to distract or a whirlwind. What was the use of healing with herbs and manipulating circumstance with tea when your immediate life was in danger?

'Well, witches didn't succeed with our ancestors. You won't succeed now. I should punish you. Destroy you as you were—' Willow dodged him as he launched towards her, knocking into a sideboard and dislodging a large glass vase. It hurtled towards the tiled floor with a crash. She screamed and the door connecting to the staff area flung open. A maid rushed in.

'I'll just clean this up, señor,' Rafe spun round to face the surreal guardian angel proffering a dustpan and brush. He froze, struggling to retract his thunderous rage to pass off the altercation as a lover's tiff. Noting the slight nod the newcomer directed her way, Willow ran.

Adrenaline flooding her body propelled her through the house to the hall, leaving bloody footprints from cuts on the sole of her foot on the expensive rug. Yanking the front door open, wearing only her bikini, she fled.

# Chapter Thirty-Five

'Y̲ou haven't got a tattoo.' Nate's voice brought her back to the present with a jolt. The more she'd spoken, the further she drifted away from herself. Was this what it was like when Amber astral projected for the first time? If so, she could keep that talent to herself. Disorientated, it was a relief to be still cocooned in his arms. He hadn't let her go. The pillow beneath her was wet from tears she had no recollection of crying. She sniffed.

'No, but I do have a scar. Every time I saw it, I remembered him, that day, so I had it removed.' She shuffled away from him and turned to show him the silvery mark on her back. He trailed his fingers over it, circling the blemished skin as if he could erase it and her painful past with his touch alone.

'The bastard,' he muttered, his hatred for Rafe brewing under his breath. 'How did you escape? The vineyard sounds isolated.'

'It was.' Willow returned into his arms. He needed to know the rest of the story and the present. Taking a deep breath, she plunged back to the past. 'Again, it was the maid.'

\*\*\*

Disorientated, exhausted, and inexplicably cold despite the blazing sun burning her skin, she froze with the sound of an engine creeping closer. Despite her heart holding on to a slim foolish hope this was all a bad dream and Rafe would arrive on his bike to confirm it, the bruises blooming under her skin and sharp pain in her foot with every step proved otherwise. She needed to hide. But it wasn't the sound of the roar of a motorbike or one of the sleek cars seen in the Amenábars' extensive garage but the rumble and clatter of a small compact tractor.

'Senorita Willow?' A man with a weather-beaten face gazed down at her. Deep lines forged in his brow as he scanned her injuries, and a flurry of what she suspected were expletives caught under his breath. She stepped forward to accept his proffered hand but paused, clocking his dark green uniform emblazoned with the Amenábar Vineyard logo. Was he a friend or a foe? He registered her dilemma.

'Maria sent me. The maid at the house. Please. Get in. Quick.' His panicked expression as he looked around spurred her on to make a decision. She levered herself into the cabin next to him. 'And put those on.'

Willow ripped open the cellophane wrappers of a spare uniform matching his own and wrangled herself into it, shuddering at the thought of wearing something that branded her as part of the Amenábar workforce, but a bikini-clad woman on a tractor would be conspicuous even from afar. She stuffed her now-dry halo of curls under the baseball cap, hoping the drive through the fields would deliver her to safety and it wasn't part of a twisted game where a predator played with its prey before delivering its death pounce. Again, she cursed her magical restrictions and lack of foresight to check the weekend with her tarot cards or ball. Both now stuck in Rafe's room with her—

'My passport.'

'In there.' Nico, according to his name tag, pointed to a black rucksack by her feet. Opening it, she saw a small collection of her clothes, including the sandals she'd mislaid days before, and new toothbrush and toiletries. Her journal.

'You're not the only witch in the house. Maria has dreamt of this day for weeks and set a rescue plan into action.'

***

'And it worked like clockwork,' Willow said back in York. With her back against Nate's chest, he kept her in the twilight of truth, one foot in the present and the other teetering on the edge of the past. Rather than consume her like before, the images of the rescue played out like a movie on a screen. She could no longer smell the earthly smell of the vineyard or chlorine clinging to her hair. A smell that still turned her stomach decades later.

'On an isolated road on the edge of the estate stood an old beaten-up Renault Clio with its engine idling. Maria's cousin Raquel took me to her apartment in Zugarramurdi, which I now know is the town of the witches. She removed fragments of glass from my cuts, bathed them and applied balm to my bruises, all the while berating me for getting involved with one of the Amenábar clan. According to her, their ancestors were instrumental in some persecutions of supposed witches in the seventeenth century. Only happy when they were burned at the stake. They never left that mindset behind, and their paranoia about witches cursing them in revenge grew with Francesca once her husband died. I had a lucky escape.

'When Maria arrived later to update us of the reaction to my escape it was clear if Rafe ever saw me again he'd fulfil his promise of my destruction, encouraged by his loyalty to his grandmother.'

Later when Raquel cut off her curls and dyed her hair conker brown, Willow Taylor was no more. 'On the day I witnessed the persecution of our kind first-hand, I learnt about the power of many and a coven network in action. They gave me a new SIM for my phone, clothes, and helped me get a passport reissued under my father's surname instead of my mum's maiden name which she gave me, something I never shared with Rafe. My subconscious kept elements of my history safe for the future, I guess. I was shunted from one coven to the next across France and then Germany where I flew east.'

# Chapter Thirty-Six

L ying with Willow in his arms, feeling each ragged breath as she told
her story, lost in the past, challenged every fibre of Nate's willpower
not to let the building anger show. How could anyone do that? Never mind
someone who claimed to love her. No wonder she reacted as she did to his
appearance on her doorstep and portrayed herself as an ice queen when she
was anything but. He wanted to track down this Rafe, shake him, thump
him. And his grandmother, however ancient she might be. Then it clicked,
the photo and her extreme reaction to the journalist's phone call, and her
aversion to the publicity of her shop.

'He found you, didn't he?' Bile rose in his throat. What had that bastard
done to her now when he wasn't there to protect her? When he accepted
her dismissal of their fledging relationship as a rejection of him rather than
something bigger. Her nod was small.

'Yes. That night after we went to the pub, he sent a text. Innocuous but him. Then a card arrived just after Valentine's. That one sent me into a spiral of panic and depression. Waiting for him to destroy me and all I worked for like he promised.'

'And did he?' He needed to know the extent of the damage taken place in his absence however much it might hurt to hear it. The Enchanted Emporium was her baby. If Rafe had affected her business, it would hurt just as much as a physical blow.

'No, not yet anyway. It's gone quiet.'

'You think he's decided to leave you alone? What did the police say?'

'I've not been to them. Not much point: apart from the text and card and my own fear, there isn't much to go on, and I destroyed the card to make a protection spell.'

'So, you're saying it worked.' Relief swept over him, his belief in magic was tentative but he believed in her; if she said it was real then it was good enough for him, especially after hearing her experience in Spain.

'It didn't feel like it at the time. When magic works, there's a distinct shift in the air, an audible click as subtle as placing a jigsaw piece in place followed by a flood of empowerment or exhaustion depending on the spell. This time there was nothing.' She shrugged, and a frown formed as if she was debating the situation, but then it was gone. 'But it must have done. Or he's given up.'

She couldn't disguise the doubt in her voice and the seed nestled in his own mind. Would a man like that just let things go? With a heritage built on hate and fear, he doubted it. If she was safe, it must be the magic.

'Would your coven help?'

'My what?' A smile danced at the edges of her lips. Lifting his own heart, it was absurd. Months ago, he'd have baulked at the idea of those words coming from his mouth. 'I don't have one. No, as much as I appreciated the help, apart from Louise and now Amber, I work better alone. Like Jax.'

'Well, will Amber help?' The Goth princess with her raging loyalty would conjure a dozen hexes to rain on the Amenábar family.

'She doesn't know. No one knows. Only you.' He was under no illusion that her trust in him was momentous, a precious gift she gave nobody.

'Enough now.' She reached up and caressed his face. 'You're all caught up with the dark depths of my past and more recent. It's all fine.' She kissed him and he breathed in the lingering aroma of the shower gel, reminding him of their shared moments in there which he wanted to relive.

'Oh my God, I've covered you with snot and tears. Not quite my best look.' He handed her a box of tissues from the bedside table and she dabbed her red swollen eyes and blew her nose.

'I've seen you worse and so have my shoes. You could've told me when you got the first message. I'd have supported you.'

'I didn't know you.'

'Yes, you did. We bonded over cheese on toast and tea. Besides, I knew we had something as soon as the Enchanted Emporium threw me out of the shop. It was more meddlesome than your cat.'

'The store didn't throw you out. You slipped.' Her playful retort eased the heavy tension hovering over them, easing her back into the present and emotionally calmer.

'With a helping hand. It was either the shop, a ghost, or you. I'd rather believe you don't hide a murderous streak for strangers disrespecting Vincent. Whoever did it, it worked. I fell in love with you. Even at your most frosty.'

\*\*\*

He fumbled with his shoes, looked over Willow's sleeping form, and resisted the temptation to slip in beside her. She shifted and lazily opened her eyes. 'You're going?

'I need to be back in the office. Finish off some stuff for Henry before he takes over.' And seal the deal on Jamie's ludicrous scheme that had kept him apart from Willow for months. George and Jamie, through all their teasing, were right. They knew his heart more than himself and now he'd admitted he loved her, when he returned to Whitby it would be for good. Once he had got this weekend over and untangled all remaining threads of his London life, he would be free.

Down in the foyer he waited at the reception for the receptionist to finish her call. He slipped her a small package, with instructions for it to be placed on Willow's breakfast tray. He'd arranged for room service. A small gift insignificant to many but he hoped she'd see it for its true intention. That she had captured his heart. And his future.

# Chapter Thirty-Seven

'Where's Willow?' Amber tied on her apron before scooping up her now-blue hair into a ponytail. 'And why is Vincent so clingy?'

To her surprise, when she arrived, the feline launched himself at her and wound himself round her legs, orange fur clinging to her fresh black tights. After yesterday's disapproval of her plans, she expected him to switch between a soul-searing scowl to shunning her for days. His quick forgiveness concerned her.

'Has Black Cat been around causing chaos again?'

'No, Vince's sulking. Willow didn't come home last night, and he's not impressed despite me coming in early to feed him. She's allowed to have fun, you know.' Rosa wagged her finger at the sullen cat, who glared and slunk away with his fluffy tail hanging low.

'But she never stays away,' Amber said, biting down on the ensuing panic of the change of routine. And failing. 'Is she okay? Have you heard from her?'

'Of course I have. Don't you get yourself wound up about it like that bloody cat. As I told him, she's having some fun. I don't think I've ever known her to be out with friends, have you?'

'Exactly. No wonder Vincent is concerned. Anything could've happened.' The threats in the letters pierced her mind. Maybe he'd hurt her and was using her phone to divert attention. Maybe ... Amber wanted the customers to vanish so she could interrogate Rosa, rather than rely on snatched sentences between serving.

'I spoke to her. She was happy. Between you and me, I think there's a man involved. Maybe Nate has come up from the city? From what I heard, they were good together. She needs someone like him.'

'No, she doesn't. Why does everyone think he's so perfect? You haven't even met him,' Amber snapped, pushing panic about the stalker aside. Willow mustn't meet Nate again. Fate wouldn't be that cruel.

'What's wrong with you?' Rosa spun around to face her once the last customer left. Cornered, Amber sighed.

'He's just not what everyone thinks he is. She's better off without him.' *And with my dad.* Thank goodness her plan was in action. One more night brewing and it would be ready to use and then—

The door jingled and Willow bounced in, her skin flushed and her eyes sparkling like Amber had seen at Christmas. *Shit, Rosa was right. A man was involved.*

Amber polished the glass jars on the shelves. A daily mundane chore Willow insisted on, a task she usually found relaxing as she connected with each herb and blend, feeling their energy and acquainting herself with their uses. The calmness refused to come. *Everything will be okay. Despite how it looks, Rosa is wrong.*

Willow cooed to Vincent, and he chattered in return. Her absence was forgiven. All the weight and darkness crushing Willow for the past few months had disintegrated overnight. She shone with happiness. Amber's stomach churned as dread descended on her.

'Well, I never thought I'd see the day that Willow Anderson did the walk of shame,' chuckled Rosa.

'I'm not,' Willow replied, straightening up and detaching herself from her purring familiar.

'You're in yesterday's crumpled clothes. Your eyes are sparkling without a hint of a hangover. If that isn't an indicator of a night of passion, I don't know what is.'

'You will never guess who I bumped into? Nate. I'll tell you all about it, but first I need to get changed. Put the kettle on.' Calling Vincent to follow her, Willow swept out of the shop floor on a high.

Amber swore under her breath, while fury sparked in her blood. *This can't be happening. Not now.*

'You'll rub the glass away if you carry on polishing that jar any more. What is up with you? She's happy.'

Amber reached into her apron and pulled out a forbidden mobile, and swiftly scrolled through her apps. She thrust it at Rosa and watched her pale as Amber had that morning.

'Fuck. You need to tell her.'

'Tell me what?' Willow returned, changed into her uniform, holding a tray of three drinks, ready to spill her news. Amber's eyes darted from her mentor to Rosa, who nodded. With no other option, Amber reluctantly showed Willow the phone.

Amber felt her heart break as Willow's face slid from joy to despair the moment she comprehended what she was seeing. The cups slipped from the tray and crashed onto the floor. She shrugged off both employees rushing to her aid before pelting across the courtyard through Black Cat Alley.

Rosa grabbed Amber's arm, stopping her following. 'Leave her. She needs time alone. Let's clear this up before a customer arrives.'

\*\*\*

Amber's intuition had niggled when she returned home on Christmas day. As much as she enjoyed Nate's company, something was off. A secret unsaid. A quick online search gave her more information, his business credentials and job title. Impressive, but she needed to delve more. Flicking through Facebook profiles, she checked those who could be him. Unlike Willow, who shunned all social media platforms, Nate had an account. Annoyingly, he'd set it to private, but it still revealed his friends' list. Rookie error. This led to the beautiful Rebecca McLeod, who had no qualms in sharing her relationship status and snippets in her corporate life of lavish dinners and business events. The quickly accepted friend request gave Amber an insight into her private life and Nate's world. From moaning about her workload to cosy nights in with accompanying stylish photos, and drunken nights with friends, Amber could see it all, including the incriminating photo posted days before Christmas—dressed in a closely fitted red ballgown, she linked arms with a dashing Nate Reynolds smiling at the camera. He was a two-timing cheat. He would have been hexed if he hadn't abandoned Willow days later. She had had a lucky escape and Amber decided this secret was best hidden.

Amber wasn't sure why she'd checked Rebecca's newsfeed that morning. Perhaps it was the certainty that her matchmaking plan would be a success and she needed to check the opposition to Willow's heart for one last time, or the pesky algorithm flagging a meme reminding her of her existence, but when she saw Rebecca's excited post, she felt relief. Nate was no longer a threat to her father's future. She never guessed that hours later, she would break her friend's heart all over again.

# Chapter Thirty-Eight

Willow fled from the shop, ignoring the gaping customers in the courtyard and Amber's call to wait. She needed to be alone. The streets heaved with chattering tourists, lingering outside shops admiring the produce on sale, eating chips or ice cream. She ignored the tuts as she weaved through them, reluctant to lose any speed. Humiliation burned her skin, crushing any joy and empowerment she'd experienced earlier. How had her life escalated out of control within minutes? One minute she was making tea, bursting to tell Rosa about her night with Nate, the gherkin bauble she'd found nestled in a box next to her breakfast tea with the promise of many Christmas trees to come, confirming his proclamation of love he said as he left, and the next she was overhearing frantic whispers between her employees, Old Percy flickering out of focus with the tension building in the air, and Mrs Marley wringing her hands in anticipation. Amber's face reflected her own horror when she saw the Facebook post.

Nate was getting married. No wonder he couldn't visit her at the weekend, he was too busy walking down the aisle.

She ran up the steps towards the Abbey, past the Celtic cross, until she reached the top to sneak over the crumbling wall to the edge of the headland. The sea crashing beneath her matched her mood.

'Oh Lou, I've made such a fool of myself. I trusted him with everything. Everything. Told him things only you and Marian know. Things I can't even tell Glenn, and now I discover he's a liar. A snake. Charlatan and a cheat. I'm such an idiot.'

Tears cascaded down her face and, trembling in the North Sea breeze, she wrapped her arms around herself. How could she have got it so wrong? Yesterday he declared he loved her and only that morning did he hint at their future together. He gave her a gherkin for their future trees. Yet, it was all a sham. She was just a final fling before he tied the knot. Forget being in York for business. He was probably on his stag night and now laughing with his friends at her expense.

Her phone buzzed in her pocket over and over like an incessant bluebottle demanding attention. She checked. Several missed calls from Amber, Glenn, and a text from him saying how glad he was she was home safe and would see her soon. No chance. Twice bitten, she never wanted to see him again. One click deleted the text, and she wished her memories were as easy to remove.

If only she were tech savvy like Amber, none of this would have happened. She'd have revealed his cheating ways at Christmas. As tempting as joining Facebook was to see the scale of the deception herself, there was no need; the images from Amber's phone were tattooed in her mind. His arm draped over another woman's shoulders at a Christmas Ball days before they met. Her dark hair cascaded over her shoulders, and her smile revealed perfect white teeth. As a professional lawyer, according to her biography, she was everything Willow wasn't. There was no competition and his loyalty was obvious as Rebecca McLeod proudly declared in less than forty-eight hours she'd be Mrs N. Reynolds. An enormous diamond shone on her finger in the classic black-and-white shot. Her friends' excited comments about how they were the perfect match seared Willow's heart further. Was this what a heart attack felt like? A clenching tightening in the chest and inability to breathe. She wanted the ache to stop, to rip her heart out. It wasn't fair. She berated herself for being with him, her instincts failing her at a crucial time. Again. What was the point of having witch senses if they didn't prevent heartbreak? Her knees buckled, and she fell forward, her body refusing to hold itself up. A hand pulled her back from the cliff edge and strong tanned arms embraced her. Turning, she sank and sobbed into Glenn's shirt.

'It's okay. Hush now. I've got you, Willow.'

***

'Next time you have your heart broken, please can you retreat to somewhere less dangerous? It would've spoilt quite a few holidays if the tourists witnessed you slam headfirst into the rocks below.'

'I won't have my heart broken again. I'm done with men. Love is not for me.' Willow stared into the steaming cup of Yorkshire tea. With luck and a nod of recognition from the owner, Willow and Glenn had been guided to the corner of a busy café. The hubbub of the other customers drowned out any conversation. 'I just didn't see that coming. I loved him and he said he felt the same.'

'I saw the spark between you at Christmas. I never suspected him to be a cheat. Maybe there's been a misunderstanding.'

'I saw the photo, Glenn, and the post. He's getting married tomorrow. I was just his final notch on his bedpost. What a fool.'

'He had us all fooled.' Glenn nodded to the waitress, who brought them both a full English breakfast. Willow nibbled a piece of toast despite the tantalising aroma of bacon. Her appetite had deserted her.

'Except Amber. She knew something was amiss. She was right. I should have listened to her.'

'I guess we should know by now; teenagers are always right.'

'I told him everything. Things only Lou and one other knew.' Willow looked at Glenn. He'd bared his soul to her two years ago. Now it was her turn. For the second time in twenty-four hours, she revealed the secret she'd held close for twenty years.

# Chapter Thirty-Nine

Amber waited until she heard the gentle snore from Glenn's bedroom. He'd arrived home looking drained and tired, but he assured her Willow was fine and stronger than anyone gave her credit for. Amber only hoped he was telling the truth. She wished she could sneak into the Cobble for the *Mend a broken heart* brew the engaged witch had marked as a perfect cure. Instead, she wished upon the lone shooting star streaking across the black sky.

New moon, the ideal time for spellmaking and, being Friday, Amber prayed to Freya, the Lady of Love, to make this potion work. The look on Willow's face when she saw the Facebook post was still fresh in her mind. How dare Nate break her heart? After all that was happening, he did that. She hated him. The possibility of a revengeful hex was considered, but he wasn't worth it. He deserved Rebecca McLeod with the high-maintenance life and opinions. But if she ever saw him again, she'd make sure he felt the same crushing pain as Willow.

Her space was prepared in silence. Textbooks stacked haphazardly were pushed into the corner and tubes of paints and pencils thrown into a drawer. Opening the Old Apothecary box, Amber paused, fascinated by the contents. Her own Enchanted Emporium. Not for the first time did she trail her fingers over the bottles, wondering who they belonged to, but Willow's cleansing had wiped the energies clean. Shame, she thought, they might have given her guidance or a kick to make this spell work. She cast a circle, lit a pink candle, and ticked off the list of the spell's ingredients, including the fresh catnip. On this private occasion, she hoped to feel a connection with her mum, but there was no additional hum of a spirit close by. She was alone.

The scratch on her hand still stung when she unscrewed a glass vial, making her curse that cat. Was this Vincent's way of warning her to stop? She groaned and slammed her hands on the desk in frustration. The pewter goblet wobbled precariously, forcing her to grab the cold stem before it fell over. Water sloshed onto the desk and a drip rolled down the metallic curved cup. Amber drew the goblet closer, watching the water settle, mesmerised by the movement.

In the goblet's depth, an image emerged of Willow sitting in deep concentration staring at her laptop, her hand clutching a locket worn around her neck. She looked up, her forehead furrowed as she sensed she was being watched. Amber jolted back on her chair, snapping the connection. This was a sign. She'd bought the locket with her dad the first Christmas they were all together. On one side there lay a photo of Willow and Louise from their student days, and the other was Glenn and Amber. She'd worn it ever since. Willow was the glue holding the trio together, facilitating healing and a future. Her resolve boosted, she knew bringing Willow and Glenn closer was the correct way to go; with this potion's nudge, they would be the family they were destined to be.

The crunch and grating of the pestle grinding the herbs against the stone mortar calmed her and pushed away her final doubts. A pinch here and a dash there. She whispered her incantation, adding the dry ingredients to the brew simmering over the camping stove borrowed from Jack's dad. Once cool, she decanted the clear liquid into small glass vials. It was ready. Now all she needed to do was slip it into the lovebirds' drinks and make amends with Jack. The next stages would work better with two people.

# Chapter Forty

Nate pulled at his tie as he waited at the altar. Whose idea was it to wear a full morning suit at the height of the blistering summer? Rebecca. Her plans for this wedding had begun in her childhood and these outfits had been on display in the wedding magazines cluttering his flat for months. The open pages sending subliminal messages of her expectations of her perfect day. He loosened his tie that felt more claustrophobic than those he wore at the office, and they were bad enough. But not long now, soon he would relegate the ridiculous pieces of fabric to the bin. What purpose did they have? Nothing, a bit like the top hat he held. What was he supposed to do with it? He shifted uncomfortably under the watch of the congregation. Some he recognised, many he didn't. They'd invited how many people? His mum stood in the first pew dressed in the outfit he knew she bought while Rebecca chose her wedding dress. As soon as the engagement was announced, the pair announced a giddy shopping trip.

His parents were gaining the daughter they always wanted. Rebecca got on better with them than he did. Reaching into his pocket, he rechecked his phone. The screen was blank. No messages. No missed calls. Since his return to London, he'd tried to contact Willow with no luck. The uneasy silence hung over him. Had she changed her mind about his feelings for him? His latest messages were unread. He should never have come back. He should have contacted Jamie and made his excuses, reneged on the deal he'd made in the shellshocked days after Christmas, he should have—

Jamie nudged him with his elbow.

'For God's sake, Nate. Stop fidgeting and put that away. Rebecca said strictly no phones in the church. She'll kill you. Besides, there's no time.'

The church organ sprang into life with Wagner, and the door opened. His mum grabbed the hat Nate still held, shaking her head at his incompetence. Jamie mouthed, 'Are you ready?' and he nodded. Rebecca glided down the aisle towards him, looking radiant in the elegant ivory fitted dress. He smiled at her glowing happiness as she was moments away from marrying the man she loved and gaining the Reynolds name.

*\*\*\**

Nate held Rebecca in his arms as they danced. Live music played in the background, and chat and laughter filled the exquisite ballroom decorated to her high expectations. Like the rest of the day, the venue was perfect.

'Thank you,' she said, her eyes sparkling as they spun.

'What for? Dancing with you? I've danced with you many times,' Nate said.

'Reluctantly, yes. You know what I mean. Today mustn't have been easy for you. I'm aware of what you gave up. Jamie told me.'

Shrugging, he bit back his anxiety over Willow's continued silence. 'Are you happy?'

Without hesitation, she answered, 'Yes. Yes, I'm very happy.'

'Then that's all that matters.'

Rebecca reached up and kissed him on the cheek.

'May I have a dance with my bride?' Jamie approached them as the music slowed into a romantic ballad.

'She's all yours.' Nate slipped out of Rebecca's embrace, patted Jamie on his shoulder, and strode towards the bar. He needed a drink. Or two.

'Are you all right?' Henry stood next to him at the bar looking worse for wear. His eyes glazed, his tie skew-whiff, and his words slurred, his brother was drunk. He must be to be bothered to talk to him. Unlike with Jamie, Nate's relationship with his middle brother was uneasy, a one-sided sibling rivalry he never understood. They actively avoided one another at every opportunity. Nate nodded, flinging back another shot of whisky, and ordered another.

'Of course. Rebecca's had her perfect day. Mum has got the daughter-in-law she wanted, to a different son than planned, but hey, the result's the same. So, all's good.'

'Exactly. Everyone thought it would be you walking down the aisle with her, not Jamie. He's only been home five minutes.'

'Exactly. It only takes five minutes to know when you have fallen in love,' Nate explained. Henry looked no wiser, making Nate sad for him and his wife. They were coming up to their tenth wedding anniversary without feeling that spark. No secret smiles or caresses exchanged between them. 'Look at the pair of them,' Nate pointed to Jamie laughing at something his new wife said. 'They're made for each other. Rebecca and I just took a while to realise it wasn't working. And our hearts lay elsewhere. Now excuse me, I need to make a phone call.'

***

'God, you look rough.' Jamie bounded over as Nate stirred his black coffee in the hotel dining room. Many other guests were doing the same, all suffering from the wedding reception continuing until the early hours of the morning. Hangovers shaded their faces a tinge of green.

'Whereas you're bouncing like bloody Tigger. Aren't you supposed to be somewhere else with your new bride?' Nate said as his brother dragged a chair out and flopped down. He stole a slice of Nate's toast.

'Becky and I are leaving for the airport soon. Just wanted to say bye. And thanks. None of this would have happened without you.'

'Sure, it would. You'd just have had a more low-key event at Gretna Green or Vegas.'

'Becky would have hated that. All this finery and show was important to her. Still no news?'

'Nothing.'

'I still don't understand why you didn't bring her. All chicks like getting dressed up.'

'I don't think she would appreciate being called a chick, and I only rekindled our relationship a couple of days ago. And bizarrely you weren't high on the agenda of conversation. Besides, it would've been like bringing her into the lion's den with Dad, Henry, and everyone commenting about my ex walking down the aisle with my brother.'

'Her appearance would've helped me. I'm seen as the evil one breaking up you and Becky's relationship. Christ, the lecture I got from Gran. But, if you're worried about Willow, why are you here? Just go. There's nothing stopping you now, Henry's got his backside firmly under your desk and I'm married to my beautiful bride.' Jamie's phone buzzed and he leapt up from the table. 'Becky's waiting at reception. And you've gotta go to Whitby. Let me know how you get on. I'll send you a postcard.'

Nate shook his head at his brother's retreating form. Throughout their entire five-year relationship, Nate had never called Rebecca 'Becky'. Despite the shock revelation about Jamie's and her relationship, he was glad she'd found someone to calm her edges so she could relax. Nate picked up his phone and dialled a number. 'George. May I speak with your wife?'

# Chapter Forty-One

Willow's head throbbed as she tipped the herbs into the simmering cauldron. The intoxicating smell turned her stomach. Maybe this wasn't the wisest choice of stock production, but at least she was away from the bright lights of the shop floor. How much did she drink last night? Time had blurred after she opened the second bottle of wine.

Despite her resolution on the train journey back from York to take control and stop hiding from Rafe, face the situation head-on, typing his name into the search engine proved too much. Heartache over Nate was bad enough without battering it further with images of Rafe. Defeated, she added Speedwell Cottage instead. Maybe luck would be on her side, but it refused to flag up any clues. Maybe it was as Louise once suggested and warded with protective spells that made it vanish soon after she last saw it.

A gentle knock on the workroom door interrupted her thoughts; Amber came in, gingerly closing it.

'Hi. I wasn't expecting you in today,' Willow said.

'I'm just passing by and thought you'd need this. Tea and a bacon butty are the perfect hangover food according to Dad and he should know. I brewed the tea myself; I hope it helps. Are you okay?'

'Apart from a horrendous hangover? Yes, I am. Well, I will be. This will help, I'm sure. Thank you. I'm sorry if I scared you yesterday. It was a bit of a shock.'

Amber shrugged, brushing the apology away. 'Anyway, I'd better go. Dad says can you meet him at Monique's at seven?'

'Monique's? Are you sure? Why would he want to meet there?'

'Dunno, maybe making sure you eat. I'm just the messenger. Enjoy.' She left before Willow asked for more. She must have misheard. Monique's was the newly opened restaurant famed for fine dining and its romantic setting, not a place she considered Glenn suggesting, especially in the current situation. The last thing she wanted to see were couples gushing over each other. If Glenn was insistent she eat, fish and chips on the harbour would suffice.

Her appetite woke with the tantalising aroma of bacon and the nausea faded with every bite. It really was the best hangover cure. Willow smiled, picking up the teacup Amber had chosen; decorated with yellow roses, it symbolised hope. It was a relief to see Amber taking an active role in blending again and using her natural flair for herbs. If this tea soothed her broken heart, it could be a hit brew in the summer when holiday flings came to an abrupt end. She stirred the liquid, breathing in the aroma. What had she used? Chamomile, of course, raspberry, interesting. Willow picked out each ingredient. There was something else, a very subtle mint fragrance. Vincent bounded onto the bench, nudging the cup.

'No. Vince, you're not allowed up here. Shoo.' She forced him onto the floor, but he returned again and again.

'What's up with you?'

She took another sip, detecting a hint of catnip, and glanced at her cat. Catnip? It did have calming qualities useful in tea, but something niggled about the combination of flavours. A forgotten conversation between Willow and Lou at uni about her excessive use of raspberry came forth.

'Everyone loves raspberry. It's useful to disguise magic and tastes you'd rather people didn't know about,' Louise explained when faced with Willow's complaints. If Amber had read Lou's journals, it was a nugget of knowledge she would know and use. What was she hiding?

Willow took another whiff, digging deeper behind the ingredients, to the spell itself, the intent.

'Oh Amber, tell me you didn't?'

Rushing to the sink, Willow emptied her cup before she dialled Glenn's number; she had to warn him not to drink or eat anything Amber had made. His phone went straight to voicemail, forcing her to leave a message and hope he listened to it in time.

***

Going out was the last thing Willow wanted to do. An evening in with more wine and a box set appealed more, but with the high possibility Amber had drugged Glenn with a love potion, she had no choice. There would be strong words with her apprentice when she saw her next about her misuse of spell work, however well intentioned. All day, Willow's attempts to contact Glenn had failed. Who knew what damage the spell had caused between him drinking it and now? She only hoped Amber's knack for potions meant her timing for it to activate was as meticulous as her blending skills.

She found Glenn sitting at a table near the window. A pleasant spot, it allowed diners to watch the activity on the street outside and suited her fine. Once seated, she could avoid the smooching or gooey-eyed couples around them. Who needed a love potion when the busy room buzzed with pheromones?

Glen rose from his chair before she could say hi, and he kissed her on the cheek before pulling out her chair. His eyes dilated. She didn't need to ask if he'd received her message. The potion was working as intended. *Thanks, Amber.*

The server arrived to collect the drinks order. Glenn ordered a fresh Diet Coke and Willow ordered herself a wine. She needed something to calm her tumult of emotions; worry blended with the brewing annoyance at being put in this position. Thank goodness she wasn't also under the spell's effects otherwise tomorrow could have been awkward. No good would have come out of it, whatever delusions Amber might have.

The reversal potion she had hidden called for it to be mixed with red wine, but since that was off the agenda Diet Coke would have to do. She just needed to distract Glenn long enough to slip it into his drink undetected.

'Good day at work?'

'Not bad. I popped into Mr Garner's to see if he needed anything. His daughter's a lovely woman, don't you think? Very underappreciated, you know.'

'Really?' As far as Willow remembered, she was a replica of her mother—an old bag who ruled her husband's life with a firm hand. Mr Garner had flourished since her death six years ago, revealing a cheeky sense of humour that attracted all the ladies into cooking for him and helping with his chores.

'Yes, such a shame she's married. I hope he loves her; do you think he does?' Willow choked back a giggle at his sincerity and the notion Amber might have wound up with her father getting it together with the woman from hell.

'Of course he does.' Marriage was the last topic she wanted to discuss. She'd deleted several more unread messages from Nate and he had the gall to phone the Enchanted Emporium.

Luckily, Rosa answered and slammed the phone down.

'What about you? I've been worried about you,' Glenn slurred. 'You do know Nate didn't deserve you. Not one bit.' He reached over and caressed her hand. 'You need—'

Willow snatched her hand away, relieved the waiter had arrived with the drinks. Glenn needed the antidote fast. And she didn't need to hear his views on what she needed.

Glenn looked momentarily confused before he began a tirade about Nate's behaviour. Willow wanted him to stop. She thought things couldn't get worse until Glenn leant over and tapped the woman on the neighbouring table to tell her all about Nate's deception, but it was fine as it meant he could marry Willow instead. She cringed and her skin blushed until it matched the red flocked wallpaper behind him. Using his animated storytelling as a distraction, she poured the liquid from her vial into his Coke.

'Glenn.' She pulled him away, apologising to the couple. 'We need to decide our order. You look thirsty. Have a drink.' He drank some Coke and scrunched up his nose.

'Does this taste okay to you? It's bitter.' He offered her his glass and she pretended to take a sip.

'It's fine.'

'No. No.' Glenn shook his head, unconvinced. 'I think I'll get him to change it. Maybe it's the glass.'

'Glenn, it is fine. I think it's because you're too thirsty to taste it right. The more you drink, the better it'll taste. In fact, I think you may have sunstroke from working too hard outside. The best thing you can do is drink up and then we'll go for a walk on the beach for some fresh air.'

'If you say so, Willow,' he replied, looking deep into her eyes, and followed her advice. The spell was working so well, if Willow asked him to stand on the table and tap dance to impress her, he would. 'You're so wise. It's because you're a witch. Are all witches wise? They must be except the one in that fairy tale. The one with the mirror. The mirror conned her, didn't it?'

*Just like Nate conned me.* Willow indicated to the staff they wanted the bill, and she registered their relief they were leaving.

'I love witches. I love you. And I loved Louise, I still do. She was a witch, you know.'

'Yes, I know. She was very much a witch,' Willow said, linking arms with him to guide him to the beach in the hope the sea air would quicken up the reversal. His bewitched speeches continued, hardly taking a breath.

'Except I didn't believe in magic then. I didn't believe her. It was all hocus-pocus baloney until you came along and showed me differently.' He stumbled over a rock. His misstep caused her to step forward to prevent his fall. 'You saved me. Again.'

He spun Willow round to face him and gazed down at her with devotion, intensifying the air between them until his mouth met hers. The remnants of potion lingered on his lips, its magic urging her to respond, and powerless, she kissed him back.

\*\*\*

Amber couldn't believe her luck when she discovered Monique, the extravagant chef and owner of the self-named restaurant, was Artie's aunt. Its reputation for quality, extraordinary food, and intimate atmosphere had cemented it as the go-to venue for romantic evenings to impress your loved ones. Over the last few weeks, Amber had volunteered at Bones Ink in exchange for knowledge and experience, and Artie knew how much her dad and Willow meant to her. A quick word to his aunt and he wrangled her a reservation for them. A tiny white lie about the occasion might have been told. While setting a surprise blind date would have raised eyebrows, a fortieth birthday was acceptable.

Jack readily agreed to meet that evening and Amber found after weeks of not seeing each other, she was eager for his company. From seeing each other daily their contact had dwindled to occasional texts. There were no fireworks at the end of their relationship, if it was the end. Amber was unsure, but hoped tonight would reveal all and allow her to monitor her dad. She enjoyed Artie's company, and he crowded much of her thoughts, but she missed her best friend.

On her way to meet Jack, she passed Monique's and saw her dad leaning towards Willow, deep in conversation and holding her hand. Her plan was working. Her bubbling excitement was hard to contain while catching up with gossip with Jack at the local pub. Along with the dream where he snubbed her, the covert meddling blocked the path of their natural chat.

'Come on,' Jack said, putting his empty glass on the bar. 'You're too fidgety. Let's walk.'

So they did, but Amber remained distracted, knowing metres away her magic was taking hold.

Sitting near the beach huts overlooking the sea, Jack and Amber ate chips with lashings of salt and vinegar. From the corner of her eye, she saw her dad and Willow stroll onto the sand, arms linked and her dad looking longingly at Willow.

'Is that—?' Jack asked.

'Yes. Come on, I don't want them to see us.' Amber jumped up, grabbing Jack, urging him to leave, but her eyes didn't leave the pair. Her dad stumbled and Willow held him up. The atmosphere changed, magic danced in the breeze as he leant forward and kissed Willow. Amber's stomach churned. It really had worked.

'See I told you. They're made for each other.' Amber turned away, no longer wanting to witness her dad's affection. It felt wrong, voyeuristic. Her job was done. 'Come on.'

Jack followed her off the beach, shaking his head. His mood changed from happiness to puzzlement and sadness.

'What's up?' said Amber.

'I can't help thinking it should have been Nate. There was chemistry in the photos. They fitted together. This feels odd.'

'Nate is a cheat. A liar. You just don't like admitting you were wrong and I was right.'

Jack froze and stared at her as if searching a for a clue. A chill crept up her spine. 'You did something. Didn't you?' Amber kept silent. This wasn't how she wanted things to go. 'None of this is real. They aren't and nor are we. I bet you only phoned me as an excuse to spy on them.'

'They are real. I was just speeding things along so I can go to uni happy,' Amber defended her actions, but Jack's face showed his disappointment, his anger.

'So, you are going to uni now? Not waiting for Artie to notice you. Or be his next assistant?'

'If my grades are okay and things work out with them. Artie says—'

'Yes, you will do anything Artie says, won't you? So far, all I've heard about is him and his shop. Him and interfering in other people's lives is all you care about.'

'That's not true. I—'

Jack threw his arms in the air, cutting her off. 'Enough. I don't want to know.' And with a deep sigh he stormed down the road, leaving her wondering how a perfect evening had fallen apart with one kiss. Was this the beginning of her debt's repayment for using the spell?

# Chapter Forty-Two

A ripple of laughter broke free as Willow stepped back from the embrace. Glenn stood, his eyes wide as his glazed look faded into shock. His bewilderment made her laugh more, as unfair as it was.

'Did we just kiss?'

She nodded. 'But in our defence, we were both under the influence of a love potion brewed by your daughter. And I don't know about you, but this will be an experience I don't want to repeat.'

'Me neither if it induces you into a fit of giggles. My technique must be off.'

Willow mentally counted down to the moment he would comprehend the first part of her declaration. Obviously, male pride about performance trumped being drugged.

'I assure you, your technique is just fine.'

'I can't believe you laughed. At least you didn't wipe your mouth with the back of your hand.'

'What, like this?' Willow did as he suggested, wiping any remaining potion molecules away.

'Just like. Hang on, did you just say my daughter cast a spell on me? On you?'

Willow nodded, grabbing hold of his arm. 'Mainly you. I sussed something was going on in a couple of sips. Still enough for me to kiss you back, though. She's exceptionally good at magic. I tried to warn you, but you didn't look at your phone.'

'It was out of battery. Shit. I'll kill her. Why an earth would she—?'

'Go easy on her. She had her reasons. I think she wants us both to be happy and secure, especially you. She doesn't want you to be lonely when she goes to uni. She did it with love and best intentions.'

'How come you're so calm about this? Doesn't this violate some witchy human right laws?'

'I've had the day to think about it and while love potions aren't to be played with, they're not banned. They have consequences, but free will still exists. It lowers inhibitions, like being drunk.'

'Well, I did some pretty shit things while I was drunk. I don't feel drunk now.'

'The kiss stopped that and the antidote I slipped into your drink.'

'Great, so you drugged me too. It's like living in a spy novel. I love you, Wills, but this would never happen normally. You're my best friend, but—'

'I agree,' Willow said. 'Anything more than friendship would be too weird. I mean, after all the things I heard Lou say about your life together, I could never compare and nor would I want to. She'd haunt me if I ever hurt you.'

'Hang on. What exactly did she talk to you about?' Glenn studied her as she blushed. Louise was never one for holding back on her emotions or experiences. Willow bent down to remove her shoes. The damp sand squidging between her toes was a welcome distraction.

'Everything. Nothing,' she mumbled. 'Girl stuff, you know.' To avoid deeper interrogation, she ran down to the seashore. He quickly pursued. They walked, arms linked at the water's edge. The waves lapping over their feet with each ebb and flow.

'How do you think Amber will react when she discovers her plan didn't work?'

'To be fair, Glenn, after her embarrassment fades, she'll be okay. She's torn—she wants you to be happy, and not alone, but also doesn't want to lose you. I am the easy, safest option. She knows me. Another woman might take you away from her when she has only just found you.'

'No one can do that.'

'You need to tell her, convince her, and then maybe you'll get to choose your own dates.'

'I'm not going on any more dates. I told you.'

'You did, but that was when you thought Amber was hurting herself.' An image of Glenn laughing with another woman flashed through Willow's mind.

'Who is she?' she asked.

Glenn looked down at his feet and smoothed out the sand with his foot before answering. 'Lorna. I met her at AA and have been helping her out in her garden. She's lovely, caring, and fun.'

'And pretty. But is she a witch?' Willow needed to check.

'No. Two witches in my life are enough, but she knows about Amber and you. She's intrigued but unfazed.'

Willow listened and watched his face light up as he spoke about Lorna. Amber need not have worried. Without her help, Glenn was happy.

# Chapter Forty-Three

The stunning display of orange, pinks, and reds promised a glorious day for the tourists waking in the town. Nate sat on the sea wall dressed in his crumpled clothes from the day before, his rolled-up trousers damp from walking in the shoreline, contemplating the scene he saw the previous evening. When he'd found the Enchanted Emporium empty, he decided a stroll on the beach would clear his head after the long drive and give him the courage to phone her. His heart leapt when he saw Willow in the distance and plummeted when he recognised Glenn. After witnessing the embrace, he knew sleep would be elusive and dreaded returning to an empty Sand Dale Cottage, so he had walked over the River Esk and climbed the 199 steps. The town fell behind the higher he went. On a bench, he watched the sun set and darkness fall. Lights shone in houses and the soft sound of laughter and chat rose as people returned home from the restaurants and pubs. They were getting on with their lives while his stood still. Any plans he'd made during his journey up the country vanished with that kiss. The kiss he expected to receive was given to someone else, and it was all he saw when he closed his eyes, on an endless loop. The clouds cleared, revealing the stars he never saw in the city. They failed to bring joy, only memories of Willow, teaching him the constellations and their related stories. He should have come back sooner and followed his heart. Instead, it had shattered in two.

He couldn't hate Glenn. He liked him, and he knew he would care for Willow as she deserved. They had a history, lived close by, and Amber would be happy. They were, after all, a ready-made family.

The fishermen's chat and laughter while they brought in their catch drifted in the refreshing breeze, and Nate witnessed the hubbub of the smokery processing the famous kippers and shops opening early. Whitby was waking up. He strolled to a small café offering takeaway coffee and then returned to the beach, cradling his hot drink. He doubted he'd ever return to this coastal town and wanted to soak up its atmosphere before he left. A familiar figure strode along the shoreline, her chunky boots leaving distinct marks in the wet sand before they were washed away by the waves. Her hair was longer than before and a vibrant blue instead of red. It compelled him to walk over.

Amber jumped as he approached, her blood draining from her already pale face. He apologised for scaring her, which she shrugged off, gathering her defiant demeanour.

'I just wasn't expecting to see you,' said Amber, swiping strands of hair away from her face before stuffing her hands in her pockets.

'It was a surprise visit but an enlightening one. How's college?' They walked side by side as he listened to vague updates until he couldn't wait any longer. 'How's Willow?'

'You haven't seen her?' Amber scrutinised him, taking in his dishevelled appearance.

'Not to talk to, but I saw your dad and Willow together last night.'

Amber nodded. 'They had a celebratory date at Monique's.' Her smile confirmed what he suspected. While he'd given Willow his heart in York and she gave him her trust, her heart already belonged to someone else. How had he got it so wrong? It explained why his calls and messages had been rejected. Their night together must have been a mistake, in her eyes at least. A goodbye.

'How long have they been together?' Nate asked, unsure whether he wanted the answer, but he needed to know whether he could have done things differently.

Amber paused before delivering the words that punched deep into his soul. 'Just after Valentine's Day.

***

The Moors rushed by in a green-and-brown blur. Jealousy and anger urged him to drive faster on the winding roads, descending and ascending the dramatic landscape. He'd trusted her and thought she cared for him. How could he be so stupid? The warning signs were there at Christmas, telling him she and Glenn were more than friends. He should have listened to them.

His brakes screeched, and the car jolted to a stop as a sheep wandered onto the road. It glared at him before continuing to the other side. The shock of a near miss forced him to slow down. He needed to take a break before he hurt himself or someone else, and he needed a drink stronger than his lacklustre coffee. His phone shrilled, and taking it as a sign, he pulled into a layby.

'Nate Reynolds.' He answered the number he only vaguely recognised.

'Mr Reynolds, it's Joanne Dawson from Parson's Investigations. I'm just enquiring whether you've received our preliminary report you requested on a Mr Rafael Amenábar?'

Nate's mouth went dry and he clutched the steering wheel tight as he told them he'd read it later and no he didn't need to hear a recap. It wasn't his business anymore. He'd forward them to Willow for her to deal with. 'And also, we've found Speedwell Cottage.'

***

At a crossroads, Nate turned right down a nondescript lane far away from the main through road and a chill passed through him, reminiscent of his introduction to the Emporium and its homicidal matchmaking ghost. Not that it did much use, Mrs Marley and Vincent should have focused on someone closer to home and his heart wouldn't be hurting as much. His life would have continued as before, the office, networking and, well, not Rebecca, she'd still have had an affair with Jamie, but he might not have reacted the same, raged instead of giving his blessing and help. Love had touched him, and he couldn't stand in his brother's way. And he was doing it again. Willow, like Rebecca, had made her choice.

'Recalculating. Recalculating,' screamed the usually calm voice of his sat nav.

'I'm in the middle of nowhere, now is not the bloody time for you to bloody recalculate.'

Maybe he should turn around, back to a familiar road, and continue home. Willow had waited this long to find Speedwell Cottage; a few hours wouldn't matter. He could forward the details to her as a final farewell. But after all her enthusiasm, he needed to see this place that had captured her dreams and heart. The place she called home. He switched off the sat nav, checking his phone which had no signal and was unresponsive, meaning he had to follow his instinct.

Unlike the stark landscape he'd left, trees lined both sides, the canopy forming a verdant tunnel, providing a welcome dappled shade from the blazing sun. He approached a single-track stone bridge rising over a rambling stream Joanne Dawson described in her call. He was close to the mythical place. A flash of vibrant blue and orange streaked past his windscreen. A kingfisher. Encouraged him further. Even if he didn't find the cottage, Parson's did say there was a village nearby and he could fuel up and dose up on caffeine. The narrow road twisted and turned back on itself, before opening up to moorland and fields. A tractor approached, forcing Nate into a layby. Over the lichen-covered stone wall, he saw it in the distance. A squat tree with a distinctive swept canopy he recognised from Willow's photo. He'd found Grandma Jax's.

A mile later, he pulled down a dusty track. The car bumped and jolted with every pothole forcing him to question his wisdom at his detour, but there it was. The abandoned low stone cottage of Willow's dreams. It even had the traditional, much sought-out rose climbing above the front door in full bloom.

He parked the car and walked to the house. Left to nature, the front garden resembled a meadow, an explosion of colour and a hive of activity with butterflies and other insects. The windowpanes set in the thick walls were intact and there was no sign of vandalism, much to his surprise. He peeked inside to see the shadows of the basic furniture hidden under cloths. No one had lived here for years. Whoever Willow saw moving in hadn't stayed despite the building's potential for a family home. The stunning secluded location with the Moors rising in the background and front alone would attract buyers. Maybe it housed more sinister ghosts than Old Percy.

Nate turned the corner of the house. The overgrown garden and brambles formed a narrow walkway over the cracked path. He cursed as thorns snagged his trousers and scratched his legs. He ploughed on. It was a larger property than the photo suggested, each generation adding extra rooms for their requirements. Ivy grew up this side of the house, covering any windows. A whistle alerted him to a presence ahead. What did he expect? A house owned by a witch was bound to have a ghost, maybe Grandma Jax, but did he really want to meet one? He began to retreat. The brambles had settled across the path, blocking his way. He had no choice but to continue forward. The bright sunlight blinded him as he entered a walled garden, conjuring up memories of Willow's yard at the Emporium. She'd love this. Flagstone paths formed sections devoted to vegetable plots, espalier fruit trees grew up the red brick wall, and there was a knot garden for the herbs. It was perfect, too perfect. Where were the weeds and brambles?

Were some ghosts capable of gardening?

*Snip, snip, snip.*

He followed the sound of secateurs shaping a hedge. The man looked down from his stepladder on hearing Nate's footsteps. In his mid-twenties, with a tan from working outside and blonde hair suited to a surfer, he was no ghost.

'Can I help you?' the man asked with a local burr and scrutinised Nate from head to toe.

'Sorry I wasn't expecting anyone to be here,' Nate said, unsure how to explain his presence. Should he admit Willow's search? No, it was her story to tell. 'I was just passing by. Saw the property with its stunning views and I thought ...'

'You'd trespass onto the land.'

'No. Not at all. I—'

'Don't worry, mate, I'm only kiddin'. You don't look like a squatter. Anyhow, if you were, it wouldn't like it. Not one bit. Some have tried.' The man placed his secateurs into a sheath attached to his belt and climbed down the ladder.

'What do you mean?'

'This place tends t'look after itself. The reason it's not been vandalised or owt. It's protected by its reputation.'

'Which is?' Nothing would surprise Nate now. Seven months ago, he would have laughed at the idea of spooks, spells, and magic, but a lot had changed, which brought him back to her—Willow. He needed to tell her about this sooner or later. She might not want him, but he owed her this. Maybe this was the way back to her heart? Jealousy twisted in his gut. No, she had made her decision, Amber was clear about that. He had to let her go.

'It is a witch's place—has been for generations, centuries. These gardens are wonderful—herbs and plants you see no more but are ideal for herbal remedies and the like. Got spells on it, I reckon, don't you feel it? It's just waiting. The air zings with anticipation when a visitor approaches, then shrinks in disappointment. M'dad thinks I'm mad, but he never listened to Grandad's insane ramblings. He knows all about this place. Milly, my sister, reckons he was sweet on the old lady who owned it. Always doing odd jobs for her. We've kinda taken over for a while.'

Nate tried to feel what the lad had said, but nothing. Willow would feel it—she had said something similar about the Enchanted Emporium. 'Grandma Jax,' he mumbled.

'Yeah. Jax—that was her name. How do you know? Not exactly from these parts, are you?' the gardener said.

'I think I know a friend of her family.'

'Jax's? Really? Grandad would love to talk to you.' He looked at his phone. 'You're not heading off, are you? He'll be in the pub this evening if he can escape the old bird. It'd make his day to speak to you.'

'I guess I could. If I can find somewhere to stay.' Nate had nothing better to do, and the more information he had the better before he contacted Willow, and a drink would be welcome to clear his head.

'There's always the Old Ram in the village. He'll be open tonight. Give me a mo.'

He strode away with his phone clutched to his ear. He returned in minutes. 'Milly's reserved you a room. She works there sometimes. It's nowt fancy, but we'll make sure Grandad's there tonight. He loves a good natter, especially if he's given a pint.'

'Why are you so helpful? I could be a property developer for all you know.'

'Milly and I love this place. We know it better than most and you're the first person who hasn't made it groan in disappointment.'

\*\*\*

The gardener wasn't joking about the pub's accommodation's lack of opulence. Milly greeted him as he parked his car and guided him up the creaky stairs to the attic.

'Sorry. It's tiny, but it's tourist season, so the other rooms are fully booked. Jez says you knew Jax. She's a legend round here. Gramps will be thrilled to meet you.' Like her brother, Milly dressed as if she was ready to catch some waves.

'I know someone who knew her.' To his mortification, his stomach growled loudly, reminding him he hadn't eaten since saying farewell to the honeymooners, a lifetime ago.

'Pop down to the bar when you're ready and I'll rummage you up a bacon butty or something. You sound hungry and a friend of Jax's is a friend of ours.' The door closed after her, shrinking the room further. The Old Ram was a quaint timber-framed building which had served the villagers of the picturesque Mexenby for centuries. With its low ceilings and sloping floors, it wasn't designed for anyone with Nate's height, and the pitched roof gave little space for any furniture beyond a single bed, a chest of drawers, and table and chair under the dormer window. At least it was clean, and he could stoop for one night. Once he spoke to Jez's grandad and emailed Willow, he'd head home. He doubted he would see Yorkshire again. It was time to let her live her life and begin his.

The Old Ram was packed when Nate entered that evening. He weaved his way to the bar and was met by a booming voice belonging to a short, balding man with his stomach straining against his shirt. He shook Nate's hand in a firm grip.

'You must be Nate. Our Milly's told us all about you. I'm the Ram's landlord, Arnold Leeson, but you can call me Arnie. Harry's over there near the hearth, with the old Jack Russell. He likes this pint.' He pointed to the pump of strong local ale. 'Do you want one too? And the dog is rather partial to ready-salted crisps. Shall I add them to your tab?'

'Better had. Do you do other food?' Hours had passed since Milly's doorstopper sandwich and Nate would need to line his stomach if he was drinking Harry's favourite tipple. Arnie gave him the menu and Nate's mouth watered with anticipation of proper food. 'I'll have a steak pie and chips, please. Does Harry ...?'

'I'll bring two over. Just don't tell the old bird. She wouldn't like it. Keeps putting him on a diet. If you can't eat what you fancy when you're as old as Harry, what's the point?' Harry's wife sounded a right dragon.

Harry sat in the corner with the tatty terrier sitting in the seat next to him. Nate took the opposite chair, sliding the beer over.

'Cheers, lad,' Harry said raising his glass. The foamed head of ale formed a white moustache on his wrinkled skin. 'Our Jez said you were sniffing about old Jax's place but more importantly said you were a friend of the family.' Harry studied him over his glasses. 'Who exactly do you know?'

The resemblance to Jez and Milly was uncanny. They shared the same ocean-blue eyes, though Harry's peered through extensive wrinkles, his story etched in the grooves. Nate hesitated. It was Willow's story to tell.

'I'm not sure. My friend may have nothing to do with the place. Maybe if I know more about the property and the lady who lived there, I could tell you if it fits together. It's just a hunch. That's all.' He cringed at the word *friend*. It didn't cover his emotions for her.

'Mexenby likes people with hunches. It makes life easier—as long as people follow them. It's a strange place, but nowt so strange as Jax's place. Never called by its correct name of Speedwell Cottage now. Rumours of witchcraft have plagued it for years. Centuries. But instead of ostracising the persecuted women, we accepted them as our own.

'Of course, there were always some who feared them but in the main they were part of the community, if on the edge. Called wise women by some, we all knew they were more than wise. Witches. No doubt about it, lad. All of them. It helped the lady of Mexenby Hall was one. Instead of priest holes, it's rumoured the manor has a witch one. And used to hide from the Witchfinder himself.'

Harry took a slurp of his pint and a mouthful of his pie. Nate let the old man talk, amazed by all he had to say. No wonder Willow felt at home here.

'Sad times when Old Jax died. She was strange, aloof, and kept herself to herself, but in times of need, she was always there. Her son died before her—a car crash. Was never the same after that, but he had a daughter. A wee bairn she was. Slight and shy, as if she would blow away in the wind, but she flourished when she came to stay in the summers. 'Twas the highlight of Jax's year. Shame her mother remarried. The visits dwindled to nothing. Never saw her again. It broke Jax's heart. She did always say to me; "She'll come back." That's why me and my family continued to look after the place long after we stopped being paid. Can't do much but have tried to keep it ready for her if she did. I'd hate to think of Jax as the last Mexenby Witch. Many here feel vulnerable without one.'

'Well, I don't think Jax was the last.' Nate placed his empty glass on the table and grinned. 'I believe my friend Willow is Jax's granddaughter.'

Harry's face lit up. He clasped Nate's hands.

'You know Willow. Oh my, you've found her. Arnie, he knows Willow,' the old man shouted across the pub. Many stopped and turned to stare at Nate as a hush fell across the room. Arnie came over.

'Really. You know her?' Arnie said. Nate's nod was rewarded with a forceful slap on the table and a declaration there would be no tab to pay, and the next round for all was on the house. 'Do you think she'll come back?'

'She remembers being there as a kid and always wanted to come back. She dreams of this place, longs for it. It's in her blood.'

'Then you need to bring her home,' Harry said.

'She found it once, but then it disappeared.'

Harry laughed. 'Mexenby has a habit of that. It's like Yorkshire's own Brigadoon. It's the witch thing, I'm sure. They hid it from danger so often, remnants of the spells still work today. Sometimes in our favour, mostly not—it plays havoc with the postal service and sat nav.'

'Just like the Enchanted Emporium. When she was here, she saw people were moving in—it broke her heart.'

'People have tried renting it, but they never stay long. The house isn't for them.'

'Yet it's never come on the market? She's scoured house retail sites and estate agents hoping they'll give a clue of its whereabouts. She's desperate to buy it. And come home.'

'Buy it?' Harry looked puzzled. 'Why would she do that? She owns the bloody place.'

# Chapter Forty-Four

Willow messaged Glenn and Rosa as requested, informing them she was fine before switching off her phone. All she wanted was to block out the world and soothe her troubled heart. She soaked in a hot bath with calming bath salts and herbs until the water cooled but it failed to erase the images of Nate, no matter how often she screamed, 'He's married.' Exhausted, with insomnia looming, she brewed herself a potent sleeping draught and swallowed it in one go. Within minutes, she sank into the oblivion she longed for until the sun rose the next day.

Her phone screen lit up with numerous messages and missed calls from Nate. Fuming, she pressed *delete*. How dare he contact her while he was with Rebecca? When she didn't respond, he had the nerve to call the shop. Ignoring the phone became impossible. Rosa's temper frayed each time she answered that Willow was not there or busy. It rang again.

'Enough. If you don't tell him to stop, I will.'

Words failed Willow. It was too soon to speak to him coherently, and she didn't want to hear his voice or make excuses. She shook her head and Rosa strode to the phone and slammed the back room door shut. Muffling her angry tone.

Willow turned up the music and overcompensated her cheery chatter to a customer to prevent any eavesdropping. She'd witnessed Rosa's temper before and she'd hate to be Nate right now. The door opened and Rosa returned, her face flushed.

'He'll no longer contact you, but insisted I tell you he found it.'

Willow followed the detailed directions he messaged to her phone. He had found Grandma Jax's cottage. The needle in the haystack. It was surreal, and a doubt planted by Rosa niggled. Was this an elaborate, cruel trick? An excuse to see her he knew she couldn't refuse. She shook her head, hating the cynical thinking. He might be a cheat, but she knew he wasn't intentionally cruel.

***

As Nate predicted in his texts, the sat nav became useless as Willow descended into a dip of the Moors. The road twisted with only sheep for company until she saw a stone bridge. Once over, the village came into view.

The high street bustled with tourists, and she found the Old Ram with its faded signage. She squeezed Mavis into the only available parking place before taking a deep breath, unsure what would happen next and why Nate was so insistent she came here. Wouldn't it have been better to meet her at the cottage?

A hush fell over the bar when she entered. Several men and a woman with a mop of vibrant red hair Amber would have loved spun round in their chairs and stared as if she'd entered a scene from a horror movie and she'd soon be warned not to go out on the Moors. What was going on?

'You must be Willow!' A man appeared from the back, rubbing his hands on a cloth before flinging it over his shoulder. 'I'm very pleased to meet you. Nate won't be a minute. I'm Arnold but call me Arnie. How about I get you a drink? Cold drink or tea? In a pot, of course. J—' A woman in her twenties nudged him quiet.

'Coke will be fine. Thanks.' Willow slipped onto the stool someone offered her, and she waited for Nate. Each excruciating minute appeared to stretch into hours. Sipping her drink, she listened to Arnie babble, and watched people study her as if she was an exhibit in a zoo, nudging each other as they stared.

Nate bustled into the bar, grinning when he saw her. For a moment, she thought he'd kiss her, but he stepped back.

'There's someone I'd like you to meet.' He took her by the arm, sending the familiar electricity through her. Seeing him again was a mistake. Married or not, her body hadn't caught up with the situation. Once she saw the house, she'd make sure she never saw him again. They weaved through the clientele, who still watched her, to the corner table where a young couple, no, she decided, a brother and sister were settling an elderly gentleman down, much to his protestations. A terrier bounded from beneath the table, sniffed her shoes before jumping up, wagging its tail until she responded by rubbing its ear.

'Willow, this is Harry and his grandchildren, Jez and Milly. And you've met Chalky. Harry, this is Jax's granddaughter, Willow.'

Harry clutched her hand in both his aged, papery-thin ones and studied her with tears in his eyes. 'You look just like her. I always thought you did, but now it's undeniable.'

'You know me?' Willow struggled to accept this man knew her grandmother, never mind her.

'Aye. I doubt you remember me. Picked you up from Whitby Station sometimes. I was younger then and still had my hair.'

'That was you?'

'It was.'

Nate guided a bewildered Willow onto the spare chair next to him. He squeezed her hand, and she didn't flinch away. The old man in front of her held her attention. He knew her. Memories of her past weren't a figment of her imagination as she somehow feared. If Nate found Harry, it meant he'd found Speedwell Cottage.

'So, my dearest Willow, how much of your family history do you know?' Harry asked.

'Not a lot about my dad's side.' Willow had often asked her mum endless questions about her dad when she was small but received few answers. They stopped completely when her stepfather arrived, after curt responses of 'You have a new father now.' The only time she saw a photo of him was at Grandma Jax's, but Willow picked up the sorrow his name caused and never asked. She'd regretted it ever since.

'Well, let's see if we can change that.' He reached for his pint, preparing himself for a lengthy conversation.

'As I told your Nate, there have always been witches in Mexenby. We think they were all descended from one family—your family. It's hard to trace them all as most talents were passed down the maternal line, so the names changed with every generation until your dad. He was the first male born with magic for centuries.'

'Dad was a witch?' Willow choked on her drink. This was too much to take in. Jez spread out several faded photos of her family on the table. She picked one up of Jax on her wedding day with the grandfather she never knew. Harry was right; she did resemble her grandmother.

Another photograph showed Jax, and with Willow's dad outside the cottage. They both shared a familiar smile. She wished she'd had the chance to know him.

'Where do you think you get your powers from? Your mum? No, she didn't share his abilities. Jax doubted she ever knew about them until he died leaving her with you. Your differences were noticeable when she brought you to Jax's for holidays. You shone magic under Jax's care. It was always obvious to see what Jax was and, ultimately, what you were. Mexenby witches have never been ones to hide away even when it leads trouble to their door.' Willow shifted in her seat, flushed with guilt, aware hiding had been her default all her life, but trouble still found her.

'M'dad knew your grandmother from school. Were in the same class and close friends. Many people, I imagine, thought they'd get married at some point—always together strolling on the Moors, him helping on her family farm, but it didn't happen. Your grandfather, Thomas, arrived in the village and the atmosphere between them sizzled; there was no doubt who she would marry. Soon after, they had your dad, Eddie. They were happy and Jax served the village well with her lotions and potions until the day Thomas died. It shocked the village and devastated Jax. Thank goodness she had Eddie to look after. We all tried to help but you know what she was like, she retreated into the cottage and rarely came out. A recluse who refused visitors, except my dad. He'd insist I came up to the cottage rain or shine to offer help. Petrified, I was, with the rumours of her being a witch, and she had an infamous temper that came to the fore after Thomas's death.'

She picked up the photo of her grandparents, caressing their images with her finger. Poor Grandma Jax. The pain and grief must have been unbearable, and it explained much about the demeanour Willow remembered.

'It took a while, but eventually she'd ask me to do odd jobs and then help with the gardening. She taught me all I know and encouraged me to set up the gardening business that them two have inherited.' He pointed to Jez and Milly before taking the fresh pint Arnie offered him. His fatigue and toll of telling the story showed in his face.

'We can take a break or tell me more another day,' she suggested, crushing her own burning curiosity to know more.

'No!' Harry slammed his pint down on the table, making everyone jump. 'It has to be now. It's taken too long for you to come back, and the old bird will never let me out again when she notices I'm not there.'

'Harry's wife doesn't like him coming here,' explained Nate, bringing Willow another drink.

'Wife? Who said anything about m'wife? Our Nellie couldn't have cared less if I were out,' chuckled Harry, 'The old bird is the battle axe of the manager at my care home. Expects everyone to sit around playing dominoes or watch the drivel on the telly. Not allowed a laugh or a life when you get there.'

'She's not so bad, Grandad. She just cares,' said Milly.

'Cares. Cares—pah.' Harry guzzled some more beer, wiped the foam from his moustache, and carried on.

'One thing Jax was adamant about was Eddie's education. She loved the smallholding, but she knew he needed more; she was determined he'd go to university. He did, much to his surprise. He hated school and study. Even accused Jax of using magic and spells to get a place. Something Jax always denied. I believed her; he just never believed what he was capable of. He thrived. In his last year at university, he fell in love with your mother. Brought her home to meet Jax. Now love, your mum was lovely, but for reasons none of us could understand, Jax wasn't impressed. In a foul mood, she was, when the visit was over. Villagers blamed the storm that weekend on her; the poor tree in the graveyard never looked the same after it got hit by lightning. It's only alive today because she cast a spell on it so maybe there is truth in that rumour. Your dad and her refused to speak until he came back to tell her about you and the upcoming nuptials. He wanted her blessing. Your parents got married in the church in the village. Your mum looked beautiful, and they were very much in love. Jax was heartbroken and acted as if she'd lost a son, not gained a daughter. We know now why, of course.' He paused to finish his beer. 'Within weeks, we heard about the car accident and his death. Premonition, that's what she had, and she couldn't stop it. In a way, she always blamed your mum. A truce formed when you came up for holidays as a toddler, and they even became friends until she remarried. Then she lost you too.'

'I never knew,' Willow said. Tears freely ran down her cheeks.

'Knew what?' asked Harry. He rifled in his jacket pocket and handed her a clean, freshly pressed hankie, and she smiled a thank you before blowing her nose.

'Any of it. I never even knew they were married. I assumed when she refused to talk about my father, he'd deserted her while she was pregnant with me. She never gave me his name when I was born. If it wasn't for these holidays, I'd have assumed I didn't have any other family apart from Mum. Neither would talk.'

'Grief does that to some; lock their emotions in a box, they do, before pushing everyone away, even those they love for fear of being hurt again.' His words hit home, gripping her heart further, and she sneaked a look at Nate. Is that what she did?

'Not seeing you again nearly destroyed her. I was the only one she would accept help from, and that's only because I am as stubborn and hard-headed as her. She always said you'd come home and here you are.'

'Speedwell Cottage always felt like home,' Willow hiccupped. 'I tried to come back when I heard she'd died but I was too late for the funeral. My stepfather didn't tell me.'

'Nasty sod he was. Well, that's past. You're here now, and it's time to give Speedwell Cottage back to its rightful owner.'

Harry pushed a bunch of keys on a key fob she recognised across the table.

'I don't understand.'

'Speedwell is your place. It always was.'

\*\*\*

Willow apologised to Mavis as she pushed her to her limits, keeping up with the Land Rover ahead. After much fuss, Jez and Milly had manoeuvred Harry into the vehicle as he demanded. He didn't want to miss Willow's reaction on seeing the house. Nate insisted he accompany Willow, filling the car with his presence and an uncomfortable silence as they left the village behind and drove up into the Moors. Patches of purple showed promise of the stunning display of heather to come in the following weeks. They turned into a narrow potholed lane. Willow's eyes widened and she took a sharp breath. Trembling, she parked the car.

'This really is Grandma Jax's house. When you said I couldn't I ...' she garbled. Nate grinned and unfolded himself from the Morris Minor and walked round to open her door.

'Shall we?'

The house was more weathered than she remembered, but the tiled roof that she recalled Grandma Jax telling her was once thatched, the rambling rose, and the dull brass bumble bee door knocker on the door with its circular window were the same.

Harry stood next to her, leaning heavily on a stick. 'Family always came in through the kitchen door. Come with me, lass.'

The twins and Nate stood back as the pair made their way round the house into the gardens, tenderly cared for by Harry's family. She looked up to see the attic room windows. Her heart skipped a beat. Her old room.

The key turned perfectly in the door, and they entered the kitchen. The dresser from her childhood still dominated the room, as did the large farmhouse table. The Belfast sink and Aga remained, but someone's attempts to update the cupboards and the haphazard addition of a modern oven filled her with distaste. She sighed and tears threatened to fall as they went into the other parts of the house. Her grandmother's belongings had been stripped away, leaving a shadow of the home it was. Harry touched her arm.

'They put that in to encourage the rental market. It failed. People never stayed long. Quite a lot of her stuff is in my garage. When she passed away, the solicitors dealing with her estate let us know when the house was due to be cleared. We rescued what we could. Her books, teapots, and the like. Hope it was the right thing to do. Hate to feel we stole them.'

Willow gave him a hug. 'You did right. I appreciate everything and thank you for looking after her and being her friend. I hated thinking she was alone.'

'My dear, despite her crotchetiness and isolation, she was still part of the village; Mexenby folks always look after their own, witches included. Casseroles and cakes were left on her doorstep, and I always popped over to check up on her. Don't feel you let her down—she wasn't your responsibility; you were a kid. She understood. She'll be happy you're here now. You are staying, aren't you?'

She left the question unanswered. Nate and the others came in as Willow slipped through the back door and walked across the garden to the orchard she had seen through the window. Harry stopped him following.

'Leave her. She needs to do this alone.'

\*\*\*

The tree canopy shaded Willow from the bright sun and provided a welcome coolness. The sweet aroma of apples filled the air, and she could taste their sweetness with every breath. She walked in further. The leaves rustled and danced in the gentle breeze, providing a shimmering dappled green light. In the centre of the orchard was the tree she was looking for—old, craggy, and twisted. It bore no fruit unlike its younger counterparts. Tracing her hands across the rough bark, she could feel its life force, faint but steady under her palms. It had seen many seasons and held a special place in Jax's heart. It was mother to many of the surrounding trees and Willow couldn't help wondering if the pair had had a chance to say goodbye. She hoped so. A plan formed in her mind.

Kicking off her shoes, Willow sank her bare feet into the cold damp grass, closed her eyes, and opened her arms wide. Through a gap in the canopy, she whispered a word of thanks to the sun for the abundance of apples it provided and relished the warmth on her face, the tingle of heat spreading through her hands. She welcomed the energy flowing beneath her as she allowed herself to be connected to the power above and below and become part of the orchard. When Willow was a child Grandma Jax would bring her to the same spot and she'd watch her do the same, but now Willow was alone, feeling what Jax must have done—the welcoming the surrounding trees gave her, the sense of well-being and energy. A belonging.

Returning to Jax's tree, Willow placed her newly energised hands on the bark and closed her eyes. Her mind played out the story of Jax's life through the tree's lifespan; they had grown together—planted by Jax's father to celebrate her birth, it had seen her morph from infant to child full of mischief playing games and then to an adolescent hiding with a book in hand to escape chores, chaste kisses with boys to the proposal of marriage followed by the joy as she presented her own child to the tree. She saw the tears fall when Jax, dressed in black, mourned her husband, and then years later with greying streaks running through her hair, her only son. Jax's smile returned when she presented the tree with her newborn grandchild and Willow saw glimpses of her own childhood, of her dancing among the trees collecting blossom or windfall. It was Jax who ate the first apple the tree had ever produced, and the last. Jax was the one who wassailed to it every year. Willow felt the tree's sorrow at the loss of its friend, but the joy at Willow's return.

Willow opened her eyes. Buds of white blossom appeared on the branches and unfurled into full bloom. She reached up and picked off a sprig with a whispered thank you. Moments later, the blossom fell like confetti over her feet and the fruit it bore ripened to match those in the neighbouring trees. With another word of thanks and a bow, she caught one as it fell. Harry had asked if she was staying, and the trees had given her their opinion.

Nate and Harry, along with the twins, stood on the threshold of the cottage to see Willow walk towards them biting into an apple, apple blossom tucked behind her ear. Nate had never seen her so happy and alive, relaxed and radiant.

'Well,' said Harry, 'it looks like a witch has returned to Mexenby and a new chapter has begun.'

Chalky greeted Willow with an excited wag as she approached the house, followed by a slower Harry.

'That's a sight,' he said, pointing to the blossom in her hair. 'The orchard must be as pleased as I am that you're here.'

'It is. I just don't understand how I didn't know this was mine. I've been searching for it for a long time.'

Harry went quiet, considering his response. 'I have my suspicions it was something to do with your stepfather. Jax made sure your inheritance was put in a trust until you were old enough. Twenty-one, I believe. The Brownes from the village dealt with it all acting on your behalf but must have consulted him. If he kept Jax's death a secret, it doesn't surprise me he did the same here. When it was your birthday, we expected you, but you never came. Then when we heard he died, the Brownes tried to find you again, but no joy.'

'Wait. Stuart is dead?'

'Yes, love, didn't you know?'

'No. We became estranged when I left home at sixteen.'

'Oh my. I'm sorry, but glad you got away. Jax always said he was a bad sort. Your mum never saw it and it caused a right row. That and Jax's use of magic.'

'I can't believe he is dead. When?'

'Christmas after your twenty-first birthday.'

'I was travelling, India then China. I love tea. In fact, I have a shop called the Enchanted Emporium in Whitby. Specialises in tea and magic.' Willow struggled to comprehend the turn of events. He was dead. The last part of her childhood was over. Three bombshells had hit in the last few days, which must mean she was due for calm, and here was the ideal place for it.

'Jax would be proud. Never wanted you to hide who you were. It's not the Mexenby way. She'd be happy to see you in love and settled too. Nate's a good sort.'

'There's no Nate and me. He's married.'

'Really? He never said. Well, my old bones are getting tired and so are Chalky's. By the time the twins drop me off, it'll be time for a siesta, then afternoon tea. The old bird will be fussing about my whereabouts. Worse than my grandchildren. Please visit me soon.' With a promise made, he walked away, paused, and called back.

'Advice from an old man. When someone talks, make sure you listen with your heart.'

# Chapter Forty-Five

'I don't understand how you found this place. Do you know how many hours I've spent searching for it using maps and the internet?' Willow watched the water bumble over the rocks and pebbles, and the ripples extend from the stick she threw in before it floated down the stream and tangled in the weeds. On the edge of Grandma Jax's land, it was a place she believed fairies played and lured travellers away. Being there after all these years felt surreal, especially in the presence of Nate.

'I could say serendipity. A wrong turn here and there. But.' He ran his hand along the back of his neck and shuffled his feet on the riverbank. 'I'd be lying. I hired a private investigator. They phoned me just as I was leaving Whitby.'

'You hired a PI? For me?'

He nodded. 'I knew how much it meant to you. It was the least I could do. Thank goodness, Jez didn't phone the police accusing me of breaking and entering when he caught me snooping around the cottage to check whether this really was the place. Found it yesterday. Don't you ever answer your phone?'

She ignored his question. He'd found this for her. Her heart pounded with a reignited emotion for him, but her head screeched at it to stop. 'Wait. What are you doing up here? You're supposed to be on your honeymoon with your new wife.'

'My what?'

'Your wife, Rebecca. The one you rushed home to marry after your last night of freedom. I can't believe I was so stupid. I trusted you, shared everything with you, and foolishly believed what you said.' Rage boiled up inside her, pushing gratitude aside, and a rush of electricity spread to her fingers. Sparks of magic longed for a release.

'I meant everything I said.'

'You're married, Nate.'

'Where did you hear that from?'

'Amber. Don't deny it, Nate. I saw the photos. You and her at the Christmas Ball days before we met. Her recent declaration of love and joy at being Mrs Reynolds. Both times we were together, you were with her.'

'Shit!' Nate raked his hand through his hair, grabbed her arm, but the jolt of energy forced him to release it. 'Ow. Fuck. It's not what you think. Did you see the photos uploaded yesterday?'

'No. I saw enough. Besides, you know I don't use social media.'

'Which is why I never thought it'd be a problem. I mean—' Nate frantically scrolled his phone, cursing the lack of signal under his breath, '—I bet Amber wouldn't show you the new ones, even if she checked. She hates me. Yes, I took Rebecca to the Christmas Ball and yes, we were engaged. But by Christmas Day, as far as I was concerned, it was over. I promise.' He braved touching Willow again, turned her towards him, and lifted her chin up so she could see the intensity in his eyes. 'Rebecca married Jamie, not me.'

'Jamie?' He gave her his phone, allowing her to scroll the wedding photos. Willow was transfixed by the stunning bride she recognised, beaming at the camera, wrapped in the groom's arms, with Nate standing to one side.

'Jamie, my globetrotting influencer brother, swept her off her feet when I was too busy at work trying to provide her the lifestyle she declared she wanted. The brother who, unknown to me, was the man I caught in my bed on the day of the Ball.'

'He did what? That makes no sense.' Yet the photo proved otherwise.

'What doesn't? The fact she fell in love with him and married him months later? If you saw his Instagram feed, you'll know many women want to marry him. He receives several proposals every day.'

'I've seen his Instagram. I can use Google, you know, I'm not a complete Luddite. Besides, her post said Mrs N. Reynolds, not J. And there were no photos of him anywhere on her page. Just you.'

'His full name is Noel James after being born unexpectedly on Christmas Eve. He detests his name and has always been Jamie. Rebecca has been on a social media blackout since Christmas, and they've kept their relationship secret from everyone except a select few.'

'Why?'

'You've seen what the media's like. A scandal about him having an affair with his brother's girlfriend would've ended his career. Sponsors would run a mile. Rebecca also wanted a fairy-tale wedding without the press. Now they're married, the media will focus on that. I'd no idea it looked like me and her were still together on bloody Facebook. Or it'd affect us. I had to go back for the wedding. I was his best man.'

'His best man? How could you do that? They cheated on you.'

'They did, but meeting you made me realise you can fall in love deeply in a moment and I never had that with Rebecca. Why should I stand in their way? They deserve happiness. They followed their hearts. Like I should have done. When you told me to leave, I decided to let the dust settle instead of fighting for you. And then, I worried what would happen if the media linked you with the potential Jamie scandal. With the Clara feud, they'd have had a field day. Instead, I tried to forget you. Which is impossible. I never realised by waiting I'd lose you to Glenn.'

'Glenn? What's he got to do with this? We're just friends.'

'So you said. Yet I saw you kissing on the beach.'

'You were there?'

'You didn't answer my calls or messages, so after the wedding I came up to check you were okay and tell you everything. I bumped into Amber, who said you've been together for months. Yet you call me a cheat.'

'She what? I'll bloody kill her. Amber lied. There is no me and Glenn, there never has been and never will. That kiss you saw was thanks to her slipping a love potion into our drinks. I can just about forgive her that, every witch gets tempted to meddle in other people's lives with good intentions, but lying...' Anger flared, sending a blue ball of energy flying from her fingers. It skipped across the stream until it scorched a patch of grass opposite. Stunned, she froze. Her magic never did that before.

Nate stepped forward, wrapped his arms around her, and drew her into an embrace, distracting her from the damage.

'I could have lost you.'

'But you didn't, Willow, I'm here. Speedwell Cottage is here, and you've discovered your family history,' Nate cajoled. 'Everything has turned out okay.'

His words and embrace soothed her, and any remaining anger directed at Amber notched down to a simmer.

'I love you, Willow Anderson, even when you're angry.'

'You do?' His fingers caressed her face and brought his lips closer to hers so she could feel his words dance in the air between them.

'I do.'

\*\*\*

Willow grabbed Nate's hand and led him up the stairs of the Old Ram, away from prying eyes. With the apple blossom still tucked behind her ear, the energy and sense of well-being from the orchard pulsed in her blood; she felt alive. The world was calmer, colours brighter, and her more acute senses tuned into the hum of the earth, of nature. She could hear each individual note of the birds' melody outside, the soft creak as a rosebud in a vase opened, and smell each component of the blend of Nate's aftershave. The electricity she'd experienced the first time she held Nate on that cold night was nothing compared to this. She needed to share the energy buzzing through her, and allow him to feel the power. She longed for his touch. To feel the intensity of each stroke, caress, and kiss.

Locating his room, he wasted precious minutes rummaging in his pocket for the key before she led him into the bedroom. She slammed the door behind him, securing the lock. Wasting no time, she kissed him. The heat and passion made him respond instantly. Clothes flew across the room, as they both undressed, eager to touch each other with no barriers. Her skin shimmered with magic and any ghosts in the Old Ram soon averted their eyes, allowing the Mexenby witch to claim her man in peace.

'Well, that was different,' Nate said, holding a contented Willow tight. 'I could get used to sleeping with the Mexenby witch.'

'I don't think you could call that sleeping.'

'So I wasn't dreaming the sparks, lights and—'

'No, you weren't. Who knew what a walk in the orchard could do?' said Willow.

'Maybe we should do it again just to make sure I wasn't asleep.' His fingers trailed across her back, sending shivers through her body. She edged away.

'I can't. I have to go back home. Vincent needs me, and I need to lock up.' *And tackle Amber.*

'Phone Rosa. She'll do it. Just say you've some amazing gossip to tell her tomorrow. She'll be more than happy to help.'

'I guess.' He was right. Without details, today's events would satisfy Rosa's desire for juicy gossip.

'Come on, Mexenby needs its witch to stay the night, even in a bed that isn't made for one, never mind two. I suspect Arnie wants to celebrate your return, and so do I.'

Willow picked up her phone and dialled the Emporium.

# Chapter Forty-Six

Amber fled the Emporium, feigning illness as the reason she couldn't stay. Rosa, full of concern, let her go, adding to the guilt she already felt. After the in-depth lecture she'd had from her dad about inappropriate use of magic and his confession about his feelings for a woman called Lorna, Amber had welcomed Willow's absence when she arrived for her shift. It was short-lived, cut short by Rosa's overflowing need to gossip about Willow rushing out to see Nate, of all people.

Another wave of nausea threatened as she hoisted her rucksack on her shoulder and attempted to ignore Beetle squirming and protesting at his containment in her side bag. Running away unnoticed was hard enough with bright blue hair, but a ferret draped around her shoulder would guarantee attention. Once Willow spoke to Nate, Amber's deceit would be revealed, and however white the lie, she'd see it as an ultimate betrayal. Everything was falling apart. Glenn had a date set up with Lorna. Willow was still alone, and she still hadn't discovered who the poison letter writer was.

Garth looked up from his manga magazine as she stumbled into the shop and rolled his eyes. Refusing to react, Amber left her rucksack on one of the sofas and made her way to the back rooms. She wouldn't be long; she'd be out of his radar as soon as she collected her portfolio of designs she'd forgotten. Maybe they'd be enough for her to get an apprenticeship elsewhere. Artie said she had talent. The staffroom was spotless and sparse of furniture apart from a couple of chairs and table. A far cry from the Emporium's cosiness, but she'd miss it. The heartache of leaving Willow and Rosa was expected, but it surprised her how reluctant she was to say goodbye to this place. Bones Ink had only been part of her life for the summer, but she had no choice. She couldn't hang around.

She knew her eyes were red, puffy, and she looked a state without make-up disguising her blotchy skin, but she didn't care what he thought of her, she just needed to collect her portfolio of designs. Maybe someone would offer her a job based on them.

'Amber,' Artie's voice came from his studio, 'is that you? I've a customer who may be interested in a design of yours. What's happened?'

Holding her notebook close to her chest, she bumped into him as he came to find her. With red puffy eyes and no make-up, she couldn't hide her distress.

'What happened?'

Unable to answer, the truth too mortifying and complex, Amber burst into tears. The following hug and mug of tea made her feel worse. Any other time, his attention would have been a dream come true. But now it added to the shame.

'Look. Whatever's happened don't run away on impulse. Here's the key to my flat upstairs. Stay and decide what to do tomorrow, please.' Fatigue overwhelmed her, and with a meek smile, she reluctantly agreed.

The flat with its high ceilings and tall windows was larger than Willow's, and Artie's minimalist approach to furniture added to the sense of space; the large television, gaming console and gaming chairs showed a side of him she didn't know. The sound of her grabbing a Coke she found in Artie's fridge alongside the cans of lager woke Beetle up and he crawled out from the shoulder bag she wore. In reality, she should have left him at home, but Amber couldn't face it. He was her only friend, the one she could trust and who loved her unconditionally.

'Come on then—'she scooped him up, '—let's find our room for the night.' She snatched up her bag and headed to the room Artie said she could stay in, declaring his housemate was away. The warm feminine atmosphere with extensive cushions and knick-knacks dotted around surprised her, and despite the excess pink, it was a relief from the sweaty socks and lingering stale aftershave she'd expected.

Rummaging through her bag, Amber pulled out Jack's hoodie and slipped it on. How could she have misjudged things so badly? She bit her lip. First, she messed up with Jack and now Willow. They'd be better off without her. She couldn't fix the past, but maybe she could discover who penned the letters. Maybe Willow wouldn't hate her so much then.

She found one of the envelopes the perpetrator had written on in her book. It would have to do. The letters remained on her desk for her dad to find, so he could warn Willow of the dangers lurking in the shadows. She deserved to know the truth, even if Amber was too cowardly to tell her in person. Amber checked the time. At three in the afternoon, she doubted the perpetrator would be asleep; Whitby wasn't the Mediterranean where siestas were popular, but it was worth a try. While practising dream walking, she discovered many people drifted into daydreams mid-afternoon.

It was all she needed. Beetle stood expectantly as she cast a circle around herself, but it did little to calm her unease. With her apothecary box at home, she didn't have access to the herbs for added protection; she had to do this alone. Holding her necklace tight in one hand and the letter in the other, she closed her eyes.

The shock of arriving in his dreamscape nearly hurtled her awake. It took effort to remain. She did it. She was in his dream. The euphoria was brief. Panic set in. Instead of observing from a distance, she was sitting in the back of a car. The space was restrictive, and the overwhelming smell of new leather upholstery made her nauseous. Approaching footsteps forced her to pull her hood up further and shrink down.

*Do not look. Please do not look.*

He didn't. The driver's door opened, and he slid in. Her viewpoint gave little away. He was tall, with light brown hair, dressed in an expensive grey suit, and when he lifted his arm to rub his neck, a cufflink shone in the sunlight. She couldn't see his face. Damn it, that's all she needed.

He revved the car engine and shot down the road at speed. The landscape flew by as they drove through the countryside, tyres squealed as he took the corners without braking. Faster and faster he went. A tree loomed ahead. They were going to hit it. Amber screamed and lifted her arm to shield her face, her sleeve rolled up. He looked in the rear-view mirror and his piercing eyes met hers.

# Chapter Forty-Seven

**W**illow woke lying in Nate's arms, precariously on the edge of the bed. She feared any movement would send her tumbling to the floor.

'Do you think Arnie has another room available? This bed isn't made for two.'

'Milly said not. Maybe after we have drunk a few pints, it won't matter.'

Willow's mobile sprang to life with the rendition of Mungo Jerry's "Summer Time". She ignored it, but it rang again and again. She rolled over, refusing to acknowledge Nate's raised eyebrows at her music choice. He caught her before she fell.

'Hi Glenn. What's up?'

'Is Amber with you?'

The earlier anger she felt towards Amber threatened to flare when Glenn mentioned his daughter's name but retreated with the touch of Nate caressing her arm, grounding her as the orchard had done. The teenager's actions were foolish and ill-judged, but when the red mist subsided, she knew Amber didn't lie maliciously or out of spite. It wouldn't be fair to involve Glenn; she would deal with her apprentice alone.

'No. I'm out of town at the moment. Why?'

Glenn's silent protracted pause chilled her. She slipped out of bed to snatch her clothes strewn over the floor. Following her lead, Nate stumbled out of bed with a thud followed by a 'Fuck' as he hit his head on the sloping roof.

'Where are you?' Glenn asked.

'I'm with Nate. It's a long story. What's going on, Glenn?' She listened to him explain. 'I'll be with you soon.'

Amber was missing.

***

Nate squeezed himself into the compact car, his head touching the ceiling and knees bent ridiculously high. If she weren't so anxious, she'd have laughed at the absurdity of the sight.

'You don't have to come,' she said, reversing Mavis out of the pub carpark.

'Don't be silly. I'm not being left behind again. You have a knack for disappearing yourself. Just go slow over the cattle grids, please.' Nate buckled himself in, regretting the last pint of the Old Ram's special. 'Or better still, drive my car.'

She scowled at his request. She needed the comfort of her own car and the distraction of driving to prevent her mind from reeling with concern, rather than being a passenger in Nate's smooth top-of-the-range Land Rover.

'Let me get this straight, no one has seen her since this morning when she lied about being ill. Maybe she's gone to clear her head at a friend's place. She is eighteen. She'll be fine.' He was unsure of the need to panic.

'I hope so, but Glenn said her clothes and Louise's journals are missing and something about some strange letters that were clearly not sent to her.' Willow waited for him to make the connection that was worrying her.

'You think they're from Rafe.'

The icy fingers of fear clenched her heart as she nodded. 'And it gets worse. She's not been sleeping and having nightmares, which may make her powers unstable. The last time that happened, she was in ICU for weeks. We need to find her.'

# Chapter Forty-Eight

The beer flowed, and people huddled in crowds, laughing and talking around a small bonfire. The bass of the music from someone's Bluetooth speaker acted as the heartbeat of the party with the regular whoosh of the sea hitting the shore. Amber slipped her boots off, allowing her bare feet to sink into the golden sand, watching the people mingle. When Artie invited her, she'd jumped at the chance, but doubts formed. She didn't belong, not fully. Amber loved the conversations with Artie about art, tattoos, the world, and he didn't flinch at her witchy quirks she accidentally revealed, but his friends were older, working or not, and treated her as a kid. And that's how she felt, a child out of her depth. Home appealed, and she longed to talk to Glenn and for him to make things better. She'd messed up. Big time. Had he noticed she'd gone yet? She hoped not. Artie's invite had delayed her plan to be miles away by now.

She sat down to watch the sun's daily farewell. The bright colours were forever changing, proud to show its power and glory. Unlike Willow, who loved the moon, the sun's energy with its changing canvas and artistry attracted Amber. The summer had started with such promise and hope. It should have been the best one yet. Three months of no education or revision pressure; it was her time to have fun with Jack. To work and save money for their travels. All her plans had crumbled, and it was her fault. She turned on her phone, debating whether to text Jack an apology, explain, and confess how badly she had behaved. All she wanted was for her dad and Willow to be happy. The kiss was supposed to seal the deal and when she'd seen Nate walking on the shoreline, a spike of anger and fear flared. His presence would ruin it all. The lie about her dad's relationship slipped out before she could stop herself. Such a small lie, but it snowballed into a tangled mess of shame and deceit. His face had crumpled at the news. The enormity of her lie crushing her was made worse by the recent posts on Rebecca's newsfeed with another man as her husband. She'd completely messed up.

A woman she recognised waved to her, calling her over. Amber brushed herself off. It was time to have fun, in the hope it would wash the sadness away.

Amber swayed in time with the music, her body relaxing more as she gulped another mouthful of beer. The first sips tasted bitter, making her splutter. How could her dad have consumed so much of this stuff? The answer came as a calmness washed over her and she felt a disconnection from her thoughts. She was in her body, but not. Not too dissimilar to dream walking, but she was awake in her own life. She welcomed the numbness from pain. All she had to do was listen to the music. Artie's laughter drifted across the crowd and, like the moth to the bright moonbeams, she weaved her way through the sweating bodies towards him. She giggled. He was her moon. Jack didn't matter. Artie had invited her to the party and given her a place to stay. He cared. He'd make everything okay.

'Oh, here she is. My prodigy.' Artie draped his arm around her, making her swoon. 'I'm glad you came. Grab yourself another drink.'

Introductions made, a new confidence emerged as she spoke about her designs to interested bystanders. Why did she think she didn't belong? They listened; Artie listened. In the light of the bonfire's flames, Amber studied him. He was more handsome than before, but fuzzy around the edges. *I'm drunk*, she decided, *and I like it.*

A stunning woman approached, snuggled in a picnic blanket. Artie's eyes lit up as she kissed him on the cheek, and he wrapped his other arm around her. 'Chloe, there is someone I'd like you to meet. Amber, this is Chloe, my business partner and fiancée.'

'I'm thrilled to meet you.' Chloe held her hand out to Amber and awarded her with a radiant smile. 'Artie's talked about you and your designs non-stop. It's lovely to finally put a face to the name. And I've an idea I'd love to discuss with you for when this one is born.'

Amber's heart imploded at her words and the sight of Chloe's round stomach. Not only was Artie in a relationship, but he was also about to be a father.

'I need to go.' Artie's friends let her pass, and she fled further down the beach.

\*\*\*

Cursing, Amber berated herself. He didn't see her as anything but a child. He never had. She headed towards the sea, away from the crowd. She sank onto the sand, cradled her legs, and allowed the tears to flow. The shock of Chloe's arrival, the waves lapping over her feet, and sea air, cleared some fog clouding her thoughts. A fool. She was such a fool.

The back of her neck prickled. Someone was watching from the beach huts. She turned. *Bloody Clive. Goddess, he is creepy.* No wonder Willow disliked him, though the feelings were mutual with his tales of devil worship and Hell he spewed whenever he saw her. Amber chuckled every time she passed the estate agent's with the witch ball hanging in the window and the horseshoe above the door designed to keep witches away. They meant nothing, a false hope to make him feel better. A witch could enter and purchase a property from him, and he wouldn't even know. He arrogantly strolled around the town, in his highly polished Italian-made shoes, bespoke suits, and slicked-back hair, as if he should be adored. He tracked her as she stood and walked along the shoreline. It didn't surprise her when she heard and felt the thump of his footsteps behind her.

'You look like you have the world on your shoulders. Awful day?' he said, approaching her. 'Why not have another beer? It helps you relax.'

He was being nice. Why was he being nice? Where were the anger and declarations of abomination? 'Go on,' he urged. 'You'll feel better.'

Amber's eyes blurred and struggled to keep him in focus. Swaying, she prepared to argue, but resigned, she just took the beer and took a long swig.

'Do you want to tell me about it?'

She shook her head. Nothing made sense. He continued to speak, and his nasal whine mellowed. Maybe he wasn't as bad as she thought. Attractive in a way Artie never could be. A breeze picked up, whipping her hair across her face; she swiped it away.

His hand shot out and grabbed her arm, twisting it to reveal her dragonfly tattoo. His face filled with a white rage.

'It's you! You're the witch who has been haunting my dreams.'

# Chapter Forty-Nine

Nate watched Vincent's emotions flick from overjoyed to see Willow to concerned and on guard in an instant. The witch and her familiar were clearly attuned to each others moods, and he knew it would take a while to get used to the close bond. Glenn remained at his home in case Amber returned, as the police assured him she would. The hope she'd be at the Emporium faded when they came back to darkness.

'Tea,' Nate said, sliding the cup over to Willow sitting at the table with several cream letters in front of her. She paled, reading each one. They were vile rants and threats, and each letter began with *Dear Goldilocks*.

'I don't understand why she has them and they weren't delivered to you. Or why she didn't give them to you?'

'Protection. They wouldn't have been able to get to the Emporium because of the property's protection spells. I cast them after the first letter, and she bolstered them up while I was ill. Unlike the first letter, he posted these. My guess is he tried to hand deliver the second one, but the spells repelled it, so he used the postal service, assuming the postal workers to be immune.'

'But they're not?'

'No, but ever since I moved in, our regular post-person developed a system which has worked for years. He must have told Amber about it, allowing her to intercept the letters. When we first opened, I had a flurry of letters objecting to bringing magic to the area, especially with the shop's terrible reputation. Some were horrid. A similar protective spell was cast. Any letters unable to pass through the alley are left with a neighbouring shop. The Emporium doesn't react well with negative energy.'

'What happens if they try to deliver?'

'With my spell, a sense of unease, extreme anxiety and nausea. Enough to warn people to back off. Amber's spell, I'm not sure. All I know is it's more powerful than mine.'

'She's that good?'

'More than she knows, which concerns me. If she has tried to deal with this on her own, I dread to think what she could've done.'

'Her disappearance may be unconnected. It looks like she's run away.'

'But where to? Something's not right. What happens if Rafe has found her?'

Rafe. 'Shit.' Nate scrambled for his phone and opened his emails from Parson's Investigations. The report of Rafe Amenábar, forgotten in the excitement of Speedwell Cottage and lust. He scanned the document, his hold on his phone tighter the more he read.

'It isn't him.'

'What?' Willow looked up from the altar she was creating on the coffee table with crystals, a shell filled with water, candles, and other artefacts he didn't recognise.

'Speedwell Cottage wasn't the only thing Parson's Investigations were looking into. After you shared your story, I thought it would help you to know where he was. If he was still a threat. This is the report.'

Willow grabbed his phone, and while she read, he scanned the room. It had changed since he was last there. A large map of the Yorkshire Moors covered part of the wall. Pins dotted the potential places of Speedwell Cottage where Willow had checked and dismissed. Mexenby was nowhere to be seen. He peered closer, finding Fetherby, its nearest village, and tracked the main lane with his finger and smiled. It truly was hidden in plain sight, with Mexenby tucked away in the central crease. So easy to miss. Thank goodness Parson's had found the old rental advert in an archived local newspaper. Was Amber another case for them?

'He's in prison.' Willow's voice shook, Rafe's life in black and white bringing the fear back.

'Yes, for GBH of his current wife and assault on his previous one. Your Zugarramurdi witches were right when they said you had a lucky escape. With his grandmother dead, the Amenábar estate is run by his sister, Anna.'

'He could still be pulling strings inside jail. If he saw the photo, he could—'

'He didn't see the photo, Willow. Scroll down to the amendment on the last page. He lost his sight in a violent attack in his last jail. Witches aren't the only people to hate him.'

'But if it's not him, who has Amber?'

Nate wasn't sure anyone had Amber, but the threat to Willow was closer to home than a Spanish jail. Someone who knew her hair formed ringlets when it grew like the fictional thief. From her uni days? He sank down beside her on the floor to comfort her, but Vincent had the same idea. Leaping off the sofa, he dislodged the pile of scrapbooks perched there, and a box of old photos, obviously part of Willow's search for Grandma Jax's cottage. Letting Vincent soothe Willow, Nate gathered the scattered images up. Faded ones of the Emporium before she weaved her magic and made it into a success. They documented its revival.

'When was this?' He showed her one of her standing by a more sprightly Mrs Ramsey in front of the shop with its peeling paintwork but sparkling windows.

'When I first returned. She wanted to know what I'd bought. And ...' Fear crept across her face. 'My hair was longer. In the excitement of owning the shop, I forgot to cut and dye it. My roots and curls show. It could be anyone local.'

'We need to update the police. And Glenn. Is there anyone you remember from that time you befriended? Those trolls, did you—?

'Paint. I decorated the shop myself; it got everywhere in my hair. The night after that photo was taken I shaved it off when—' Willow paused, grasping a memory. 'No, it can't be. He's annoying, but a harmless creep.'

'Who?'

'Clive.'

'I disagree, Willow. He was full of malice that night in the pub. He hates you. Most places in town embrace the gothic atmosphere. Mercer's is a different story. It's the only estate agent's I know that takes active precautions against witches.'

'It's all talk. He wouldn't risk doing anything.'

'Are you sure? What did he do to make you cut your hair?'

'It was a misunderstanding. I wasn't lying about the paint in my hair, it was a nightmare, but soon after I moved in Clive paid me a surprise visit. Surprising because when I viewed the property, I could've sworn he feared the place, and he lost out on the commission because of his attitude. But he acted nice, charming even, so much I agreed to meet him at the pub after he said he'd found some information about the history of the place. It was an okay evening. I met some locals, except he was under the impression we'd been on some sort of date. When we left the pub, he tried it on. I rebuffed him but then he touched my hair. I reacted without thinking. The memories of Rafe overtook me, and I kneed him in his groin. As soon as I was home, I cut my hair. He has disliked me ever since. Later he was part of the campaign to close the shop until he became convinced I'd cursed him. His belief in hexes is quite handy as he stays out of the way.'

'So, nothing happened until Christmas?'

'Only glares and snide comments as he crossed the road to avoid me. I scare him.'

'What changed?'

'Nothing except you.'


The fire died down, leaving a chill in the air. Nate hoped it wasn't an unseen ghostly presence. Who haunted upstairs? Mrs Marley? He couldn't remember. He covered Willow with a blanket while she slept on the sofa, Vincent tucked in next to her, providing comfort and security. Overwhelming exhaustion hit after she'd performed a location spell with limited success. All she could detect was water, which being on the coast gave little information. Was she still in Whitby or had she travelled elsewhere? In desperation, Willow attempted scrying. While being more Amber's expertise, it had worked when Amber got into strife before. Images shimmered in the black mirror, showing water lapping over sand, a dragonfly tattoo. A man's hand. Willow's shock broke the tentative connection. Repeated efforts failed, but she kept trying until she keeled over.

Not prepared to leave her, he updated Glenn and hoped he'd persuade the police to search the beaches.

The banging on the shop door vibrated the old windows, waking Willow. Nate rushed downstairs first, trembling as he ran through an ice patch near the counter. 'Not now, Percy,' he muttered before taking stock of what he had said. He was talking to a ghost!

Willow threw him the keys as she entered the shop. He unlocked and opened the door.

There stood Amber, propped up by a man at least ten years her senior.

'Oh my Goddess, what's happened?' Willow sprang into action, wrapping her arms around the sobbing teenager who looked younger than he remembered, like the child she'd only recently left behind. Her pale skin was nearly translucent in the light of the old gas lamp, emphasised by the dark streaks of mascara and eyeliner. Amber crumpled against Willow, unable to speak for shivering. Nate noticed the dried blood beneath her laddered tights and her grazed elbows. He saw red.

'What have you done to her?' he snapped, taking in the stranger's dark clothes, tattoos snaking up his arms and neck, and his ponytail. If this man had hurt her—

'Nothing, mate. It wasn't me. I just brought her home. She's had too much to drink,' the man said, cradling his hand, bruises forming at his knuckles. 'And as for him, we sorted it.'

'It's true,' whispered Amber. 'Artie saved me.'

# Chapter Fifty

'Amber's still asleep. And Glenn will be over later to pick her up,' Nate said, placing a tray loaded with fresh croissants, jam, and tea brewing in a pot on the bed. He'd added a small jug of dahlias and valerian, hand-picked, she assumed from her yard.

'Interesting choice of flowers,' she commented, shifting further on the bed so he could sit next to her. Was he aware they meant commitment and readiness? Was it a message for him or her?

'What? I just thought they were pretty,' he replied, breaking open a croissant.

'They are. I love them, and breakfast. It was a late night. Thank you.' She leant over and kissed him. 'Amber and I spoke for hours but she's still adamant she won't talk to the police or press charges.'

'Why not? The more trouble that bastard gets into, the better.' Ever since he saw Amber's vulnerability last night, and heard her muffled anguish over Clive's letters, he'd wanted to grab Clive and finish what Artie started. One black eye wasn't good enough for him. Only Willow's insistence not to stopped him. He'd nearly lost her twice, he wasn't prepared to risk it again.

'In the scuffle before Artie arrived, Clive released her because Beetle bit him. Ferrets can be ferocious biters if provoked. And they are very loyal and protective. Always a good choice for a witch, I think. She believes if she presses charges for assault, Clive will respond by taking action against her for his injuries.'

'Well, if that's the case, I wonder what's going on at Mercer's Estate Agency. When I walked past to the bakery, the police were there and the staff look worried.'

'Maybe we should go there.' Willow ripped apart a croissant, releasing the warm, yeasty aroma, and smothered it with raspberry jam. 'After breakfast, of course.'


Their arrival at Mercer's Estate Agency was met with a flurry of frantic activity. Paperwork piled high on desks and a computer was in the process of being taken away by a police officer. Cold mugs of coffee remained on the desks of the pale, anxious employees.

'I'm sorry, we are closed today,' an agent, Laura, according to her name badge, said.

'We're looking for Clive,' Willow explained.

'Aren't we all? You'll have to join the queue.' Laura indicated for them to leave.

'What do you mean?'

'He has scarpered, hasn't he?' Laura said, ignoring the police officer's shake of the head. 'Head office flagged up an anomaly in the accounts yesterday. Before we had a chance to look at it, he'd gone. Disappeared with yesterday's takings too. It wasn't the only anomaly either. His business side is rife with them. Siphoning money meant for rental repairs into his own account and more. So, you'll just have to wait.'

'Can you tell me if my property, Speedwell Cottage in Mexenby, has been affected, please?'

Laura paled and the police officer came over. 'It was one of the first.'

*\*\**

Speedwell Cottage felt different from Willow's first visit. Was it because she was alone or had her orchard experience connected her to the house, making it truly hers? It welcomed her with the warmth she recalled as a child, and the sense of emptiness had receded. Dust motes still danced in the muted sunlight creeping through the grubby windows, several bleached shapes still lined the wallpaper where pictures once hung, and indented marks were all that remained of much of her furniture. But overnight, Grandma Jax's rocking chair had appeared near the hearth, as had the patchwork quilt folded on the seat. Picking it up, Willow stroked the threadbare material and tears threatened to fall. Many evenings, Grandma Jax wrapped it around herself while immersing Willow in the world of the fae, giants, and the Moors. The rhythmic creak of the chair and crackle of the fire added to the experience. This was home.

The large box on the kitchen table confirmed her suspicions the twins had been there under Harry's instructions. Written in a shaky cursive was a note.

*My dearest Willow,*
*These belong with you.*
*Love Harry x*

Removing layers of newspaper dated decades before, Willow peeked inside. She beamed with the unwrapping of a small red teapot and several cups she recognised, followed by a battered metal kettle with its accompanying whistle. Tears flowed as she discovered Grandma Jax's preferred cup and saucer as well as her own. A cloth bag next to the box held more treasured gifts: a bag of loose-leaf Yorkshire tea, sugar, biscuits, and the promise of milk in the fridge. With a thanks to her newfound friends, she did what she needed to do and put the kettle on.

Sitting in her childhood's favoured spot, the back doorstep, Willow sipped her tea. The fresh air enhanced the clarity of the taste, making her sigh with pleasure. She viewed her garden, as confirmed by Jax's solicitor that morning. After years of looking, Speedwell was hers. Mr Browne, Junior, also apologised for their handling of Jax's affairs and confirmed this cottage had been part of Clive's simple scam to divert money meant for repairs and upkeep of empty and rented properties on Mercer's books into his own bank account. No one had checked whether repairs were made or even needed. They trusted his word and the fake receipts he gave. She doubted Clive's threats were ever about her witchiness or jealousy as Nate speculated, but greed and fear they would uncover his fraud once she found Mexenby. No wonder he'd reacted on Boxing Day while Nate and she discussed her dreams of finding this place.

Strips of land lay fallow like the front garden, allowing nature to take over, rewarding her with a vibrant display of colour and sound. Her sharpened senses had not dampened overnight. The whistle of the swaying grasses and percussion of insects' wings as they darted from flower to flower accompanied the orchestra of birdsong. It was a perfect start of the day.

With the walled garden full of traditional herbs and plants, the orchard and small woodland, she could harvest her own ingredients for remedies and tea. A plan began to form for the future. They could extend the range offered at the Enchanted Emporium. Maybe even open a second store in the village. To the side of her property lay the smallholding area where Jax had kept her sheep and chickens. Speedwell Cottage was a place to be self-sufficient. The house required love and renovation to be habitable and become a home. She longed to start, but could she really leave her flat and ghosts behind?

***

The car door slammed. Nate walked round to the back, seeing Willow standing tall with her arms outstretched, looking into the distance. The gravel crunched beneath his feet, alerting her to his presence.

'When I was little, every sunrise Grandma Jax and I would say hello to the sun and at sunset she'd welcome the moon. I never realised the significance until I was older. Despite her sorrow and crotchetiness, she remained grateful for all she had. And harnessing their power. This place is special, don't you think?'

'Are you any closer to knowing what you want to do?'

'Maybe. Shall we go to the orchard?'

Holding hands, they walked down an avenue of trees. Willow reached to catch a ripe apple before it fell to the ground and gave it to him. The fresh sweetness took his breath away. There was only one tree in bloom.

'This is Jax's tree. Planted for her birth and I doubt it will see another year. It's having a final glorious farewell before it returns to the earth.'

She guided him further into the orchard to a smaller tree, smothered in fruit.

'This is mine. Not that I knew it until Harry told me. As much as I adore living in the Emporium, this is where I belong.'

Nate nodded and wondered why she sounded so surprised. Everyone saw it the moment she arrived at the Old Ram. He just hoped the ghosts at Whitby understood.

# Chapter Fifty-One

'What if they don't like me?' Amber said. The closer the starting date for university came, the more nervous she grew. Following her surprised success in her exams, her dream of studying fine art was becoming reality.

Willow put down the pestle and mortar to look directly at her apprentice; noting her damp eyes she felt a sudden tug of love. 'Ambs, phone your dad and tell him you're staying over here tonight?'

'But you and Nate are planning to go out.' She wiped her face with her sleeve, ruining her immaculate eyeliner.

'Just do it. Nate can fend for himself for the night. There is something we need to do.'

With her old backpack on her shoulder, Willow led Amber through the town with Vincent not far behind. The pubs were closed, and the few drunken customers staggered home. Tourist season was nearly over for another year. Darkness cloaked the quiet streets except for the occasional burning lights and flickers of blue screens. The sea crashed on the harbour and Willow tingled with a familiar anticipation. They reached the bottom of the 199 steps.

Amber stared at them. 'We're going up there?'

'Oh yes! I'll race you!'

'Are you trying to kill me? My lungs are burning,' moaned Amber, struggling to catch her breath. Willow had won by many steps. They strolled to the headland with the Abbey behind them.

'Stop moaning. You're young, you'll live. Now—take your boots off and socks. No excuses—just do it.' Amber followed her mentor's lead, muttering under her breath.

Willow's bare feet revelled in the dampness as they sank into the grass and her shoulders relaxed. Being here was the right thing to do.

'Do you know me and your mum would come up here every summer until I went travelling? The first time she demanded I took off my boots and socks. She rarely wore shoes if she could help it. She also suggested going sky clad, but I've only done it once and Yorkshire air is too cold to ever do it again. Anyhow, it was her who told me what I am telling you now. You are a witch! It's in your blood, your soul, so don't hide it. Those who are worthy of you will love you, witch or not, and they'll accept who you are. Feel the vibration of land under your feet, the connection to the universe above and the power of the feminine moon, but most of all be you.'

'But Dad didn't accept Mum as a witch,' Amber whispered.

'Maybe she didn't give him the chance. She never fully told him. Louise was great at giving advice, but when it came to her relationship with your dad she failed to take it for herself. As soon as they met, she fell hopelessly in love and was desperate to keep him. Despite her soul tingling with the knowledge he was the one, she didn't trust her instinct or him to reveal her true self. The depth of her feelings scared her. She hid most of her witchiness away, forced it into a box in fear he'd reject her. All her talents she revealed could be easily explained by her bohemian personality. Many people are attracted to crystals, gifted in gardening, and highly intuitive. And interested in herbal remedies without being a witch. Louise buried her magic and her beliefs until you came along. Then she needed her power to keep you safe, but even then, she was torn. Your dad loved her deeply. He felt the strength of the connection despite the lack of witch blood. He's learnt to accept your magic; he'd have accepted all of her if she'd trusted him enough. Their relationship would've been stronger for it.

'You'll be fine and will find friends who will become your support network. Trust your instincts and your magic. Your mum will always be with you as she is with me guiding the way, and I'm only a phone call away. So is your dad. He'll collect you anytime. Yes—' reading Amber's cynical mind, '—even with Lorna in his life. You are his girl. No one can take that away from you.'

'Do you feel that with Nate? The connection—the knowledge he loves you—all of you?'

'Pardon?'

'You heard. Do you?' Caught off guard, Willow couldn't answer. He said he loved her and was moving into her flat, but was that enough?

***

The two witches drank mugs of hot chocolate watching the sunrise from a bench overseeing the town. Beetle curled up on Amber's knee, tired from his joyful exploration of the surroundings. The night passed with Willow reminiscing about her university days with Louise, and Amber sharing her fears and her dreams. A hovering ball of witch fire cast by Willow kept them warm. For a witch who could rarely light a candle with magic, Speedwell Cottage had given her power a boost. It suited her, mused Amber, as did Nate. Now she knew the truth.

Whitby woke with the boats arriving at the harbour, attracting the screeching gulls circling above and a certain ginger tom. The distinct smell of smoked kippers rising to the clifftop made Amber's stomach growl.

'Come on, Vincent's hungry and so am I. Race you down to the bottom!'

The large breakfast served in the café sated Amber's and Willow's appetite, invigorated from the sea air, any remaining tension from the last few months dissipated. Amber felt lighter and the excitement of new beginnings returned. Her friendship with Jack was back on track after an intense heart-to-heart where he revealed his parents had separated, sending shockwaves through the perfect family. He'd been juggling with caring for his siblings, college work, and his own emotions. It hurt that he didn't confide in her, but who was she to talk? Dad was happy with Lorna, Willow had Nate for now, and university loomed. There was only one problem remaining.

'Any news about Clive?' she asked, biting back the fear his name still conjured.

'No. The detective in charge occasionally contacts me, but no new updates. Clive is still hiding but at least it's calm,' replied Willow, mopping up her last few baked beans with her toast.

Calm didn't stop Amber's worry a storm would brew again. Nor stop his face appearing in her dreams, reliving the moment on the beach. She needed to finish what he started. How could she move on without justice for what he did to Willow and her? She'd finally given a statement to the police, but it wasn't enough.

'Doesn't it make you angry and want to do something?'

'Of course, but I've Grandma Jax's now, and you are safe. They're the most important things.'

If Willow had no desire to act, Amber would act alone, but it'd be better with two. 'I've an idea to speed the investigation along.'

'No, Amber. Whatever it is, let the police deal with it.'

Willow's stern tone irritated Amber, but she remained calm. 'Please listen to what I have to say. You've just told me to trust my instincts, so I am. Clive will scam other people, and this will stop that. It'll be better with you, that's all.'

Willow leant back into the chair and folded her arms, glaring at her charge. 'So, you're saying whatever I think, you'll do it anyway? Didn't you hear what I said earlier about staying out of trouble?'

Amber smiled, nodding. 'I did, and agreed I'd stay out of danger while away. But I won't be at uni or alone if I'm with you at Speedwell Cottage.' She continued to talk.

# Chapter Fifty-Two

The brief rap on the Emporium's door interrupted Willow's thoughts. Grabbing the bowl of sweets, she glanced in the mirror to adjust her black velvet pointy hat. Halloween was the only day she dressed in the full garb of a stereotypical witch from her black dress and hat to her purple stripy stockings. Another drunken tradition Louise started, and Willow had revived to reward the few brave children who ventured into Witch's Yard. She was unsure which they preferred, the old, abandoned building hidden in darkness and cobwebs perpetuating the haunted legend, or the current one with the window display alight with candles, pumpkins, and bats.

She opened the door. A chill swooped around her ankles with an unusual display of affection from Black Cat. No one was there. An amber flicker on the doorstep caught her eye where the largest, most perfectly formed pumpkin she had seen glowed. She crouched down to see it more clearly. It was a work of art, the intricately carved design of a heart filled with ivy and flowers danced in the candlelight. A figure stepped out from the shadows in the courtyard.

'It nearly weighs as much as that blasted cat of yours,' said Nate, swooping down to pick it up and rotate it to reveal more carvings. Written in calligraphy, *Will you marry me?*

Words failed her as she reread the message again and again before stepping aside to allow him in. As the flickering pumpkin sat on the counter and illuminated the store, Nate knelt on one knee and held her shaking hand.

'I've loved you ever since I saw your dancing silhouette behind the Emporium's blind and heard your rendition of Boney M's 'Mary's Boy Child' through the door. It was untuneful, but blissfully happy. A complete contrast to the grouch who flung the door open. But she soon faded away. You and your magic captured my heart. I want to wake up with you every morning, debate the properties of tea vs coffee, and face any challenges ahead together. I want to see you sparkle every full moon when you return from the orchard or the headland. Willow Anderson, please, will you marry me?'

She stood in silence studying him, the curve of his face, the faint shadow of stubble on his chin that would be rough against her touch, and the scar on his hand holding a black box. He wanted to marry her. Be with her. Her heart skipped a beat, followed by a flood of warmth and happiness. This man she knew every inch of and thought she'd lost wanted all of her.

He snapped open the box to reveal a simple platinum diamond ring on a bed of velvet. 'It's beautiful,' she whispered.

'Come on, Wills. It's Samhain and a new moon. According to my trusted source, it's the ideal time to release the past and begin new projects and adventures. How about doing them with me? Vincent tolerates me—' nodding to the cat who edged closer to her, '—and the ghosts agree. I know they're here. Just like I know Mrs Marley watches me in the shower until she's dragged away. There is a distinct chill on my left side.'

Willow chuckled at Mrs Marley stammering to her husband. Nate asked again, 'Will you, Willow Sarah Anderson, marry me?'

She looked around. The old apothecary had paused his duties at the counter. Black Cat sat upright next to the orange pumpkin while the previous owner and wife stood side by side nodding. 'You always know the one, dear, and when you do it's time to share your heart,' said Mrs Marley, beaming.

Willow knew. She'd always known from the moment she reached out to help him from the tangled fairy lights.

'Please give me an answer. This floor is uncomfy and if they were not dead already, those three will die of suspense.'

'You want to marry me? Even with the ghosts?' Willow clarified.

'Even with added house guests.'

'And the teacups?'

'We can add to them if we must when we make memories together. But we need some mugs too.'

'Compromises have to be made, I guess.' Willow conceded and grinned. 'Yes. I'll marry you.' She squealed, pulling him up, and welcoming the familiar tingle flooding her body when she drew close. 'But no fancy churches. Or ...'

'Whatever you want.' He kissed her and lifted her onto the counter. The hat slipped off, but Nate caught it and placed it firmly on her head. 'Keep it on. It suits you. When I imagined this moment, I never once saw you in an outlandish outfit.'

Their kisses deepened until she pulled away. 'I think we need to stop. You're making Mrs Marley blush.'

'Maybe we should go upstairs to celebrate?' His fingers caressed her back and hovered over the buttons of her dress. It was tempting to agree, but she shook her head.

'You will have to wait. It's Samhain. We witches have things to do.'

# Chapter Fifty-Three

The orchard glittered with the fairy lights strung between the bare branches and they illuminated the sparkling frost crunching beneath their feet. Magic and apprehension hung in the air. The winter chill forced Willow to tug her ruby-red cloak tight around her as they approached the clearing and the altar Glenn had made from a fallen tree. Grateful for its warmth, she still thought dressing like an extra for *The Lord of the Rings* was ridiculous and unnecessary, but Amber insisted it was crucial to the plan. Dressed in an emerald cloak, Amber wore hers with a confidence Willow wished she had. Her doubts grew about the idea when she discovered the finer details, particularly the part involving Beetle who was currently raiding Amber's bag on the floor. His bushy demeanour reflected his excitement at the current adventure.

'You're asking me to put my life in the paws of a ferret,' Willow said.

'No. I'm asking you to trust me with your life. Beetle is just backup and knows what to do if he senses danger here. He'll alert me, and we'll be back here in a blink.'

'And vomiting.'

'You're only sick if we come back too quick. I've prepared peppermint tea just in case.' Amber shrugged, undeterred by Willow's hesitancy and risk aversion. Dream walking was safer than soul walking, and she'd survived that. If anything went wrong, all they needed to do to come out of the shared dream was wake up. Beetle knew to nip Amber if danger approached. And Vincent would follow suit.

Willow looked at Amber and saw the witch she was and the witch she would become. Her chin thrust upwards, absorbing nature's energy, and her fingertips tingled with magic; she was no longer the gawky teenager she first met. The wings on the dragonfly inked on Amber's arm fluttered, and it preened its feet, ready for flight. To do this, Willow needed to hand over control to her young charge. Could she trust her? How could she not? This was Louise's daughter, the child Willow promised to look after not realising how much she'd receive in return. The one Louise knew had more magic potential at four than she knew how to handle. If anyone could do this, Amber could. And if she walked away, Amber wouldn't. She refused to let go of the desire to bring Clive to justice with a stubbornness on par with a terrier in a shed full of rats.

Music drifted from the cottage and the fairy lights flickered as ghosts of the orchard materialised, emerging in the shadows of the tree, Willow's ancestors drawn out by Amber's power to offer their support. Vincent settled on the limb of a large apple tree, watching the two witches cast a circle.

With Beetle curled around Amber's neck, she set out the altar while Willow lit the candles with witchfire, in awe that it was successful. Louise was right, Willow's innate magic just needed to come home to flourish and once tonight was over she'd experiment to know how far she'd come. Candlelight bounced off Willow's ring, making Amber squeal with delight.

'He did it and you said yes.' Incantations were temporarily forgotten as she grabbed Willow's hand. 'It's beautiful. I'd have preferred a skull myself, but it's perfect for you. I have so many questions about the proposal.'

'Which can wait until we've done this. Come on, let's do it. I want to celebrate with Nate,' Willow said.

Amber nodded and stepped away.

It was time to trust Amber and herself. She poured the swirling potion she'd made earlier into the goblet. Magic rumbled beneath their feet, with an incantation and plea for guidance from the Goddess; the spirits gathered around the cast circle, adding an extra layer of protection from outside danger. Willow reached for the lone apple on a nearby tree and sliced it open. She dripped the potion onto the creamy flesh and watched it take a blue hue as it soaked in. Each took a half, and while holding hands, they simultaneously took a bite. In seconds, they slumped to the ground, sleeping while Beetle guarded them until their return.

\*\*\*

Their arrival was quick and simple. There were no flashing lights, spiralling tunnels, or the visual disturbances Willow had imagined or seen on TV. One minute, she was in the orchard, and the next she was in a landscape not of her own making. She looked round at the Mediterranean villa with its whitewashed walls and rustic furniture.

'That's a relief,' Amber said, releasing her hand. 'Buildings are easier to navigate and safer with more places to hide. I was concerned we'd end up in his driving dream. He likes fast cars and is a reckless driver. This location will be fun. Come on, we need to find him.' They crept down an empty corridor with silent footsteps, looking into every room.

'Stay out of sight. For now. You'll be the last flourish,' said Amber said. Willow bit her lip and silently apologised to Louise, fearing this would be the night she witnessed what her friend's daughter was truly capable of. Wide-eyed, the teenager resembled a child given permission to run riot in a sweet shop or a witch given unrestricted access to ancient grimoires.

The kitchen looked out onto an idyllic scene of a clear blue sky and an orchard of orange trees. After the freezing conditions at home, she welcomed the dry heat and her mouth watered at the vibrant fruits' citrus fragrance in the air. Peering round the door, she watched Amber enter the room. Clive stood at the sink with his back to them. He paused at a sound or unexpected breath above the chirp of the cicadas outside. Water flowed over his hands into the bowl of soapsuds.

Who washes up in their dreams? Amber was right when she declared some dreams were mundane. It was time to add some excitement. *Come on, turn around*, both witches urged. All they needed was an acknowledgement or a simple response like eye contact for the fun to begin. Nothing. He continued to stare out of the window. It wasn't going to work. He was trying to wake himself up. Willow stepped back. Something darted and zipped in the air towards him. Amber's dragonfly had released itself from the confines of her skin. Clive flung his arm up in defence as it flew around him.

'Get it off me.' He spun round and stared at the figure cloaked in green. The game could commence.

The insect retreated at Amber's command. Clive ran through the open kitchen door to the terrace with the young witch in pursuit. As she raised her arms, dark clouds rolled in. A flick of her wrist sent a fork of lightning down from the sky. The loud crack echoed through the orchard and the smell of burning confirmed a tree took a direct hit. Clive turned. His pale face was visible in the glow of witch light Amber held in her hand.

'What do you want from me?' he said.

'It is not what I want. This is about her.' Amber smirked, nodding in Willow's direction.

She stepped forward, releasing energy balls from her fingers, and willing them to morph into woodland sprites. Imagination was key, and the sense of power it produced was intoxicating. No wonder Amber fought against reining it in.

The creatures flew around him, poking and prodding, forcing him to back up against a tree. They shrieked with laughter as they surrounded him. He paled further and stammered incoherently. Another flash of lightning lit up the sky.

'One elephant. Two elephants. Three elephants. Four—' Amber counted. The roar of the thunder vibrated across the landscape.

'Look, I don't know why you're haunting me. I've done nothing to you. You witches are all the same. Hateful creatures.'

His rant stopped as more lightning flashed, and Amber counted up to three elephants tracking the storm. 'You don't like storms, do you? Made you quiver under the bed as a child. Even locked yourself in the cupboard once, much to your brother's delight. Made you wet yourself. Shall we see if we can do it again?'

'No more. Please. How did you know?' he pleaded.

'I don't know, us witches know things. See things and know when you hurt another,' Amber replied, striding closer to him.

'As she said, this isn't about her. This is about me,' Willow said as she stepped forward and flipped down her hood.

On recognising her, Clive's hatred replaced his fear. He stood taller and more defiant. 'Should have known you'd be behind this. Not content with ruining my life, you are haunting my dreams.'

'Ruined your life? How have I done that?' she said.

'As soon as you came into the agency, you ruined it. No commission on the sale of the Old Apothecary or bonuses that followed. No. All that went to Michael. I showed you the property. Me. Not him. It was my commission, my promotion he took. You always thought you were better than me. Well, you didn't know about Speedwell Cottage, did you? So much for witches knowing things. You know nothing. Your constant need for updates on sales of farms in the area made diverting the repair costs into my account all the sweeter when I realised you were the missing grand-daughter connected to Speedwell. Two properties connected to witches, both connected to you. Bloody witches, but someone knew how to get under your skin, didn't they? Who was it that first called you Goldilocks, eh? Who was it that first made you scared?'

He spat onto the ground. His words empowered him when she remained silent, an icy rage running through her. 'Whoever it was, they kept you in line, hiding. Despite hexing me, my nest egg was safe. I learnt how to protect myself from you vile creatures. Witchcraft couldn't touch me, and then he turns up with his posh boarding school accent. He gives you a black eye, yet you fawn all over him, telling him about the cottage. My cottage, my income. And now you've made me lose my job, my car and house. You're in league with the devil.'

The mention of the devil sparked an idea. The gytrash of her own nightmares, with its glowing red eyes and sharp teeth, crashed through the trees at her command. It circled Clive as the sprites scuttled away. Its mouth drooled as it snapped its powerful jaws shut.

Willow walked closer and closer until she could see the beads of sweat running down Clive's face and the tremble in his hands. He shrank under her gaze.

'No. You ruined your life. Your greed. Your hate. You didn't do a thing the day you showed me the apothecary. You were too scared of the rumours of harmless ghosts. You will find witches are not so docile. No protection you can find here will keep us or the devil away.'

The gytrash growled and lumbered closer. Clive scurried up the tree, higher and higher, into the canopy.

'We'll be back night after night until you confess everything to the police. And we mean everything. Every scam and dodgy deal you've made, every assault, every time you hurt another person. They need to know it all before we back off. See you tomorrow.'

Willow strode away, her cape flying behind her, and nodded at Amber who beamed as she commandeered the weather. In sync, the next flash of lightning streaked down and thunder boomed as she said, 'No elephant.'

It hit the tree. Clive flew into the air, his limbs scrabbling to find something to grasp. His bloodcurdling scream echoed around the garden. Both witches wondered if he'd wake up before he fell into the gnashing jaws below.

***

They didn't have to wait long. Willow's phone rang shortly after she woke up to sun streaming on her face. The detective in charge of her case informed her Clive had staggered into a Greek police station, clearly intoxicated, demanding to see someone. Aside from his ramblings about witches and the devil, he confessed to multiple fraud over many years, theft, stalking Willow and two other women, blackmail, and the assault of Amber and multiple speeding offences. As the detective listed his crimes she cringed. No wonder his dreams were as warped as Amber confessed to seeing on her quest to find him. It was over.

# *Epilogue*

S now formed a white blanket over the village with the laden clouds threatening more. Watching from the kitchen window, Willow saw Nate tug his coat tighter around himself as he waited for the gangly puppy to finish investigating the newly formed landscape. His small paw prints created an abstract piece of art on the blank canvas. She smiled and cradled her mug of tea in awe at her happiness. If only she could bottle the emotion to sprinkle in the Wishing Spell products or happiness tea, her bank balance would be healthier. Speedwell Cottage demanded more money than her current budget dictated to bring it into the twenty-first century, but together she and Nate would make it a home, starting with a new bathroom suite and boiler. It was one of life's joys to sink into a hot deep bath to read without her knees getting cold and her breath forming a plume of mist in a freezing room. The sprig of blossom she'd plucked from the tree on her arrival still bloomed in a jug on the dresser. A contrast to the mistletoe hanging above the doorways and holly decorating the rooms.

Vincent chirruped beside her, demanding his breakfast. Concerns he'd feel pushed out by Merlin's arrival went unfounded; he accepted him as part of the family, and they often curled up together in front of the fire. Time would tell what his reaction would be when the puppy grew bigger than him. Apart from an occasional gentle swipe, the feline and canine companionship worked well. Merlin accepted his place at the bottom of the hierarchy, and Nate was getting used to the questioning looks he received when he walked Merlin because Vincent insisted on sauntering a couple of metres behind or along the walls.

The kitchen door flung open. The sub-zero gust of air made her wince as she was bulldozed by a flurry of black before it shook itself.

'Bloody dog took ages. It's freezing,' Nate grumbled, grateful for the mug of coffee she offered.

'He's excited. Besides, you decided you needed a dog.' The smell of turkey wafted from the new range. A far cry from the small oven they'd roasted dinner in last Christmas. Who knew one year could change so much? Speedwell Cottage was also undergoing a transformation, with the kitchen the first place they renovated, determined to keep its beating heart. On Jax's Welsh dresser stood a small collection of Willow's teapots, cups and saucers. Others lined the bespoke display shelves along another wall with many hidden in unpacked boxes in the workroom where Grandma Jax prepared her remedies and dried her herbs. She'd confess to their presence one day.

'Any news from them?' Nate wrapped his arms around Willow, drew her close, and kissed her.

'Roads are clear enough, so their arrival is expected as planned.'

'Still enough time to show you how much I love you and how cold my hands are then.'

She shrieked as he placed his icy hands on her stomach. 'Sorry, Casanova, we have Christmas dinner to prepare for, starting with your specialty—extra mince pies.'

Willow placed the last present under the tree they'd decorated days before, with the gherkin hidden in its depths for someone to find. The roaring fire in the stone hearth, started with the Yule log made from a fallen tree on her land, added heat and ambience to the picture-perfect room. Muted lighting and decorations hid the faded wallpaper, cracks in the ceiling, and the cobweb she struggled to remove. Vincent relished the heat, after squeezing himself onto Grandma Jax's chair while Merlin barked at the sound of vehicles arriving and the slam of their doors. It was time to bring the house to life with people Willow loved.

Everyone sat at the farmhouse table with little room between them. Glenn and Lorna chatted to Jez and Milly about the garden and their common business interests while Harry kept Mrs Ramsey entertained with tales of Mexenby and the local witches. Amber brought Willow up to speed with her adventures at university with her new friends. Speedwell soaked up their cheer into the fabric of its walls to feed its warmth and sense of home.

'It's a beautiful house, dear,' Mrs Ramsey said while Nate poured her a glass of wine.

'It will be when it's finished, and the other rooms are habitable. Harry's family and Jax's magic did a grand job of caring for it, but time took its toll on the roof and upstairs.'

'Stop moaning,' Willow butted in. 'The holes in the roof are fixed, we have heating and electricity now. It'll happen.' Willow's determination to celebrate Yule and Christmas in her family home had paid off even though late and she spent the nights on an inflatable mattress in the sitting room.

They were making memories to enjoy in the future. 'Have you decided what you're doing with it?' Amber asked.

Willow had known the answer as she placed the sprig of apple blossom in her hair on the first day in the orchard; accepting it was harder. Every time she saw it on the windowsill, it urged her to make a commitment. This was the home she had longed for all her life, but the Enchanted Emporium was her baby. It had provided a sanctuary and a place to grow when she needed it most, but as she saw Amber flourish and the Cobble call to her, Willow realised she was just the custodian until its true witch was ready.

'This is my home, so once finished, Nate and I'll move in permanently.'

The house sighed with relief.

'The ghosts will miss you,' said Amber into her drink, 'and so will I.' Others murmured their agreement. Nate squeezed Willow's hand to encourage her on.

'You're at uni most of the time and I'll still be at the Enchanted Emporium, though I'll have to devote some time here to get the growing side of things going. Why buy from suppliers when I can grow my own? Besides the Marleys were happy before I arrived. She'll miss the romcom movies she insists I play, though. I was thinking of renting out the flat.'

Amber and Glenn choked on their drinks, and Mrs Ramsey looked unconvinced. 'You can't do that. People won't want to share with its extra guests,' Amber argued.

'They're harmless,' Willow said.

'They're still ghosts,' reiterated Amber.

'It just needs the right tenants. Like Rosa and Alejo. They've been looking for an affordable home for ages and I'm sure we can come to an agreeable arrangement for monitoring the place. It'll enjoy having a child around.'

'Rosa would do I guess,' Amber conceded, 'but there's one problem. It only one bedroom.'

Nate coughed, and Willow looked down at her plate and mumbled, 'There're two.'

'No, there aren't, which is why I sleep on your sofa after late-night spell sessions,' said Amber.

'Actually, there are two. The second's just full of ... things.'

Nate had discovered her secret the day he moved in. In a small room hidden in the Emporium's eaves were stacks of boxes and packing cases. Treasures she collected while travelling but mainly cups with their matching saucers, tea caddies, and teapots she rescued from car boots and online auctions. A hoard of old and new items she couldn't resist, hidden away like a dirty secret. She didn't want anyone to know the extent of her tea obsession. Willow blushed. 'You can never have enough cups.'

'Obviously,' said Nate.

'Just like Jax. Our Jez discovered more boxes of hers in the loft. Full of the things they were. You'll bring them over, won't you, Jez?'

'We'll be drowning in the bloody things.' Nate shook his head when Jez agreed.

Chatter continued to fill the room with a backdrop of Merlin's and Vincent's loud snores, their rounded bellies full of turkey treats. Amber passed round the crackers with a smile. 'I made them again this year.' With a countdown from three, they pulled them apart. Giggles ensued as they read their gifts. Lorna shared hers with Glenn. With a snap, a bag of herbs tumbled to the table. Willow picked it up and sniffed. A carefully blended mix containing everything for fertility. She chuckled and handed it to the woman who had stolen Glenn's heart.

Glenn unrolled the tiny scroll to read the message. 'To new beginnings. That sounds fair enough for me.' Ignoring his daughter's pale face and the magic brewing in the air.

**The End**

# About the Author

Kate Kenzie may not be Yorkshire born and bred, but it's where her heart is and why her fictional worlds are set in the Moors and her favourite haunt, Whitby. Creator of the Enchanted Emporium and its residents, she blogs book reviews and author interviews at The Enchanted Emporium Bookshelf.

Part-time writer, and full-time dreamer, if she's not reading from her ever flowing TBR pile, she is writing or drinking tea. Like many, she always dreamed of being an author but notebooks of half-finished novels and children's stories were pushed aside in adulthood until a random Facebook conversation rekindled her passion for world building. By receiving a bursary for the RNA New Writer's Scheme, she found her tribe.

Awarded the Katie Fforde bursary this year, she writes romantic and paranormal fiction, especially witch lit. Her short story, *The Ghost Writer* available in an anthology, *Byline Legacies* by Cardigan Press.

Find out more and stay in contact through katekenzie.com or on social media as @kakenzie101

# Acknowledgements

L ike many people I've always dreamt of writing a book and finally forty years after writing Brambly Hedge fan fiction with my Victoria Plum pencil, I've done it. *A Blend of Magic* has been years in the making but it wouldn't have evolved from the original short story without the support, and regular kicks to just get on with it from the following people. They all deserve my gratitude and if I've missed anyone out, it's not intentional, I promise, you should know by now my dysfunctional brain cell is always forgetful.

First, it has to be Debi McFarlane who witnessed Amber's initial incarnation while at school and always said I'd publish a book one day. I'm sorry there are no mangled piranha bitten feet in this version but maybe next time.

Catharine Ramage and Maria Sinclair whose serendipitous conversation and box of unfinished work brought me back to my writing and stopped me procrastinating. The writers at my local writing group who helped me gain my confidence and skills with writing prompts, laughter, a and lots of biscuits, but especially Kris Egleton, Cath Louth, Nick

Watts, Steve Southcoat, and those who aren't with us anymore Evelyn Robson and Marion Cherill.

My Auntie Ann who bought me my first novel writing course and has kept me supplied with monthly writing mags. And my father-in-law, Gordon and friends Charlotte Cartwright, Liz Carr and Graham Hill for their unwavering belief. Liz, I'm sorry you never got to read the finished version but your enthusiasm for the Emporium kept me writing.

Thank you to my writing tribe, the wonderful Barbabes, Emma Wilson, Emma Jackson, Sandra Forder, Julie Morris, Jenny Kennedy and Kate Baker who've witnessed the tears and frustration experienced bringing these worlds to life. My beta readers, Rosetta Yorke, Emma-Louise Smith, Sharon Booth, Kate Baker and Lizzie Thornton. My local RNA chapter who've been supportive and welcoming from the moment I joined. Jeevani Charika/Rhoda Baxter for your Canva tutorials and Lynnda Worsnop for your tech help. Kimberly Adams for sharing your publishing tips. Fellow spoonie writers who understand the exhausting rollercoaster ride it is to write while living with a chronic illness including Rebecca McDowall, Jeanna Louise Skinner, Clare Wade and those in ADCI group. You showed me it is possible to achieve the author dream from beneath a duvet.

The Foxes at Foxes Retreat who kept me going with laughter throughout lockdown and beyond. Your friendship is invaluable.

Those at Mythic Alley -Jessica Haines and Emma Jackson – it's your turn next, Jess.

While writing, the universe has nudged me along by offering several opportunities I would never have dreamt of including a NaNoWriMo mentorship with Megg Geri which gave me a very rough first draft, guidance from Alison May, Stephanie Butland and Miranda Dickinson. Bursaries from Milly Johnson, and Katie Fforde allowed me to be in the RNA with their wonderful readers and encouraging members.

Also, I want to shout out a thanks to Kiltie Jackson whose Twitter (or whatever it's called now) cinnamon roll challenge many moons ago gave birth to Nate's fascination with baking. And thank you to the book bloggers and booksellers who are the unsung heroes for many authors new and old, including the lovely Tea, Leaves and Reads. The admins for the online book groups who help share the love of books to the community especially Chick Lit and Prosecco, The Fiction Café and Heidi Swain and friends. Wendy Clarke, your group and FB lives were an integral part of my fledgling writing journey. And Nafferton Feoffees – if it wasn't for you helping me with my laptop and dictation software this novel wouldn't have existed.

Thank you to Imogen Howson for the editing and Luisa Galstyan for my gorgeous cover.

As you can see, writing maybe a solitary activity (apart from the characters living in your head) but it takes a village/city to bring it into the hands of the reader. Thank you all including those reading this, my first novel.

If you loved the witches, please share the love by telling friends and leaving a review.

Love

Kate x

# Mythic Alley

## Who are we?

A consortium of fantastically-minded writers who thought three was definitely the magic number. After many years of seeing the publishing industry in the UK still unsure where to put romance books that were a little bit different from the norm, we decided to band our knowledge and abilities together and see if we could spread the love for all things romantasy a little further.

And so, Mythic Alley was born.

Find out more here: https://mythicalley.co.uk/

**Coming Soon with Mythic Alley**

Heart of Stone by Jessica Haines

# Heart of Stone By Jessica Haines

## Chapter One

### Nyssa

"The rest are almost here." Seren jumps down from her perch on the tower's windowsill, slamming her viewing glass back together with a metallic thud. "Jack already saw several slipping into the back ramparts, if we don't leave before these ones hit the gate, we'll never make it."

I move to the make-shift crib, my hands shaking as I reach inside and collect the sleeping bundle. I wanted to let her rest as long as possible before I said goodbye, but the warning from our sentries in the forest came too late. We're out of time.

Juniper squirms a little as I raise her to my chest, resting her head against me for a second. Long enough for me to catch the hint of honeysuckle that clings to her soft hair.

Her eyes flicker open to reveal a sky-blue gaze, so pure it's like being greeted by something sacred. "Hey little one, how was your sleep?" I ask, rocking and cooing in that gentle tone that makes her grin. Even though I know she doesn't understand the words, I hope one day she might remember my voice.

A battle cry erupts outside, shaking the once impressive fortress. Mortar rains down and I dip sideways, still crooning and smiling as I dodge the debris. Juniper doesn't need to know how our once great home has been pilfered and ransacked until it's nothing but a husk, she might never even be told her real name.

"Nyssa, we have to leave now." Ryley comes close, her silver hair is covered in a dirty white coif, an ankle-length brown dress shrouds her body and hides what's left of her wings and concealing her fae heritage. She'll look unremarkable to anyone who happens to see her, a nun out with one of her orphaned charges. The sackcloth and linen can only hide so much though, the tears resting on her lower lashes show the heart that is breaking beneath.

I feel it too. My heartbeat stuttering as I ease Juniper away from me and place her securely in my friend's tender embrace. Our time is up.

"You have the letter?" I ask, needing the distraction now the warm bundle is gone. The heat of her small body disappearing too fast, like she's taking every ounce of my warmth as she goes.

Ryley nods as she wraps her arms underneath the blanket, already edging away. "I'll make sure the sisters keep it safe."

A tiny hand rises from the mass of fabric, reaching for something I can't see. But it feels like it's pulling at my insides, drawing the love and rightness that finally came into my life when she burst into it. The last bit of humanity I've clung on to fizzling out as she's moved toward the back wall.

"Good luck out there," Seren says, moving to the wall. She searches in her pocket, retrieving one of her large crystal orbs, cradling it in her palm like Ryley holds my half-sister.

I smile, not knowing what else to do. There are no more words to say, we've said them many times over. We only have our actions now. They'll be what carries on our legacy, or leaves it crumbling in the dirt. Just like the castle around me.

Seren lifts the sphere, the inside a whirlpool of blues and greens, like an ocean battling the surface, fighting to escape. With a twist of her wrist she smashes it into the brickwork, the water surging up the wall like a wave rushes toward the shore.

Errant drops land on my bare skin, but they are soon pulled back by the sway of her magic, weaving upwards across the mortar until they merge and spread, creating a vertical pool on the walls surface, like a distorted mirror. I stare as my reflection swirls in the liquid, before a pinpoint of darkness appears in the centre. It spreads, devouring the crystalline squalls only to replace it with a forest of sprouting jades and ambers. The portal keeps rushing until it's wide enough to allow the women to slip through.

"Stay safe," Seren says, her eyes filled with the usual intensity she gives all things, pushing away the weight of uncertainty that I know sits in her chest. We've all felt the strain of it since we realised there were gargoyles heading our way, their granite bodies filling both the horizon and the woodlands, turning our futures into a dull, stone grey.

They've come to take what they believe is theirs, come to claim a due that my unworthy father offered over twenty years ago.

Me.

Printed in Great Britain
by Amazon

40143033R00219